GETTING
SASSY

GETTING
SASSY

D. C. Brod

TYRUS
BOOKS

Published by
TYRUS BOOKS
1213 N. Sherman Ave. #306
Madison, WI 53704
www.tyrusbooks.com

This is a work of fiction.
Any similarities to people or places,
living or dead, is purely coincidental.

Library of Congress Cataloging-In-Publication Data has been applied for.

12 11 10 09 08 1 2 3 4 5 6 7 8 9 10

978-1-935562-22-1 (hardcover)
978-1-935562-21-4 (paperback)

In memory of my mother,
Ruth Elizabeth Ditzel Cobban

Acknowledgments

Many thanks go to writer and reader friends, and those who have supplied much-needed support and encouragement: Maria Alderson, Susan Anderson, Miriam Baily, Don Berk, Kathy Boller, Ann Brack Johnson, Mary Brown, Brian Davis, Ceclia Downs, Susan DeLay, Gail Eckl, Carol Haggas, Bob Keegan, Beth Mottashed, Patrick Parks, Laura Pepin, Joan O'Leary, Rachael Tecza and Laura Vasilion.

My husband, Don.
Ben LeRoy and Alison Janssen of Tyrus Books.

All the folks at Town House Books and Cafe in St. Charles, Illinois.

And, finally, thanks to Susan O'Neill for introducing me to Spud, Sassy's inspiration.

CHAPTER 1

The idea of stealing the money first came to me as I stood in line at Lundergren's Liquors, my fist wrapped around a six-dollar liter of Chablis. It hit without warning and bored into my brain like a tiny meteorite, forever changing the landscape.

I quickly assured myself this was an intellectual exercise and not an actual idea. My mind tends to wander in bizarre places, but it usually comes home when called. I tucked a strand of hair behind my ear and focused on the squat little woman in front of me who was grabbing items from the counter displays and tossing them onto her pile. To her two six packs of Miller Lite, she added four Slim Jims, a bag of beer nuts and a lemon. Behind me, a man seemed to be carrying on an animated conversation with himself. But when I turned, I saw that the young, bald guy sported one of those ear phones. He looked like he was being assimilated into the Borg collective.

"I gotta stop at the deli for Carlisle's liver scraps," he was saying. I hoped Carlisle was their dog and not their two-year-old.

Robbing a store—how hard could it be? What would I use as a weapon? Not a gun. Those things can go off. Then what? Did anyone ever get away with the old stiff-finger-in-the-pocket ploy? The clerk calls your bluff with a Louisville Slugger and then what do you do with your finger? Nothing dignified, that's for sure.

I watched as Marv Lundergren keyed in the woman's purchases. Deep lines creasing his rough, reddened skin weighed down his features, rendering his expression immobile. When he'd rung up a total, the woman began rummaging through her purse, finally emerging with a checkbook. "Can I write this for twenty over?"

"Sure." Marv caught my eye and winked.

I tightened my grip on the Chablis, digging my nails into my palm. Of course I'd never rob a store in Fowler. Not only could I be recognized, but I'd never take money from someone I knew. Not that the folks up by the Wisconsin border or wherever I decided to pillage were any less deserving of their money. That was the problem: who did deserve to be robbed?

Having recovered a pen from her purse, the woman asked, "What's the date?"

"August third," I told her and added the year.

"Where does the time go?" she muttered as she began to fill out the check.

Indeed.

The cell phone talker behind me had moved on to another call. Maybe someone who bought dog food at the deli and couldn't wait to get home to consult his stock broker deserved to be robbed.

As I watched Marv glance at the woman's driver's license and then pull two tens out of the till, it occurred to me that a liquor store heist would be pointless anyway. Even on a good day, the till probably didn't contain more than a few hundred dollars. Most people used credit cards or wrote checks. In order to get the kind of money I needed, I'd have to rob a bank. And that was way too daunting. I sighed, more from relief than disappointment. That was when I realized I actually had been considering it. My scalp tightened.

"Robyn?"

I jerked out of my reverie and set the Chablis on the counter. "How's it going, Marv?" I dug a five and two ones out of the canvas laptop satchel slung from my shoulder.

"Can't complain. How's your mom doing?"

Marv's long, knobby finger punched open the drawer and plucked out my change.

"About the same." I pocketed the coins and collected the bottle, now concealed in a paper bag.

"That's a pretty nice place, isn't it?"

"It is. She likes it real well."

"Marcy Spender's mother moved in there, didn't she?"

I nodded. "I see her sometimes." What I didn't add was that my mother had pronounced Cloris Spender "duller than dirt."

"Well, you give Lizzie my best."

"Thanks, Marv. I'll do that."

As I stepped outside and into the damp heat, a wave of shame nearly flattened me. Whether I robbed Marv or a total stranger, I'd be turning someone into a crime statistic. The world was a scary enough place already.

Believing that ended my flirtation with crime, I filled my lungs with the muggy air and welcomed the return of my sanity.

A light rain began to fall. I tilted my chin up towards the solid gray sky and enjoyed the soft punches of cold against my face.

Rainy days accentuated Fowler's blandness, which had to work some to get to pleasant on a crisp spring morning. Except for an occasional splash of color—a turquoise scarf, a basket of purple flowers in the florist's window and a neon bar sign—the town looked like a film noir set. Along the wide, mostly empty sidewalks, a disturbing number of storefronts had a "to rent" or a "space available" sign propped or taped in their windows. I lived above a picture framing store that, in the two years I'd lived in Fowler, had also been a clothing boutique and a shop selling religious artifacts. Liquor stores and bars did well, and the coffee shop was always busy. A psychic had rented a retail space a half block from my apartment, so maybe that was a good sign. She ought to know.

Now that I'd determined that robbery was impractical, not to mention just plain wrong, I felt almost giddy. I didn't want to steal anything. Aside from a souvenir ash tray and maybe a bar glass, I'd never stolen anything in my life. Even when the girls I'd aspired to hang with in middle school dared me to steal—or "lift" as they'd eu-phemized—a tube of Yardley lip gloss, I'd declined. They'd called me "chicken" and shunned me at the lunch table. I suppose I was scared, but I also believed it was wrong. So why had it even occurred to me to knock off a liquor store? Maybe it was easy to claim the higher ground when you didn't need the money. Or the lip gloss.

I considered walking to my destination, Dryden Manor, but de-cided I didn't have the time. Not only did I have a three o'clock ap-pointment with my accountant/financial advisor, but I was hoping to avoid April Clarke, Dryden's director. I had a pretty good idea of her schedule—it paid to be attentive—and knew she usually took a late lunch. So if I got in and out of there by two thirty, I shouldn't run into her.

I cut down the alley between the florist's and the Depot to the small lot where I park my eleven-year-old Civic. The little green ma-chine has got only thirty-five thousand miles on it, and I don't think my mechanic believes me when I tell him the speedometer has never turned over. It hasn't. The low mileage attests to the fact that I love to walk, don't care to drive, and on most days I don't stray far from home. The exception was taking my mother for a drive. There were times she got so antsy she couldn't stand being indoors and around people. On those days we'd go for a long ride, usually out in the coun-try, and the miles worked on her like a mild sedative.

I listened to a Vivaldi guitar concerto as I drove. He usually light-ened my mood. As opposed to Beethoven, who made me want to conquer something. Or someone. I pulled into the lot at Dryden and let the strings crescendo and fade before turning off the car.

One of the things I liked about Dryden Manor was that I could honestly say I wouldn't mind living there myself when my body and mind couldn't make it on their own anymore. Not that I was planning for that to happen. I've never been able to imagine myself old, and I think there's some timer in my head that keeps me from becoming too enamored with the idea of a long dotage.

From the outside, the building resembled an English Tudor estate surrounded by a thick, manicured lawn, mature oaks, pines and ashes, and seasonal gardens, now vibrant with purples, golds and pinks. Walking paths wound through the grounds and bordered the Crystal River, which ran the gamut from a meandering stream to a rushing torrent, depending on the amount of rain and the snow runoff. Today it flowed at a good rate, attesting to the wet spring and summer we'd had, and I took a moment to watch the current carry a narrow, twisted log downriver before I turned and headed up the walk.

I signed my name in the visitor's register and rounded the time up to 2:15. The receptionist wasn't the usual woman, but she seemed to know who I was and, with a wry smile, directed me toward the first floor lounge. "I think Lizzie's holding court."

That's the thing about being Lizzie Guthrie's daughter. People know me.

Two years ago when she moved to Dryden, I thought my mother was on her way out. She has chronic obstructive pulmonary disease, brought on by years of smoking, and was wasting away, both physically and mentally. I believed that my mother had chosen her time, and while I wanted to respect that decision, I also wanted to see that she got some of the luxury and pampering she'd missed out on in her retirement. Dryden Manor was the place.

But then, instead of continuing her downward spiral, she'd thrived at Dryden. After a rocky start, that is. Smoking was not allowed on the premises, and my mother was an unapologetic smoker. She had to go cold turkey. For a month she called me daily, alternately begging, cajoling and commanding me to buy her a pack. Many a day I wanted nothing more than to march down there, jam a Virginia Slim between her lips and light it for her. But then the calls became less and less frequent and eventually they stopped. And once her doctor sorted out her medications, her mental state improved some. Her short term memory was still diminished and evenings, when her confusion was most profound, could be surreal, but her memory of events in the distant past was still good, albeit selective. For example, she frequently spoke of the luxuries she enjoyed as the wife of a banker, but had forgotten that Wyman considered many luxuries to be Satan's temptations. (I'll never forget the battle over the bidet. Wyman won.) Then, after he died, she'd worked for a couple of tight-fisted dermatologists until she was in her seventies, starting as a clerk, a secretary and finally retiring as an office manager. And now she ruled Dryden as lady of the house. This didn't win her a lot of friends among the residents, but she had her fans among the staff members who liked the feisty ones with delusions of grandeur.

I would have loved watching her occupy this role if it weren't for the sad, stark fact that her worst fear had come to be: she had outlived her money. She wasn't aware of this—a small gift the dementia offered—and I'd only begun to realize the lengths to which I might go in order to keep her from knowing.

Last month I'd been a week late with her rent. I'd used up the last of her funds and emptied most of my checking account as well. I knew all I was buying was time and that the days until August rent was due would creep up on me like hyenas smelling a kill. Now it was here—three days ago—and I'd squandered the time, visiting a few nursing and assisted living homes that accepted public aid residents and, at the same time, wondering how large an apartment it would take to contain the two of us. I'd even resorted to purchasing lottery tickets, a practice I'd always scorned. And speaking of practices I tend to scorn—robbery would be near the top of that list.

"Robyn."

I froze, hearing the soft thud of footsteps coming up behind me on the plush carpeting. Drawing in a deep breath, I turned to face April Clarke, who approached with a handbag slung over her shoulder and a set of car keys dangling from her right hand. Timing was everything.

Her smile didn't seem forced, which was more than I could say for my own. She gestured with a nod in the direction of her office. "We need to talk," she said. "It won't take a minute."

When I hesitated, she added, "I've been leaving messages on both your home and your cell phones."

I nodded—I know when I've been busted—and followed her into the small office next to the reception area.

April closed the door behind us and moved into the middle of the room, pushed aside a coleus plant on her desk to make room for her purse. But she held on to her keys as she leaned her butt against the desk's edge.

I swallowed. "I just need a few more days to find a place."

"Are you looking?"

When I'd made the decision to move my mother into Dryden, April had been one of its assets. I'd watched her chatting with residents, and she'd never given me the impression that she wanted to be somewhere other than with her old people. Fully involved and focused, she could not have not been faking. And now, as she waited for my answer, I didn't see any anger or sign that she viewed me as a deadbeat who had let it all come to this.

"I, um, yes. I've got an appointment this afternoon with Willoway Care Center."

"They have a bed available?"

"Yes." I paused. "Middle of the month."

She nodded. "They're good. I've heard good things."

"That's good." I blinked and looked out the window, past a vase of black-eyed Susans.

"She'll do okay, Robyn."

"She doesn't like change."

"People of her age usually don't. But give her a little time. She will adjust. Lizzie's tough."

My shoulders bobbed once in a half-assed attempt at a chuckle. "Yeah." The elm outside blurred and I looked down at the floor. "I know."

And then, because I figured April shouldn't have to ask all the tough questions, I said, "I've got some money coming in next week. Can I pay you then for the days she's still here?"

"Robyn, don't do this to yourself. Your mother doesn't want you to go into debt over this."

I shook my head. "I won't." I wondered what April would have thought about my criminal inclinations. I could hear her: *Robyn, your mother doesn't want you doing hard time over this.*

After studying me for a few moments—I didn't blink—she sighed and said, "Okay. I'll tell Connie."

"Thank you, April." Connie—Dryden's financial manager—was the one who did make me feel like a deadbeat. But I had to be grateful for any time they gave me and, if necessary, I knew how to grovel.

On my way to the lounge, I stopped in the women's room to pull myself together. While my mother has never been good at reading my moods, this afternoon I was sure I wore defeat like a cast-iron choker. Here I was—forty-five years old with no one in the world depending on me except for my mother and my dog. And I'd been a disappointment to at least one of them. Some days I hated what I saw in the mirror. I blew a puff of air up toward my bangs. Maybe there was still a chance. An outside chance that was as stupid as robbing a bank, but at least it was marginally legal. I swiped my lips with a stick of gloss and went to see my mother.

I found her sitting with three women in the lounge. As usual, she wasn't behaving. The fact that she is far from the most popular resident at Dryden Manor doesn't faze my mother one iota. I think she sees herself as a firm but benevolent monarch who doesn't expect to be adored by all.

She's a small woman, made smaller by bones that were collapsing into themselves. But she held herself as straight as her C-shaped spine would allow. Today she wore the powder blue terry pants and hoodie that I'd gotten her. She sat with her legs crossed and her fingers laced around one knee. Her chin was lifted so she could look down her petite nose at the women sitting in a semi-circle around her.

If I could have chosen the physical traits I would inherit from my mother it would be her near immunity to wrinkles—at eighty-two, her face was almost without lines—and her hands. They were slim, with fine, blue veins and were seldom still, punctuating her sentences and grasping the air for forgotten words.

Of course, there were also days when I wished I'd been adopted. As I came within earshot of her little group, I conceded that this might be one of those days.

"Of course it's not pizza, Effie," my mother was saying. "You need more than cheese to make a pizza. It's got to have sausage or those pepper things on it. Why if—" She broke off when she saw me, and the moment of confusion she often had when I arrived unexpected passed—like a cloud lifting from her eyes—and, without getting up, she opened her arms to me.

"This is my *beautiful* daughter, Robyn." She often introduced me this way. It made me feel schizophrenic—as if there were a homely but more compassionate daughter who showed up more often.

I took her hand and gave it a little squeeze.

The three women looked at me with varying degrees of skepticism. Effie, whose hair was dyed a harsh shade of brown that matched her perpetually arched brows, looked up at me and said, "What do you think, Robyn? Can a pizza have just cheese on it?"

My mother's grip on my hand tightened. I swallowed. "It's not a very interesting pizza." A nail dug into my palm, and with some effort, I pried my hand from hers.

"I brought your wine, Mom. Should I take it up to your room?"

Her eyes locked on mine. Glaciers exuded more warmth than those pale blue stones.

"So it *is* pizza," Effie crowed, proving herself as pugnacious as her soft, square jaw implied.

"It's a sorry excuse for a pizza." I turned toward my mother. "Why don't you come up to your room with me?" I asked, offering her a way out of this deteriorating situation.

Bestowing a gracious smile on the women, my mother said, "Syl, Vera, do come to my room before dinner for an aperitif."

Before either Syl or Vera could respond, my mother took my arm and, steadying herself with her cane, allowed me to escort her out of the lounge.

I glanced over my shoulder and saw the three women huddled together, talking, glancing our way. Effie was smiling.

"Would it have killed you to agree with me?" my mother said.

"Pizza's important." Then, because it never hurt to remind her, I added, "You don't always have to be so confrontational."

"I'm entitled to my opinion, aren't I?"

"You are. But you stated it as fact."

"I see." She nodded as though this angle required careful thought. "So what I should have said was 'that's not pizza *to me*.'"

"That would have been more diplomatic."

"The hell with being diplomatic. I've been diplomatic all my life."

Hardly.

My mother's room on the second floor overlooked the river and the walking path. When she'd moved in, we sat together with the binoculars I'd given her, watching the ducks and geese. A pair of cardinals frequented a nearby yew, and she referred to them as "my cardinals." I was grateful that the couple had chosen a tree near my mother. Not only were they fun to watch, but their antics provided conversation fodder.

My mother settled into her rocker by the window, and I checked her tissue and hand cream supplies and rinsed out her wine glass, using my thumbnail to rub the tinge of red from the rim. I always felt like I should do more to make this a home for her. But there wasn't any more to do.

This was what getting old was like. Everything got smaller—our homes, our freedom, our bodies. After my stepfather died, we had moved to a three-bedroom ranch house. When I went to college, my mother gave me as many of her belongings as I would take and moved

to a two-bedroom apartment and then later to a one-bedroom retirement condo. Now her home consisted of a square, beige room
with a microwave and mini-fridge in one corner and her bed, a chair
and television in another. She'd jettisoned everything else, donating
most to Salvation Army. She did give me her jewelry and a Wedge-
wood plate. And even though she'd instructed me to throw away a
box crammed with old papers and clippings, I'd stashed it in the basement of the building where I rented. I didn't want to throw away anything I hadn't looked at, but out of sight was out of mind, and I
seldom thought about it.

I adjusted the angle of a photo—my mother in her mid-thirties
in front of the Trevi Fountain—on the wide windowsill. Her life had
been distilled to a few mementos: a picture of me, some figurines—
two dachshunds and three finches. And, of course, there were my biological father's remains, which currently resided in a raku vase she
kept on the window ledge. He died just before I was born, so I have
absolutely no memories of him, but every year on his birthday I buy
a new vase for his ashes. I'm not sure why I do this, but I think it's
both a way to honor my father and an excuse to buy pottery. Plus the
fact that my mother seemed to enjoy the ceremony where we removed
the plastic container holding his ashes from the one vase and put it
into the new one. We would toast him with wine and she would tell
me a story about him. It's usually the same one—how he proposed to
her—but she likes telling it.

After I'd poured her a glass of wine, I told her I had to leave. Then
I braced myself. My mother hated being alone, a time when she was
more likely to get confused and anxious. It was as if this worrisome
voice in her head started in on her when she was by herself. In order
to combat it, she'd usually turn on the television. But she couldn't
converse with the TV, and so there were days I nearly had to fight my
way out her door.

"Where are you going?"

"I've got an appointment with my accountant."

"Why do you need an accountant?"

"Because I was a journalism major."

"I don't know why you didn't study something more difficult. Like finance. Or medicine."

I clamped my mouth shut.

She paused for a moment, and her thin white brows drew together as she posed a question to herself. "It's not tax time, is it?"

"No," I said, hoping she'd drop it.

"Then why do you need an accountant?" For an eighty-two-year-old woman with encroaching dementia, she sure knew what questions to ask.

"He's also my investment advisor."

"Oh." She pushed herself up from the chair. "Take me with you."

This was what I feared. "I don't know, Mom. I'm just going to be sitting in an office."

"I don't care. I need to get out of here." Her tone had taken on a panicky edge. If I hadn't known better, I'd have thought she was teetering on one of her anxiety states. The signs were there. But I figured it was more likely she didn't want to return to the lounge, where she'd have to face Effie and friends and might have to acknowledge her erroneous take on pizza. Losing face was not something that Lizzie Guthrie did gracefully.

But before I could come up with a reason for her to stay here, she had propped her cane against the wall and was zipping up the front of her hoodie.

CHAPTER 2

The Arthur Floyd Tart building, Fowler's tallest, was named after the architect who designed it. The big, black slab of stone had tinted windows and an impervious look to it. Several floors of the building once housed a prosperous computer software company that made the kind of computer games that were probably inciting children and other impressionable types to violence. But they were quite successful at it, so Fowler took the attitude, if they're not designing cyber characters who gleefully disembowel each other here, they'll be doing it somewhere else. Which is exactly what happened after they were bought out by a larger company. So now those floors were empty, and the darkened windows looking down on Fowler's business district reminded me of some carrion beast waiting for the town to gasp its last breath.

The Tart's remaining businesses occupied the lower and upper floors, and my money man was on the tenth, and highest, floor.

Unlike his persona, Mick Hughes's office was unassuming. It consisted of an outer room where his secretary du jour plied her trade and his own office, which gave him a view of Fowler's skyline, such as it was, and the expressway extension beyond it.

Since I'd been his client, he'd had three different secretaries. Different and yet not. As though they had all risen from the same gene pool: tall women with athletic builds and blond hair. They were polite enough, but smiles were hard won.

The current secretary's desk plate identified her as Myra Quill, and she peeked into Mick's office before waving me in. No way I was letting my mother sit in on this meeting, so I settled her into one of the armchairs in the outer office and selected three magazines for her. She discarded *Southern Living* and *Time* but opened *In Style*. I left her in Myra's care.

When I walked into Mick's office, he stood—not something he normally did—and whistled under his breath—not something he ever did. "What happened to the rest of you?"

Since I'd seen him in February for my taxes, I'd lost the thirty pounds I'd been carrying since my divorce twelve years ago. It was a combination of things—walking, a little weight training, less fast food. And there is no underestimating the toll that worry can take on a person's metabolism. Nerves apparently speeded mine up. I might have been a happier person a year ago, but I did like being able to fit into smaller jeans.

"I donated it to Models without Hips," I said as I drew the big envelope filled with my finances from my satchel and set it on his desk.

"You look good." He said it like I was a Philadelphia cheese steak sandwich.

"Thanks." I dropped into the chair and patted the envelope. "And I'm hoping you can find some money for me."

I noticed he had his own "Robyn Guthrie" file opened on the desk. After allowing his gaze to linger on me—on my chest in particular—for another moment or two, he settled into his chair. I knew I'd overdone it with the knit top, which was a snugger fit than my usual sloppy Ts. I was here hoping he'd offer me a loan, not a romp in the sack.

But Mick moved on, picking up the top sheet from his file and placing it squarely in front of him. "This looks pretty good," he said, after perusing it for a moment. Then he glanced up at me. "You planning on taking early retirement?"

"No," I said with the sigh of a person who knows she'll never retire. "My mother lives in Dryden Manor, and she's running out of money." I hated telling anyone this. "If I can come up with some of it, maybe I can get a bank loan to cover the rest."

He folded his arms on the desk and leaned toward me. "How much you talking about?"

"It costs roughly five grand a month."

He whistled again in a different kind of appreciation and looked down at the figures.

"I'll do anything to keep her out of a Medicaid bed," I said.

Shrugging, he said, "Have her move in with you."

"I'll do anything but that."

He was right—I should find another apartment—one on the ground floor with an extra bedroom—and move her in with me. The "sandwich generation" did it all the time—three generations under the same roof. I didn't have kids, so I guess that made me an open-faced sandwich. The guilt and shame I felt over my own ambivalence was eased slightly by the knowledge that my mother didn't want to share an apartment with me any more than I did with her. I knew that because we'd tried it once.

"Okay," was all Mick said with a nod. He opened the envelope I'd given him, then sat back, smoothing his tie against his chest. Neither of us spoke for several minutes as he went over the papers I'd assembled, which laid bare the state of my financial affairs.

Having someone peruse my finances felt a lot like getting a pelvic exam, and to keep from squirming, I glanced around the room. Mick had no photos on his desk, and his bookshelves were filled with thick, imposing tomes. The only items interrupting the monotonous beige of his walls were his degree from U of I, which hung on the wall next to his desk and, beside that, a watercolor of a chestnut horse in a white-fenced paddock. I suspected that Mick, or someone else he held dear, had painted it. It wasn't very good. The horse's legs were short in proportion to the rest of its body, and its tail was inadequate. But I've never asked about the artist, because I was afraid he might ask for my opinion. And I would have to tell him the truth. Because that is what I do.

Rumors swirled around Mick Hughes like flies around a rotting peach. He'd been a jockey—that much was known fact. I'd heard that he walked with a limp, although I'd never seen him walk far enough to determine the veracity of that rumor. I seldom saw him without the desk between us. The source of that limp was up for debate. One story had him mangling his leg in a bad fall during a race. Another had someone mangling his leg for him when he refused to throw a race. I find the former story more credible, since I couldn't believe Mick was familiar with the higher ground. He seemed to revel in his role as Fowler's bad boy. He was probably a few years younger than me—early forties—with a broad forehead and bright, rather intense, eyes. I always thought his sandy brown hair needed a combing, but he may have been going for the unkempt look, because he sometimes looked like he could use a shave as well. As far as I knew, he'd never married, but I doubted he had qualms about dating women who were.

Until today, I'd been content to know nothing of Mick's life outside this office. An editor at the *Fowler News and Record* had recommended Mick Hughes to me when I'd first gotten to town, saying that Mick earned money on the side as a bookie and as a loan shark, but that he kept his various enterprises separate. This convinced me that reasonable people benefited from Mick's financial acumen. The rumors didn't bother me. Besides, I figured the more shady his extracurricular doings, the harder he'd work at keeping everything above board in his legitimate business.

"If you didn't need five grand a month, it'd be a pretty good year for Robyn Guthrie, wouldn't it?" Then he leaned back in his chair and raked a hand through his hair.

In fact, it was a good year. I'd ghosted a book and had established myself as a stringer at several magazines that paid well. In addition I was earning some money as a freelance editor. If you ignored the fact that I needed sixty thousand dollars to keep my mother at Dryden for the next year, I was doing great.

Just as he began punching my numbers into his computer, his phone rang. He answered, saying, "I'm busy here, Myra." As he listened to her, he picked up a slip of paper, tapping it against the edge of his desk. Then, abruptly, he said, "Send him in."

He gave me a thin smile. "You mind waiting outside for two minutes, Robyn?" He wagged his head toward the door. "Gotta see this guy."

"Sure," I told him, relieved that I didn't have unfinished business with Mick.

The man waiting for Mick carried a black briefcase and wore a black suit with a bright white shirt and a stern look. I got a whiff of a spicy cologne as he brushed past me on his way into Mick's office. I had an image of the two of them exchanging wary looks along with thick wads of money.

My mother had nodded off, head resting on one shoulder. It was a position I often found her in, and one that looked like it would give her the neck cramp from hell. But I let her sleep and picked up *Time*. To be honest, I was also more in the mood for *In Style*, but would've had to extract it from beneath my mother's hand, possibly waking her.

Myra seemed interested in what was going on in the other room, but since there was a closed door keeping her out, she had to content herself by keeping watch on her side. She reminded me of an overeager Doberman—alert and all jittery with stifled energy. Like she was just waiting for an excuse to throw herself at the door.

I didn't have long to read. No more than five minutes passed before the man left Mick's office. He glanced at me with eyes the color of washed-out cornflowers. Myra watched as he walked out the door then settled back onto her haunches.

My mother roused from her nap.

"Who's bringing the salad?" I heard a trace of panic in her voice. "I am, Mom."

She nodded, murmuring, "Don't put any grapes in it," and went back to sleep.

"I'm good, but I'm not a magician."

Back in his office, Mick delivered the bad news as he studied my life on paper. He shook his head and went silent for several moments, tapping his pencil against the edge of his desk. He had rolled up the sleeves of his shirt and pulled his tie down an inch or so.

There was an edginess to him now, as though he was a doctor about to tell me I had better get my affairs in order. Then his lips moved slightly as though some new thought struck him, and he began plugging more numbers into his computer. I noticed a sheen of perspiration on his forehead. At least he was working hard.

I surveyed the room again—anything to distance myself from the edginess. That was when I noticed that the painting of the horse was crooked.

It hadn't been crooked before the man with the briefcase stole a few minutes of Mick's (and my) time. Or had it?

I quickly added together a number of facts: Mick made book on the side, therefore he dealt in cash; the man had something in the briefcase, which might well have been cash he was bringing to Mick; Mick had to put the cash somewhere, and the painting was large enough to hide a small wall safe. More insane justifying: while money made on illegal betting wasn't exactly stolen, it wasn't obtained in a legal manner either. Therefore, it was okay to steal it.

Then the cautionary, albeit underdeveloped part of my brain kicked in, and I reminded myself that Mick's reputation was due, in part, to the gusto with which he pursued deadbeats. One persistent rumor had him kidnapping the mistress of a man who hadn't taken his debt seriously enough and he had threatened to return her to the man's wife one digit at a time. I had no idea how that particular ploy ended and wasn't even certain it had occurred.

Images of my own shattered kneecaps were enough to restore reason. You are nuts, Robyn, I told myself, adding a mental thump upside the head.

Just then he looked up, and for a second I thought he was seeing right into my mind where my felonious thoughts screamed in 72-point type. But he pressed his mouth into a narrow line and swiveled his computer screen so I could read it.

"That'll buy you three, four months."

I sighed. And waited.

With a quick glance at the horse, I told myself that if he was going to offer me the loan, it would be now. And accepting a loan from Mick Hughes would be only slightly more sane than stealing the money from him. Maybe he'd give me a decent interest rate because I was a client or because he thought I looked good in a snug shirt and minus the thirty pounds. And then what would I do? That kind of loan—even one with a reasonable interest—would keep me in debt for most of my life. But if it would keep my mother in Dryden, maybe it was worth it.

His chair squeaked as he leaned back, hands clasped lightly as he studied me. Finally, he said, "I've known you about a couple of years, right?"

"About that."

"And I know you're a pretty smart lady."

I nodded. "Thank you" didn't seem appropriate.

"Smart enough to know that nobody could squeeze that kind of money out of your portfolio."

I swallowed.

Mick continued. "That's not why you came here, is it?"

It was all I could do not to look away. "I guess it's not."

Neither of us spoke for several moments. Finally, he said, "You don't want to do this."

My face grew warm and I swallowed again. Of course he was talking about his loan service, but I figured if anyone could spot a larcenous thought, it would be Mick Hughes.

"Trust me," he said.

Nothing more. Loan not offered, therefore not taken. Last chance down the tubes. I managed to convince myself that he wouldn't give me such a great interest rate. He probably saved his "specials" for women a lot better looking—not to mention younger—than me. There was still the bank. But even if I could get the loan there, I had to wonder if the amount would outlast my mother. How much was enough? Weighing her days left against a loan—God, there were times I despised myself.

He was right, of course, and I'd been nuts to even consider such a thing. Embarrassed by my own presumptions, not to mention foolishness, I began stuffing my papers back into my canvas satchel. "Well, thanks anyway. Maybe I can get a bank loan."

"You don't want to do that either."

"What I can't do is nothing." A sheet of paper slipped from my pile and wafted to a graceful landing on the other side of the room, one corner curled against a black file cabinet.

"Shit," I sighed, slumping back into the chair. It was just a piece of paper, but, at this moment, I was no more capable of retrieving it than I was of swimming the English Channel.

He was up and moving around his desk before I could stop him. I noted that he did limp, but it wasn't—at least in those few steps—pronounced. "I got it."

He had some trouble bending over; apparently his bad leg didn't bend very well. But he returned the errant sheet—a copy of the letter welcoming my mother to Dryden and a listing of the monthly charges. I love irony. I stuffed it, along with my other papers, into my satchel.

"Just sit for a second," he said, returning to his chair.

I gestured toward the door. "My mother's out there." In truth, I had no desire to stand, to leave, to maintain any momentum.

He glanced in that direction then shrugged. "She can wait."

I took a few deep breaths, trying to collect myself. I had no idea what Mick was thinking until he said, "There are some pretty nice places out there. Dryden's not the only option."

"I know," I said. "I've got an appointment at Willoway this afternoon. Just to check it out." I'd gone through the public aid process and my mother had been approved, but I hadn't yet fully resigned myself to moving her to that bed that was opening up in a week and a half.

He waited, as though he knew I wasn't finished.

"The thing is, she likes Dryden." And that was all I trusted my voice to say.

He leaned back with a sigh, nodding as though he sympathized. But then he said, "I can't help you. Sorry."

"Okay. I understand." Then I added, "But I am going to need to buy her two more weeks at Dryden."

"We can do that."

Like it was *our* money. But I just nodded and said, "Let's do it then."

"I'll work the figures up here." He seemed eager to be able to help me with something. Maybe he was just showing a nice side I hadn't known existed before. But then he added, with a small grin, "You need some distracting."

I looked at him, saw the spark in his eyes. "You think?"

"Cubs are playing the Cards tonight. Got tickets behind the Cubs dugout."

Yeah, that was all I needed, I thought. Like nine innings with my accountant was going to solve my problems. "Sorry. I've got an interview tonight."

His brows pulled together, and he tapped his forefinger on the mouse. "Job interview?"

"Oh, no." I shook my head. "Not a job. Well, kind of. It's for an article."

He waited.

"I'm doing an article on a new business in town. The woman's a psychic. A medium." I hurried on before he could snort. "I'm going to witness a séance."

"No kidding," he said, cocking his chin. "What's her name?"

"Starwise. Erika Starwise." I added a small shrug. "I doubt that's her real name, but that's her business."

"Can't you reschedule?"

"No." I tried sounding regretful but firm. "If I were just interviewing her, that would be one thing. But this séance is supposed to connect this client with her late husband, and there's something to the timing."

"You're shitting me." He leaned back, folding his arms over his chest. "He's dead, right? What else has he got to do?"

I laughed. "Good point, but I'm just—"

"Miss Guthrie?" Myra had opened the door just enough to stick her head into the room. "Your mother is getting a little anxious. I wondered …" She trailed off, her eyes wide with desperation. Behind her, I could hear my mother: "Robyn? Robyn, hurry."

"Gotta go," I said.

"I'll call you when I figure out the best way to do this."

I smiled my thanks and left. I should've anticipated this. I doubted Myra was much in the way of company.

My mother was standing, her cane forgotten, *In Style* on the floor. Her knees buckled, and she started to go down, but I got to her first and managed to settle her back into the chair.

"I'm here, Mom. Now, let's sit down. We'll be going right away."

"Why did you leave me?" Her tone was harsh, accusing.

"I didn't, Mom." I had to grit my teeth, biting back words.

I sat next to her and rummaged in my satchel for a stick of gum. "How does spearmint sound?"

"Get me out of here!" She was yelling.

"Okay, okay," I said, my hands fumbling to unwrap the gum, knowing she'd have trouble walking in her agitated state. "How about we stop for a glass of wine and some nacho chips?"

I handed her the gum. Hands trembling, she folded it twice and put it into her mouth, chewing it several times before saying, "Where will we go?"

"Ernesto's?"

As I steered her toward the exit, Mick stood in the doorway to his office, watching us. He nodded at me, and it seemed like there was some regret in the gesture, but by the time we'd reached the elevators, I'd decided that I didn't know Mick Hughes well enough to be interpreting his gestures.

My mother insisted on walking across the lot to my car rather than letting me pull it around for her, so it was a slow journey. It had stopped raining, but I kept my hand wrapped around her arm. To distract her, I mentioned that Mick had asked me out.

She stopped, the tip of her cane centered in a puddle, and looked up at me. "He did not."

"Yep. Asked me to a baseball game."

"Well," she said, shaking her head and moving her cane forward another six inches. We followed. "You're not going, are you?"

"No," I answered, but was a little puzzled by her question. She usually didn't miss the opportunity to tell me I should date more.

"People are just too familiar these days. Take that woman who came to see me this morning. Calling me Lizzie—"

"What woman came to see you?"

She stopped again, puzzled. "What was her name? I can't remember, of course."

"Was she in your room?"

"She was quite pleasant, you know."

"Was she in your room?"

"She came to my room, but I entertained her in the meditation room."

"What did she want?"

"She knew Robbie."

"My father?" She seldom talked about my father, and when she did she usually referred to him as Robert.

"Did I say Robert? I mean Wyman." She took another step. "Yes, she was here about Wyman."

"How good a friend was she?" Wyman, my stepfather, did have a history.

I took her arm and she slumped against me. "Oh, my. I'm very tired. Is it far to the car?"

I found it mildly amusing that my mother wanted me to think she'd gotten the names of her husbands confused, and yet I knew if I drove past the nacho place, she'd remind me to stop.

"It's right here." I steered her around the silver Mercedes parked next to me.

"Oh, good." She gave me a sweet smile. "Would you get the door for me?"

CHAPTER 3

I took my mother to Ernesto's for her wine and chips and for the inter-rogation I planned to give her. She must have sensed my motives, be-cause at first she insisted she was tired and wanted to go home. But when I sweetened the pot by suggesting we get cheese on our na-chos—an extravagance we frequently pined for but seldom indulged in—I knew I had her.

I waited until the waitress had set the plate of cheddar-smothered tortilla chips (jalapeno peppers on the side) on the ceramic-tiled table and my mother had filled her little plate. But before I could open my mouth, she began her own line of questioning.

"Why don't you get a job at the *Tribune?*"

"What? What's this about?"

"That's what this appointment was about, wasn't it? You're having money problems."

"I'm not having money problems."

As if she didn't hear me: "I'm sure the *Tribune* would pay better than that freelance work you do."

"This isn't exactly a good time to apply for a job at the *Tribune.*"

"Of course it is. You just have to march down there and show them how good you are. You'll never get anywhere in this world, Robyn, if you don't put yourself out there. Why, I'd never have got-ten my job at the bank if I hadn't stood up straight, tossed my head back, walked in there and told them they needed me. And do you know what they did?"

"They hired you."

She nodded as though she'd made her point.

When she paused for a sip of wine, I jumped in before she could swallow. "Tell me about this woman who came to see you."

"What's to tell?" She set her glass down, broke off a corner of one chip, dipped it in extra cheese and thrust it into her mouth. I could hear the slow crunch as she chewed.

Normally, she gave me a numbingly detailed description of the rare visitor to cross her threshold.

"Where did you say she knew Robert from?" I asked, hoping she would lapse again.

She licked a smear of cheese off the tip of her finger. "Wyman. It was Wyman she knew." Giving me a look, she added, "Which one of us is senile?"

I nodded, smiling. "Sure. Wyman."

"Her father knew Wyman from the old neighborhood. He lived outside Los Angeles."

"Wyman was from Cleveland."

"What did I say?"

"Los Angeles."

"Hmm. I think perhaps this woman lives there now."

"But you called it 'the old neighborhood.'"

"I misspoke," she snapped. "I'm an old woman." She added that haughty glare of hers but was the first to look away.

When my mother cannot remember something, she usually gets upset, almost to the point of tears. I say "almost" because her eyes are quite dry. Which is too bad. A good sobfest can be therapeutic. I extracted a chip from the nacho pile that was large enough to feed a family of four. "What was her name?"

She shook her head, then she took a dainty sip of wine. "You know my memory."

"What did she want?"

"She was just paying her respects."

"What did you talk about?"

"Oh, I don't remember. It's not important." Then she slipped into her whine mode. "I don't know why you question me so."

"I'm just trying to jog your memory."

"I'll thank you to let me jog my memory on my own, if you don't mind."

She bit off the point of a chip and chewed it carefully. "I believe her father knew Wyman from church." She nodded as though she liked the fit of this story. "Yes, I believe that was it."

I gave her a dubious look.

"He was a very devout man, Wyman was," she said, and added a bitter little smile that suggested she didn't forget what else he'd been.

Wyman did have fierce religious tendencies. Until I was old enough to rebel, he forced me into church every Sunday. It was some odd offshoot religion that was okay with dancing but drinking was out of the question. To this day I won't go near a dance floor or a church, and my beverage of choice is Famous Grouse. But seeing as this is the worst my stepfather ever did to me, I haven't got much room to complain.

When I was sixteen, he died of a heart attack, much to the dismay of Greta Evans, the church organist, who was beneath him at the time. That turned my mother off to church.

Almost thirty years later, the memory of Wyman's funeral was still quite vivid. When Greta had the nerve to show up, my mother presented her with the funeral bill, saying that if it weren't for Greta, Wyman would still be alive, therefore Greta had better pay up. Wyman must have had a thing for in-your-face women because Greta stepped right up to my mother and said Wyman wouldn't have strayed if he'd been getting some at home. My mother, her face pinched tighter than a gibbon's, told her that she and Wyman had sex three times a week. And then, caught up in the moment, she added that only a month before they'd made love in the vault of the First National Bank, celebrating Wyman's promotion to vice president. At that point, the funeral director and his assistant had, much to the mourners' disappointment, intervened. We'd never know how many other local landmarks bore Lizzie and Wyman's mark.

At the time, I was mortified. At sixteen I didn't want to be identified as the daughter of the couple who had sullied the vault, and I was relieved when my mother moved us, presumably for financial reasons, from upscale Oak Brook to middle-class Westchester. Still, for a long time I could not even approach a drive-up bank window without putting my mother and Wyman in there, rolling in dough. It took me years to gain enough perspective to find the humor. Although my mother and I never discussed the incident, I hoped it was a memory that hadn't been lost to her. She and Wy may never have gotten to Paris or even Montreal, but at least they had the bank vault.

The incident had made my mother bitter enough for her to shed Wyman's last name and go back to Guthrie. I had never been legally adopted by Wyman—neither of us considered it much of a priority, I guess—and had always gone by Guthrie. I didn't know much about my biological father, but being Scottish appealed to me.

"This cheese is too salty," my mother said, curling her lip. I considered returning to the stranger who had called on her, but knew it was pointless. I just hoped this woman wasn't someone trying to sell my mother a time-share in Vail or a set of encyclopedias. My mother did like to buy things.

We talked about the weather, and I reminded her again that I was taking her out for her birthday dinner in a couple of weeks so she should start thinking about a place. And I told her about the articles I was writing and the magazines that would be publishing them. She asked if I had been paid for the book I'd ghosted, and I told her I had; she said she thought I should think about investing in a house. I told her I'd think about it.

And then, as the mention of money often does, she was reminded of her own financial state. She'd had a decent savings when she retired—a combination of her own retirement fund and the money

Wyman left her, although she'd had to dip into the latter on occasion. Monthly assessments on the retirement condo she moved into five years ago had nibbled away at it. But then there had been a series of scams she'd fallen prey to: telemarketers promising her riches and mailings targeting her distrust of any state or federal institution. But the T-Rex among the carnivores had been a disastrous real estate deal in which she'd lost thousands. Lots of thousands. I blamed myself for much of this; I should have been paying closer attention to her finances, but she'd always been so sharp in that department. I hadn't wanted to see her decline, so I'd ignored the signs. I finally realized what was happening when one day when I called her and it was like talking to a character out of *Alice in Wonderland*. She was babbling about Robbie taking her for a ride on his sail boat and how she'd gotten sunburned. My parents had lived in Colorado Springs. At the time I hadn't seen her for a couple of weeks, but she'd been okay then. But after I hung up I drove out there and found her playing solitaire in a threadbare robe with food rotting on the counter. I'd taken her to the ER and they'd admitted her at once. She had a temperature, was dehydrated and confused. She spent five days in the hospital and two weeks in a nursing home getting her strength back. It had all happened so fast, but her doctor told me that wasn't unusual. I swore it would never happen again.

While I was sorting through her finances, trying to figure out what she could afford, I learned about her "investments." My mother hadn't put up an argument when I suggested she make me power of attorney and had let me move her to Oak Park and into the two-bedroom apartment I'd been renting. To say it was a disaster was to say that the Civil War was a misunderstanding. Part of the problem was that she had no one, except me, to talk to. She refused to go to the senior center, which she said was filled with "old, simple people." (I'm sure they missed her too.) But she hated being alone— which seemed odd for someone who had lived a significant part of her life alone, but her doctor assured me that this was fairly normal. When she was awake, she needed to be talking to someone, and I was it. And she could be awake most of the night. I hired a series of caregivers to spend some time with her, but my mother drove one after the other away, like a batter fouling off pitches. I wasn't sleeping much and found myself snapping at her for no good reason. I had trouble concentrating and wasn't getting my work done. In short, I was becoming someone I didn't recognize. And then she wouldn't quit smoking, which wasn't helping her health or my asthma, not to mention the fire hazard risks. During the two and a half months we'd lived together, she had deteriorated, I was losing my mind, and I didn't know how to stop either. And she seemed miserable as well. Getting smaller and hardening as I watched. Her doctor told me she probably didn't have more than six months. That was when I looked into the assisted living option. I figured her savings would last six months, but I wasn't sure that I could.

We found Dryden in Fowler, which was a ways west of Oak Park. The deal was that I'd move out to Fowler with her and she would quit smoking. So that's what happened. I was proud of her for quitting. I guess her (and my) health wasn't motivation enough, but 24/7 companionship was. And I watched her savings dwindle. And now, although she freely admits she's not up to handling her finances, she always asks about them.

"I know I've asked this before," she said, "so please forgive me, but how are my finances holding up?"

"They're doing fine, Mom." I drained my glass of cabernet. "You're in good shape." So we both lied to each other. All the time.

After getting my mother settled in her room, I drove across town to meet with the manager at Willoway Care Center. It was an appointment I'd put off making for way too long. I needed to make a decision on where to move my mother, and I needed to make it now. I should have begun looking for a place sooner. When I first realized that my mother's physical health was improving, I did look at a few places. None of them measured up to Dryden. I felt good about her being there. Now, I had no choice but to move her, and I didn't want to confront the options I had.

Willoway Care Center had the advantage of being close. It was clean. It came with good references. And it was about to have a vacancy.

The woman who showed me around, Jane Goodwin, smiled a lot and called the residents by name. She wore a bright yellow suit with a black blouse and reminded me of a goldfinch. In order to evaluate my mother, she had interviewed her a week ago, under the pretext of being a social worker studying the ageing process (more lies).

Her make-up was dramatic—dark eyes, arched brows and fresh lipstick—and her skirt was snug, almost tight.

"This is the first floor dining room." It was large with lots of windows looking out on a garden. The morning sun would make it a cheery place. She showed me the physical and occupational therapy rooms and then took me to a room that would soon become available—half of it, that is.

"Hello, Irene," Jane said to the shape beneath the coverlet on the bed next to the window. The gray-haired thatch poking above the green duvet turned and a sharp-nosed woman squinted in our direction, her mouth drawn inward over her gums.

"Who's that?" Irene groped for her glasses on the laminated table next to the bed.

"It's just Jane," Jane said, bending over Irene and giving her shoulder a pat. "You go back to sleep."

Irene's mouth twitched in annoyance, and her little head turned away.

"She's a dear," Jane said to me, keeping her voice down.

"Is she the one who's leaving?"

"No. That would be Phyllis who's checking out."

And before I had to ask why, Jane added, "Her family is moving out east. Vermont."

A hospital-type curtain hung between the two beds, and I couldn't help but wonder how long it would be before Irene checked out and my mother got a bed with a view.

The accommodations weren't awful, but they weren't nearly as nice as Dryden. Her living space would, once again, grow smaller. I couldn't imagine a queen living here. Then I asked the question I dreaded.

"If my mother's dementia worsens, will she have to be moved from this area?"

Jane barely hesitated. "The second floor is our special care unit. Would you like me to show you that area?"

"Yes."

We walked down the hall to an elevator where Jane had to punch a code into a keypad before the doors would open. She gave me a quick, nervous smile before pressing the button for the second floor.

We rose one floor to the special care unit. The moment the doors opened, the smell hit me. It wasn't overpowering, but no amount of disinfectant will mask the smell of urine, feces and decay. But the walls were painted with murals of meadows and waterfalls, and near the nurses' station was a large cage containing a dozen finches in varying colors.

We passed a common area where about ten residents were seated in a circle in their institutional blue plastic padded chairs. A woman who I assumed was the physical therapist tossed a large beach ball to each resident. Some caught it, others let it bounce off their laps and onto the floor.

Jane showed me a room similar to the one downstairs, only without any personal touches.

"But my mother is very aware of what's going on around her. She's sharp. These people don't seem to be … really sharp."

"She is feisty," Jane allowed. "As I said, we evaluate and make decisions based on what is best for her."

"Who would she talk to?"

"These people talk to each other." She seemed surprised that I'd asked.

"I don't see anyone talking." Another lump was rising in my throat, and it hurt to swallow. "My mother loves to visit with people."

"Your mother isn't ready for this floor, Robyn." She put her hand on my shoulder. "In many cases a patient with encroaching dementia never has to move up here."

I nodded. What she didn't have to say was that they died before their dementia got bad enough, which might have been preferable.

As we approached the elevator, I looked back and noticed a man strapped into a pale blue vinyl armchair, his chin on his chest and his hands twitching as if they were the only part of him still alive.

If she lived long enough, this was where she would wind up. That was the sad, sad thing about dementia and ageing. No one got better.

When I got home I took Bix for short walk and tried not to think about my mother's living situation. But it was like trying to ignore a big spider on the ceiling in your bedroom. When I finally managed to turn my thoughts elsewhere, they wandered only as far as Mick's wall safe, which was, I'd come to realize, another pointless intellectual exercise. Because even if I could break into his office, even if I could figure out the safe's combination, and even if I could do all this without being caught by building security or by Mick himself, what good would it do me? I needed *a lot* of money. So even if he had ten grand in there, what would that buy me (aside from ten years in prison and/or a violent death)? Ten thousand would be devoured by Dryden Manor within two months. Still, it was disconcerting for me to acknowledge that I might consider jail time before having my mother move in with me again.

The sun was making a feeble effort to leak past the clouds, which only served to make the air heavier. I flapped the bottom of my T-shirt for a little air conditioning. Bix teetered as he lifted his right rear leg over the curb in order to urinate into a storm drain. In spite of my mood, I had to smile. He's a pudgy, short-haired terrier mix, and with his round little stomach and dainty paws he's a rather comical looking sort. He's also the most angst-ridden, fastidious dog I've known.

We passed the Psychic Place on our way home. The curtains were drawn and the silver writing on the window sparkled. Erika Starwise had moved into the shop in the middle of the night a couple of weeks ago. One afternoon the storefront was bare, the window a large pane of dirty glass with a view of a small anteroom empty except for an electric pencil sharpener, still plugged into the wall, sitting on dirty taupe carpeting. A door leading to the back of the shop was open, and the space behind it dark, as though it led to nowhere. The next morning when I took Bix with me to the Wired Lizard, a mural of stars and moons spanned the purple-draped window, and what appeared to be a nebula surrounded the words painted over the glass: The Psychic Place. Beneath, in smaller letters, was: Erika Starwise, Medium.

When I'd called her to ask for an interview, we'd talked about a good time to do it. She told me she was lining up a séance that I might find interesting. And, since that had to be better than just listening to her tell me how clairvoyant she was, I agreed. Three days later she'd called back and invited me to a séance being held tonight. The invitation came with specific conditions. I was not to use the real names of the attendees, nor was I to take any photographs. I'd asked Erika if I could come early so I could interview her prior to the séance, but she told me that would not be possible. "I must distance myself from the living prior to a séance. Perhaps, if I'm not too exhausted, we could talk afterwards." Then she'd asked me if I'd arrive a little later than the others—say, seven fifteen—so she would have time to assure her client that she would remain anonymous in the article. Erika Starwise's behavior left me a bit suspicious of her, if not of her profession.

I do believe in psychic phenomena. There's more to this world than what we can see—at least I hope there is—and I suppose that some people can peer over that fence, so to speak. But I was raised and schooled to be dubious. My mother blew the Santa myth for me when I was seven, and journalism school taught me to check things out. But Erika Starwise had an impressive website, chock-full of recommendations. She'd had a successful business in California, and I made a mental note to ask her why she'd moved from the L.A. area to Fowler of all places. Further Googling revealed a number of conferences where she'd been featured and a yearly retreat she'd helped to establish.

When Bix and I returned to the apartment, I checked my voicemail while Bix retired to one of his two doggie beds. He has identical beds—one in the living room and another in my bedroom—so he doesn't have an anxiety attack when he wants to be in the same room I'm in, but has nowhere to curl up.

I had two voice mail messages. The first was from Connie telling me that the leniency Dryden was giving me in paying for my mother's room was "highly irregular," but April had made the decision and now Connie must abide by it. But if my mother had not been moved out of Dryden by the fifteenth, Connie would see our feckless butts in court. Well, those weren't her words exactly, but the sentiment was there.

The second message began with: "Hey there. It's me." Before I could ponder the possibilities, he added, "Mick. Mick Hughes." I assumed he was calling about the money we were diverting to Dryden. But then he went on, "How about I take you to the casino on Saturday night. A little gambling, dinner …"

Sighing, I punched "7" to erase the message, then "off" and returned the phone to its charger. Mentally, I dusted off my file of excuses, knowing I'd go with the truth. There were variations on the truth, of course, but wasn't it always the hard one that worked the best? While it was true that I experience a Bix-like state of agitation the moment I set foot in a casino, that was only a stop-gap excuse. Mick would suggest another baseball game or maybe just dinner, and then I was busted. No, it was best just to say outright that I liked him as an accountant and money manager, but his personal life made me a little nervous. Maybe my honesty would cost me an accountant, but we'd both move on. I wasn't the kind of woman who men pursued beyond the end of the block.

I still had an hour before my meeting with Erika, so I made myself a light dinner of grilled chicken on romaine with black beans and a few toasted walnuts, topped off with a balsamic vinaigrette I'd been trying to perfect. It wasn't there yet, but I was getting close. Maybe a little more pepper. I ate the meal at a small, ceramic-covered café table wedged into a corner of my kitchen while listening to a Runrig CD and watching for crow activity in the birch tree. I used to eat on my couch, off of the coffee table, while watching television. Then about six months ago I decided if I kept up the habit, I was going to need a bigger couch. At the same time, I stopped buying take-out and introduced myself to the stove, and what developed was, thus far, my most satisfying and longest-lasting relationship, which really wasn't saying much. I am challenged in that area. Seventeen years ago I married a guy who I'd known for three weeks. I was bowled over by his charm, sincerity, and the way he looked at me. The day after the wedding he dropped the charm and the look changed from adoration to predation. I left after twenty-three days, and there are times when I wonder why it took so long. When you step into a river and see the bulging eyes and double-barreled snout of an alligator, you don't continue wading to the other side on the off chance that he's just eaten. No, you turn tail and run. And while I believed that everyone was entitled to at least one colossal mistake in her life, the experience left me thinking that there was something basic about the institution of marriage that I just didn't get.

I added my dishes to the nearly full dishwasher, slammed the door shut and set the cycle to quick wash. What was it about me that attracted shadowy guys like my ex and Mick Hughes?

CHAPTER 4

When I arrived at the Psychic Place the outer office was empty and the door to the back area closed. I thought about knocking but didn't want anyone to think the spirit had arrived early, so I browsed around the office, trying to get a sense of Ms. Starwise. I smelled food—burgers?—and wondered if Erika had indulged before company arrived. The office looked better with furniture in it, although the carpet still needed cleaning. The pencil sharpener had found a new home on a black metal desk with a wood veneer top along with a phone and an appointment book. I glanced at today's entry: "Patricia Melcher, 7 pm" it read. Not that I'd ever use it for the article, but I liked knowing a person's name.

A certificate from the Psychic Institute of Cambridge hung on the wall above a metal bookcase. Closer inspection revealed its location to be the Cambridge in England, although I saw no claims that it was associated with the university. On top of the bookshelf, a short row of volumes shared space with a photo of a pretty young girl—maybe twelve—with long, dark hair and a sweet smile. She stood in front of a wooden bridge, and orange and gold leaves covered the ground.

I had just picked up the photo for a closer look when something touched my shoulder. I jumped and spun around for my first eyeful of Erika Starwise.

"I startled you." She retracted her hand and folded it into her other.

"I didn't hear you," I said, thinking she might have cleared her throat and at the same time sensing she'd known exactly what she was doing. I replaced the photo on the bookcase, adjusting it so the angle was as I remembered. "Your daughter?"

Her gaze wandered toward the picture, then back to me. "Yes," she answered.

She was a tall woman, around fifty. Her conservative beige linen jacket and slacks contrasted with her short, spiky red hair and penciled-in eyebrows. Bright red lips curved into a cool smile, and she said, "I am assuming you're Robyn Guthrie."

"I am," I replied, then added, "And you're Erika Starwise," feeling the silliness of the name as it tumbled off my tongue.

She assured me that she was, then said, "We first must settle a few things."

I nodded, noting the precision in her speech, almost as though English wasn't her first language. But I detected no accent.

"Sure."

"This is an intimate experience you've been invited to share. My client was not at all eager to have you here."

"I thought you okayed this with her." I hooked my thumb around the strap of my shoulder bag.

"Of course I did. You see, when she told me she had two friends who wanted to share the experience, I asked if she could find another. I explained to her that an odd number of participants is the most welcoming number for spirits. Five is an especially meaningful number." She paused, then added, "As in the five points of the pentagram."

"Of course," I said, not sure if I should be playing it straight here. Did she really believe this or did I detect a wink and a nudge in her delivery? "So she was willing to let me join the group."

"Correct." She hesitated. "Although she was not pleased to have a journalist among us."

"Is that going to be a problem?" I was on the verge of adding: because if it is, I'd be more than happy to go home and scrub grout.

She sighed deeply, but I had the feeling this sigh wasn't aimed at me. Then she said, "I convinced her that you would follow the terms

I mentioned, and I have promised to return her money if we are unsuccessful."

"Okay," I said, hitching my purse strap up on my shoulder. "Let's do it."

"Yes," she said, eyeing me up and down. Then she walked to the back door and opened it, allowing me to enter the sanctum of her offices, which, until only a month ago, had been the Embroider Me Emporium.

I stepped into the narrow hall and said, "Do I smell hamburger?" The aroma was undeniable back here.

"Whopper with fries. It was the deceased's favorite." Then she added, "We must make his spirit welcome."

I looked at her, trying to decide whether to ask her how ghosts ate. She must have picked up on the question, because she said, "Scents are highly evocative."

"Of course," I said.

"Patricia is asking her late husband for permission to remarry."

"And she's going to do what he says?" I found myself whispering.

"That will be her decision." Erika reached in front of me to open the door to the room on the right then gestured with a nod for me to enter. "I only form the conduit."

As I stepped in, the rich, grilled smell nearly knocked me over. If this guy died with his sense of smell intact, he'd show up, and if I were him I'd be madder than hell that I no longer required food.

Three women were seated at a round table, and as I walked in, one stood. I wasn't sure what I expected of the person who was paying a psychic so she could talk to her late husband. Certainly not this small, scrubbed woman with shiny chestnut hair who seemed more inclined to light a candle in church for her dead husband than to pound on his door.

"You're the reporter?" Patricia said, making it sound like an accusation.

"Yes." I introduced myself.

"Erika told you I don't want my name being used. Our names."

"That's not a problem," I told her.

I glanced at the other two women. One, I'd have bet, was Patricia's sister—she was heavier but had the same close-set eyes and thin lips. In contrast to these two women, the other appeared somewhat disheveled, with her straight blond hair pulled back into a pony tail. I wasn't expecting Patricia to bother with introductions, but she nodded at the one who looked like her and said, "This is Cynthia," then at the other, "and that's Laura." Both women said "hi" but only Laura offered a smile.

Then Patricia addressed me again. "I'd like to make one other thing clear. This is my séance," she said. "If Daryl doesn't show up it may be because of you." Then she turned to Erika. "I don't think I should have to pay if that happens."

"As I said before, Patricia, I will refund your money if your husband does not join us." Erika pulled out one of the chairs and indicated for Patricia to plant her butt in it. "You will sit here." She continued, placing us around the table so that I sat between Cynthia and an empty seat that I assumed was Erika's. Laura was to Cynthia's right.

"Patricia," I said, scooting my chair up to the table, "may I ask you a couple of questions?" I pulled a reporter's notebook from my purse along with a pen.

Patricia glanced toward Erika, who was closing the door. Then she said, "No," and added, "I'd rather you didn't. Maybe when we're through."

Smiling, I nodded my understanding and shoved my notebook and pen back into my bag. Then I cleared my throat in order to mask the sound of me pressing the "record" button of the digital recorder I carried with me everywhere. I know I should have asked permission to do this, but I was certain Patricia would have said no to that as well. But recording an encounter I'm going to write about is something I usually do so I can make sure I've got the quotes straight, and I also like to listen for the things I didn't pick up the first time. I set my purse on the floor and pushed it beneath my chair.

The room was small—the table just about filled it. A gauzy, lilac curtain hung over a shade covering the room's single window. Beneath the window was a small, half-moon table on which a short candle burned atop a wrought iron pedestal. I thought I detected a whiff of cinnamon, but it was mostly masked by the burger's smell.

Five more candles—three white and two purple—were strewn about the table, and as Erika lit each one, she explained that spirits seek light and warmth. I studied the group with whom I would be reaching into the hereafter. Patricia and Cynthia had their gazes fixed on the table's surface—not like they were praying, more like they were avoiding the rest of us. Laura caught my eye, but I couldn't read anything in her expression.

Erika crouched in one corner of the room, and with one red-shellacked nail, punched a button on a small CD player. The room filled with the sound of wind in trees and a gentle rain, and I hoped the ambient noise didn't interfere with my recorder. With a click, Erika flicked off the light switch, and the room was illuminated only by candles. Then she took her place between Patricia and me.

"As I explained earlier to Patricia, I cannot know how a spirit will contact us. I may see him and be able to speak with him—although that is not common."

"If you see him—" I interrupted "—will we be able to see him?"

"Probably not," Erika said, and went on before I could ask why not. "It is possible that we will see something—faint lights or shadows. Do not be frightened by this. It means that the spirit has found us worthy. I may hear a voice in my head. All of you may experience thoughts that are not your own. I urge you all to keep your minds open. Listen to these thoughts. There may be rapping sounds. Perhaps not. All we may feel is a presence." She turned to Patricia. "It may take some urging. Some spirits are eager to communicate; some are more reserved." She paused. "If there is skepticism in any of you—if any of you doubt there is a spirit world—I ask you to leave now."

Erika wasn't the only one looking in my direction. I just nodded.

"Very well," she said. "Let us hold hands. Join in a circle." We did. Cynthia had a light, wet grip, while Erika had a firm, cool hold on me. Following Erika's lead, we all placed our clasped hands near the edge of the table. "Now, let us close our eyes and embrace the silence."

It was a long silence, and I could hear the grilled chicken rioting in my stomach. I opened my eyes just long enough to see that the others were following orders.

Finally, Erika took in a deep breath and said, "Our beloved Daryl Melcher, we bring you gifts from life into death. Commune with us, Daryl, and move among us."

As I said, I was dubious, but I was also a little nervous. Part of me did believe in this—or at least was afraid to deny it. And who knew what kind of guy this Daryl had been? Why did Patricia need to ask his permission before remarrying? I began to write the article in my head and realized I was having a hard time making it a fluff piece. Between the medium and her client, this had become a rather edgy experience. And I had my doubts that Daryl would redeem it.

Mainly I was aware of Cynthia's wet hand. The back of my neck prickled, and I could feel the warmth of the candle burning inches from my arm.

It was a moment before I realized Erika was talking. "… slowly. Breathe in through your nose … and out through your mouth." I tried keeping my mind blank or at least open, but all I could think of was that maybe I should have cut back on the garlic in that vinaigrette.

After a few minutes of breathing, Erika spoke again. "Our beloved Daryl Melcher, we ask that you commune with us and move among us." Seconds passed, and she repeated the words.

Aside from a sharp stab of pain that hit me in the stomach, then quickly passed (the garlic again) I felt nothing. It had gotten a little cooler in the room, but maybe the window was open a crack. I peeked and saw the curtain lifting away from the wall. Erika gave my hand a sharp squeeze, and I closed my eyes and concentrated on my breathing.

"If you are with us Daryl, please make us aware."

Nothing. My Cynthia-side hand was drenched, and it was all I could do not to disengage myself and wipe my hand on my jeans. I tried—I honestly did—to pick up stray thoughts in the room. Thoughts that couldn't have been mine. But all I could sense was the mix of burger, fries and melting wax. I heard a gentle, low rumble of thunder, and it was a moment before I realized the CD was giving us a spring rainstorm.

Erika repeated her request. I peeked again and saw the curtain move away from the window, and this time I was able to see that the window was not open. I squeezed both hands and pressed my feet into the carpet. Probably a drafty window. My curtains did that all the time, and I never suspected a ghost.

The third time Erika asked, there was a single knock. It sounded like it came from within one of the walls, and at the same time it reverberated throughout the room.

I looked and saw Patricia's eyes squeezed shut so tight her face was contorted. Careful what you wish for, Patricia.

"We welcome you," Erika said for most of us. "Are you Daryl Melcher?"

Nothing.

"Please respond with one rap for yes and two for no." She paused. "Do you understand?"

One rap.

I checked to make sure all our hands were still on the table.

"Are you Daryl Melcher?"

Who else would it be? I couldn't figure out which wall the knocking emanated from; it was sort of like "surround sound" on a high-end TV.

One rap. And then another. Patricia's eyes sprang open, and she turned toward Erika, who shushed us all.

"Are you Daryl Melcher?" she asked again.

No.

Interesting. Now Laura was watching Erika. The pressure in the room seemed to increase. I felt a little like I was rising rapidly in an elevator. One of my ears twitched. All the while Erika's hands remained in plain sight.

"Is someone at this table known to you?"

Yes.

"Is it Patricia?"

No.

"Well, I—" It was Patricia, probably about to ask for that refund, but Erika silenced her with a hiss and a pointed look. The candlelight cast Erika's narrow features in shadow.

"We have invited a guest; we will be polite."

Jaw locked, Patricia leaned back into her chair and heaved a disgusted sigh.

Then Erika proceeded to go around the table, asking the spirit if it knew any of us. As she did, I watched Cynthia and Laura for signs of relief as the spirit passed them by. Laura nodded as she released her breath, and Cynthia eased her grip just a tad. I was the last person Erika asked about, and by then I was convinced this was a random spirit, bored with the hereafter and looking to frighten some middle-aged women.

"Are you here for Robyn Guthrie?"

One rap.

I waited for a second knock, but it didn't come. Shit. What was this woman trying to pull?

"Robyn," Erika said, as though inquiring about a ringing doorbell, "who could this be?"

"I have no idea."

"Are your parents alive?" Erika asked.

"My mother is. My father isn't." If this was Wyman coming back to do some explaining, he'd better give it a second thought. Ghost or not, I was fully prepared to take a bite out of his sanctimonious, two-timing ass.

"Why don't you ask if it's your father?"

"No," I said. "I don't think I can."

Erika did a little throat clear and then said, "Are you Robyn's father?"

Yes.

"Ouch," Cynthia whispered. I loosened my hold on her.

"What was your father's name?" Erika asked.

"Wyman," I said.

"Wyman, have you come to see Robyn?"

Nothing.

I was not going to make a fool of myself by talking to some guy Erika paid to lurk in the walls.

"Something's not right," Erika said, her painted brows pulling together. "Is your name Wyman?"

Two knocks and that prickly feeling began to work its way down my back.

Erika was watching me.

How could this woman have known about my biological father? Although, we did share the same last name.

"Robert," I managed to croak. Swallowing against the dryness in my throat, I added, "He died before I was born." In a flash I remembered how my mother had mentioned his name just this afternoon. A slip, she'd said. Maybe it was. Maybe he'd been bugging her.

"Are you Robert?" Erika asked and was answered by one knock.

"Do you need to speak to Robyn?"

Yes.

Oh, Jeez. My breathing had gone shallow. I wanted to take a sledge hammer to the walls. Someone had to be in there.

"This spirit is strong," Erika said, closing her eyes. "He will not be denied."

I willed the heaviness in the air to go away, but the sensation only became more intense. And, instead of smelling a Whopper, I now smelled some cologne or aftershave. Or maybe it was a flower.

"Robyn, why don't you try talking to him?"

My mouth was dry. For starters, I didn't know what to call him. I had no memories of him, and I didn't know what I would have called him. Wyman had insisted on "Father."

So I said, "Dad?"

The responding knock came almost before I'd gotten the word out.

"How are you doing?" What a stupid thing to ask a dead person. I tried again. "What do you want?"

I counted my heart beat three times and was sure everyone else was keeping time by its thudding. If this was fake ... if I was being played for a fool ... Erika would be sorry she ever loosed a journalist on her seedy little endeavor.

"Ask him if Daryl is there," Patricia said in an urgent whisper, interrupting my internal rant. God, what a silly woman, I thought.

"You will do no such thing." Erika shot Patricia a look.

Then she said to me, "Try to ask questions that can be answered with a yes or no," she said, her tone implying that she shouldn't have to tell me this.

Of course. "Have you got something to tell me?" I asked.

Yes.

I tried to convince myself this was not happening. This was not what it appeared to be. A guy was in the walls with some kind of amplifier, and I was the dupe because I was writing the article. Nothing like some free publicity. I could see the headline: Medium Channels Reporter's Father. Erika and the knocker would be guffawing over this once I was out the door.

But what if it was real? I couldn't ignore him. I tried to think of a question only he and I would know how to answer. Something that Erika couldn't have found through research. But that was hard, seeing as I'd never met him. Was there something he left me? My mother?

"Okay, Dad, how do I know it's you?" It wasn't until I noticed Patricia drilling me with a glare that I realized I'd spoken aloud. Well, I couldn't suck the words back. Nothing to do but press on.

"I have a locket you gave my mother. Is it in the shape of a heart?"

No.

Maybe a lucky guess. If he was guessing, his luck would have to run out.

"An oval?"

No.

"A teardrop?"

No.

Erika said, "There is no locket, is there, Robert?"

No.

Okay, he passed that one. Still might be luck. "Did we have a cat?"

No.

"A dog?"

Yes.

"Was her name—"

Erika jerked my hand. "Don't waste this, Robyn. He's here for a reason. Is there some decision you're trying to make? Some change in your life?"

I thought for a second. What if he really was trying to tell me something? "Do you know where my mother is?"

Yes.

"Should I move her?"

No.

And then, because that was awfully easy for him to say, I asked, "Okay. Can you pay for it?"

Erika jerked my hand again; at the same time Robert said: *Yes.*

"How?"

"Yes or no," Erika reminded me, then added, "Quickly, his presence is fading."

I could feel the pressure in the room easing. "The money exists?"

Yes.

"Does my mother have it?"

Nothing.

I repeated the question and thought I heard a single knock, but it was a faraway sound and could have come from anywhere.

"He has left us," Erika said, although I knew it already. He was gone—if he'd ever been here at all. The room felt different—all I could smell was char-grilled burger—and the back of my neck wasn't tingling anymore.

I tried to pull away, but Erika held onto me. "Thank you, Robert. Go in peace."

Whoever you are, I thought.

Across the table, Patricia made a clucking sound and said, "Well, that was a complete waste of time."

"I will happily return your money, Patricia," Erika said, then added, "Or, we can arrange another session. At no charge, of course."

Patricia mumbled something that was drowned out by Erika instructing us to sit for a moment and remember our feelings, thoughts, visions. I desperately wanted to disconnect from everyone here. The only visions I had were of me fleeing the room and these strange people. I didn't often think about my biological father. I'd never met him. I needed a photograph to see what he looked like. At times I thought I could see him in my mind, but when I focused on his face, he would morph into someone else. For a while there he'd looked like George Harrison.

Screw the article. Let one of the other stringers do this. I glanced around the table and saw four women with their eyes closed, no doubt searching their minds for visions or thoughts left by some spirit. Not one of them looked ready to stand up and say this was a sack of shit, and let's not let this food go to waste.

Maybe they were all in on it. Maybe they were all pseudo psychics, and this was the kind of favor they did for each other. Maybe there was a way to find out.

I ripped my hand from Erika's grip and slid the other out of Cynthia's, then stood and wiped my hand on the seat of my jeans.

"Don't worry," I said, "I won't need any quotes."

As I walked out of the room, I heard the squeak of a chair.

I'd almost reached the street entrance before Erika stopped me. "Robyn. Please."

I turned and watched her cross the small room.

"What?"

"Your father tried to speak to you. And if you hadn't been so intent on proving he was a fraud, you might have learned something." She picked up her appointment book and flipped a couple of pages. "I will need a day or two to recover. But I can make room for you on Monday."

I'd seen her appointment book. It looked like my social calendar. "I don't think so."

I put my hand on the doorknob, but she stopped me again with: "He will give you signs, Robyn. Watch for them. He is near. He has something to tell you, and his soul will not rest until he does."

"He's been dead for forty-four years. What the hell took him so long?"

She hesitated. "That is unusual."

I waited.

"For a spirit to not have moved on after so many years."

"Maybe he had nowhere to go," I said, good agnostic that I am.

She shook her head, more out of pity than disgust. Then she said, "I'll be here when you're ready."

"Thanks," I said, and grabbed the doorknob again, then released it and let my hand flutter at my shoulder for a second. "Shit," I muttered. "Forgot my purse."

I retraced my steps to the séance room. When I opened the door, all three women looked up. Patricia's mouth was open, but she snapped it shut when she saw me and gave me a narrow-eyed look of resentment. Cynthia had her wet little hand on Patricia's shoulder in a feeble gesture of comfort. Laura was helping herself to the French fries.

"Forgot my purse," I said, reaching behind the chair I'd vacated.

I hooked the strap over my shoulder, turned to Patricia and said, "Life is way too short, girl. Marry the guy."

Bix met me at the door doing his terrier toe dance, but I urged him to give me a minute before he got his walk. I was suspicious of anything that went on in Erika's little psychic den. And that included the three women there for the séance. So I dug out my recorder and reversed a short ways—just enough so I could hear what had been said right after I left. If I was expecting a psychic conspiracy, I was disappointed. Although, I was a little surprised to hear that kind of language coming out of Patricia's mouth. Clearly, she didn't have much use for people who upstaged her. I was okay with that but wished I hadn't offered her a little sisterly advice there at the end.

By now Bix's stiff little tail was experiencing tremors, so I grabbed his doggie pack and my keys, and we went for a walk. It was dark and rather cool as Bix and I headed down to the park just a block east of my apartment.

And while Bix marked every third tree along way, I mulled over the evening's events. If Erika was a fraud at least I wasn't the only mark—Patricia was too. But I'd been the target. Patricia had simply been wasting her time. And what I couldn't figure out was why Erika would go to the trouble of conjuring up someone I'd never known. And if she knew enough about me to know that Wyman wasn't my biological father, then she also knew that Wyman was the only father I'd known. Why not conjure him up? And why conjure anyone up? I had a hard time believing it was just for a sensational story.

It had started to drizzle, and so Bix turned and began leading me toward home. He just doesn't like the rain much.

By the time we got home and I'd toweled down my dog, I'd forced myself to examine the possibility that Erika, despite her absurd last name, might be the real thing. And if she was … then the man who had died before I was born just remembered he had something to tell me. And as soon as I stopped doubting, as soon as I let a little hope seep in, it overwhelmed me. Then I told myself I was being silly—the dead don't talk—and all that hope whooshed out of me, leaving me so empty I thought I would deflate.

And then there was what he said—don't move your mother. The money exists.

"Right," I said to Bix, who continued chomping on his rubber rabbit.

I poured myself a scotch over ice and dribbled a tablespoon of water in it, then scrolled through the caller ID numbers. There was a cellular number I didn't recognize, a call from M Hughes and then there was my mother's number on the monitor, which made my stomach clench. When she called at night, she was invariably more confused, anxious and demanding than usual. Sometimes she'd accuse of me things I couldn't possibly have done, like stealing her money or moving her car. They call it sundowning; I call it heartbreaking.

Voicemail had two messages for me and, as I feared, one was from my mother.

"Robyn? Where are you?" Her voice had a panicky edge. "I'm ready to call the police. And your father … he hasn't come home from work yet. I've got a pot roast in the oven? …who is going to eat it? … Robbie? Is that you? … I'll call you back, Robyn. I think he's at the door."

Robbie? I quickly dialed the nursing station on my mother's floor, talked to Vera, the night nurse, and learned my mother was napping. Crisis had passed. Yes, she'd been agitated, but not beyond the usual.

"Did she have any visitors tonight?" I mentioned the interruption.

"No," Vera said. "That must've been me checking up on her."

I thanked her and asked her to call me if things got rough again and then said a silent prayer that my phone was through ringing for the night.

I had one other message. This one was from Mick.

"Hey, how'd talking with that dead guy go? Can't wait to hear. Oh, and I've got a way for you to take a few thousand out without paying any penalties. Call me."

For a second, I almost did call him. Just to have someone to tell this to.

Instead, I changed into a pair of cut-offs and a T-shirt, pulled my hair up into a pony tail, then curled up in my comfy chair with my laptop and drink and brought up the internet.

The circumstances surrounding my father's death had been a fact of my life that I'd never questioned. Why would I? He had died just outside of Colorado Springs, where my folks lived at the time. He'd been delivering mail when a guy driving a Chevy Impala swerved to miss hitting a turtle crawling across the road and plowed into my father. I was probably the size of a cantaloupe in my mother's womb at the time. She moved to Illinois right after I was born and married Wyman a few years later.

In the past I had used the internet to search for records of my father, but had always come up empty. I had chalked this off to bad record keeping on Colorado Springs's part. But now I began to wonder. And since my mother was less than forthcoming these days, I knew of only one other source where I might find some answers. That paper-filled box she'd asked me to get rid of was probably just that—a bunch of miscellany I could toss with impunity. But maybe now was the time to see if that was the case. I dug my key to the basement door out of the kitchen drawer where it had spent the last two years.

The picture framing store I lived above had taken up most of the basement, which was lit by two naked bulbs with long, beaded pulls. My corner was still there, although I had to move a large oil painting of a clown's face—rather creepy, actually. But there I found my two suitcases, a few pots for planting and the box. While it wasn't large or particularly heavy, it smelled moldy and I hoped no creatures had taken up residence in it.

I hauled it upstairs, sneezing as I went, put on a pot of coffee and settled in for a long night.

Around one thirty, I unearthed a nugget that sent me scrambling for my computer.

CHAPTER 5

Although my internet search kept me up past three a.m., I was out of bed by seven the next morning. I showered and threw on a pair of jeans and a T-shirt and hustled Bix out the door for his morning walk. If I timed my visit right, I could get to Dryden Manor before my mother had breakfast, and then it would be easy to lure her into a meal of blueberry pancakes with maple syrup at Malone's. I wasn't craving her company; I was itching for a showdown. And I had no qualms about my plan to pump her for information while pumping her full of flapjacks. After my night of research, I was convinced that your average supermarket tabloid contained more facts than my early recorded history.

Bix cooperated and finished his business quickly, and we were on our way back to my apartment when a red Porsche drove by, then slowed and pulled over to the curb about ten feet in front of me. I'm generally not impressed by cars. It's not that I'm above all the superficial materiality that has made us the greatest consumers in the history of the world. Possibly the universe. Hardly. If I had the money I'd buy the same digital camera every time it got upgraded. But I am not a car person. To me, driving is overrated. But this little convertible—black top up—perched beside the curb and humming at me, made me wonder if maybe I'd just never driven the right car. As I slowed, the passenger-side window slid down, and I saw Mick Hughes behind the wheel.

It was too late to run or walk away. His Porsche had snared me as surely as a grappling hook.

"Hey," he said, smiling as he twisted in his seat, one arm draped over the steering wheel. "That your dog?"

No, it's the badger I've leash trained. "Yeah. This is Bix."

"Hey, there Bix," he said, then lifted his chin toward me. "I was on my way to see a client and I saw you. Wondered if you got my message. About the casino."

"I did. But I got home kind of late last night. I was tired."

Bix, affable to a fault, was trying to pull me toward the car. But, small as he is, he didn't stand a chance against my desire to remain inert.

"Sure," Mick said, sounding not at all convinced. Despite the fact that the morning had brought with it a thick layer of gray clouds and a fine mist, he wore a pair of sunglasses that prevented me from reading any further. "So what do you think?"

"I really don't like casinos. They're too … discordant."

He removed his sunglasses and squinted up at me. "Discordant, huh?"

I nodded. My feelings were difficult to describe in one word, but that came pretty close.

He rubbed his thumb across his lower lip. "Do you like to eat?"

I considered telling him I was on a macrobiotic diet, eating only that which I grew in jars in my apartment, but lies always came back to bite my ass. "I've been known to."

"I'll pick you up at seven. We can talk about your money. And other stuff."

I hesitated, then nodded. "Okay." Clearly, I would have to spell it out for this man. But not until I had the money to keep my mother from being put out on the curb. And the place for either of those subjects was not on a public street with him leaning across the passenger seat of his hot little car.

He put his sunglasses back on and as he pulled away the passenger window slid up. It occurred to me that having a client in this area was a bit of a coincidence. Unless Mick lived near here. And one didn't see many red Porsches parked in the apartment lots.

It was at this point that I began to wonder if I was being stalked by my accountant.

I spent the brief drive to Dryden deciding if it would be worth going out with Mick just to see if he had anything to contribute to my mother's housing. Maybe he'd invite me back to his place. That could be dangerous, but I could handle him. Like Bix, he was small. Maybe he had a priceless coin collection he wouldn't miss immediately. Or a Monet in an out of the way corner. I thought of that little safe in his office—if there was a safe. For all I knew he had a tiny plasma television behind the painting. Or a blank wall. Still, I let my imagination toy with the possibilities. Mob money? Money from gamblers using him as a bookie? Blackmail money? I was truly ashamed of where my thoughts wandered these days, but Mick's intentions toward me probably weren't any more virtuous. What did any of it matter? With her medications and all, I would need close to sixty thousand dollars to keep her in Dryden. And that was just for one year. My mental activity was merely intellectual aerobics, albeit larcenous aerobics. At least it kept my mind occupied, and that was a good thing. Because it was easier for me to plan a robbery than to imagine where my mother would be living in a matter of days.

I arrived at Dryden in time to see my mother emerge from the elevator with a group of the second-sitting breakfast eaters. Wearing a bright red blouse over black velour slacks, she bulled her way through the small crowd using her cane and repeating "Excuse me" in a loud voice along the way, her knitted brows reflecting her intense determination. She earned several glares, none of which she seemed to notice. When she saw me standing by the desk, she stopped, confused, as though she knew the dark-haired woman from somewhere but couldn't place me. This confusion lasted only a few moments, and then her features relaxed. By the time she reached me, she was nearly giddy. And when I suggested we go out for breakfast, she clasped her hands together and her eyes widened behind her large-framed, pink glasses. It was like I'd just asked her if she wanted to meet Santa.

"Oh, that sounds lovely, dear. Let me get my sweater." Her abrupt turn nearly caused a collision with a walker-wielding woman, and there was no telling how many others that mishap would have taken out.

My mother gave the woman a dismissive look and said, "Excuse me, Betty, I'm going out to breakfast."

I wasn't sure, but it looked like Betty mouthed the word "bitch."

My mother caught the next elevator up, leaving me to collect the nasty looks from those she left in her wake.

As I waited for her, one of the nurses came out of a back office. A huge woman with a lumbering walk and narrow eyes that harbored no nonsense, Lorena was actually a favorite among residents, including my mother. I think my mother liked the bigness—the safeness—of Lorena, and saw her as a benevolent bear in a white dress and Rykas. When Lorena saw me, she came right over. "We need to talk," she said, almost under her breath, and my heart began pounding—a natural reaction when someone says those four words to me. Then she motioned me away from the desk and toward a grouping of three Victorian chairs, currently unoccupied. What had I done? How could she know we were running out of money?

When she began with: "I really should be telling April this, but I'm going to hold off," I tried not to whimper. She glanced toward the hall leading to management's offices. "We don't make our money here by fining residents we catch smoking in their rooms."

My jaw dropped, and I flapped it once before I said, "Smoking?"

"I didn't catch her at it, but I know what it smells like. God knows, Lizzie's not the first here to try it." She paused and took a breath. "This morning when I stopped in on Lizzie, I know I smelled cigarette smoke."

"No," was all I could manage.

She nodded. "Afraid so. She used to be a smoker, didn't she?"

"Before I moved her in here. But that's been more than two years." Of all the things to worry about, the one that had not occurred to me was my mother sneaking smokes in her room.

Sighing, she twisted her mouth as she shook her head. "It happens sometimes. Maybe she bummed one off a resident."

"How many residents smoke?"

"Not many. But there's a hard-core group and, believe me, they know who's carrying."

I couldn't imagine anyone would give my mother the time of day, let alone a cigarette. She wasn't exactly in the running for Miss Congeniality.

"Did you say anything to her?" I asked Lorena.

"'Course I did. And she acted like I'd accused her of boiling babies. Got all indignant." She gave me one of her rare smiles. "You know how she can be."

I assured her that I did and said I'd talk to her.

"You understand," Lorena continued, "this rule was in place long before the state made it illegal."

"I know."

"And the fine has to be high to make the point."

"I completely understand," I assured her. And I did. "Thank you so much for telling me. And not April." Who, at this point, might not fine us, but would have one more reason to see my mother leave. "I'm taking her out to breakfast, and I'll talk to her."

Just then I noticed that my mother had gotten off the elevator and was watching Lorena and me have our little chat. Her sparse brows were pulled together as though trying to recall an errant thought.

I gave her a little wave, thanked Lorena again and walked over to collect my mother.

"Blueberry pancakes?" I straightened the collar of her blue sweater.

She watched as Lorena walked past the reception desk and out of view, still searching for that thought. But then she finally looked up at me and smiled, hooking her arm in mine. "I think I'd like bacon today too."

"I can arrange that."

While signing her out, I took a minute to check the register of Dryden's guests from the day before.

At Malone's Pancake House, as I reached out to open the door for my mother, I said, "Smoking or non?" I was certain that she could not remember that Illinois had removed all options.

Her beatific smile, no doubt inspired by the warm, sweet smells, faded into a tight frown, and she drew herself back, removing her hand from my arm. "Why would you ask such a thing?"

"Smoking or nonsmoking?" I repeated.

"I haven't smoked in years."

"Nonsmoking," I said to the hostess, who gave me an odd look but grabbed a couple of menus and showed us to a table.

As soon as we were seated, my mother picked up the menu and held it like a laminated curtain in front of her face.

Once the busboy filled our glasses with water, I said to a photograph of the triple cheese omelet with salsa, "You know why I asked, don't you?"

"Asked what?"

"If you wanted the smoking section."

"I'm sure I have no idea."

"Mother, lower your menu, please."

After a few seconds, she lowered it only far enough for me to see a pair of pale blue eyes sparking with anger.

"I'm sure I have no idea," she repeated.

"Don't give me that, Mom." I rested my folded arms on the table's edge. "Lorena says she smelled smoke in your room."

"Well, that's ridiculous. I don't know why she'd lie like that. I thought Lorena and I were friends."

The fact that she sounded genuinely hurt attested to my mother's latent acting abilities.

"She's just worried," I said. "Not only is there a thousand dollar fine for smoking, but smoking in those rooms is dangerous."

When she continued to smolder, I asked, "Don't they have someplace outside where you can smoke?"

Making a sour face, she folded her menu and set it beside her. "Oh, just a little area in the garden. The way the wind whips through there, it's a wonder anyone can keep a match going long enough to light up."

I pictured those elderly women, standing around the garden, the edges of their coats flapping in the breeze, hands cupping matches to their cigarettes, and it was my turn to hide behind the menu.

Then my mother muttered, "With what I pay for that room, I should be able to smoke."

I remembered the rule was if a resident was caught smoking in her room twice, she was out. And for a fleeting moment, I thought I had *my* out. If my mother was the reason she would have to move into a less appealing place—if she did it to herself—then I could shed a little of the guilt. But the moment that bubble surfaced, it burst, and I knew it was wrong. All wrong.

I lowered my menu and saw that she was sipping her coffee, which was pale with cream.

While she still hadn't admitted that she did sneak a smoke, I conceded that I wasn't expecting a mea culpa. I just wanted to make my point. Besides, she was going to have plenty to feel defensive about in just a few minutes.

We both stuck to neutral ground as we chatted. She told me about the lecture they'd had on migratory birds that would pass through northern Illinois in a month or so, and I told her about an article I was writing on a woman who collected kaleidoscopes. She told me she thought a woman in her forties shouldn't be wearing her hair as long as I did; I told her that the rules had changed. Then she conceded that it wasn't the length that bothered her so much as the fact that I often wore it in pony tail. It was easy, I told her, fully knowing she would next mention that if I didn't want to spend the rest of my life alone, I needed to put more time into my appearance. She didn't disappoint. But this time she added, "You're not getting any younger, you know." *By the minute*, I said to myself, almost looking forward to our imminent confrontation.

I waited until the waitress had delivered her stack of blueberry pancakes and rasher of bacon, then watched while my mother poured a generous quantity of syrup over the pile. I even let her take a couple of bites and commented on how good my scrambled eggs and dry wheat toast were.

I took a sip of the strong, hot coffee, set my mug on the edge of the red paper placemat, and said, "I need to talk to you about my biological father."

Barely glancing in my direction, she dabbed a chunk of pancake in the syrup and thrust it into her mouth.

"Robert," I added, then pressed on. "Maybe you could start by explaining why you told me he was a mailman who died in the line of duty." I paused and waited for her to look at me. When she didn't, I said. "Neither is true."

She stopped chewing and glared at me, her jaw locked.

I pressed on. "And you were living in Cortez, Colorado, not Colorado Springs."

Nailing me with her frostiest look, she said, "You were born in Colorado Springs."

"You moved there from Cortez."

Her hand trembled slightly as she picked up the mug of coffee and took a sip. I waited for her to return it to the table.

"Mom, I just want to know why you lied."

She carefully chewed a bite and didn't make eye contact with me until she'd washed it down with another swig of coffee. I was always a little surprised at how her watery blue eyes could harden and turn flinty.

"What difference could it possibly make?"

"He was my father."

"You never knew him."

"So?"

I'd already decided I wouldn't tell her about the séance. And after my night of research, I didn't think I needed to. "He was my father. Don't I have the right to know?"

She just glared, and now the little muscles around her mouth were working.

"Didn't you think I'd *want* to know?" I pressed.

"You never questioned me."

"Why should I? You tell me my father was a mailman, why would I doubt you? Why would I think you were feeding me a lie?" I took a deep breath. And then another. If I lost it now, I'd regret it.

"What did he do," I asked, "that made you think a lie would be better?"

"Who did you talk to?" she asked.

"I found your divorce papers in the box of stuff I've been keeping for you."

She drew in a deep breath and released it slowly. "The one I asked you to throw away?"

"Don't change the subject." I hurried on. "You were divorced in Cortez. I wondered why I'd never heard you mention Cortez. Once I Googled Robert Guthrie in Cortez, I learned that you haven't been very forthcoming about him. For one, he didn't die there."

Her mouth twisted into a bitter smile. "And what else do you *think* you know?"

The way she stepped on the word "think," I knew she was angry. Probably more angry than upset at this point. Which was good, because once she started to make her little sobbing noises, I'd have to stop.

"Well, that woman you talked to yesterday …"

She drew back, and though some of the anger left her features, I couldn't quite read what replaced it. "I won't discuss that."

"I need to, Mother. I need to talk to her." Then I added, "And I will."

"Well," she broke off an end of crisp bacon and popped it into her mouth, "you're going to have a hard time doing that without her name."

"It's Mary Waltner."

Her eyes narrowed, and I could hear the bacon crunching in her mouth. "So," she said, "now you're spying on me."

"No. All visitors to Dryden have to sign in."

She glanced out the window, which was covered in fat raindrops. "She won't tell you anything you want to hear."

"Yeah, well, maybe it's something I need to hear."

She studied me for several moments, and I tried not to cringe under her glare. Then she dabbed her lips with her napkin, and set it beside her fork. She kept her hand on the cloth, gently kneading it. "I see," she said, with a sigh.

"What do you see?"

"You didn't take me to breakfast because you wanted to visit with your mother." A brief, chilly smile was offset by her eyes, which had softened and turned moist. "You wanted to make me talk about things that are hard for me to talk about. I don't have much of my life left, Robyn. We both know that. And I don't want to spend it weeping over my past. I see too many of the women do it at that place."

"Mom—" I put my hand on hers, but she snatched it away, then reached for her purse.

"I'd like to go now."

"Come on, Mom. I'll drop it." For now. "You've hardly touched your pancakes."

"I don't have a taste for them anymore." And her look added "thanks to you."

She was slipping her arm into the sleeve of her sweater, and I knew there was no turning her around. I fished a twenty out of my wallet and dropped it on the table.

"I don't want to go back there just yet."

We'd been driving in a silence I was determined not to break.

"Where do you want to go?"

She didn't speak for another minute, and then she said, "I'd like a cigarette."

I glanced at her, but she kept looking forward.

"You know they're bad for you. You've got COPD."

After a moment, she said, "What does that stand for again?"

"Chronic Obstructive Pulmonary Disease."

She sniffed. "Fancy words."

"For a long time there, you weren't smoking at all. I thought you'd beaten it."

She looked at me sharply, "I will choose what I want to beat, thank you."

The light drizzle had intensified, and I moved the wipers up a notch. "I don't want you getting sick again."

With a sigh, she said, "Everyone has to die of something."

I didn't need to tell her that suffocating in your own body had to be an awful way to go; she knew that.

"I miss them," she said, as though she were talking about some friends who had moved away. "They calmed me."

Another half mile down the road was a convenience store. I pulled into the lot.

"Virginia Slims, right?"

She nodded without looking at me.

When I got back to the car I was reeling from sticker shock and thinking if she were to keep this up, I'd have to add a couple thousand per annum onto the amount I needed to steal.

I settled into the driver's seat and looked down at the beige and gold pack I held. My mother was watching me, expectant, but not willing to snatch them from me. "I hate these things," I said.

"I know." She sighed. "I do too. In a way."

But there were days when I hated how much I needed a scotch.

"Some ground rules," I said, and she nodded like an obedient school girl. "I keep them. You only smoke when you're with me." I waited for another nod. "If I hear you're smoking at Dryden, it's over."

"Yes, *Mother*," she answered.

"I'm serious."

"I know."

Neither of us spoke for several seconds. Then she said, quietly, but with some dignity, "I'd like one now."

"I don't want you smoking in my car."

"I understand. If you'll just drop me off in that park we just passed, I can sit on the bench."

I gave her a look. The rain hadn't let up. "We'll go to my place." It would be easier to air out than my car.

We drove the rest of the way in silence. I didn't often bring her to my apartment. I guess I realized it was kind of a sad little place and figured she'd look at it and start telling me what I needed to add, when the truth was I really didn't want to add anything except maybe more books.

Bix greeted us at the door, wiggling his little terrier butt. My mother scooted him out of the way with her cane. "Aren't you an odd-looking creature?" she said in the way she did every time she saw Bix, then settled onto one end of the couch. Bix hopped up next to her, found no welcome, and retreated to the other end where he curled himself into a ball.

She regarded the dog, her lip practically curled in disgust, and said to me, "I can't believe you let this animal on your furniture."

"It doesn't bother me a bit," I said.

"Hmph."

I dug the pack of cigarettes out of my purse and handed it to her, then went into the kitchen in search of some matches and an ash tray.

When I returned, she had the pack open and one of the long, slender cigarettes wedged between her first and second fingers. I set a small plate on the table next to the couch and handed her the matches.

"Thank you, Robyn."

I nodded. "The cigarettes stay here."

She shot me a look, then averted her eyes. "All right," she said, as though resigned to gruel three times a day.

I opened the two windows behind the couch, then sat across from her in my purple reading chair and watched as she lit up, taking the smoke into her lungs like she was inhaling sweet mountain air. She held it in for a moment, then exhaled in a rush and coughed a couple of times. It was a thick, phlegmy sound, and I tried not to think about what it was doing to her lungs.

She swallowed and said, "You never smoked, did you?"

"No," I told her.

"You were smart."

I shrugged. "There are other vices."

"Oh? You have some?" she said, her tone arch.

"None I'm telling you about."

For the first time that day, we both smiled at the same time.

Then my mother glanced at her watch. "I suppose it's too early for a little glass of Chablis."

I kept my sigh on the inside, and when I stood, I said, "It's five o'clock somewhere."

She gave me an odd look. "Your father used to say that."

"Wyman?"

She snorted a laugh, and a puff of smoke came out her nose. "Hardly."

Silly me. Wyman didn't smoke or drink but compensated by screwing the organist. "Yeah," I said with a smile. "I should've known better."

I returned with a glass for each of us.

"I thought you only drank red," she said, reaching for her glass.

"It's early."

We sat in silence for several minutes, watching Bix, who had fallen asleep on his back with his skinny legs in the air. One paw was twitching.

I was sometimes amazed at how much of her distant past my mother remembered. Her short-term memory was on its way out, but she held onto the past like a jeweler unwilling to give up her most precious pieces. This was what I was counting on. I needed for her to share a few of those gems.

Finally, my mother said, "If Wyman had known about your father—what he was—he never would have married me."

"Why didn't you ever tell me about him?"

"You were three years old when I married Wy. How could I expect you to keep a secret like that? And then, well, it never came up."

That was true. She had seldom spoken of my biological father. I never mentioned him in front of my stepfather, because Mom said it made him feel insecure.

"How did you learn this?" she asked.

I gave her a brief explanation of how I was able to access the Cortez, Colorado obits and found no records of a Robert Guthrie dying there at that time. "And then," I said, "I found his name on a police report. He robbed a gas station."

"Yes," she nodded. "I remember." She stared off in Bix's direction.

"Did he do time?"

"Yes. He was sentenced to eight to ten years."

"Is that when you divorced him?"

"Yes."

I waited for her to continue, and when I began to wonder if she was going to, I prompted with: "Is he still alive?"

She was slow to focus on me, and when she finally did, she spoke as though not quite detached from a dream. "No. No, he isn't. At least that's what that woman told me."

And then she told me what else Mary Waltner had to say.

CHAPTER 6

"You know, Wyman could certainly be a pain in the tutu, not to mention a philanderer, but he was a good provider." My mother sighed. "He was also a very proper man."

Yes, I thought, he may have been a self-righteous, philandering jerk, but he put up a great front. Too bad he hadn't been able to cover his final set of tracks.

"If he had known about Robert—and Robert's difficulties—I'm certain he never would have married me. And I needed to be married. For us." She looked at me. "I wanted what was best for you."

I nodded, noting the progression there.

She was silent for a long time, and I didn't push it. As long as she stayed awake, I figured she could still be gathering her thoughts. Who knew where she had to go to do that.

Finally, her brows scrunched together as though this particular thought had been a painful extraction, she said, "He was a cruel man."

I felt a chill snake its way up my spine. We Guthrie women had a way with these types. Forcing myself to concentrate on the here and now, I thought of how she'd never had a bad word to say about him before this. And even after my research the night before revealed that he had been an armed robber, well, I still thought he could be decent. I mean, here I was, trying to come up with a means and the wiles to steal thousands of dollars, and I considered myself a decent person. Nice, even. "My father?"

She looked at me slowly as her eyes focused. "Yes," she said. "Robert."

"In what way was he cruel?"

Tapping an ash from her cigarette, she took a sip of her wine, making a sour face before returning the glass to the cork coaster.

When she didn't continue, I prodded with, "Why did Robert rob the gas station?" wondering if it was only about the money.

She blinked and said, "He liked to scare people."

The image I'd held in my mind all these years shifted a little more and darkened considerably.

"How do you mean?"

"Oh, you know … like a bully." She nodded to herself and then looked up at me. "He was a bully."

I tried to read the answer to my next question in her eyes so I wouldn't have to ask it. From what I saw, she wanted me to keep my mouth shut. But I couldn't.

"Was he abusive?"

Her lips pressed together and she closed her eyes. I thought she was going to cry and then remembered that she couldn't. I knew I should go over there, scoot Bix off the couch and put my arm around my mother. But I couldn't.

"I've forgotten so much," she said, "so much of the good things—why do I have to remember that?"

"Bad things can make us strong."

"Either it's made me strong or it hasn't," she snapped. "I'd like to forget it now."

I nodded. "Good point."

"Thank you," she said, as though my approval wasn't at all necessary.

I knew my mother—or at least I thought I did—and I knew how to get her mind out of the sad places. Either make her laugh or make her angry. Just now I couldn't think of a way to make her laugh. So, I said, "As bad as he was, why didn't you think I should know about him?"

Faster than a sparrow's blink, her head shot up and her mouth hardened. "What difference would it have made?" She went rigid with anger, one arm crossed tightly over her chest and the other holding up the cigarette like a flag. "It's not as though you've got his blood in you."

"Then whose blood do I have?" *And don't tell me I'm one hundred percent Lizzie.*

She faltered, but then the hardness returned to her jaw. "That's *not* what I meant, and you know it. I-I meant you're not a violent person. You're not a thief."

My next breath caught in my throat. I swallowed and continued. "Didn't he ever try to find me?"

"As far as I know he never tried to find either of us. Until now." Her eyes locked onto mine. "You were better off, Robyn."

When I didn't respond, she added, "He never saw you."

That was probably true. He'd been arrested two months before I was born.

"What kind of work did he do?" I asked.

An impatient sigh. "Oh, I don't remember. I think … I think he was an auto mechanic."

"He fixed cars," I said, more to myself.

Her chin puckered again. "Bastard," she said and tapped her cigarette so hard, part of the burning ember dropped onto the plate.

"Why did you marry him?"

She shrugged and sighed. "He was charming. Handsome. I hadn't known him very long." Another shrug. "I made a mistake."

Wow, did that sound familiar.

She smashed out her cigarette and took a drink of wine. I wondered how long she'd stay awake; wine had a narcotic effect on her. But she lit another cigarette and eventually, through the haze of smoke, her gaze settled on me.

"We all make mistakes," I offered, as much for myself as my mother.

She cocked her chin and said, "And I thought you were perfect."

I chose to ignore the sarcasm and asked instead, "The urn, who's in the urn?"

She coughed twice and then said, "Just ashes from a fireplace."

All these years and I'd been buying pottery for cordwood remains. The urge to point this out was so strong I could almost feel myself twitching. But, again, this wasn't about my anger. My issues. I told myself to deal with it later and simply asked, "Why bother?"

"If I could take his grave with me, you wouldn't ever need to go looking for it."

Of course. That fit perfectly into the legend of Robert Guthrie. And if I hadn't saved that box of stuff she had asked—no, *told*—me to throw away, I would never have known to check Cortez records. Still, I couldn't help thinking of all those pieces of pottery I'd purchased, always picturing the tall, ruddy-faced man in the one photo I had of him. I'd wonder if he'd approve of my pottery selection, imagining that he liked shades of purple and blue—maybe because I do—and curved, flowing shapes with no beginning or end. Now that I realized I'd spent all these years talking to a pile of soot, while my living, breathing father was out there, well, I had to work even harder to keep a lid on the anger.

"Silly, I suppose," she said.

"That's okay, Mom." But it wasn't. Not at all. "Was his birthday June twentieth?"

"I doubt it."

Move on, I told myself.

"What about this woman who came to see you? Mary Waltner."

She brightened. "Mary. She was quite nice."

"What did she want?"

"Well, she said she knew your father. And she told me that he died about a month ago."

"How did she find you?"

She paused. "I don't think I asked her."

"Where did this woman live?"

"Oh, I don't remember what she said. Nebraska, I think." As though it wasn't of consequence. I recalled that earlier she had said Los Angeles. The woman was creeping east.

"Who was she to my father?" How strange that a man who was a thief and an abuser had a friend who cared enough about him to cross (at least) two states in order to tell the wife he'd deserted forty-some years ago that he was dead.

"A friend." She paused. "Or maybe she was his lawyer."

"There is a difference.'"

"I suppose. Well, she was quite a nice woman."

Lawyer made more sense. And why would a lawyer be there if not to give her something?

"What happened to him? To Robert?"

"I told you. He died. He was almost ninety."

"No, I mean, what happened after he got out of prison? What did he do? Where did he go?"

"Oh, I don't remember what Mary told me—you know my short-term memory. Something to do with used cars."

My real father—a thief, abuser and now a used-car salesman. I leaned back and sighed. We can't all be the children of astronauts, I told myself.

"How did he die?"

She gave me one of her looks. "He was older than me by several years. At that point what difference does it make? I believe they call it 'natural causes.'"

I pushed myself up in the chair, crossing my legs under me. "So why wouldn't this lawyer—or whoever she was—just call you?"

She took a deep breath and expelled it through her nose along with a trail of smoke. "Robert left me something."

I waited, barely breathing, and I couldn't help but think about what Erika Starwise had said. Or, rather, what my rapping father had told me. "What did he leave you?"

"A little money."

"How little?"

Her jaw trembled and she took several moments before trying to speak. When she did, her voice cracked and broke over the words. "When Robert and I had been married only a few months, he stole some money I had stashed in the coffee can." She swallowed. "I was hoping to buy a new sofa with it."

I waited a beat. "How much?"

Twisting her mouth in annoyance, she said, "A hundred and fifty dollars, if you must know." Then, "I suppose you want me to give it to you. Seeing as I'm not allowed to have anything to do with my own financial matters anymore."

"No, Mom," I said, trying to keep my disappointment from showing, "just keep it someplace safe."

She patted her purse.

I was having some trouble digesting all this, and the questions just kept popping out of me. "Why would he leave you that money?"

"This woman—Mary—told me that Robert had a religious conversion at some point. Turned his life around, he said."

"Hmph," I said. "You'd think if he really had, God would have told him to add some interest to that buck fifty."

She chuckled and then, as I watched, her eyelids grew heavy.

"I wonder why," I paused, "if he had this conversion that made him pay back his debts, then why didn't that same conversion make him want to find his daughter?"

I didn't think she was going to answer me at first. But her eyelids fluttered and she said, "I don't know. But I suspect child support payments had something to do with it."

"Yeah," I said after a moment. "I guess it was easier to send you the sofa money and call it even."

The combination of wine and being up more than two hours without a nap had nearly put her to sleep. With her eyes still closed, she sighed and said, "He could be very sweet."

"I thought you said he was a cruel man."

She looked at me, confusion shadowing her eyes. "Well, yes, that's true. In a way." The she sighed again and said, "I'm tired."

"Do you want to lie down, Mom?"

"Yes, I think I would."

"I'll help you to my bedroom."

"No, that's all right." She glanced at Bix at the other end of the couch. "I can lie down here if you can move him and get me a blanket."

"Sure thing." I scooped Bix up and deposited him, a bit dazed from his own nap, on the floor, and when I brought an afghan in from my bedroom, my mother had her feet up on the couch and two throw pillows situated beneath her head.

"Robyn," she said, the sound of sleep in her voice.

"Yeah, Mom?"

"My finances are all right, aren't they?"

"You're doing fine." I tucked the blanket around her.

"I want you to tell me if there's a problem."

"I will."

"Good."

Soon she began snoring softly.

I watched her sleep for a few minutes. Sometimes it was hard to remember that this fragile, confused, frequently exasperating woman had once been my age, younger. Prettier. I thought of the hundred and fifty dollars nestled in the coffee tin. I remembered that tin—with the farm scene on it: blue sky, white clouds and a red barn. Chickens. It was where she kept her "laundered" money—leftover grocery and household cash that Wyman never knew about. She must have been good at it because she had enough to afford riding lessons for the two of us. That was one thing we shared—a love of all things equine. And now I'd learned that before the riding lessons, she had set aside money for a couch and someone stole it from her. First the hundred and fifty and then, years later, many times that.

And I thought about my own marriage, when I'd been the one to bolt. I'd left with little money and had called my mother to ask if she could loan me a couple thousand and also asked if I could stay with her until I got back on my feet. While she'd sent me the money, she'd made it clear that there wasn't room for me in her apartment. This shouldn't have surprised me. I think we do love each other, but most of the time we don't like each other very much.

I paid her back every penny and swore I'd never ask her for another thing again. And I haven't. But now she needed my help, and I was as confused as hell as to why it was so important that I be there for her. Maybe because I felt I needed to atone for my own ineptness as her daughter. I should have known where her money was going. I should not have let it come to this.

In that moment I knew where I'd get the money. Or I would die trying. I wouldn't take it from Mick, or from anyone else who hadn't taken anything from my mother. And I knew I could do this, because it wasn't stealing … it was taking back. And I knew exactly who to take it back from.

While my mother napped, I dug out my files on her finances. When I'd first learned, to my horror, the extent of damage that these "investments" had done to her savings, I was ready to track down each and every scam maggot, and if I couldn't get the money back, I intended to make them very sorry they cheated someone's mother. Especially mine. I saw the whole lot of them as this giant, hissing hydra that I—Robyn the Righteously Vengeful—would do battle with. I really hated seeing the bad guys win. But it wasn't long before I learned how difficult it was to track these people down. How adept they were at tossing snarls of obfuscation behind them, which one needed to fight her way through in order to hack off one of their heads. If I'd had the money and the time, I would have done whatever it took. But I didn't have either. And, in the past couple of years I'd managed to relegate the knowledge of what they'd done, and my unknowing complicity, to the part of my brain that allowed me to live with it.

But there was one guy whose name I had managed to track down, and I consulted a lawyer concerning any recourse I had. Piddling little. The situation had involved a proposed shopping mall in which, over the course of several months, my mother had invested more than fifty grand before the company had gone under and filed for bankruptcy. The investors were the only ones who lost anything in the deal. The company had been a minor piece of a large conglomerate owned by William "Bull" Severn. Recovering the money would have been difficult, seeing as, for all his wealth, none of this was in his name. His wife's name was on most of these holdings, with some consigned to a cousin and a half brother.

Maybe I had consulted a spineless lawyer, but he had me convinced there was no way I could win without bankrupting myself. And even then there were no guarantees. I hated that about the system—the people who'd stolen from my mother would never pay for it because they had money and/or sleight of hand on their side. Being right had nothing to do with it.

I thought about writing an exposé. Figured a magazine would love a piece like that. And, while there was some interest, in the end no one would touch it because of the potential for libel suits from wealthy folks with deep pockets.

Now I decided that perhaps my mistake had been in pursuing only legal options.

I peeked in on my mother. Her mouth hung slack and she was snoring. Bix had managed to squeeze his plump little body between her feet and the back of the couch where he slept.

I got on the internet and Googled Mr. Severn. I knew that he lived in the Chicago area, but I didn't know what he'd been up to lately. And by the time I heard my mother's groan, which accompanied her rise from the couch, I had the seed of a plan. At least I knew how I might worm my way into Severn's company. Severn, like any self-respecting mogul with more money than he knew how to spend, had bought himself a racehorse. Once I learned that, I Googled William

Severn and Mick Hughes. I shouldn't have been surprised to find the two of them linked in a number of articles; horseracing was a small, tight world, and I assumed one never got over being a jockey. But when I saw the photo of Severn and Mick in the stable with Severn's horse, I read the caption and then the article. A plan began to form in my mind. It needed definition—an object to be precise—and I didn't know exactly how I would pull it off. But I did know where to start.

It was early afternoon, and I sat with my mother as she smoked another cigarette and we chatted about little things—the Cubs' season, Bix's snoring and the loud ticking of my cuckoo clock—and then she asked to be taken home. While she was in the bathroom, I peeked in her purse and found a cigarette that had "fallen" in there. I almost checked her wallet, but knew that was a line I didn't want to cross. So I just removed the smoke and slipped it back into the pack, which I tucked into a kitchen drawer.

After she pulled her sweater on, she opened her purse, shoved her hand down into it and felt around. Then she looked up at me with knowing, angry eyes. "I see you've been through my purse."

Crossing my arms over my chest, I said, "I see you tried to smuggle a cigarette."

"That hellhole," she muttered. "What's the harm in letting us smoke?"

"I'm sure it has to do with safety, Mom."

"It's ridiculous." She spat the word out as she hooked the strap of her purse over her forearm and picked up her cane.

"You know, Mom, if you don't like where you are, if you need to be someplace where you can smoke and fart to your heart's content, then we'll find somewhere else for you to live."

"Hmph." She glanced around my apartment, stopping to straighten one of the throw pillows she'd used. "If I lived here I could smoke."

"No, you couldn't."

"Oh, I forgot. Your lily-white lungs."

"I've got asthma, Mother," I told her for, perhaps, the thousandth time. "Smoke doesn't help."

"Well, I didn't know you had asthma. How long have you had it?" she asked, and I didn't think I imagined the dubious tone.

"I was diagnosed about seven years ago," I said, daring her to challenge me. Daring her to give me a reason to thank her for her contribution to my asthma. But she backed down, and I was glad, because I would have been sorry. I always was when I did something like that. Although I doubted she'd remember for more than a minute or two. And the next time I mentioned it, she'd be asking me all over again when I learned I had asthma.

When I got home from dropping my mother off, I debated whether to run over to the Psychic Place again. Not only had I neglected to get a photo, but in light of my mother's revelations, I had a few more questions for Erika. Even if the money hadn't been significant, the spirit of Robert—or whoever had been behind him ... or it—had been right. And then I remembered when my editor had assigned me the story, he'd told me that Erika had requested me. Seeing as I usually do the "Welcome to Fowler" pieces, it wasn't an issue. At the time, I'd assumed that she liked my writing. Maybe I should have been more suspicious than flattered.

But when I called Erika, I got a recording and decided not to leave a message. I'd wait until Monday and just drop in on her. If she really was a psychic, there'd be no surprising her.

I spent the remainder of the afternoon attempting to track down Mary Waltner, convinced that my mother would never come clean about the woman's visit. As open as my mother had seemed, I knew better than to be certain this was the final word on her past. I started with the assumption that Mary Waltner was a lawyer, which made sense. Lawyers were often involved in wills and other after-death details. But my Google searches turned up little. If she was a lawyer, she was pretty low key. Then I did a white pages search of the entire United States and found there were quite a few—all over the country—from Alabama to California. After a bit more Googling, I determined there was nothing to do but pick up the phone. Damn.

I leaned back in my chair and looked up at the ceiling. When I found no divine inspiration up there, only a wisp of a cobweb, I decided I really did have to start punching numbers. Cold calling is something I detest—I'd make a terrible telemarketer, I fumble on the phone. But, I wrote out a script and got started. The first Mary Waltner, who lived in Ames, Iowa, assured me she hadn't left town in five years. Sounded like me. The next two didn't answer—I left messages, asking them to call me collect and briefly explained why I wanted to talk to them, mentioning my mother and her failing memory. The next woman answered, and she required something of an explanation, so I went with the truth—more or less. But most of them didn't want to know about my mother and her memory problems, and all I had to do was apologize for bothering them. I had a brief but pleasant chat with a Mary Waltner from Freeman, South Dakota. She'd been on her way out the door to her book club when I called, and we exchanged a couple of titles before hanging up. But mostly it was a series of short calls and left messages. When I recited my message into the last Mary Waltner's voice mail, in Thousand Oaks, California, I conceded that this was a pointless exercise—for all I knew the woman I was trying to reach had an unlisted number, or only used a cell phone. But I had to go through the motions.

When I disconnected from my last call, I looked at the number again. Where had I seen the 805 area code recently? I punched the button on my phone for missed calls and went back to last night when I'd gotten the call from my mother. There had been another caller who had left no message. A cellular call. With an 805 area code.

CHAPTER 7

As the hour of Mick's arrival approached, my nerves were thrumming at high pitch. I didn't have much experience at subterfuge, so I didn't know if I had a knack for it.

Mick was good at what he did. With my modest savings, he had helped me build a respectable portfolio. Although he had this "I'm just one of the guys" air to him, I suspected he was smarter than most of "the guys," and I cautioned myself to remember that.

The fact that I hadn't been out on anything resembling a date in almost a year added to the jangling nerves. That ill-fated venture turned out to be my first and last attempt at internet dating, which left me leery of mixing my personal life with the computer's. Not an awful experience, but the man and I had disagreed on so many issues that we spent most of the evening discussing the breadsticks.

Tonight I spent a long time staring at the contents of my closet. I considered a black and white halter dress, but decided that was best worn when I was feeling less ambivalent. I finally decided to face Mick in a pair of black slacks, a turquoise cami and a black and white silk shirt I tied at the waist. I wore my silver raven necklace, which I've always considered lucky. After a moment's indecision, I slipped into a pair of black sandals without a heel. I doubted that Mick had issues with height—he had more than enough self-confidence to compensate—but I wanted to be safe.

I assaulted my hair with a curling iron in an attempt to subdue its locks, which have a tendency to go all wild and frizzy when the weather is humid. Failing, I pinned it all up and hooked on a pair of silver, dangly earrings. As I examined my image in the mirror, wiping a smudge of mascara from the corner of one eye, the door buzzed.

Bix charged up to it, as is his habit, barking and prancing around, looking back over his shoulder at me, who he expects to open the door.

"Hush up, little man," I said.

I'm not sure what I imagined Mick would be wearing, or how I expected him to look on a date. But, seeing him standing there in a short-sleeved shirt over dress khakis gave me an entirely different image than the one of him in his office. It was as though he'd left his sleaze at that office when he'd discarded the professionally laundered shirt and the knotted tie.

Bix, indiscriminate charmer that he is, wriggled in ecstasy as Mick bent over to scratch behind his little pointed ears. "Cool dog."

"He's good company." There was something in the texture of the pale green print shirt he wore that made me want to touch it—to see if it was as soft as it looked. But I restrained myself.

Bix leaned against Mick's leg, soaking up the attention.

"Do you have a dog?" I asked.

"Nah. I've got a ferret."

I waited for him to say he was kidding—Mick didn't seem a pet kind of guy let alone a ferret man—and when he didn't, I shifted to my other hip and said, "I hear ferrets are good pets." This was only for the sake of conversation, because there was no way I believed a weasel would lick your chin.

"Name's Fredo." He gave Bix a final pat and slipped his hands into his pockets as he righted himself.

It was the first time I'd stood beside Mick, and while I didn't tower over him—at five-five I had about two inches on him—I had to resist a temptation to slouch.

"He's okay," Mick added. "Old girlfriend gave him to me." He paused. "She wasn't old. It was just a while ago."

"I get it," I said, and realized, again to my surprise, that Mick wasn't totally at ease. I wasn't sure what to make of that. I am not the intimidating type.

"So," he made a show of glancing at his watch, "we'd better get going. Got seven-thirty reservations."

"I'll grab my purse."

On the way to the restaurant, Mick explained how I could get a quick five thousand out of my savings without accruing any penalties. It was complicated but legal. I told him to "make it so" and said I'd sign any papers. It would take a few days, but I figured I could hold off the Dryden collectors for that long. While I was glad it was doable, I kind of wished he'd saved the topic for dinner. I wasn't sure how long I could sustain a conversation with this man.

Mick pulled the Porsche up to the door of Galileo's, and a valet leaped from the shadows. As he surrendered the car, Mick slipped the young man a bill along with his key.

The valet showed remarkable restraint as he pulled away.

"Do you ever worry about getting it back in one piece?"

"Nah, that's what insurance is for."

He held the door open for me.

I'd never been to Galileo's, but I'd been in town long enough know that it was one of the best—if not the best—restaurants in the area. It's one suburb west of Fowler, which doesn't boast much more than a Red Lobster, and a million miles away in terms of the social strata.

The maitre' d greeted Mick by name and led us to a table for two by a large window overlooking a pond arched by a white bridge. Subtle lighting cast the scene in an otherworldly glow. As I sat I could see myself in the glass, and above me hung the disembodied red letters of a reflected Exit sign. I chose to ignore the warning, and when the waiter asked what I'd like to drink, I said, "Famous Grouse. On the rocks."

After Mick ordered a bottle of wine, the waiter left us with a basket of bread, the menus and silence. Mick set his menu aside, and I squinted out the window toward the bridge and watched a pair of mallards waddle from the marshy grasses and into the shiny, black water. When I turned back to my menu, Mick was eyeing me. I gave him a brief smile and concentrated on the black, seriffed letters on heavy, cream-colored paper. I did not know how to make small talk with this guy—breadstick man and I probably had more in common—but I knew it was way too early to bring up racing.

I selected a heel of crusty Italian bread from the wire basket and poured a pale green pool of fruity-smelling olive oil onto my plate.

As I set the bottle down, Mick said, "You didn't really want to go out with me tonight, did you?"

Before I had to answer, the waiter delivered my scotch, a bottle of wine and two stemmed glasses. As he uncorked the bottle, he recited the specials. After giving Mick a taste of the wine and getting the thumbs up on it, he offered me some, but I waved it off. I asked him to repeat one of the specials. No matter how dire my situation, I am never too distracted to appreciate good food. As he walked away, I asked Mick if he'd ever had the trout.

"Everything here's great," he answered, "and how about my question?"

The scotch tasted strong. "I'm here, aren't I?"

"You ever give a straight answer?"

I hadn't anticipated playing defense tonight; in the script in my mind I led Mick on a winding path where in the last scene I got what I'd come for. He wasn't supposed to have the advantage. Ever. After casting a glance in the waiter's direction and seeing no help from that quarter, I looked Mick straight on and said, "I guess I just had to know why you were trying so hard." His bland expression didn't change. "I'm not beautiful; I'm not rich, and I'm not young. If you'll tell me what it is, I'll run home and bottle it."

I caught a flicker of something in his eyes—I wasn't sure if it was the sheepish look you get when you've been busted or if he was a little hurt. "Hey," he said, his voice soft, "that's not fair. I asked you out because I thought you were nice. And you're pretty." Then he added, "That color's real nice on you."

I glanced down to remind myself of what I was wearing.

"And then you lost that weight," he said, giving me an appreciative nod. "Don't sell yourself short. You're looking fine." He rested his arms on the table, leaned toward me and said, "What I can't figure is why a woman like you would even wonder."

In the face of his apparent sincerity—and he was oozing sincerity—I wasn't sure how to respond. I drank. "Thank you," I said, thinking how nice it felt to be flattered, despite knowing I was being played. Or was I?

He smiled and leaned back, taking his wine glass with him. He'd moved on too fast, I thought. If he'd really been worried about my believing him, or if he'd been sincere, he'd have said something else or at least kept his eyes on me longer. Or, maybe he was just that confident.

I returned to my menu and attempted to herd my scattered wits, reminding myself it was still early. I had plenty of time to focus the conversation. I saw the waiter approaching and decided to delay my offense until after we'd ordered.

The waiter had a silver crumb scraper clipped to his shirt pocket, and now he swooped in and removed all the unsightly bread debris with three deft swipes. I reminded myself that a place cannot be judged solely by the absence of crumbs, but I placed my order for the trout with high expectations. Mick ordered a steak, rare, and poured some wine into my glass. I nodded my thanks but thought it would have been nice if he'd asked me first.

As I was about to ask him about his career as a jockey, he said, "You ever been married?"

I considered telling him it was none of his business—not yet, anyway—but thought that was exactly what he expected me to do. I'd already succumbed to his flattery. Now perhaps he was trying to intimidate me.

"Briefly," I said, noting I was almost out of scotch at a time when I needed it the most.

"How brief?" he asked.

"Very."

He gulped down some wine and poured himself a bit more. "Bet I can beat you."

"Try."

"Thirty-six days."

"Twenty-three," I said, not at all proud of my win.

He nodded, conceding the contest to me with frank, albeit misplaced admiration. "What happened?"

"You lost, you go first." I drained my scotch and pulled the glass of wine closer.

"I caught her giving my buddy a blow job."

Judging from the way his eyes hardened, this was a true story. "What did you do?" I asked, wondering if the rumors I'd heard were confused and this was the woman who had lost a digit.

"To which one?"

"Let's start with her." I started on the wine.

"Divorced her."

Our salads arrived and I shook off the waiter's offer of cracked pepper and asked Mick, "That's all?"

He shrugged. "There's other women out there."

"What about your friend?"

"He's not my friend anymore."

"Is he still alive?"

Mick chuckled. "What? Now you're on the attack?"

"It's called ambush journalism," I said, getting into it. "So is he?"

"Last I heard." Then he shrugged and added, "It's not like we exchange Christmas cards."

Before I could get another question out, he said, "Your turn. What'd he do?"

I took my time, chewing and swallowing a bite as I considered my answer. Even after all these years, it still felt like I was getting kicked in the gut whenever I thought about him. I'd been running on instinct when we'd married, and it had gone wrong so fast that it made me question forever my instincts. And that was a lousy place to be. Finally, I said, "He had some habits I really hated."

"Like?"

"Cocaine."

"Yeah," he nodded, "that's a bad one. What else?"

"He hit me. Once." Actually, it was more than once, but I'd never admit that to anyone.

"That when you left?"

"Damn right."

"Did he follow you?"

I plunged my fork into a nest of arugula. "Not far."

He studied me for a moment, as though considering whether to follow up on that. I hoped he wouldn't, because then I would have to lie. There was no way I was letting Mick know how scared I'd been.

To my relief, he asked, "How long you know him before you got married?"

"Almost a month."

Yes, that was me, I thought. Important decisions—like who to marry, whether to have children, whether to divorce—tended to be split-second choices, once made, never reconsidered. Wrestling between the pasta puttanesca and the pecan-crusted trout had taken longer.

We polished off our salads and when the waiter arrived with our dinners I waited for Mick to dig into his steak and shove a piece into his mouth before asking, "You used to be a jockey, right?"

He nodded as he finished chewing, swallowed and said, "I've ridden a few horses."

"More than a few from what I've heard."

He shrugged, but I could tell by the sliver of a grin that he liked the fact that I knew. And that I'd asked about it. At that moment there was something slightly disarming about Mick, and that surprised me. "Twelve years' worth."

"How'd that happen? How'd you become a jockey?"

"Well," he said with a grin, "it's not like the Bulls were trying to recruit me."

I wasn't going to let him get off that easy. "Oh, I see. So if you're under five foot five, the career counselors send you to the race track."

"Yeah, something like that." But then he said, "I don't know. Always liked horses. Hung out at the track. Got to know some trainers who'd let me exercise their horses. Riding came natural." He shrugged. "Then I stopped growing." He looked at me and added, "I wasn't born to it so much as it fit."

"Where did you race?"

As we ate, he gave me a brief summary of his career—starting out in Mexico, moving up to California and finally winding up working for an Arab sheikh in Dubai who owned a stable of thoroughbreds. "Those horses had better accommodations than most people I know."

It wasn't hard for me to imagine a horse living in more luxury than Bix and me. "Did you live there?"

"During the season, January through March, I did."

"Why'd you stop racing?" I figured I knew, but this was part of that winding path.

He jerked his head to his right and down toward the floor. "This."

I glanced at the teal-green and tan carpeting, and he lifted his foot as though to acknowledge my assumption.

"What happened?"

"It got between the ground and fifteen-hundred pounds of horse."

"So you didn't get your leg broken because you refused to throw a race?" That was not on the script. The wine must have been getting to me. It wasn't the scotch. The scotch I could trust.

He reared back his head and gave me an "are you kidding" look. "Wow. I hadn't heard that one."

I doubted that.

Then he said, almost to himself, "That'd make me kind of heroic, wouldn't it?"

I nodded. "That would indicate lots of scruples."

He chuckled dryly as he lifted his glass of wine. "Yeah, that's me." He took a drink and kept eyeing me.

"When did you find time to go to college?"

"After the racing." Then he added, "I was around twenty-eight."

"Are you still involved in it? The racing?" I asked, using my fork to nudge off a piece of trout, which was flakey and moist. Perfect.

"Sure. I go to the track."

"Do you own a horse?" I paused, tried to appear thoughtful, and added, "I saw that painting in your office. Figured maybe it was yours."

"Yeah, it is. It's not the greatest work of art. But my niece painted it." He shrugged.

The fact that he hung bad paintings done by his niece was intriguing, but I couldn't let it sidetrack me. "Does this horse race?"

"Sure," he said around a bite. "Just not very fast."

"That's too bad."

"She's got good blood, so she's good breeding stock."

"Yeah," I said, nodding. "Sometimes talent skips a generation."

He lifted his glass as though toasting my thought. To be agreeable, I sipped some more of my wine, which had a pleasant, slightly spicy taste. "Amen to that."

I needed to get him back to the races, but before I could, Mick asked, "You like horse racing?"

"Yes, I do."

His eyes narrowed. "But you don't like casinos."

"That's right. If you'll recall, I said they were discordant."

"Oh, yeah." He chucked. "I remember you using that word. I had to look it up."

That I doubted.

"I don't like the chaos. The overstimulation."

"That's intentional."

"I'm sure it is. And I guess it works. Just not on me." I shrugged. "But, personally I could care less if people want to throw money away." Then I added, "Better them than me."

"If you don't like to throw money away, what're you doing at the track?"

"I like to watch the horses."

He looked up from his steak. "You like horses?"

"When I was a kid, my favorite book was anything by Walter Farley."

"No kidding."

"I read everything he wrote." I forked a piece of trout. "I also remember cherishing an orange and black book called *Horse Fever*." I popped the bite in my mouth and watched Mick as I chewed.

"You ride?" he asked.

After swallowing, I said, "I used to," and hoped the accompanying sigh sounded regretful. "When I was a kid my mother popped for lessons. For both of us. But that was awhile ago. Other stuff got in the way."

"Like?"

Now he was trying to shift back control. I didn't want to get too far off course before reeling him back. "Oh, making money. Eating. That kind of stuff. Horses are an expensive calling." I set my fork down and folded my hands under my chin. "But I always take time out to watch the Triple Crown. It's a celebration. I make myself a mint julep while watching the Derby."

He glanced at my empty scotch glass. "I'll bet you do."

The path was heading into the home stretch. I busied myself with a pile of couscous as I asked, "You said you were still involved in racing. Without a racehorse, how do you do that?"

"I do some consulting. I've got a reputation for knowing a good horse when I see one."

I wondered how he explained the slow mare, but that would take us off the path again. I thought I could see where it ended. "You tell other people what horses to bet on?" I tried to sound a little dubious.

"Sometimes. And sometimes I tell them which ones to buy."

"Really?"

"Sure. You think all these rich guys who own a line of thoroughbreds know anything about them?"

"They don't?" I cocked an eyebrow—a gesture that had taken me three months to perfect.

He shook his head as though amused by my naivety, picked up his wine glass and said, "You ever heard of Bull Severn?"

I clung to my own glass of wine and forced myself to take a sip before saying, "You mean William Severn, as in Severn Construction, Severn Realty, Severn Dynamics …"

He chuckled. "That's the guy."

"He's got horses?"

"Just one. Right now. But it's one of the best horses in the country. Favored to win the Plymouth Million next Saturday."

I sat up. "Bull's Blood?"

"That's the one."

"I didn't realize Severn owned that horse." I set my drink down. "And he consulted you when he bought the horse?"

He nodded once.

I leaned on the table. "Get out. You did not."

"Sure I did."

"Wow." I leaned back in my chair, my fingers resting on the edge of the table. "From what I've read, that's an incredible animal."

He finished chewing his last bite of steak as he watched me. After washing it down with a gulp of wine, he said, "Maybe someday I'll introduce you to Bull. And his horse."

Someday. Someday was not acceptable. I was inches from the wire, but I'd risk it all if I sounded too eager. "I'd like that," I said, introducing a slice of asparagus to my couscous.

I could feel Mick watching me closely, but I concentrated on my plate, waiting for his response, which I hoped would be an invitation.

As it turned out, it was, only not the one I'd spent the entire evening attempting to wheedle out of him.

He leaned toward me. "When we're done here, do you want to come back to my place? We can talk about it."

CHAPTER 8

He watched me, apparently waiting for a response. My thoughts spewed in so many directions, I didn't know what to say. After several heavy moments, I shook my head and sighed. "I don't know if that's a good idea."

"How come?"

"You know that marriage I mentioned earlier?"

"Yeah." He drew the word out, and I could tell by the way he cocked his jaw that he couldn't wait to see where I was going with this.

If only I knew.

"Well," I said, "ever since then I've made it a point to never go home with a guy on a first date." I drank some water, coaxing an ice cube onto my tongue.

"I'm not going to ask you to marry me."

I stuffed the cube in my cheek. "You say that now."

Silence hung between us like a noose. But then he laughed, and I joined in, relief flowing to my fingertips as I thought that now we'd each chuckle this off and go to our respective homes.

Unfortunately, Mick proved more resolute than I'd anticipated. "I'm not scared," he said. "Are you?"

"No," I replied in all honesty, because "scared" wasn't the word I'd use. He didn't scare me. Unfortunately, he didn't exactly attract me either. I did find him kind of interesting and would have said yes to a second date. Maybe even a third. But my goal had been to gain *entre* to Bull Severn without compromising my tarnished virtue, at least not until I was ready to do so.

On the other hand, it wasn't like I was saving it. That train had left the station, so to speak, long before I'd met my ex. And when I played the progression through in my head—sleeping with a man in order to meet another man from whom I intended to steal a large amount of money in order to enable my mother to continue to live in an assisted living home because I had neither the space nor the inclination to move her into my home—well, in a way, being bedded by Mick Hughes would be the least of my indiscretions.

Where does a girl take her moral compass for adjusting?

All of this rumination hadn't taken more than a few seconds, during which time Mick continued to watch me. At the end of it all, I knew what was at stake here. In spite of, or perhaps because of the fact that I was brimming with self-loathing and desperation, I was able to look him straight on when I said, "Okay. But don't say I didn't warn you."

I expected Mick Hughes to live in a condo. Maybe one of the new ones on the west side of the river. I figured he lived the life of a libertine and couldn't be troubled with mowing lawns or cleaning gutters. So I was surprised when, at the end of our brief journey, he turned onto an older, tree-lined street and then pulled into a driveway leading to a garage set behind a narrow, Victorian-style home.

It was dark and I couldn't be sure how well the outside was maintained, but I could see the gingerbread detailing and the darker shade in the trim.

We stepped onto a lighted porch spanning the width of the house where a couple of green wicker chairs flanked a wicker table with a glass top. He unlocked the door, reached in and flicked on a switch that illuminated a foyer opening onto the living room.

With a wave, he gestured for me to go first.

"Does your ferret live in a cage?" I asked as I set foot into his house.

"Most of the time," he said without elaborating.

He directed me through the living room, toward the kitchen, and I got a brief look at his rather sparse, brown furnishings in the front room.

The kitchen and family rooms were another story, and I assumed that this was where he did most of his living. A huge fireplace anchored one end of the slate-floored room, and pots and pans hung from a rack above a center island with a sink and a breakfast bar.

I had a moment of envy then. I've never allowed myself to think much about owning a home. I could probably buy a small place, but something inside me insists on being mobile. Also, I take some pride in being able to fit the items in my life into a one-bedroom apartment. Maybe I was afraid I would expand my possessions to equal the size of my home, and that made me uncomfortable. That was why I'd gotten rid of most of my old clothing as soon as it became too big for me. Still, there was a warmth to this place that wasn't present in my three rooms.

I found the powder room off to the right and excused myself. More to gather my wits than to relieve myself, although I was more successful in the latter. I spent much of the time hoping I wouldn't come out to find him spread out naked in front of his fireplace.

In the end I decided that since he had pursued me with some diligence, he wasn't going to sever our budding relationship because I didn't sleep with him on our first date. And, if he did, he was too easily discouraged, and I would simply have to find another way to meet Bull Severn. Now, if only I'd thought of all that before I'd accepted Mick's invitation.

When I came back out into the kitchen, he offered me a drink and, although I wasn't thirsty, I asked for water. Declining might indicate I was ready for the upstairs tour.

He had poured himself a brandy and taken a seat at the breakfast bar.

I sipped water that was nice and cold, set the glass on the granite-topped island and said, "I shouldn't have come back here."

He regarded me for a couple of moments, swirling his brandy in the bowl of the balloon snifter and then said, "But you did."

"Yes," I conceded. Then, "I had a nice time. I'm not sure I expected to, but I did. And I'd hate to ruin anything by moving too fast."

He didn't respond, just kept swirling and watching me.

Typically, I would have continued babbling. To keep from doing so, I drank more water.

Mick finally set his glass down and said, "That mean you don't want dessert?"

I smiled, trying to let him know I appreciated the effort.

"I'm serious," he said, patting a carton of vanilla ice cream I hadn't noticed sitting on the counter.

"Oh," I said. "Dessert. Sure."

He got up and removed a plastic bag full of pastries from the fridge. It wasn't until he pulled a few of the small, golden orbs out of the bag that it began to fall into place. And when he dropped blocks of dark chocolate into a saucepan filled with cream that had been heating on the stove, I nearly gasped.

Oh, sweet Jesus, I thought. He was making profiteroles.

I crossed my arms and leaned against the island. If the prison kitchen was out of sticky toffee pudding, this was my "last-meal" dessert.

While the chocolate melted into the cream, he cut four pastries in half, situating four halves on each of two plates.

"The worst thing about being a jockey," he said, "was not being able to eat anything but salads dressed in lemon juice."

I wondered if that was worse than getting your leg mangled, imagined the warm-cold sensation of melted chocolate and vanilla ice cream and thought that maybe it was.

I assisted in assembling two of the treats on each plate, placing a scoop of vanilla ice cream on each crust, covering it with the other half and then let Mick apply the finishing touch with the melted chocolate. My mouth was watering as he led me out onto an enclosed porch off of the family room. It was small with a couple of chairs crowded by a three-level ferret cage, a virtual playpen, outfitted with ramps, benches and toys. Fredo, long and squirmy with pale whiskers, sniffed my hand, and Mick said he'd take him out after we had dessert.

As we settled into the chairs, Mick said, "You always have a dog?"

"No. Bix is my second." I slid my spoon into the ice cream. "When I was a kid," I said, "my mom finally broke down and let me get a dog. Wyman—my stepfather—wanted one too, so that helped. Rochester was a dachshund. He barked a lot, but he was a neat little guy."

"Your mom doesn't like dogs?"

I shrugged. "She doesn't dislike them. They get in the way and they're dirty. She just doesn't see the point in pets."

"That's too bad," he said, and I nodded in agreement.

Dessert was better than the meal, which was saying something, but I didn't tell Mick that, figuring that admitting to a ravenous sweet tooth showed a weakness I didn't want him to know about. I did praise it, however, and, once again, the food distraction let my guard down.

We'd been having an innocuous discussion regarding his backyard and its three maple trees, when, after a few moments of silence, he said, "You want something from me, and I can't figure out what."

I swallowed a bite. "You're the one who asked me out. Remember?"

"Yeah—"

"And don't tell me you just happened to be driving down Forest Lane when you saw me walking with Bix."

"What?" He cocked a grin. "You think I'm stalking you?"

"I wouldn't use that word, but—"

"You're the only reason I might be driving down that street?"

"Well, when you put it that way …"

"Damn right," he said, but I could tell from his twitching grin that he found this exchange amusing. "You do remember that I'm a financial advisor."

"Yes, but—"

"So you probably figure you're not the only person I advise."

"Well—"

"And despite my reputation, I'm not a guy who makes little old ladies roll down to my office in their wheelchairs."

I stopped, a spoonful of chocolate-drenched ice cream inches from my mouth. "You were making a house call?"

"Sure."

Sure he was. I stuffed the spoon into my mouth.

"Speaking of old ladies," Mick said, "how's your mom doing?"

I glanced at him, puzzled but relieved by the abrupt change of topic. Whether it had been wise or not, I had invited Mick into this part of my life. "She's as well as can be expected, given her age and deteriorating mind."

"That's tough." He nodded, as though to himself. "You gonna move her?"

"I don't want to." I paused. "I've got a couple ideas."

"Like?"

I shrugged and then went with the only legal idea I'd managed to come up with. "I thought I'd write a book. Real fast, you know. One of those topical tell-alls that's written and published in a month. If I keep cranking out a book every month or two, I'll have money to put away."

"Yeah, right. I can see you doing that," he said in a tone implying he didn't believe me for a minute.

I wasn't sure whether I should be insulted or flattered. "Maybe not," I said. "But I have ghosted a book. I can write one on my own. I just need a good subject."

"And that's why you're here?"

"Okay," I set my plate on the table. "I admit I'm fishing for a story. Maybe a book. Being a jockey—the whole horse racing industry— that's something that would be interesting to write about."

He nodded. "You weren't after a glimpse of Bull's Blood just because you had a crush on horses when you were a kid."

"Well, not exactly. But I wouldn't be pursuing this subject if it weren't for that 'crush.'"

He nodded. "So you're using me."

"Very gently."

He regarded me with, I thought, dispassion, but then reached over and wrapped his hand around mine. With a slight squeeze, he said in a soft voice, "So what am I gonna use you for?"

I resisted the impulse to pull my hand away. "Why is it—just when you start being appealing, you get a little ..." I sought for a word other than "creepy" and settled on "... sinister."

He sat back, taking his hand with him. "Hmph. Nobody's called me 'sinister.' 'Shifty,' yeah. But sinister?"

I shrugged, but couldn't imagine legions of women rejecting Mick's offer to show them his ferret.

"What are you going to write about? I mean, horseracing is a pretty big subject."

"I'm not sure," I said in all sincerity. "I'm thinking something about the relationship between horses and their owners." I had no idea where that came from.

He looked at me as though he could tell. "What kind of 'relationship' do you think they have? One runs and the other pays for its hay."

"I mean, why do some people go into racing?"

"The money."

"That can't be the only reason." I shook my head. "There's lots of easier ways to make money."

With a sigh, he shrugged. "Yeah, that's for sure." He gave it a few moments. "It's exciting. At least from the outside looking in. And a horse—especially a stallion like Blood. He's ..." He trailed off.

"An extension of Bull's manhood?"

Mick chuckled. "Yeah. Something like that."

I figured a guy with the nickname of "Bull" and a namesake stallion had serious manhood issues.

The buzzing echo of a katydid accompanied our silence.

Finally, Mick said, "How about I take you to meet Bull's Blood. Tomorrow? Severn's having a cookout at the farm."

If I'd had a football, I'd have spiked it. "Sounds good," I said.

In the dim light I could see him nod.

"But you're having a good time?"

"I am," I said, eighty-five percent truthful.

"So," he said, canting his head, "you ready to meet Fredo?"

CHAPTER 9

The August heat had begun to build when Bix and I went for our morning walk. At seven thirty, a sepia film covered the cloudless sky, and sweat prickled my skin as we circled the block. A cool front was headed this way, and there was a good chance we'd get a storm in the late afternoon. I hoped it would hold off until Mick and I had been out to Bull Severn's farm.

I felt, deep down where my feral inclinations resided, that this trip would give me an idea—some way to take back from Severn what he'd taken from my mother. For my part, I didn't consider it theft anymore. Reimbursement. Of course, I couldn't ignore the very real possibility that I would be caught at whatever crime I decided to perpetrate. Probably jailed. And my mother would find herself in the first empty bed available in a state-run facility, preferably near Joliet, or whatever state-run facility I landed in.

But I couldn't let fear, no matter how reasonable, deter me from my mission. And, today, I was confident that an opportunity would present itself. I believed this mission was righteous.

Unfortunately, I couldn't muster this confidence for my planned encounter with Erika. And the more I thought about it, the more I realized that I needed to reconsider my objectives. So while Bix stopped to mark every sapling along the way, I attempted to put together a new scenario.

My original intention was to show up, unannounced, at the Psychic Place and see if I could either bully or bullshit Erika into telling

me how she'd engineered those knocking sounds. The further I was
from the séance, the more I was able to convince myself that it had
been an elaborately staged ruse. But now I realized that what really
mattered was how Erika had known about Robert and the money—
who cared how those sounds were made?—and I wanted to know
what else she knew about me. And why had she bothered with the
ruse? It may have been as simple as wanting to set up a reporter, hoping for a convincing article, and since I was the stringer who did these
"Welcome to Fowler" articles, I was the one she'd researched. That
made sense. But even if it was as simple as that, I wanted to know
what else she'd dug up about me.

But that didn't explain why Robert had shown up at the séance
and mentioned money. If it was all based on Erika's research, surely
she would have come up with something more concrete. I began to
wonder if Erika had known my father. If that were the case, there was
a lot I wanted to ask her. But I needed some background information
before grilling her. The only source I could think to tap was my
mother, and I wasn't sure I was up to digging into her secrets again.
Yesterday had been painful for both of us, and we needed a break
from each other. But after examining my options, I conceded that I
didn't have much choice in the matter.

I found her in her room, watching John Wayne in *Rio Bravo*. I'd given
her a collection of his movies when I bought the DVD player for her.
Wayne had always been her favorite, and now his work seemed to
hold her attention more than most of what television offered. Still, it
was hard to know how much she got out of these movies, with her
nodding off and fidgeting. But he could still make her smile, and
every now and then she'd comment on his manliness in relation to
today's "cinematic sissies."

I did so much tongue-biting when I was with her that it was a
wonder I hadn't bled out.

When I walked into her room, she perked up, hands clasping the padded arms of her chair in edgy anticipation. I knew what was coming.

"Did you bring my cigarettes?" she asked with the eager anticipation of a child expecting a present.

I let her read my answer in the glare I aimed at her. Then I added, "You know what we agreed on. You do not smoke here."

She sighed, her thin chest deflating. "That's right." She folded her hands, obedient, as though I'd snatched away her last ounce of pluck.

I'd never had children and never been the boss of anyone, so I had no practice at being the bad guy. I didn't care much for the role.

"I'm hoping you can help me with something, Mom." I took the remote from her table and muted the Duke.

With a sharp glance at me and then at the TV, she heaved a sigh, signaling her defeat, adjusted her position so she faced me and said, "And what is that, *dear?*"

I couldn't figure how to broach the subject, so I just blundered into it. "Do you believe in psychics?"

"Do I believe in them?" From the puzzled look she gave me, the question had caused her some confusion. "Well, I suppose they exist."

"No, I mean do you believe they can do what they claim they can do—communicate with the dead, see into the future? Things like that."

"Oh, all that's ridiculous." She dismissed the entire field of parapsychology with a wave of her hand. Then she peered at me and said, "Why are you asking me about this?"

"You know I often do interviews with new businesses in town. For the *News and Record.*"

"I believe you may have told me that."

"Well, the night before last I interviewed a psychic."

"A psychic in Fowler?" She considered that briefly, then sniffed. "I knew this was a strange town."

"A lot of people use psychics. I imagine they had them in Westchester."

"A psychic would've been run out of Westchester."

Not wanting to wander off track, I conceded, "You're probably right."

"That's very generous of you." She added a faint, tight smile.

I hurried on. "Okay, let's say they're all charlatans. But they do know things—I mean they find things out about people so they're able to make these people believe what they're being told. It's all part of the con."

It took a minute for all that to compute, but finally she nodded slowly and said, "Perhaps. And, so?"

"Well, this woman knew something about Robert."

She sat forward. "What did she say about him?"

"It wasn't what *she* said so much as what *he* said."

"He spoke to you?"

I shook my head. "No. I'm sure he didn't. But I was supposed to think he was talking to me."

"How did he sound?"

"Well, he wasn't talking really. Knocking. He was one of those knocking spirits." When her expression didn't change, I added, "You know—one for yes, two for no."

"He believed in that sort of thing," she said, almost to herself.

"He did?"

"Yes. He did." A little smile curled the corners of her mouth as though she were reliving a pleasant memory. "He used to say that we get a second chance after we die."

"Robert said that?" The little I knew of Robert, especially what I'd most recently learned, didn't make him sound like the kind of guy who'd given this much thought. At least not while my mother was in his life.

Her gaze wandered back in my direction and then she started as though she'd just noticed I was there. She crossed one leg over the other and smoothed the pale blue fabric of her pants before cupping her hands around her knee. "But it's all silly, of course."

"I tend to think so too. And I'm guessing that this psychic must have known a few things about me—about us—in order to keep it going. And I want to find out how she knew what she knew about Robert. There must be some way she got information on him."

"What did she know?"

"This rapping spirit knew that you had some money."

When she didn't respond, I hurried on. "Money other than your savings. I guess I thought it was a lot of money, but then you told me about the sofa money, and I realized that must have been it. But how did she know about it? And then I can't figure out why she'd want to lead me on. I mean there are other ways of trying to convince me—easier ways—that she's the real thing. Why did she think she had to? And why me? I was set up, Mom. And I need to find out why."

In the midst of my babbling, I realized that my mother was looking at me in a way I'd never seen her look at me before. And I thought I'd seen them all. Her mouth was open just a little and her features seemed frozen except for her eyes, which were rounded with either shock or fear. Was she having a stroke?

"Mom!" I launched out of the rocker and reached for her hand. When I touched it, she started, snatching her hands back and clasping them together at her chest.

"Are you okay?"

"Yes, of course. I just felt … dizzy for a moment." She blinked rapidly.

"Are you sure?"

"Yes," she snapped.

Definitely not a stroke.

"Okay, I need some information from you. That woman who came to see you the other day—Mary Waltner—the one who gave you the sofa money, she must be involved in some—"

"Will you get me my purse?"

That stopped me.

"My purse," she repeated. "It's on the table next to my bed."

When I didn't move, she leaned forward and cocked her chin. "If what you want is the sofa money, then you should have just asked for it."

I took a deep breath. Then another. "I don't want the money, Mother. I want to know how this woman thought she could con me. Mary Waltner knew Robert. I can't think of another place to start."

"Well, I don't have his address. Why should I have his address?"

"I didn't ask if you had his address. But I thought you might know where he was from."

"I don't remember."

"Mary Waltner. Was she from California?"

"I don't remember."

Her emotions had gone raw again, and she pulled herself up the way she did when slipping into her martyr role. "How do you expect me to remember these things?"

"Sorry, Mom." I paused. "But I need to know these things."

The rocking chair had developed a creak—just since I'd been sitting in it. I listened to it screech for what seemed like several minutes.

My mother was the first to break the silence. She'd been looking out the window where a sparrow perched on one of the yews. Finally, she turned back to me and said, "What was the name of this psychic?"

"Erika Starwise."

Instead of us having a chuckle over the woman's name, she nodded and said, "I'd like to talk to her."

I stopped rocking. "Mom, she's a—"

"I don't care what you think she is. I want to talk to her."

"Why?"

"I want to see what else she knows about Rob-Robert," she said, faltering.

"Why do you care?"

My question was met with stony eyes and a firm jaw. "It's none of your business."

I hadn't heard that line in several decades, but it had the same effect. I was twelve years old and asking a question that wasn't covered in *Growing Up and Liking It*. Challenging her would be pointless, but I could not let this meeting happen. "Yesterday you were saying good riddance to the bastard. He stole from you. He hurt you."

"I want to talk to him."

I settled back into the rocker, using my toes to keep a slight motion going. "If you think psychics are con artists, then why would you bother?"

My mother looked down at her hands and chipped away at the pink nail polish on her right thumb. Friday was manicure day.

I pressed a little harder. "You know she's just making it up."

After a moment, she looked up at me, gave me a self-satisfied smirk, folded her hands together and said, "I know her name. I can make an appointment. Take the courtesy bus."

She reached in front of me to snatch the remote and turned the sound back on.

Knowing when I've been beaten and that I had to be there when this meeting occurred, I slumped in the chair and, watching John Wayne sneer at some bad guy, I said, "I'll talk to her."

My mother turned to me and, with exaggerated politeness said, "Thank you."

Then she turned back toward the screen and added, "Don't slouch."

CHAPTER 10

Halfway to Bull Severn's cookout, I ran out of small talk. Strange. I never imagined that keeping up his side of the conversation would pose a problem for Mick Hughes. But after an uninspired discussion of the weather and the state of the Cubs, we now both stared straight ahead in silence at the asphalt, shiny in the dripping temperature. I saw no sign of impending thunderstorms, not even a wisp of a cloud against the blue.

I needed to talk. My gut was churning, and I couldn't stop fidgeting with the strap of my purse. I kept replaying the voicemail message I'd found when I'd gotten home from Erika's. It was from the goldfinch woman at Willoway Manor, Jane Goodwin, sounding sweet and sincere as she asked if I'd made the "difficult decision" yet. Then, in a less syrupy tone, she added that there were a number of people waiting for that bed.

I doubted this. If there were really a line of people waiting for the bed, Jane would have told me to pound sand by now. Still, that didn't mean there wouldn't be a taker tomorrow.

Part of me wanted to call her and say, "Okay. We're taking it." I'd forget this half-baked idea of mine. But then I thought of my mother's sunny little room at Dryden and the nuthatches and cardinals that visited the yews, and I knew that moving her to Willoway would be putting her away to die. And while she was failing in so many ways, she still had her pride and her nastiness sustaining her.

I would wait until the next morning to return the call. So I had until then to figure out how to steal a hundred thousand dollars, which was the amount I'd decided on. (This was more than what my mother lost, but when you figured in pain and suffering, not to mention interest, it squared pretty well.)

I drew in a breath of air and expelled it in another, deeper sigh. Then I glanced in Mick's direction, hoping he hadn't heard me. I didn't want him interpreting a sigh as boredom. Or, worse, for what it was—despondence.

But Mick hadn't looked my way in some time. I took the opportunity to study him—something I'd never done up close. I guess I'd figured he might notice and then be encouraged, and I was afraid to let that happen. Today he'd made some effort to tame his unruly hair, which was that shade between blond and brown that contained a profusion of colors. He was chewing on the inside of his mouth as he drove, apparently unaware that I was studying his profile, which included a sharp chin with a flick of a scar on it.

I returned to the asphalt. Maybe some of my agitation involved guilt. Mick was taking me to meet a friend of his who I was intent on stealing from. I didn't care about Severn's feelings, but I was using Mick, who had been a good accountant and financial advisor to me. Rumors aside, he'd never done anything to hurt me. Unless you wanted to count the calories in those profiteroles he'd whipped up the night before.

I didn't think he was reacting unfavorably to my appearance, seeing as I dressed for this event using the same care and precision with which I would have costumed up for Lady Macbeth. If he liked last night's Robyn, he should have been thrilled with today's. I'd curled my hair and, with the heat and humidity in mind, piled it up with some strategically placed hairpins, one of which had a tawny agate affixed to it. I kept makeup at a minimum—again I didn't want it melting off me—using some soft colors on my eyes and cheeks. My outfit consisted of a pair of cropped khakis, cheeky flip flops, and an off-white, low-cut cami, over which I wore a filmy sleeveless top, which was splashed with the colors of the desert after a rain. I'd spent less on a week of groceries than I had on that top, and I trotted it out only for special events. The weight training I'd been doing had paid off, and I had actually passed my own muster.

I looked at him and said, "You're kind of quiet."

"Huh?" As he turned, he seemed surprised to find me in the passenger seat.

"I said you're quiet."

"Oh. Yeah." He went back to the window. "Just thinking about something."

"Must be important."

He shrugged. "Yeah." Then he said, "Sorry." He glanced at me. "You look nice."

"Thank you." Now he was making small talk. "Tell me about Bull's Blood."

A rueful smile pulled at the corner of his mouth, almost as if he were thinking about a dear but troubled friend.

"Blood." He breathed the name with a sigh as he shifted in the driver's seat. "He's one helluva horse. One of the best I've seen in my years. But he's also one major pain in the ass."

"How's that?"

"Fussy about what he eats. Doesn't play well with others. He's wound tight as a Stradivarius string and he bites."

"Sounds like a girl I knew in high school."

He chuckled. "But he is the real thing. His line goes back to Man o' War. He's big like he was. Loves to run."

"I've seen photos of him; he's a beautiful horse. A roan, right?"

"Yep. He's a blue roan. Grey on black."

"Ooh," I said.

He nodded. "Yeah, he's a looker."

"He won the Preakness, ran fourth in the Belmont, but he wasn't entered in the Derby. How come?"

"Yeah." He rubbed a hand over his mouth then tugged at his chin. "He was recovering from a leg strain."

"He got it running?"

Another chuckle. "No. I think Blood got it kicking in the side of his stall."

"Oh," I said, knowing exactly how the creature felt.

The farm was about thirty minutes west of Fowler in Seton Springs, an area where white fences lined the roads and parceled thick, green pastures into paddocks.

We turned on Loris Road and then again onto a wide drive that passed under a white sign spanning it. Old English lettering painted in black informed us we were entering Severn's Acres. From the looks of the property, the sign could have read "Severn's Many Acres."

We paused at a wrought iron double gate, which, after a few moments, must have sensed we were there because it opened toward us, and I had a creepy feeling as we drove into the estate. Something like being swallowed into the belly of the beast. I guess I have some of my mother's dramatic tendencies. It was just a security gate.

We drove around a couple of bends and then the road forked, and Mick took the south road, which landed us in a parking area. Cars filled the paved lot and overflowed onto the lawn, which was where Mick parked, pulling his Porsche in next to a Lexus.

While I had expected the house to ooze opulence, I did not anticipate the degree of oozing. It was a massive, single-story stucco with shallow roofs covered in burnt sienna tile. Red stone surrounded the arched, double doors. This place belonged in Morocco. It left my senses battling between disgust and envy. But it was easy to dismiss ten thousand square feet of living space as wasteful and ostentatious when you were confined to six hundred.

Mick stood with me for a few moments as I took it all in. "Yeah," he said with a sigh, "this is the house that Bull built."

Indeed.

We didn't go in through those doors, but took a flagstone path around the estate—and there was nothing else to call it—leading to the back. For about fifty feet, the path ran alongside a second drive, which Mick explained led to the stables. Once we rounded the house, I got my first glimpse of a catered cookout. And again, "yard" didn't cut it here. There was a pool, and behind the pool and to the south was a pond spanned by a footbridge for those who didn't care to wade. The stables—painted that red-brown shade of the roof—began at the north end of the pond. Beyond the stables were paddocks.

And the people. I guessed a couple hundred of northern Illinois' thoroughbred set had come to Severn's cookout. And they were all as sleek and beautiful as the horses they raced. In a matter of seconds I conceded that I was out-dressed, out-tanned and out-toned.

We hadn't progressed five feet into the area when a guy wearing khakis and a white, short-sleeved shirt presented us with a tray full of foaming beers. Mick took two and handed me one. I don't usually drink beer, but with the heat and all, it sounded better than wine and they weren't offering scotch.

We began to thread our way through the crowd, Mick steering me by my elbow. The beer was cold and tasted surprisingly good. I took another sip.

Mick nodded at a man wearing thin, round wire-rimmed glasses the exact same silver shade as his hair. His date looked like she should have been home studying for her ACTs.

My confidence left me. First in a trickle, then it virtually gushed from my pores. I was not in the same league as these people, and Bull Severn was their leader. What was I thinking? Mick's gentle pressure on my arm kept me moving. Smiling. Nodding. Apparently, as Mick Hughes's date, I was generating some interest. Or maybe it was the cropped khakis. They probably thought Mick was escorting one of the waitresses.

At some point during the crowd walk, I decided to leave my mission to the fates. Despite the fact that I have no use for psychics, I look for signs in everything. I don't consider them signs from God—I think the whole universe is talking to me—but I do pay attention. This isn't an egotistical assumption, because I believe the universe talks to everyone. And today, as out of my element as I have ever been, I figured I would see a cosmic nod if and when I got a sign. Without one, I would abort the mission.

A number of people greeted Mick. They seemed pleased and maybe a little surprised to see him, and Mick acknowledged them all with a friendly response, but he kept us moving. We crossed the terrazzo patio, heading toward the smoke. I smelled grilling meat and caught whiffs of basil and tomatoes. This was no simple cookout. Severn had an outdoor kitchen, complete with range, stove, what looked like a pizza oven, and aluminum cabinets.

I wondered if it would be feasible to simply ask Severn to give me a hundred thousand dollars—maybe I'd explain about the "misunderstanding"—because, clearly, he wasn't going to miss it.

Then the crowd parted enough so I could see the grills—there were several of them—and I spotted Bull Severn hoisting slabs of raw meat onto a king-sized gas grill. I'd seen photos of him in the newspaper, but he was more impressive in person. I hadn't realized he was this tall—well over six feet. His height, combined with his barrel chest and powerful build, would have made him a serviceable battering ram. He smiled as Mick and I approached and, shifting his fork to his left hand, he extended his right to Mick and they shook. "Glad you could make it, Mick," he said, sounding genuine. Then he turned his attention to me and said, "You must be Robyn?"

When I nodded, he reached for my hand. "Great to meet you. I'm Bull."

His grip was gentle for a man that size, almost as though he modulated according to the person whose hand was involved. I fought my initial urge to like the guy.

Sweat dripped down his cheek, and he brushed it off with a shoulder swipe while plopping another slab of meat on the grill. I glanced around and saw there were several other smaller grills, each manned by a guy in khakis. One wrestled a chicken breast onto the grill, and I noted that Bull's was reserved for steaks.

While Mick ragged him about using gas instead of charcoal, I pondered why Mick had mentioned me to Bull. Again, I'm not anything special. Really. But I was beginning to wonder if maybe Mick thought otherwise and was in the midst of trying on that notion to see if I liked it, when I noticed a familiar-looking man. I didn't anticipate seeing anyone I knew here, so I gave him a second look. It took a moment for me to recognize him as the guy who had been at Mick's office the other day. The rude one who had interrupted my appointment. He was standing under a birch with a plastic cup in his hand filled to foaming with beer and talking with a middle-aged guy with a long, thin beard that pointed at his protruding belly. Then he glanced our way, hesitating as he saw me watching him. Those washed-out blue eyes were all the more obvious because of the thick, dark brows bunched above them. Even the pale blue, short-sleeved shirt and sueded twills didn't soften him. He gave me a slight nod and went back to the chubby guy.

"I want you to take a look at Blood," Bull was saying. "He's antsier than usual. Almost like he knows this is a big race coming up."

"Sure he does," Mick said. "They always know."

At that moment, I could feel his attention shift. He gave my arm a squeeze and said to Bull, "'Scuse me a second. Somebody I need to talk to." And then he left me alone with the man from whom I planned to steal a hundred grand.

"He's a great guy," Bull said, flipping a chunk of steak. "How long you two been together?"

"Not long," I answered, drawing my gaze away from Mick, who was being greeted warmly by a young couple.

Bull nodded in a way that implied he wasn't surprised.

"How do you know him?" he asked.

"He's my accountant."

"Oh, yeah?" He regarded me with renewed interest. "Mine too. What kind of business you in?"

"I'm a journalist." I took another sip of the beer, which was tasting really good.

He adjusted a steak on the grill. "No kidding."

"Absolutely not."

Now he smiled. He was a nice-looking man and, to my dismay, he had a friendly way about him. I told myself he needed that in order to con people.

"Newspaper?" he asked.

"Mostly freelance. Magazines, newspapers, the internet. I've ghosted a book." At this point I decided to leap in, figuring if I waited for Mick to come back and broach the subject, the opportunity might never be as good. "Actually, I'm working on a book now on the relationship between thoroughbreds and their owners and trainers."

As he flipped a large filet, I continued. "I'm thinking it could have wide appeal. Racing fans, of course. But there are a lot of women who grew up loving horses—who still love them—and who want to read about more than the racing. Sort of a relationship book, you know."

Just then a small, blond woman came up to Bull and put her arm around his waist. Small enough to tuck her head under his arm, she was pretty in a polished sort of way, and I suspected the flawless bronze tint of her skin had been sprayed on.

"This is Robyn Guthrie, honey. She's with Mick. Says she's writing a book on horses and their owners."

"And trainers and jockeys," I added. "And maybe their grooms. I figure those are the people most likely to know the horse." I paused. "Most owners aren't all that involved, but Mick tells me you are." Mick had said no such thing, but I guessed that Bull liked to think of himself as a hands-on kind of owner.

"Where is Mick?" the woman said, looking around.

"He's talking to Rudy," Bull told her.

She must have spotted him then, because I saw her focus in that direction just before she turned back to me.

"I'm Gwen Severn," she said, taking a sip of her wine. She wore a white silk halter dress with a four-strand necklace comprised of polished blue stones with diamond-set spacers. At least, I assumed they were diamonds and also assumed that the blue stones weren't glass. In all, it was a bit much for a cookout, and I had to wonder what she reserved for fancy occasions.

"So," she said, "tell me about this book of yours."

"I'm just starting it. I want to write a couple of chapters, put together an outline and see if my editor likes the idea. I figured Bull's Blood would make a great first chapter."

"Who's your publisher?" Gwen asked. Her nails were manicured and polished a shell pink color, and she tapped one against the side of her wine glass.

I named the publisher I had ghosted the book for and added the name of the editor I'd worked with. I'd anticipated this question, just not from Bull's wife.

She nodded as though she'd heard of both.

"Gwen here is a publicist." Bull had released her and gone back to the slabs on his grill.

"Do you work for yourself or an agency?" I asked.

"Myself," she said. "I've got a few clients in publishing." Then, "Have you heard of Reginald Simms?"

I had. Simms had latched onto the coattails of the second-coming publishing phenom. From what I'd read about it, his book told the story of the apocalypse from the point of view of an escaped convict. The lukewarm reviews were no doubt assuaged by the fact that it had been lounging in the middle of the best-seller list for a month.

"I've heard some interesting things about the book."

"Thanks to me," she said with a smile. Her eyes were just a little too cold to pull off gracious.

"So honey," Bull said, "do you think a book about racehorses and their relationship with their owners and trainers is marketable?"

"Maybe," she said. "All depends on how it's done. I heard you mention it's a book that might appeal to women."

I nodded. "Relationships."

She shrugged. "Could work."

"What's the name of the book you ghosted?" Bull asked.

"I can't say," I replied. "Part of the contract." Actually, that was a blessing. The book I'd ghosted for a psychologist, *12 Ways to Let Love into Your Life*, had nearly put me into a diabetic coma.

"That's why it's called 'ghosted,' honey," Gwen explained. "No one's supposed to see or hear from the real author."

"That's right," I said. "We shed a little ectoplasm on the pages and move on."

Bull chuckled while Gwen eyed me in a way that could only have been sizing me up. Without turning toward her husband, she asked, "Are you going to introduce her to Blood?"

"I'm thinking I might let Mick do the honors."

I looked around for Mick. Didn't want to lose track of him and be stuck here dodging eye daggers from Gwen. Just then I saw him coming toward us. He started to smile, but then something—or someone—caused it deteriorate into a scowl that didn't abate much as Gwen released her husband and hooked her arm through Mick's—she was adept at latching onto men—and gave him a peck on the cheek, which he accepted without overt enthusiasm. Even in heels, she was an inch shorter than him. They made a cute couple.

"Haven't seen you in ages, hon. What's been keeping you away?"

I swear she almost drawled the words.

"Guess you haven't been looking hard."

She peered into his eyes. "You know, I've been meaning to talk to you about this Arabian I've got my eye on. I'd really like you to come take a look at her some day soon. I want to make sure I'm getting what I'm paying for."

Bull glanced in Mick's direction before skewering a chunk of steak.

"Who's selling her?" Mick asked.

"Russell Williams."

Mick shook his head. "You don't have to worry about Russ ripping you off. He's as honest as they come."

"This is a very expensive animal," she said, leaning into Mick and pressing her breast into his arm.

If I'd been at all possessive about my date, I'd have had my claws drawn. Instead, I was amused by the display, wondering how far this rich little tart would go for attention. I also wondered why Bull appeared to be paying more attention to his steaks' doneness than to his wife's flirting. Maybe I just didn't get how these people lived.

"Well, Mick, you know where Blood is." Bull turned a couple of steaks and removed another two to a platter. Two new ones filled those spaces. "Help yourself to some food and then take Robyn down to the stables."

I felt as though I'd been dismissed, but Mick took it in stride. It gave him the opportunity to disentangle himself from Gwen.

I wondered if she was a little drunk—this hanging on men thing seemed a little odd for a career woman of her proclaimed caliber. But she wasn't slurring words, and her eyes were clear, so I chalked it up to either the heat or her personality.

As we started to walk away, Bull called after us, "Mick, find me before you leave."

Mick nodded.

We picked our way along the food table, and I made a plate of grilled chicken, baked beans, fruit and salad.

I noticed that Rudy had joined a clutch of people around a picnic table. This time his gaze found mine and he kept staring, and I could still feel it long after I'd looked away.

Mick and I ate with two other couples at a wooden picnic table with a nice view of the pond and the bank of dark clouds muscling in from the west. Sometime in the not-too-distant future, we'd be moving indoors. One of the other men had also been a jockey, and they were all horse people, so I spent much of the time, nodding, asking questions, researching "the book."

I was on my third beer. They had been going down with alarming ease. I know that beer wasn't the thing to drink in order to stay hydrated on a hot day, so technically it wasn't refreshing. It just tasted that way. And it made the questions so easy to come up with. Maybe I would actually write this silly book.

By the time we'd finished eating, the clouds were upon us, emitting low rumbles of thunder, and the air smelled thick with rain. Waiters were hustling plates and bowls into the house as Mick and I headed toward the stables.

As we walked, Mick took my hand. The gesture surprised me. I could remember (vaguely) the last time I'd had sex, but could not remember the last time a guy had taken my hand.

"You told Bull I was coming?"

Mick glanced up at me.

"He knew my name," I said.

"Sure," he shrugged. "I had to call him about something this morning, and he asked if I was bringing anybody. Why wouldn't I tell him your name?"

"No reason."

The stables were L-shaped, consisting of two long wings, each containing five stalls, with a tack room and an area for washing the horses in the corner. When we went in through the south entrance, Mick stopped and scooped up a handful of pellets from a metal dish on a ledge. "Grab a few," he told me, and I did as instructed, trusting that he wouldn't expect me to offer treats to a biting horse.

We passed empty, pristine stalls on our way to Blood's abode.

"Where are all the horses?" I asked.

"Blood's the only horse Bull owns right now." The edge in his voice made me turn toward him, but all he said was, "But he's got big plans."

"I see," I said. "He doesn't believe in a starter stable."

"Nope. 'Small' isn't in Bull's dictionary."

The stable smells—horse, hay, leather and manure—combined with the earthy scent of rain, creating an aroma that was not unpleasant. Rather sensual, in fact.

Blood was next to the tack room. His stall was large, with black steel bars across the top half. The middle bars swung open like a window so he could stick his head out and enjoy the breeze from the overhead fan. The lower half of the stall—the "kickboard" as Mick called it—was oak with a curious little door cut into the lower left corner. Before I could ask about that door, Blood let us know he was home with a loud "harumph." He thrust his head through the open part of the grill. His eyes widened at the sight of me, as though he remembered me from some past, hideous experience. As promised, he was big and beautiful, and when Mick reached out to stroke his neck, Blood gave us a nice view of his teeth. Mick retracted his arm, but seemed to take it in stride. He began talking to the animal, using a soothing tone and reassuring words. Blood stamped a couple of times, tossing his dark mane so that his forelock fell over one eye. Even in the dim stable light, his powerful chest muscles were evident beneath his mottled gray coat.

"How tall is he?"

Mick held his hand out, without trying to touch the animal. "Almost seventeen hands."

I did a quick calculation and determined that Blood and I were exactly the same height, if you didn't count his head. I, too, described myself as "almost five six."

Finally, Blood consented to be touched, and Mick rubbed the length of the animal's nose in a way that seemed, after several moments, to hypnotize him. While Blood was succumbing, I noticed that he was not alone in the stall. In the back corner, curled up on the straw and displaying a look that implied that it had seen everything worth seeing and had yet to be impressed, was a goat. It regarded us for several moments before deciding we were worth closer inspection. It rose from the rear first until it was at its full stature, which was maybe a couple of feet (six hands in horse height) at its withers. Bobbing its little head, which was distinguished by formidable horns and a Roman nose, it came toward us.

"What's with the roomie?"

Now I understood the purpose of the mini-door the kickboard. Mick crouched in front of it and reached out for the goat. Blood retreated to the end farthest away from us and began yanking bits of hay from a trough, swishing his tail. The goat took one of the treats from Mick's fingers. It was a coal black goat with a white, crescent-shaped mark that ran down one side, under its belly and up the other side.

"If it weren't for this guy here, Blood would have been gelded a year ago."

"How come?"

"He keeps Blood from going completely insane."

"What's his name?"

"Sassy. Short for Sassafras."

"Of course."

"He's a pygmy."

As he fed the goat another treat, he added, "This is Blood's fifth goat. The first had horns that Blood had a habit of chewing, the second and third were scared of him, and the fourth scared Blood."

"He doesn't chew on Sassy's horns?"

"Nope. I think Sassy here's got just enough gumption so he doesn't get chewed on and not so much that Blood gets even more nervous."

I regarded the creature with new respect. "So, Sassy is a goat among goats."

"I guess."

I glanced at the pellets in my hand. "Interesting how they form these bonds."

"Yeah, it is," Mick said. "But it's in character. Horses are herd animals. As a rule, they don't like being alone. Some of them are more uptight about it than others, especially in a stall. Sassy here is an easygoing guy, neutered." He glanced over his shoulder at me. "But he's not crazy about women so don't be offended if he tries to bite you."

"I'm going to try feeding him," I said, taking up the challenge. Perhaps the beer had emboldened me.

Sassy looked up at me and that was when I noticed his eyes—set into each amber iris was a large, rectangular pupil. I held my hand out to him. After several rather tense moments, he took a step toward me.

"Hey," Mick said. "He might even like you."

I watched as the little goat lips nibbled from my hand. They tickled. "I have a way with goats."

"Like I said, he doesn't like women much." He regarded me with interest. "But you seem to be okay."

"It's what I strive for. Being okay. With goats."

I guess I was really okay, because Sassy decided to pass through his goat door and join us in the aisle. I patted his back and must have hit a tickle trigger, because he craned his neck and used his horn to scratch a spot on his back. I had to laugh. "Now, that's convenient." I gave him another treat, and as he chewed, I thought.

I assumed that Blood was going to be moved to the track a day or so before the race next weekend, and so I asked, "Will Sassy here go with Blood to Plymouth?"

"You bet."

Blood, apparently used to being the center of attention, had returned and thrust his nose in Mick's direction. Blood was huge compared to Sassy; it would have been easy for him to squash or otherwise take out the smaller creature. But he blew air out his nostrils and gave the goat a gentle nudge. Just standing next to Sassy had a calming effect on the big animal. He wasn't baring his teeth or showing us the whites of his eyes.

And there it was. The idea didn't smack me upside the head or anything, but it rose like some leviathan out of the sea—first the snout, then the fangs and finally the reptilian eyes—looked me straight on and said, "Well?"

Outside, the storm raged in earnest. Inside, my mind was also raging—finding flaws and obstacles, but recognizing that it might be a good idea. If I could pull it off.

Across from the stall were two bales of hay, one piled on top of the other. I sat down on the makeshift bench and took another drink of beer. Surely, this idea was the beer talking. I wasn't drunk, but I suspected my super ego was passed out somewhere.

Sassy's hooves clopped against the concrete floor as he approached me and nuzzled the bale of hay. I gave him the last of the goat nuggets.

Mick looked over his shoulder, saw me sitting there, my feet dangling above the ground, and he came over and took a seat next to me.

When thunder growled again, Mick said, "We'll have to wait it out."

From where we sat, I could see outside the door, and the rain was coming down in sheets. With the next clap of thunder the stables shuddered. "Yeah. I figured." I crossed one leg over the other and said, "Blood's a beautiful animal. I'm thinking this book will have photos. I imagine he's quite photogenic."

I felt Mick watching me, but he didn't say anything and, finally, when I couldn't stand it any longer, I turned toward him. "What?"

He cocked a smile. "Bullshit."

"What?"

"I said bullshit." He drank some beer and looked toward the animals. Sassy had returned to the stall, but kept his eyes on me.

"I heard you. I just don't know what you're talking about." But my mouth had started to go dry, so I must have suspected.

"Horses and their relationships with their owners," he said, and I didn't think I imagined the acerbic tone he was taking.

"So?"

"You're not writing a book." He laughed—a kind of harsh laugh, maybe a little bitter as well.

"Of course I am. I may not be able to sell it, but I—"

"Robyn," he sighed as though he regretted what he was about to say, "I'm not sure why you're here, but it's not because of a book you're writing."

"Oh?" I honestly didn't know what else to say. All I could come up with was: "What makes you an authority on my motives?"

He turned to me, chin tilted. "You're not the only one who knows how to do research."

"I'm not? I thought I was." I wondered where he was going with this and suspected he was about to zing me.

"Bull Severn ripped off your mother."

I considered saying "He did?" and acting like I didn't have any idea what Mick was talking about, but I knew how the exchange would end. So I said, "How do you know?"

"I'm his accountant."

"So you helped?"

"No, that was before my time." He shrugged. "Not that I haven't covered up a few indiscretions for him, but none of them involved your mother."

I waited.

"If it weren't for Bull, you wouldn't be trying to get a loan that would put you in debt for the rest of your life from a guy with a reputation for taking loans seriously."

"No, I wouldn't." Then I added, "The loan money would have bought me some time."

"That money would have bought you a lot of grief."

I shrugged. "But it would have postponed it."

"You wanting to meet Bull really has nothing to do with a book you're writing—the hug-me horse book—and it's all about figuring out how you're going to rip him off. With interest." This man had my number. And I knew it.

I swallowed. "Yes," I said, hearing the rasp in my voice and willing the tears away. I hate being found out; it was bringing out an emotional response I needed to squelch. Denying it was pointless. Besides, I hadn't done anything yet.

"And that's why you went out with me."

"Partly. But only partly."

He nodded as though that were acceptable. "What were you going to do?"

"It doesn't matter. I'm not going to do it." I drained the beer and set the plastic cup next to me. Sassy eyed it with interest. "I wouldn't have done it anyway. I'm lousy on follow through."

"But you had an idea."

"It only just came to me, so I haven't had a chance to find all the flaws, of which I'm sure there are many." I shrugged. "Also, I've had a few beers. Ideas I get when slightly wasted are usually also slightly wasted."

"What is it?"

I looked at him. "Why do you care?"

He shrugged. "Professional curiosity."

"You're going to tell Bull." I knew he wasn't, but I wanted to hear him say it.

"No, I'm not."

"I'm sure it's got so many holes in it ... you'll laugh."

"I won't."

I looked toward the stall. Blood had his head over the door, but seemed focused on a stray thought. Sassy was now half in and half out of the stall and was lying in an upright position staring toward us—picture the sphinx as a goat. "I was going to kidnap Sassy."

Mick followed my gaze.

"If Blood can't perform without his little friend, that would make Sassy as valuable as Blood." I took a breath and continued, "So I figured I could steal Sassy and hold him for ransom. Figured Severn would pay good money to make sure his horse raced."

Mick leaned back against the wall, the plastic beer cup resting against his chest. For a minute he just stared straight ahead, but then he started smiling and nodding. "That's pretty good."

"But it's a mean thing to do," I said. "To Blood. Who may be a pain in the ass but didn't take my mother's money."

"He'd survive," he said, then, after a few moments, asked, "How were you going to pull it off?"

"Like I said, I'm not sure yet. I just came up with the idea."

"Just like that?"

"I'd been thinking about Blood. I'm not sure why, but I thought the horse was the way to go."

After a moment he said, "I know why."

I waited.

"You don't want to just take money from Bull. You want to hurt him."

After giving that some thought I had to concur. "I guess so. A man as rich as Bull shouldn't be able to steal thousands from a little old lady and get away with it. And just taking some money from him wouldn't hurt him like I want to."

"So think about it now. How would you do it?"

I felt as though we were equals on that level—one con artist talking to another, and I was kind of flattered. I gave it a minute's thought before saying, "I don't know. I suppose I'd do it at night. But I imagine there's some kind of security network. I don't know."

"You got that right." He swallowed some beer.

"This place isn't bugged is it?"

He chuckled. "No."

Now that it was no longer going to happen, it had become an intellectual exercise. Apparently, when it came to crime, I was an "all talk" kind of gal.

"I'd have to figure out how to get past those front gates." I paused. "I assume this place is all fenced in."

"Right."

"And then once I got Sassy—I guess I'd have to rent a van or something, because he wouldn't fit into the back seat of my Civic—I'd have to figure out where to put him. There's no way Sassy would pass for a 'dog under thirty pounds' so my apartment is out."

As I was trying to imagine Bix's reaction to Sassy, Mick said something that I had to ask him to repeat.

"I think the two of us could pull it off," he said again.

"You? Why?"

He shrugged. "You're not the only one who can use a few bucks."

I remembered old pale blue eyes and wondered if this was what he referred to.

"How?" I asked.

"It'd take two," he said.

I waited.

"One to create a distraction while the other takes the goat." As he spoke, Sassy stood and walked toward us.

"I wish Bull didn't seem like a nice guy—"

"He's not. Trust me."

"Right."

"And Gwen ..." Mick snorted. "Gwen makes Bull look like Mr. Rogers."

"Her name was on the land company Bull set up."

He nodded. "She knows exactly what her husband is doing."

"Would this hurt her as much as Bull?"

"Yeah. But in different ways. Gwen doesn't care about the horse, but she does care about the attention she'll get if he wins the Million."

"Hate to deprive her of that," I said, smiling.

Then I said, "I'm guessing it would be easier to take Sassy here than at Plymouth."

"That's for sure."

"When is Blood going to Plymouth?"

"Not until Saturday morning," he said, his inflection rising as though he just realized this was a good thing. "With most races, Blood is at the track a couple of weeks ahead of time. But he's been training at Plymouth for the past month. He likes the track. It'll be less stressful for him to get there the morning of the race. Less time to fret." He paused. "Besides, Bull's throwing a big party on Thursday night. He wants to show off Blood. Can't do that if he's not here."

I leaned back against the wall. The rain had eased up and the thunder had moved past us. The beer had left me pleasantly light-headed and full of possibilities. I wondered if Bull's party might provide an opportunity, but the combination of heat and beer was making my eyelids heavy, and I couldn't hold the thought.

"We could do this." Mick said, and his breath warmed the curl of my ear. I turned toward him, and he placed his hand against my cheek and then he kissed me. Something stirred inside me that had been hibernating for a very long time. I responded, slipping my hand around his neck.

I'd read about couples who engaged in criminal behavior mainly because they couldn't wait to get home and tear each other's clothes off. Apparently I was of that persuasion.

That was how Gwen found us. Locked in a criminal embrace with Mick's hand slipping under my filmy top to cup my breast. I may have been moaning.

"Thought you two might need an umbrella." One was at her side, still dripping and another in its nylon case.

I sat up, brushing myself off, adjusting my clothes. Mick brushed his hair off his forehead and gave her an annoyed look.

"You were always the one with the good timing," Mick said.

Gwen worked her lower jaw, her eyes practically spewing acid.

I wondered why Gwen would care if we got wet, but I quickly figured it out. Of course, she didn't. And she hadn't come out here to see me. She and Mick had a history together. Possibly a recent history.

"Yes," she said, "well I shouldn't be surprised to find you out here with your tramp du jour."

Very recent. But now she was getting personal. "Who's calling who a tramp?"

She turned toward me, and for a second I felt the heat from the searing look she'd been giving Mick. Next to me, Mick cracked up. For some reason.

Sassy bleated. It was a long, drawn out "Whaaaaaa," and it was definitely aimed at Gwen. Now I started laughing.

Gwen spun around and stalked out, taking both the umbrellas. Along with them, she took my inclination to continue where Mick and I left off. Her appearance had the same effect on my passion that a hot needle has on a balloon. Gone. Just like that. Mick's attempts to rekindle the mood were wasted. Not that he didn't try.

Finally, I squirmed out of his embrace and stood, brushing straw off my pants. "Maybe we should just leave."

He leaned back on one arm, looking up at me. "Don't let Gwen get to you."

"Speaking of Gwen, what kind of history do you two have?"

"We don't." He plucked a shard of hay from the bale. "She just can't stand it when a guy doesn't flirt back at her."

"She's awfully possessive for a sore loser."

"Gwen Severn isn't used to rejection."

"Well, Gwen," I mumbled under my breath, "practice makes perfect."

Mick flicked the piece of straw to the ground.

"Let's go," I said. Since everyone had moved inside, I figured we could make our escape without anyone being the wiser, but apparently Mick was raised to have manners.

"Can't just leave," he said, pushing himself up from the hay bales. "I've gotta talk to Bull."

"We could send him a note." I blew a lock of hair out of my eye. "Tell him what a nice time we had."

He gave me a look.

I gave Sassy a hug before we left and Blood just huffed at me.

The rain had all but stopped as Mick and I walked from the barn up to the house, my sandals squishing in the gravelly dirt. I breathed in a lungful of the fresh air and said something about the cool front arriving.

"No kidding," Mick muttered under his breath.

The inside of the house was as opulent as the outside implied. We went in through a covered porch that wrapped around the back of the home, part of which jutted out from the main building, where a number of the guests had congregated to watch the storm. The wait staff had barely lost a beat, continuing to hoist trays of beer and wine.

Some of the guests had left, but the majority carried on in the confines. Some looked a little damp, but most had survived the storm without any water damage. I couldn't say the same for the soggy caterers.

We entered a large room that abutted the kitchen. A dark wooden bar ran the length of one long wall. Above it were glass racks and behind it a mirror reflecting the bottles set up against it. Padded stools lined the bar and five or six round tables were strewn across a muted blue and green plaid carpet. There were four beer taps—Guinness and several British ales. Paintings of wildlife and fox hunts hung from the walls. It really did look like a pub, but the image kept colliding with my first impression of the house—as if a twister had snatched a pub off Fleet Street and plopped it down in Morocco.

Bull was holding court from behind the bar, gesturing with his beer toward the kitchen. "It's only fair," he was saying. "Gwen gets her room; I get mine." Dutiful laughter from his subjects followed.

When Bull saw us, he wagged his chin, and Mick nodded at him. "Give me a minute," he said, giving my arm a pat.

"I'll be exploring the kitchen."

When I stepped into the kitchen I saw Gwen standing across the room talking with a couple of women around her age. I nearly did an about face, but the kitchen looked amazing, and I was determined not to let one unpleasant person—even if she owned the place—keep me from checking it out.

Bottles and platters lined the granite island in the center of the kitchen. Dark wood cupboards surrounded sleek appliances. I ran my hand along the stainless steel stovetop. It looked like it had just arrived from the high-end appliance store. If I had a kitchen like this—and I sometimes dreamed about it—I would have copper and steel pots and pans suspended from the ceiling so I wouldn't have to dig through three others to find the right one. There'd be bottles of olive oil and spice grinders on the counter. And the stove would look like it had been used. My kitchen would not look like an operating room.

The two women with Gwen were oohing and aahing over her necklace. When Gwen saw me standing nearby, she stepped back in order to include me in the group as she explained, "Bull gave it to me last month. It's similar to one of the pieces we had stolen last year. But," she tilted her little head and clucked softly, then continued in a lower voice, "it just doesn't have the same sentiment behind it. You know?"

The two women nodded as if they did.

"I mean, that one Bull gave me after Tyra was born."

"You get jewelry for giving birth?" It just slipped out.

"It's the least I deserve," she said, and the others joined in the laughter.

I had seen no sign of children in this place. No kids at the barbeque, no photographs, no toys. But according to Gwen, there was a nice piece of jewelry in it for her every time she gave birth. I imagined there could be any number of offspring living in the children's wing.

As though she were reading my mind, I noticed a flicker of distaste as Gwen's mouth curled up into a smile and she introduced me. "Girls, you know Mick Hughes. This is his ... date. Robyn." She placed her hand on my arm. "What was your last name?"

"Guthrie," I said, and then she introduced me to Ashley and Jocelyn.

Then I looked around the sterile kitchen and said to Gwen, "You must enjoy cooking."

She glanced over her shoulder at the stove and the double oven beside it and said, "When I'm properly inspired."

That made Ashley laugh but only got a taut smile out of Jocelyn.

I quickly sized up Ashley, who was pretty with a thick shock of auburn hair that, in the minute or so that I'd been standing there, she had tossed at least seven times. Jocelyn was less flashy and had the hazy, heavy-lidded look of someone who was slightly tanked.

"How do you all know each other?" I asked.

"We went to high school together," Gwen said.

Why wasn't I surprised?

"Where is Mick?" Ashley asked, craning her long neck to get a better view of the room.

I was about to say he was talking to Bull, but then I didn't see him with Bull, nor did I see him in the pub.

Before I could answer, Gwen smiled and said, "He's one you've got to keep your eye on."

"Yes," I said with a sigh. "I worry so."

Gwen was frowning as I excused myself. I didn't see any point in continuing a dialogue with her and her friends. I had already staked out the restroom (three beers), and I found it again without a problem. Afterwards, I wandered around, looking for Mick. I knew he wouldn't leave without me, but I wondered where he'd disappeared to. There'd been that Rudy guy giving off weird vibes, and I didn't see him anywhere either.

I walked out onto the porch and stood by one of the floor-to-ceiling windows that looked out on the back of the estate. The cool breeze chilled me a little.

"You're Mick's friend."

I turned to see who the British accent belonged to and was surprised to find Rudy standing behind me.

"Yes," I said. "Robyn Guthrie."

He bowed slightly. "A pleasure."

"And you are …?" I cocked my head.

"Rudy Dresser."

"Nice to meet you." On closer inspection, Rudy proved to have a rather nice smile.

"How do you know Mick?" I asked.

"We go way back." The smile deepened. "Also, he's my accountant."

"Mine too."

I glanced around, looking for Mick. This man's eyes were disconcerting. Seeing no relief in sight, I said, "Are you a racing fan as well?"

He shrugged, and I saw a trace of amusement in those pale eyes. "Inasmuch as I enjoy beautiful things." He gave me a nod.

"Yes, thoroughbreds are amazing." I pushed a strand of damp hair off my forehead and noticed that Rudy's eyes tracked my hand.

Then he said, "Speaking of beautiful, that's a lovely ring you're wearing."

"Oh." I glanced down at my hand. "It's my mother's." It was an art deco ring—one of the pieces she had given me when she moved into Dryden. "She doesn't wear it anymore."

He placed his fingers under mine, lifting my hand and angling it for a better look. "And it should be worn. Most definitely."

"Thank you. I like it."

"It's charming." With a dry smile he added, "Could use a bit of cleaning."

As he released my hand, I took another look at the ring. Clear stones and indigo blue stones combined to resemble a small, bejeweled bow. I'd always loved it but assumed the stones were glass.

"You should get it appraised," he said.

"Really? I wonder what it's worth." The words just fell out of me and must have conveyed the wishful thinking of one who needed a serious influx of cash. Fast.

He laughed. "I doubt it's enough to retire on, but it's something you might want to consider insuring." With a shrug he added, "Perhaps a thousand or two."

No, that wasn't enough. Still, it made me wonder where my mother would have gotten such a ring. Not from Wyman. "Thanks, I will have it appraised. Maybe I'll get it cleaned too."

"There you are."

I looked over my shoulder to see Mick approaching. He put his arm around my shoulder—a little awkward given the two inches I had on him—and said, "I see you've met Rudy."

"Yes," I turned to Mick and saw he was eyeing Rudy. "I've just learned the ring I've been tossing on the kitchen counter when I make turkey meatballs should be insured."

That got Mick's attention. "Nice," he said as I flashed the ring. Then he took my hand and said, "Why don't we take you and that ring home?"

Was it just me or was Mick getting a little possessive? I decided to play along. "Can't wait to see that ferret of yours."

Mick rolled his eyes and then nodded to Rudy. "Talk to you to-morrow," he said.

"Nice to meet you, Robyn."

"Likewise."

When Mick pulled the Porsche up to my apartment, he turned to-ward me, his hand resting on the shift knob, and said, "You inviting me up?" He sounded hopeful.

"No," I answered after a moment. The beers' effect had abated and sanity had returned. Still, I remembered the taste of his mouth and his touch that was both deft and gentle, and it was with some re-gret that I stifled those second thoughts. I'd been in my apartment for two years and the only men who had been in it had been there to re-pair a fixture or to deliver a package. I knew if I invited him up we would have sex—not a bad thing—but then he would want to talk about the Sassy affair, and I would have to tell him that it was the beer talking. And then I'd have to ask myself if everything that fol-lowed had also been the talking suds. If I ever invited him into my bed it would be with a head not muddied by booze.

He pressed his lips together and sighed. "How come?"

"I'm not ready to complicate my life—not in that way."

"You were ready in the barn."

"I know." I smiled and added, "Having a horse and a goat for an audience turns me on."

"You're an exhibitionist." He nodded to himself as though con-firming a thought.

"I guess I am."

"I've got a friend who raises goats." He shrugged. "Bet I could be back with one in a half hour."

I laughed, and he lifted his hand off the steering wheel in a can't-say-I-didn't-try gesture.

"Okay, so how about I come by tomorrow, and we can talk about your idea."

"It was a three-beer idea. Worth about that much."

He frowned, squinted as he cocked his head. "If Edison thought that, we wouldn't have electricity."

"Edison drank?"

"I'd bet on it."

I leaned over and gave him a kiss on the cheek, which he didn't respond to, but continued to hold onto my gaze when I drew away. In the dim light provided by the setting sun, I couldn't read his eyes, but I didn't think I needed to.

"Thank you," I said, and then added, "I didn't go just because of Bull."

"Sure," he said.

I changed into my walking shoes and after taking Bix around the block, I checked my voice mail. None of the Mary Waltners had called, and the only message was the one from Jane Goodwin, which, for some reason, I had saved. I deleted it.

I sat down and poured myself a scotch and thought about my mother's situation. If I told Jane Goodwin yes, I would have to move my mother in two weeks—after explaining it all to her. If I told her no, I would either have to come up with the money or I would have to move to a larger place. I couldn't do that again. Could I? If that possibility—however remote—didn't give me impetus to steal, kidnap, whatever, then nothing would.

Tomorrow morning I would reevaluate the scheme. In the daylight, with my sanity and sobriety returned, I was sure it wouldn't be worth considering any longer. But I would wait until then to decide.

I watched Bix, splayed on the floor chewing a dog biscuit I'd given him. Sassy was three times the size of my dog, and probably wouldn't stop at dog biscuits. It didn't take much to imagine him feasting on furniture and peeling off the wallpaper in the kitchen. And when I considered what a goat would do to Bix's sensitive psyche, well, I knew it wasn't worth considering further.

By the time I'd worked that out, I had finished my drink. I almost poured myself another, but I try to set my limit at one, although I will admit to pouring a rather dark scotch.

I changed into a T-shirt and slipped into bed. The storm had cooled the air and it was nice sleeping with the window open. I lay my hand in the space beside me on the bed and tried to decide if I was sorry I'd rejected Mick's advances. Maybe a little. He'd kissed with passion and took his time. And, given the situation—being in someone else's barn and all, that had to take something—either incredible concentration or a complete disregard for consequences. He'd been a jockey. He probably had a bit of both.

I rolled over on my side and tucked one hand into the cool underside of my pillow. But when I closed my eyes, sleep was the last thing my body wanted to do. Images rioted in my mind—my mother, Willoway, cigarettes, Mick, Bull and Gwen, Blood, Sassy—and I didn't know how to turn them off.

I sighed into my pillow. If Mick were here, I wouldn't be counting leaping goats. That's for damned sure.

CHAPTER 11

I woke with a mild hangover. Not the searing headache precipitated by consuming too much red wine, but that "my head is stuffed with cotton" feeling and a stomach doing flip flops, thanks to the combination of beer and scotch. The scotch god is a jealous one—the unfaithful are punished. I turned off the radio and rolled over, seeking oblivion. But my brain picked right up on the looping thread from last night—my mother … Mick … goats—and I knew I stood a better chance of putting these thoughts out of my mind by getting out of bed and doing something.

So I got up, threw on a T-shirt and jeans and drank a large glass of orange juice, followed with a bowl of Cheerios and a banana.

While walking Bix, I ticked off my tasks. I had an article to finish. I had to handle my mother's demand for a séance, I had to give Jane Goodwin my answer, and then I had to deal with that decision because, in the sobering light of day, I realized the one thing I was not going to do today was steal a goat.

I decided to finish the article first because, frankly, that was the easiest to face. This meant I had to visit Erika at her shop to ask some follow-up questions, so at the same time I could talk to her about another séance.

While I took a quick shower, I thought back on that insane discussion Mick and I had had in the barn. (Not to mention the lapse of self-control.) It was a parlor game, really. Stealing a goat and holding it for ransom. Ridiculous. I would not bring it up again and hoped that Mick would do the same. And maybe it was time to change accountants.

When I arrived at Erika's shop, there was a man sitting at the desk in the reception area. He was in his late forties with broad shoulders, which contrasted with a narrow nose that was the centerpiece of an outstanding face. When he looked up from his cell phone, I had to remind myself to keep moving. I'm not usually bowled over by a man's looks, sensing, perhaps unfairly, that a gorgeous man was apt to be as faithless, and as preening, as a rooster. But his rather sharp features were offset by kind eyes, and the slight smile he gave me produced a set of dimples. His brows rose a fraction of an inch and he raised a finger as though asking me to wait a moment. Then he said into the phone, "Yeah, I know, but …"

I wondered if he was Erika's receptionist. He wore a rust-colored T-shirt that accentuated the cut of his arms. The conversation he was conducting didn't sound work-related. Although he wasn't talking loudly, and I wasn't straining to listen, I picked up words such as "next week" and "Dallas."

Nevertheless, if he wanted to give me his attention, I decided I would be grateful for it.

I felt those friendly eyes follow me as I walked past the desk, seeking some distraction that would allow me to refocus. I'd noticed the smell when I'd walked in—a mix of fruits and spices—and I saw that, since Friday, Erika had begun peddling psychic paraphernalia. I walked over to the shelves to see what was for sale. Aside from candles, incense and crystals, there were also sets of Tarot cards and a small tray of amulets ranging from pentagrams to bats. A single shelf was filled with books on Tarot cards, crystal balls and one on the psychic power of animals. I picked up the latter, thinking perhaps I was a mere 189 pages away from learning why Bix attacked the vacuum.

I was skimming a paragraph on reading a dog's body language, when the rooster spoke. "Are you here to see Erika?"

I glanced over my shoulder. "Yes. I'm Robyn Guthrie. Are you the receptionist?"

A quick smile. "No, I'm Jack Landis. Her brother." He stood and walked around the desk—I just knew he'd look amazing in a pair of jeans—leaning his butt against its edge and crossing his arms over his chest.

"So Starwise must be her married name."

That made him laugh and, although it was a little on the high-pitched side, it fit the rest of him. Then, with a sheepish shrug, he crossed one ankle over the other, grinned and said, "I'm afraid that was my idea. Not the Starwise. Just that Erika Landis didn't sound … authentic." He finished with a half-hearted shrug and then locked his gaze onto mine. "Name withstanding, she is the real thing."

I nodded agreeably.

His brows drew together as if something about me had belatedly sparked a memory. "Are you that reporter who's doing the story on Erika?"

"I am."

"Oh." He drew the word out to two syllables and just nodded, looking me over.

I glanced to either side. "Am I infamous?"

"Not really. She said it was an interesting session."

"I guess you could say that."

"She's got a client now. Shouldn't be long."

I cocked my chin. "Are you psychic?"

He laughed and shook his head. "No. I'm afraid Erika is the only one who inherited our grandmother's gift."

"Your grandmother?"

"Yeah. She could predict the gender of a child six months before it was born."

"I guess ultrasounds put her out of business."

That earned me an amused grin, and Jack looked like he was about to respond when the first few notes from the James Bond theme erupted from his phone. He flipped it open to answer the call.

I went back to the book, silently cursing the inventors of all annoying conveniences, and attempted to focus on the words before me. But that proved difficult because the paragraph I read made no sense—something about using a Ouija board with your dog. Still, I kept skimming the page. I wanted to keep busy because I figured if Jack and I continued to talk, I would blather, and he would know that maturity didn't necessarily have anything to do with social grace. As it was, he was eyeing me, I thought, with some interest, and I didn't want to disillusion him too early. I was nothing, if not patient.

Out of the corner of my eye, an item on the countertop caught my attention. I set the book down and picked up a small, gold-colored metal bowl containing a wooden stick that was padded at one end in an embroidered red and turquoise material. I lifted the stick from the bowl and stood there for a moment, not sure whether I should whack the bowl's side or just return it to the shelf before I embarrassed myself.

"It's a Tibetan singing bowl."

I looked up to find Jack standing right behind me. His eyes were a tawny shade of brown and he had long, feminine lashes. He blinked once.

"Really," I said.

"It's used for meditation."

"It sings?"

"You have to make it sing."

"Ah." I lifted the stick out of the bowl. "Does it do requests?" I asked, then instantly regretted the sarcasm.

One of those dimples flashed in his left cheek. "Just let it sit on your palm. So you're not touching the bowl part. Then rub the outside rim with the stick."

I tried, but I was holding the stick like a fork and not having much success.

"Like this," he said and took my hand, adjusting my grip so the padded part of the wooden stick circled the outside of the bowl, barely touching its rim. "A gentle touch on the rim …" He guided my hand around it. His hand was soft, but his fingertips rough, calloused. "Keep the pressure even."

After a turn around the rim, he released my hand and I kept going. The bowl began to hum.

"Increase the speed as it begins to vibrate."

Behind me, his voice was a whisper in my ear, and I believe I began to vibrate before the bowl did. But the sound grew, filling my head and then every crevice in the room with the hum and vibration. It was an all-consuming sound, but mellow. The bowl trembled in my hand.

A door clicked. "Robyn Guthrie."

I clamped my hand on the bowl—the room went silent—and lost my grip on the stick. It fell to the carpet and Jack scooped it up and handed it to me with a little smile. He then returned to his perch on the desk.

Erika now stood at the door to the back of the shop, arms crossed over her chest, watching me. "I'd like to buy this," I said, raising the bowl.

She glanced from Jack to me and then turned to the young woman standing just behind her who had purple-and-white-streaked hair and a stud in her left nostril.

"Thank you so much, Erika," the young woman said as she gripped the strap of her hemp bag with both hands.

"I'll see you next week," Erika told her.

The young woman cast more than a casual glance in Jack's direction as she walked past us and out the door.

Then the three of us stood looking at each other in the silence for several moments. Erika's arms were crossed over her chest and her posture was quite rigid. She wore a thick, gold bangle bracelet on one wrist and a ring with a large black stone.

"I'm sorry to bother you, Erika," I began. "But the other night I left in kind of a hurry. There were a few background questions I needed to ask you. And I also need to get a photo."

She shook her head. "That won't be necessary."

"It'll go with the story."

"I don't like having my picture taken."

I thought of those primitive people who, when first introduced to the camera, believed it would steal their souls. I wondered what Erika's problem was.

I slipped my hand into my satchel and pulled out a small digital camera. "I'll let you see it before I use it."

"No." Erika wore her stern look—it was one she favored, but then I guess I didn't expect someone who regularly communed with the dead to project a warm and fuzzy aura.

"You don't have to pose or anything," I added. "In fact, it would be better if you were doing something." I stepped back and looked around the office. There really wasn't much to work with here. I knew better than to suggest I get a shot of her face cast in the eerie glow of a crystal ball. "Maybe standing beside the counter with the curtain behind you. It would help the article. An article with a photo gets a larger percentage of readers than one without." While this was logical, it had nothing to do with why I wanted the photo anymore. And the more she balked, the more determined I became. I wasn't going home without a photo of this woman.

"No," she said, looking ready to flee into the back room.

"C'mon, Erika," Jack said. "It's one photo."

The look she gave him and the one he returned must have spoken volumes, but only in their language. Whatever the exchange meant, the next thing that Erika did was walk over to counter, place one arm on it and then turn to face me.

"One photo," she said.

I made sure it was a good one, offered to show her the image, but she declined. Then I returned the camera to my bag and exchanged it for a slim notebook. "Could I ask you a few more questions?"

When she didn't respond right away, I hurried ahead. "Just some background. These items in your shop are certainly worth mentioning."

"I carry those items only because my clients request them."

I stepped back and regarded the psychic paraphernalia. I picked up a small, smooth, beige stone with striations of brown and black. The lines came together in a spiral, giving the impression of a blooming flower—maybe a rose.

"What does this one do?"

She studied me for a moment, as though she were trying to measure my sincerity. Finally, she said, "It's for protection."

"Do you believe it does any good?"

She gave me a little smile, but it was impossible to tell if it was condescending or knowing. What it wasn't was warm. "They do no harm," she said.

I put it in the singing bowl.

"What's this?" I picked up a small leather pouch drawn together by a black string.

"That contains herbal charms." She approached me, arms still crossed over her chest. "Is there something in particular you're looking for?"

"No," I set it down. "Not really." Then I added with a shrug. "But I suppose we can all use a bit of luck."

Her eyes were nowhere near as friendly as her brother's. In fact, there wasn't much physical resemblance between the two. Maybe Jack's eyes would harden as he aged a few years. "Um," I said, "could we go sit somewhere so we could talk for a few minutes?"

"I'm afraid that won't be possible. I have another client coming in soon."

I'd have preferred a one-to-one talk, maybe over some coffee. But I had no choice but to make my stand out here among the crystals, Tarot cards and bat wings.

"Okay, just a couple more questions." She didn't bolt. "Why did you decide to move your business from California to Illinois?"

If my digging had surprised Erika, she didn't let on. Just nodded as though she found the question reasonable and said, "I wanted to be closer to my daughter. I've enrolled her in a school in the area."

"All the way from California?"

"It's a … special school."

Her tone implied that I had asked enough regarding her daughter, so I moved on. "Was your business in California similar to this one?"

"Prior to this, I have worked out of my home. On a referral basis only." She glanced toward Jack, who was still busy watching me. Then she said, "I have always been selective with my clients. Word of mouth. I often make house calls. Where I worked was of little importance."

"Okay," I said. "Can you talk about your gift? How long have you been psychic?"

She heaved an impatient sigh. "It's something I was born with."

"When did you first know you were—"

"When I was four and a half I foresaw the death of my younger sister."

Whoa. I blinked. "How?"

"I saw her face underwater. Her eyes and her mouth were open, and I watched as a water lily pad floated over her face."

All of this she delivered with an astonishing lack of emotion.

"At the time, I didn't realize what I was seeing," she continued. "Now, I pay very close attention to such images."

Her intensity made me want to step back. But I held my ground and asked the question I was sure she wanted me to ask. "What are you seeing now?"

She canted her chin. "Why do you think I'm seeing anything?"

Determined not to let her mess with my psyche any more than she already had, I pulled out a question I didn't think she'd expect. "You weren't born in this country, were you?"

After the briefest hesitation, she said, "Why do you ask?"

"You speak very distinctly. I wondered if English was your second language."

That earned me a stiff smile. "You are correct. I was born in Budapest."

"How old were you when you came here?"

She glanced in her brother's direction, then said, "I was barely a teenager."

Without a pause, she added, "I'm afraid I must go and prepare for my next client."

"But I don't know if I have enough for an article."

"If you don't, then that is how it must be." She turned toward Jack, but she was speaking to me when she said, "I'm sorry if I've wasted your time."

"Erika, can we do another séance?"

This got her attention. From the way her mouth was set, I thought she was about to yell at me, swear at me, tell me to get the hell out of her shop. But then, as her eyes held mine, her expression softened and she said, "I'm surprised. I didn't think that was … comfortable for you."

"It wasn't," I said. "But I've got more questions."

After regarding me for several long moments, she said, "All right. Wednesday evening?"

"Does it have to be at night?" Knowing how my mother tended to be her most confused in the evening and her sharpest in the morning or early afternoon when she was rested, I figured that would be the time to shoot for.

"No. In fact it doesn't." She regarded me. "Although many people think that spirits are only available in the evenings, I've found that the time of day has little to do with a spirit's receptivity."

"I may bring my mother," I told her.

"That would be fine. Thursday morning then. Ten thirty?"

"I'll call you if that doesn't work," I said.

"I'll look forward to seeing you both."

And with that, she retreated to the back area, closing the door behind her.

As I stared at the door, Jack said, "Are you hoping to get more for your story?"

"No. My story's due before then." I turned to him. "Why did she call the newspaper and ask that I do a story on her? She doesn't want it."

"I'm afraid that was my idea."

"Really? Why?"

He approached me again. "She deserves to be better known. She really is gifted."

"Yeah, so you say." I was annoyed and didn't care if it showed. She was hiding more than her history, and I knew I had some work to do if I wanted to get it out of her.

I said to Jack, "Can you tell me anything about her background?"

He grinned. "Not without risking my big sister's wrath."

"So you're scared of her too."

"She's a powerful woman."

"Because of her psychic abilities?"

"That. And other things."

"Such as?"

"Maybe we could talk about it some time … over dinner?"

I fished a card out of my bag and handed it to him. "Give me a call." While it occurred to me that Jack might also have some ulterior motive, I figured he deserved a chance.

Without even a glance at it, he slipped my card into his pocket. "How about tonight? Dinner." He smiled and added, "You pick the place, and I'll meet you there. Seven o'clock?"

I couldn't think of a reason not to, so I named a bar that served good sandwiches and was only a block away.

He smiled. "I'll see you then."

Before I left, I turned over the singing bowl and saw a sticker with $14.95 written on it in black ink. The stone of protection cost two dollars—quite a deal if it worked. I pulled a couple of bills out of my wallet. "Can I pay you?"

When I walked into my apartment, the phone was ringing. A check of the caller ID confirmed that it was Jane Goodwin, and I let her talk to voice mail. I stared at her name, thinking. Was stealing the goat really that bad an idea?

After the ringing stopped, I sat at my small kitchen table and buried my face in my hands and took three deep breaths. What was harder: stealing a goat or finding a dog-friendly apartment with two bedrooms in two weeks?

I stood. Procrastinate, I told myself. *Defer that decision until it's so ripe it bursts in your face.* That I could do.

I polished off the article on the Psychic Place. I didn't have much to add. My editor would just have to take it as it was. Or not. Either way, he wouldn't fire me. After I emailed the piece and the photo to him, I started on an article for a women's magazine on getting a full night's sleep and spent the morning in a writing haze, forgetting, for a couple of hours, how lousy things looked.

When I broke at one p.m. for lunch, I switched on the TV, then searched the refrigerator for inspiration.

The newscast didn't catch my attention until after her name was mentioned, and then I looked up to see the petite brunette anchor woman saying, "… Her body was found by a jogger yesterday in the Warren Forest Preserve, but she was not identified until this morning. Mary Waltner was visiting Chicago from California. An autopsy is pending, but authorities believe she was strangled. At this point, police have no leads in the investigation."

I opened the *Tribune* and found a reference in the Metro section— a body had been discovered, but no identification had been made.

I dug for my notebook with the page of Mary Waltners and found the one living in Thousand Oaks. While it might have been a coincidence, not for a second did I believe it was. And I'd called her home phone, leaving my name and number. Had she been dead when I called her? Or had she gotten my message? No doubt the police would be here to see me soon. Maybe I'd better call them first.

I thought of my mother, wondering if I should let someone at Dryden know. Know what? That a woman who had seen my mother a few days ago had been murdered? At least I thought it was the same woman. Still, I had no reason to believe that her visit to my mother and her death were connected, but again, I didn't trust coincidence. I tried to focus on action. If I went over there and pressed my mother on the visit, told her that Mary Waltner was now dead, I might just scare her enough to talk. Either that or I'd shut her down. No, I thought, it was time I stopped thinking of my mother as a defenseless little old lady. She was far from it. And maybe she honestly didn't remember why Mary Waltner had come to see her. Maybe she got short with me about it because she was ashamed of her memory. Right.

In the midst of my dithering, someone knocked on my door. I opened it to Mick Hughes, looking like he'd gotten a better night's sleep than I had.

It was way too soon to see him. I hadn't even processed yesterday yet. But there he was, a little smile pulling at his mouth.

"I hope you're not here about the goat," I said, holding my ground. People rarely stopped by my apartment unannounced, and I liked it that way.

"Keep it down, will you?" he said under his breath. As though the masses downstairs getting their Picasso prints framed would care.

He glanced over his shoulder and then back to me. "You going to invite me in?"

"I'm not sure." I leaned one hip against the door jamb. When I'd returned from the Psychic Place, I had changed into a pair of shorts and an oversized T-shirt that touted a Shakespearean festival in Anchorage that I'd never been to. So not only was I looking sloppy, I was guilty of false advertising.

But I finally relented. I guess I figured we'd have to have this discussion eventually. It was one more thing I could tick off my list. I stepped back from the door. As I did, Bix was there to greet my guest, wagging his butt along with his skinny tail.

"Hey, kid," Mick greeted Bix, rubbing behind his ears.

Bix is usually a pretty decent judge of character. It's not that he growls at bad guys or anything like that, although he doesn't try real hard with my mother, but people do give off vibes and animals can pick them up. And a dog with hyper tendencies like Bix was pretty sensitive to moods. When I'm edgy, he's edgy. Mick didn't appear edgy at all. How nice for him.

I told him I was putting a lunch together and asked if he wanted something to eat.

"No, thanks. Already had something." But he followed me into my kitchen and leaned against the counter as I placed a handful of small carrots on a plate.

"How you feeling?" he asked.

I glanced at him from the corner of my eye. He wasn't here to inquire as to my health. He either wanted to talk about the goat or he wanted to bed me. Stubborn, I was determined he would fail in both endeavors.

"Okay." I plopped a generous spoonful of hummus on the plate. "And you?"

"Good," he said. "Really good." He seemed bemused, as though he were waiting for me to do something bizarre.

When I didn't, he turned his attention from me to my plate. "What's that?"

"Hummus," I said, licked the spoon and dropped in into the stainless steel sink. And, because he looked perplexed, I added, "Made out of chick peas. With some garlic." Maybe now he'd keep his distance.

Leaning his folded arms on the counter now, he looked up at me. "You're not one of those vegetarians, are you?"

"Half-assed. I don't eat red meat, but I do eat fish and chicken."

He nodded and then after a moment said, "What do you have against chickens?"

"They make me nervous."

He smiled a little and turned again so his back was to the counter.

I waited a couple of beats and then said, "Aren't you going to ask me about fish?"

He shook his head. "No, I get that part. There's something sinister about a fish. Especially those flounders."

I swallowed a smile. Didn't want to encourage him.

When I poured myself some iced tea, I asked if he wanted some. He rejected the tea, but accepted a beer. With the aid of a hand towel, I twisted the cap off and handed him the bottle.

"Thanks," he said, tipping it toward me as if toasting.

As I placed a few crackers on my plate, Mick and Bix went into the living room and Mick sat on the couch with the Tibetan singing bowl on the coffee table in front of him.

"What's this?" He picked up the wooden stick.

I told him.

"Oh, yeah? How's it work?"

Knowing how sensual an experience playing the bowl can be when done in tandem, I demonstrated by circling the stick in mid air, and then handed it to Mick, who began running the stick around the rim.

He proved better at it than I'd been on my first try. As the intensity increased, my scalp tightened; the sound built and Bix began to howl, backing off from Mick, and the bowl. Either Bix liked it or it made him crazy. Mick cut the noise off by placing his hand on the bowl and then placed the stick in it. "Hard to tell if he was singing with it or at it."

I set out slate coasters for each of us and then settled into the purple chair with my plate.

Mick cocked his chin at me. Bix had hopped up beside him on the couch, and I swear the dog had cocked his head, too.

"You okay?" Mick asked. "Seem kind of …," he shrugged, "edgy."

And why would I be edgy, I asked myself. Let me count the ways. Instead of going with the entire truth—something getting rare these days—I went with a half-truth. "I just heard some disturbing news on the TV." And I told him about Mary Waltner's visit to my mother.

He listened, and when I'd finished, he took a drink from his bottle and returned it to the coaster. "How d'you know it's the same person?"

"I don't. But I have a strong feeling she is. I've been checking—I don't think my mom was entirely truthful about why she came to see her."

"How come?"

"I don't know. That's why I wanted to talk to her."

He nodded. "Can I do anything?"

That surprised me. "No. But thanks."

Then I said, "I should call the police. Tell them what I know."

"Can you wait until I leave?" he asked.

"I guess."

We spent the next minute or so in silence, except for the sound of me chewing my carrot and Bix cleaning his privates.

"I've been doing some thinking," Mick finally said, folding his hands as he leaned back into the couch. He crossed his bad ankle over his knee. Today's boots were a soft-looking leather in a deep olive shade.

"Have you?"

"I think we could pull it off."

I shook my head. "I think it's crazy."

"Kidnapping a goat *is* crazy." He gave me an assured nod. "But it's also a really good idea."

"The goat has a name."

"Sassy," he said, flatly. "Kidnapping Sassy."

"Listen to yourself. Let's kidnap a goat and hold it for ransom." I shoved a little hummus onto a cracker. "I'll bet in the history of the English language those words have never before been strung together."

"It's not unheard of," he said, and when I gave him my dubious look, he elaborated. "That's where the expression 'get your goat' comes from. A guy would steal a companion goat before a race to put the horse off."

"You're joking?"

He shook his head, and I saw no suppressed humor in his eyes.

"Was ransom involved?"

"Not that I know of." He smiled. "That may be an original touch." He leaned forward. "Look, maybe you were only joking. Maybe you were a little drunk. But you came up with a great idea. We could do it." He eyed me for several long moments, and I couldn't read him to save my soul. "And the thing is, whether you meant to or not, you came up with the perfect way to take Bull down a notch or two. Blood is Bull's ticket to the big time."

"I saw his house. He has already arrived."

"He's not where he wants to be. Not in racing circles. Blood wins this race and he'll be drawing top dollar stud fees. Folks will have to take Blood and Bull seriously. But if Blood gets scratched because he's too whacked out to race, well, how much is his pedigree going to be worth? What's Bull's reputation as a horseman going to look like?"

I nodded as I finished chewing. But then I said, "No, Mick. I don't think so."

"How come?" His gaze intensified. "You know he deserves it."

"What about his kids? Do they deserve it?"

"Bull ripped off a lot of people. You think he thought about their kids?"

Not as far as I knew.

"Besides," he kept going, "you're not going to break the man. His kids—who I've never seen by the way—will still go to their fancy schools, starting in preschool. What we're going to do is embarrass Bull and show him and everyone else that he shouldn't be in this business."

When I didn't respond, he gulped down some beer and added, "He deserves that."

"I'm sure he does," I said. "But, you should know this about me before you work too hard at convincing me."

Mick waited and I continued, "I learned, after trial and error, that the safest way to do something illegal or just plain wrong was to only think about it, and not follow through. The fun is in the planning. I'm one of those people who never gets away with anything. That's probably why I'm so law-abiding. I cut class one day in middle school so I could get tickets to this concert I was dying to attend. I was with several friends, and who do we run into but my neighbor. She squealed on me and Wyman grounded me so I didn't get to go to the concert."

"Did you rat your friends out?"

"No," I told him. "But that's not the only time. I always get caught."

He smiled a little. "But you wouldn't rat me out."

"True," I sighed. "But that's small comfort to me."

"Stick with me," he said. "I never get caught."

"Stick with me and you will."

"Wrong attitude," he said. "We can pull this off."

Then, as if that settled the matter, Mick eased himself back into the couch. He took a pull on his beer, then rested it on his thigh as he said, "Do you know what Bull did with the money from that real estate deal that tanked?"

I figured he didn't need prompting, so I waited.

"After a little laundering, he bought himself that stable we were in yesterday, the exercise track, and then he bought Bull's Blood."

I digested this while I swallowed my cracker. "So, really, it's my mother's horse."

"You could say that."

I set the plate down and brushed a few crumbs off my hands, then washed the cracker down with some iced tea.

"How much would we be asking?"

Without hesitation, he said, "Half a million."

"For a goat? You're joking?"

He shook his head. "It's not just the goat. It's Blood's reputation. Bull's reputation."

"Has he got that kind of money?"

He nodded. "Oh, yeah."

Maybe someone who could afford to shell out a half million dollars to get his goat back deserved to be separated from his money.

"Okay," I said, "you know why I need the money. Why do you need it bad enough to do something ridiculous?"

He studied me for several moments before he sighed and said, "Let's just say I've got some debts of my own that have come due. And I'm a little short."

I set my glass down. "Listen," I said. "You know exactly why I need the money. I don't think I'm being out of line asking what you need it for."

"What difference does it make? I'm not pushing drugs on little kids or selling virgins into slavery. Maybe I'm looking to buy my own horse."

"If that were it, you'd have told me a long time ago."

He stood and walked around the coffee table. Not wanting to relinquish the height advantage, I stood. In my bare feet, I still have a few inches on him. None of those inches seemed to bother Mick a bit as he looked up at me.

"I like you, Robyn. I do. But don't go thinking I'm ready to cut you in on my life. Far as I'm concerned this is a business proposition. You want to go in with me on it, then say so. If you don't, I think you know you'd better keep your mouth shut. You've heard rumors about me. You can figure that about eighty percent is crap. But then there's the other twenty. So don't think you've got me figured out. That'd be a mistake."

My face grew hot, and I hoped it wasn't changing colors. The tension between us tightened, ready to crack. But there was a flood of energy as well, and I folded my arms across my chest to keep from either slapping him or kissing him. Instead, I swallowed. "Is that a threat?"

He shook his head once. "I wouldn't threaten you, Robyn."

Stepping away from me, he said, "Tell you what. You think it over.

If I don't hear from you by tomorrow afternoon, I'll find someone else."

I was determined to get in the last word, but nothing came to me. Especially after he got to the door, turned toward me and said, "Don't forget to call the police."

CHAPTER 12

I don't handle confrontation well, and I sure as hell didn't expect this from Mick. In a way, it made my decision easier. Why would I want to do dishonest business with a guy who threatened me? Okay, it hadn't been overt, and there had been that undercurrent of sexual tension, which was, in a word, unsettling.

But I didn't have the time or energy to contemplate my relationship with Mick. No matter how dire my situation, I was way better off than Mary Waltner. And maybe I could do some good there. So I called the police and asked to speak to whoever was working on her murder investigation. After being on hold for about thirty seconds, someone picked up the phone and a man said, "Hedges, Homicide."

I told him my name and verified that he was handling the Waltner investigation. "I believe she visited my mother on Friday." I went on to explain and added that I thought Waltner had called me later on Friday, and I told him about my calls to the Mary Waltners.

"You really wanted to talk to her."

"Um, yes, I guess I did. I'm looking out for my mother."

"You know why she saw your mother?" From his hoarse, rumbling voice, I placed him as middle-aged with thinning hair, a healthy paunch and a lopsided walk.

"Well, my mother told me that Mary had been a friend of my late father's." I didn't mention the other story my mother had concocted, because that would have required a lot more explanation, not to mention an understanding of my mother. Let him talk to her.

"Where's your mother?"

I told him, then he asked why I thought Mary Waltner had called me. "There was a call but no message from a cell phone number with the same area code as one of the Mary Waltners."

"What's the number that called you?"

"Hold on one minute." Of course he would want to know this. I pushed the hold button and scrolled through my call log until I found that call on Friday.

When I got Hedges back on the line, I recited the number and said, "The call came in at 4:38."

He grunted as though that were interesting to him. "That's her number all right."

"Do you know what time she died?"

"Not long after that."

I wondered if my recorded greeting, which sounded as scripted as it was, had been the last voice she'd heard prior to her murderer's.

Hedges thanked me and said he'd be in touch.

"Um, could I be there when you talk to my mom? Her memory isn't so good, and I can sometimes help her out."

"No, that's okay," he said after a moment. "I'll let you know if I need you."

"Please be careful with her. She gets upset easily."

"Don't worry, I will."

Then he thanked me and hung up.

"Good luck," I muttered into the phone. As I pushed the disconnect button, it occurred to me that Hedges would probably tell my mother that Mary Waltner had been murdered. I wasn't sure whether I was concerned about her getting upset or annoyed because now I wouldn't be able to use the death to press my mother on the urgency of her telling me everything she knows. And, once again, the internal conflict left me feeling like a heel.

Attempting to regain my focus, I glanced around my apartment. A murder would certainly complicate kidnapping a goat. With a cop liable to show up at any time, I sure couldn't keep Sassy in my bedroom. Another excellent reason to pass on this caper. And why was I still discussing this with myself?

Reassured that I had made the right decision in telling Mick he'd have to find another cohort, I returned to the draft of the article I'd been writing. But I found my mind easily distracted, and it took longer than it should have.

When I was finished, I called my mother about the séance I'd arranged. I considered mentioning the cop to her, but knew that would just get her agitated. Best to let it unfold in its own time.

Skipping the pleasantries, I went right to the point. "Wanted to let you know I've arranged for the séance, and I'll come by to get you on Thursday morning at ten fifteen."

"Séance?"

"That's right. Yesterday you said you wanted to talk to my father." I shouldn't have been so blunt about it—I knew her short-term memory was terrible—but she had coerced me into this séance and now she had no memory of it.

"Oh." A long pause. "And who was it again, dear? That woman?"

"Erika. Erika Starwise."

"Of course."

I guess it paid to have a distinctive name.

"Do I need to get dressed up for this?" she asked.

"No, Mom. Just come as you are."

"Will he be able to see me?"

All I could say was, "What?"

"Will Robert be able to see me?"

"I don't know, Mom." But it was a good question. "Why?"

When she didn't answer, I prompted her again.

Finally, with a sigh, she said, "I've gotten so old."

I put a lid on my surliness, resisting the impulse to come back with: *He's dead. How much worse can* you *look?*

Instead, I said, "Mom, he knows how old you are. He was old, too, when he died. And, besides, you're gorgeous. You'd win the Dryden beauty pageant hands down."

"Oh, Rob—"

"I am serious."

"Do you think I would?"

"Absolutely." Vanity—the last thing to go.

"Well, all right."

Before we hung up, I said, "Mom?"

"Yes?"

"Wear that washed silk blouse I got you. The one with the flowers. Blues and greens. You look real nice in that."

"Perhaps I will."

As I dressed for dinner with Jack, I marveled at the turn my social life had taken in the past week. Since I'd moved to Fowler, I'd been something of a recluse, occupying myself with my work and my mother. I assumed there was a social scene to this town, but I hadn't made much effort to find it. Most of my friends were in Oak Park or the city, and to tell the truth, there weren't a whole lot of them. I've never been one of those people who can juggle a bunch of people in her life. I suppose it came from growing up an only child. Back then I had a few friends, but kept to myself a lot. Even my mother and I didn't hang out together very much. And it wasn't the teen angst thing that kept us distant. She was a beautiful, vivacious woman. A little overwhelming. I guess I always felt invisible in her presence, and she must have thought so too, because she didn't usually ask me to tag along with her. The one thing we did do together was go out and buy me new clothing at the start of the school year. To see her today in her mismatched outfits that seem to attract food stains was hard; she'd always been so well dressed. Everything matched. And she had flair. Actually, I thought her taste in clothing bordered on the bizarre, and I think to this day I dress conservatively because of that. But I could remember more than once when she'd goad me into trying on an outfit I wouldn't have given a second thought to on my own. And I'd find—to my surprise—that the short purple skirt really did make me look taller and my legs weren't all that bad. She'd rag me about wearing baggy clothing—come to think of it, she still rags me about that—and tell me there'd come a day when my figure would either sag or turn thick, and I'd be sorry I didn't show it off when I could.

These shopping excursions invariably included lunch, where she would indulge in a martini. Or two. She knew I'd never squeal to Wyman, and she had the whole afternoon to sleep it off. And I was easily bought off with a blouse or a pair of earrings. I was also someone who listened to her. She loved to talk about her childhood and the scholarship she received to college. But she was a little foggy about why she dropped out and downright evasive about the year or so before she met my father, but I guess I figured everyone was entitled to a few secrets in her past. So I nodded and listened, even when I'd heard the stories before, because I think I knew that Wyman wasn't interested—or wouldn't have approved. And my mother's small circle of friends wasn't as tolerant of the repetition. I guess I was her favorite audience.

Today I wore a fitted red jacket over a white shell and a khaki skirt. Yesterday's storm had taken the humidity with it, and I was able to let my hair fall over my shoulders.

It was a short walk to Phinny's Pub, a place I felt comfortable going by myself. Occasionally, I'd bring my laptop there and do a little work while listening to the juke box selections. In a way, I was a little uneasy introducing the place to Jack. What if he liked it and I didn't like him? I'd hate to lose a good place because I was trying to avoid someone.

As I walked past the Psychic Place, I wondered what Erika would think of her little brother going to dinner with me. Probably wouldn't care much. She was odd, but I didn't recognize anything weird in that way. Then I wondered what Mick would think if he knew I was out on a date. Not that it mattered. Our relationship was over. If you could call one dinner and one makeout session a relationship. Whatever, it had to be over. For one thing, when I refused to go in with him on the goat heist, that'd be it for us. Even if I were to lose my mind and agree to it, I wouldn't want to be romantically involved with my partner in crime. I knew little about the criminal world, but that was a no-brainer. So either way, Mick Hughes was history. And that made me a little sad. I hadn't started out interested in him at all. Never thought he was my type. But he'd surprised me. Sort of like one of those outrageous outfits my mother would pull off the rack.

Stepping into Phinny's was always a pleasant experience. It was cool in the summer, cozy in the winter and smelled of rich, frothy beer and French fries. I waved to the bartender—Kathy was working tonight—and then saw Jack rising from one of the booths along the back wall.

He smiled as I approached and let me slide into the bench across from him before taking his seat. In front of him was a mostly full dark beer.

"Glad you could make it," he said. "Short notice and all."

I shrugged. "I'm not so busy that my Mondays are booked."

"Would you like a drink?"

"Sure," I said. The waitress, Danny, was on her way over. She said hi and instead of saying "I'll have the usual," I hesitated, as though considering my options, and then said, "I'll have a Famous Grouse on the rocks with a twist."

Danny bobbed her eyebrows at me, then glanced at Jack, who was occupied with the menu.

He looked up as she walked away, and said, "I like this place. It's got a good feel to it."

"Yeah," I said. "It's comfortable."

"Food good?"

"Uncomplicated, but good."

"I'm starved," he said, returning to the menu, and I took the opportunity to marvel at the way not a strand of his close-cropped silver-threaded hair dared go astray. "Had a late breakfast and haven't eaten since." He looked up at me again and his gray-green eyes lit up as he smiled. "Want to share some nachos?"

"Sure." My mother would love this man. And I might not be far behind. But I quickly admonished myself—I had stopped being impressed with looks when my soon-to-be-ex husband back-handed me into the stereo.

When Danny returned with my drink, Jack placed the order and then said we'd graze a while before ordering dinner.

"So," I said, taking a sip. "What brings you to Fowler?" I figured it had to be Erika, but wanted to hear it from him.

"I'm in Chicago for a few days for a sales meeting. Meeting's not until Wednesday so I took Monday and Tuesday off and decided to go visit my sister."

"What do you sell?"

"I work for a pharmaceutical company," he said, and named one of the big ones.

"Miracle drugs?"

"Sure. Why not?"

He smiled when he asked a question.

"Where do you live?"

"West coast. Oregon. Suburb of Portland."

"I hear that's a nice area."

He nodded. "It is. If you like rain."

"Actually, I do."

"You'll have to visit some time."

I really wasn't fishing for an invitation. But I was reminded of how awkward first dates are. You need to get all the information out of the way before you can cut to the important stuff. When Mick and I had dinner the other night, conversation hadn't been much of an effort. Maybe because he'd been doing my taxes for a couple of years, I figured he already knew way too much about me. Still, I hadn't been at all bored that night. I mentally kicked myself. Here I was sitting across from a handsome man, with a legitimate job, and I was thinking about the average-looking, dicey one I was cutting loose.

Gradually, the conversation crept away from the mundane. And by the time we started in on our meals—a cheeseburger for him and a teriyaki chicken sandwich for me—I was feeling pretty comfortable. I guess it had been so long since I'd had a first date that I hadn't known what to expect.

Jack had transformed from an attractive stranger to an attractive man with an abundance of interests. He'd skied the Alps, scuba dived in the Bahamas and worked as a forest ranger one summer in Wyoming.

When prompted, he talked about his sister who, as it turned out, was about seven years older.

"She just about raised me," he said around a bite of his sandwich. He finished chewing and swallowed. "Our father left when I was a little kid and our mother worked two jobs."

"Was it just the two of you?"

"Yeah. Just us." He dabbed a crumb on the table and flicked it off onto the edge of his plate.

"Is your mother still alive?"

"No," he said, sighing. "She died when I was in college—Erika made sure I finished—and since then it's been just the two of us."

"But Erika has a daughter. Was there a husband?"

"Briefly. He died in a car accident. Lily—her daughter—she's great."

"That's a pretty name."

He smiled as he studied me for a moment. "So is yours."

"Yeah, I guess there are worse birds to be named after." I considered this as I chewed on a fry. "Like Grackle. Or Skua."

He chuckled, then became serious. "So you moved out here from Oak Park so you could be with your mother."

"Something like that," I said. "Actually, it was a compromise. She didn't want to move to Oak Park, and I didn't want to move to her suburb. We found Dryden and liked it, and because it was in Fowler, this is where we both landed."

"She's lucky to have you."

I laughed. "There are days you couldn't tell her that." I described our bout with the cigarettes.

"She's a feisty one, isn't she?"

I just shook my head.

"I'd like to meet her."

I gave him a look.

"No, really. I think old people are great."

"That's because you don't have one."

"Seriously," he said, laughing. "I used to play guitar and sing—you know, when we're young, we all think we can play guitar and sing. I used to do gigs at nursing homes." He frowned. "Come to think of it, I never rose above the nursing home venue."

I nodded. "That's telling you something, I think."

We both laughed a little over that and then he said, "But, you know, I liked to joke around with them. Sometimes brought pizza. They liked me. I think they just tolerated my singing, but they liked me."

I bet they did. He was handsome, personable and took time out for older people. What wasn't there to like? "Well, you're welcome to meet her, but I warn you, she hasn't got a cuddly side, and if you buy her pizza it damn well better have something on it besides cheese."

It must have been the scotch—or maybe the second one. But by the end of the evening he'd convinced me that we should stop by my mother's tomorrow at lunch and bring a pizza.

I insisted on paying part of the bill, not wanting to be indebted to him for the price of a sandwich and a couple of scotches. He didn't argue, and when he walked me home he gave me a kiss on the cheek before leaving me at my door without so much as a half-assed effort to get past that door. But he did promise to meet me at Dryden at eleven thirty the next morning, so I guess he wasn't completely turned off to the idea of being with me. Or at least he was willing to tolerate me in order to meet my mother.

When I got home, my phone was ringing and I saw my mother's phone number on the caller ID. I glanced at the kitchen clock. Nine fifteen. Not a good time for her.

"Hi, Mom."

"Oh, dear," she said.

"Mom?"

"Robbie must have loved me, don't you think?"

"I'm sure he did, Mom."

And then: "Why haven't you come home yet? I made your favorite for dinner. Steak tartar." I had no idea where that came from. Raw meat? Then she started fretting over not being able to coddle an egg. She was nearly in tears. Then, out of nowhere, she said she was going to see if she could get a banana.

"Mom!" I said before she could hang up. I heard her hesitate. "It's Robyn, Mother."

A long pause, and then, "Oh." Disappointment.

"Are you okay?"

"Well, I'm not sure." Her voice had gotten smaller and much, much older.

"I'm out of bananas and the stores will be closing." Her voice, clotted with dry tears, had become a whine. "I ... I can't remember where I parked the car."

"You don't drive, Mom."

"What?"

"You don't drive."

"Oh, thank God."

Her relief was so profound, I almost had to laugh.

"Do you think if I called the concierge they could get a banana for me?" she asked.

"You're not in a hotel, Mom."

A pause. "I'm not?"

"Look around your room. Those are your pictures on the wall." I gave her a few moments. "Are you sitting in your brown chair?"

"Y-Yes." More confused than panicky.

"Look next to you on the table. See the photo of you and me? You're wearing a mini skirt."

"Just a moment."

I heard her set the receiver down. I pictured her slowly reaching for the thirty-five-year-old picture of the two of us. A few seconds later she uttered a soft, "Oh," and then was back on the phone. "Oh, Robyn."

This was the hardest. Her whining really grated at me. She couldn't help her confusion—I knew that—but she'd perfected the whining years ago and it hadn't improved with age. But I could deal with that; the anguish ripped me apart. "It's okay, Mom."

"No, it's not."

I heard the breath of her sigh and searched for a response that wouldn't make her feel worse. But then her tone shifted as she said, "There was a man here today."

"Who was that?" I figured it was Hedges, the cop, but wanted to know what she remembered.

"I can't recall his name, but he was asking me about some woman."

She seemed to be groping for a name, so I prompted her. "Was it Mary Waltner?"

"Why, yes." Then, "How would you know?"

"I talked to him earlier."

"Oh." A pause. "Well, it's horrible what happened. But I couldn't tell him much."

I was going to ask her what she did tell him, but then she said, "When will I see you again?" and I knew we'd moved on.

"I'll be by tomorrow. Maybe with a surprise."

"Oh, good," she said without much feeling. "What time is it now?"

I told her. "And, Mom, if you still want a banana, there's fruit out on the table in the lounge on the first floor."

"Banana?" It was as though I'd said *wombat*. "I don't want a banana."

"Bye, Mom."

As I returned the phone to its cradle I thought about what the doctor had told me. How these episodes would become more and more frequent. This was the second this week. It helped if she knew she wasn't alone. That was one reason Dryden was perfect. She had her own room, but she wasn't alone. There were always people to talk to. If the residents had had enough of her, the staff was incredibly patient.

Once again, I felt the weight of the guilt for not welcoming her into my home—or into some new apartment. But I'd learn to live with that guilt, because I knew what a toll we'd take on each other's sanity. I couldn't be with her constantly, and she needed someone there all the time. And if there was any way I imagined myself pulling off a goat heist and extortion, I'd have done it. But there wasn't.

It would have to be Willoway.

CHAPTER 13

At ten the next morning, I drove to Willoway. I'd thought about calling ahead and telling Jane Goodwin that I was on my way, but decided to just drop in, perhaps thinking that I might spot the bucket of gold at the end of the rainbow on my way there.

The day had turned sunny and hot but the humidity was low. I never expect days like this in August, so I try to appreciate them when they're here.

Willoway was set off a main thoroughfare, with a long drive that passed beneath mature trees and led to a grassy area with benches and a few tables, with parking off to one side. I told myself it was pretty—and it was—and the landscaping was well kept. The drive itself was about three quarters of a mile long and in the few times I'd been to Willoway, I'd never seen anyone beyond the lawn area. Even so, I didn't think much of it when I saw the figure coming toward me, walking along the side of the road. But she was tottering a bit, and as I slowed down I saw she was wearing a blue robe, loosely belted, and white vinyl mules. She was shuffling so that her left shoe had slipped and her bare heel came down on the gritty roadside with every step. I stopped my car and lowered the window. She peered in at me, but didn't speak.

"Are you okay?" I asked, knowing that she wasn't. She didn't respond.

"Can I give you a ride?" I noticed the plastic band on her right wrist.

She squinted at me, shifting from foot to foot.

I turned off my car and got out, approaching her slowly, without any abrupt moves, much like I'd have approached Blood if I'd had the nerve.

She was a tiny, bent woman, coming barely up to my chin, and her white hair was as pure a shade as I'd ever seen. Her large, blue eyes showed neither fear nor comprehension.

"Ethel?" she said.

"No. I'm Robyn."

Her mouth puckered and her brows pulled together. "I'm waiting for my sister."

I glanced around, looking for help, but we were alone on the road.

"She's waiting for you back at the house."

"Oh?"

"I'm supposed to give you a ride."

Now she seemed troubled. "They didn't tell me that."

"It's just a short way."

She looked at my car, then at me, trying to focus. "Did Ethel send you?"

"Yes," I said.

"Oh." She looked around as though she, too, was hoping for divine intervention, then said, "Well, then all right."

She let me help her around to the passenger side, slipping out of one shoe along the way. I picked it up and tossed it on the floor. A stale, sour smell rose off her. I got her settled into the seat without much fuss. She was so tiny I could practically have lifted her. I noticed her right leg had a dark purple bruise on it and her toenails were curled, yellow claws. I took the opportunity to glance at her bracelet and saw that her name was Beatrice Hendrie.

A minute later I pulled up in front of Willoway's entrance and helped her out of the car. Once inside, I figured I'd hand her over to the receptionist at the sleek, curved desk, but that proved impossible, seeing as there was no one at the desk. In fact, the lobby, with its sparse furniture, was empty, and although I heard voices coming from one or more of the three halls branching off from the reception area, I didn't want to go in search of anyone, lest Beatrice decide to wander off again. That was when I noticed the little bell sitting on the reception desk. Perhaps the receptionist also took to wandering. I situated Beatrice in one of two contemporary chairs, and then I tapped the bell and listened to the ding echoing throughout the reception area. Beatrice was fiddling with the ends of her robe tie. She gave me a pleasant smile.

I gave the bell a swat this time and then another, and from an office around the corner, I heard a gravely voiced woman say, "Hold your horses. I'm coming."

She rounded the corner holding a large mug of coffee between her hands. I thought she was surprised to see me, but then realized it was just her penciled in eyebrows, arched like twin gateways to the west. The eyes beneath the brows were rather harsh and, right now, annoyed.

"Can I help you?"

"Well, I'm hoping you can help this lady who I found wandering down by Bolton Road." I stepped aside so she could see Beatrice.

Her jaw dropped an inch, but she snapped it shut quickly. "Beatrice, have you been wandering again?"

After setting down her coffee, she went over to the old woman, who was looking up at her with those large, blue eyes, and took her hands. "Are you all right, hon?"

Beatrice didn't respond, but the woman didn't act as though she expected her to. "You sit right here, hon, I'll give Mrs. Goodwin a call."

As she hurried behind the desk, she looked up at me and said, "Thank you so much for bringing her back. This is not at all like her."

She picked up the phone, then stopped. "Who were you here to see?"

I blinked. And then I said, "No one."

She smiled. "Well, thank you for bringing our Beatrice back."

I nodded, and as I turned toward the door, I heard her say into the phone, "Jane, it's Beatrice." A pause and then, "… Yes."

I watched over my shoulder as she steered the old woman around a corner, and then I left.

It took me the length of the driveway to make my decision. And before I pulled onto Bolton, I punched in my accountant's number on my cell phone.

"Yeah, Robyn," Mick said.

"We need to talk." I swallowed. "Shall I come to your office?"

"No, I'm at the gym. You want to meet for lunch?"

"No." I was afraid I'd come to regret this decision, and didn't want it to ruin food for me for the rest of my life. Or for ten to fifteen years.

"Okay," he said, "how about my place?" He recited his address and said, "Eleven thirty."

"I'll be there."

After I disconnected from Mick, I called Jack—my mother's pizza party would have to wait—and left a message on his voicemail. I hoped he heard that message before marching into Dryden armed only with a guitar and a pepperoni pizza.

When I got home, I parked in my usual space behind the building and was climbing the steps to the rear entrance when I noticed a man sitting on one of the chairs wedged onto my tiny back porch. As I paused in midstep, he pulled a leather badge holder from his jacket pocket.

"Robyn Guthrie?"

I nodded.

He let the badge holder drop open. "Detective Richard Hedges, Fowler PD. We spoke earlier."

"Uh, yes." I hoped he didn't notice the hesitation; I hoped it had all been in my head. I knew he was here about Mary Waltner, but I couldn't help but think that "future extortionist" was stamped on my forehead.

When I'd climbed up onto the porch, I scrutinized the badge—it looked real, but fake badges were supposed to look real.

As he pocketed it, I could hear Bix scratching at the back door.

Hedges nodded in that direction. "Someone's trying to dig his way out."

I smiled. "Yeah, that'd be Bix. We'd better go inside. He doesn't like to miss anything."

As I unlocked the door, Hedges said, "I saw your mother yesterday."

"That's what she told me."

He stepped into the narrow entryway leading to my kitchen. "What'd she say?"

Bix could barely contain his pleasure in seeing me—it had been almost an hour. Everyone needs a dog.

"Mostly, she was confused."

He nodded as though that fit.

I invited him into the living room and offered him some coffee, which he accepted, but asked for milk. "All I've got is fat free," I told him. Skim milk made for gray coffee.

He made a face. "Skip it then."

Then he bent down to let Bix sniff his hand and gave the dog a little scratch behind the ears. Bix doesn't care to have his ears fondled, but he tolerates it pretty well.

Hedges was not as I'd imagined him, which was middle-aged, with some hard years on him. In reality, he was tall and slender with long fingers and a sharp nose. I guessed he was a few years younger than me. He moved slowly, but his eyes were quick and alert.

I poured myself a cup left over from the morning pot and put it into the microwave to spin for a minute.

"I don't think your mother was being completely forthcoming with me."

I almost laughed. Instead, I turned to him and said, "What do you mean?"

"Perhaps it's her … forgetfulness."

"Dementia," I said. "That's what it is. She comes and goes. Sometimes she's clear and focused. Other times, not so much. She's much better at remembering the past than the present."

The microwave dinged, and I removed the mug and took a tentative sip. It wasn't hot yet, but was good enough for my purposes. I needed something to do with my hands besides wringing them.

We walked into the living room and he settled into my purple chair. I sat on the edge of the couch.

He wore a taupe-colored sports jacket over khaki slacks and a white shirt knotted with a blue print tie, which he'd pulled down about an inch, and he sat forward with his elbows propped on his knees, holding a small, black spiral notebook.

Frowning, Hedges said, "Is she ever …" He paused and pressed his lips together to form a thin line.

I waited.

"Is she ever intentionally … uh, vague?"

I thought about how my mother had become more and more difficult to get an answer out of. I knew that part of it was her mental condition, perhaps coupled with the questions I'd been asking. But I also believed that she'd become more and more evasive—perhaps a latent ability—the more pointed my questions had become.

"You mean evasive?" I suggested.

With a nod, he said, "I guess that's more like it."

"She can be. When it suits her purposes."

He nodded as though confirming a suspicion.

"If you're going to talk to her again," I said, "it might help if I were there. I can sometimes keep her on track."

He tapped his pencil against the chair's arm, frowning as though he didn't think much of my offer.

"Can you tell me anything about Mary Waltner?" I asked.

He removed a photo from his jacket pocket and handed it to me.

There was something about putting a face and a personality with a body you hear about on the news that makes it so very, very sad. The photo had been taken on a boat—I could see a corner of a sail off to the left. Mary was standing between a distinguished-looking older man and another man who might have been the son of the other, and they were all dressed for sailing. She had a broad smile and warm eyes. Probably around my age, she was attractive, with thick chestnut hair she wore short and wavy. She had her arms around the two men and they all looked as though they were enjoying the moment.

"How did she die?"

"Strangulation."

I nodded as I swallowed. "Is this her family?"

"No," he said, taking the photo back and glancing at it before tucking it away. "She was a lawyer and this older guy was one of her clients. I think the other is his son."

"Did she have family?"

"No," he said, then added with a sigh, "One of those workaholics. Friends say she never made time for much else." Almost as an aside, he added, "Too bad."

I just nodded. I didn't necessarily believe that lack of a family equated with a miserable existence, but he wasn't here to argue that point.

"No husband, kids." Then he glanced around my bare little apartment and shifted in the chair. "I mean, uh …"

I held up one hand. "That's okay."

He shrugged. "I've got two kids. One's nothing but trouble."

"Sorry."

"Yeah, well …"

"You said she was a lawyer?" I said, trying to steer us back on track.

"Right," Hedges said. "A pretty high-priced one at that. Your mom claims she didn't hire her."

"I'm sure that's the case. I've got power of attorney, and she'd need to let me know in order to pay a lawyer."

The chair creaked as he leaned back into it. "Has your mother got a California connection?"

"Not that I know of."

He frowned and appeared to be considering something.

I gave him a few moments and then said, "What?"

"I don't know." He rocked forward slightly. "She was kind of vague on that. Like she knew something about California, but wouldn't tell me what."

I frowned as I raised the mug to my mouth and blew on the warm liquid. "A California connection would be news to me. As far as I know she never got any farther west than Colorado."

He nodded, but his gaze wandered, as though he was trying to find some clue stashed among the spare contents of the room.

"Could it have been a random crime?"

He frowned and leaned his head to one side. "It's possible it was a simple robbery turned homicide. But we're trying to get a handle on what she was doing here. Far as I can tell, that visit with your mother was the only thing on her schedule."

"Maybe she knew someone else here. Someone who wasn't on her schedule." After I spoke, I wished I hadn't. In all the detective dramas, the murderer was just a little too helpful with the suggestions.

He looked at me carefully. "You sure your mom didn't say anything more to you?"

"Of course I'm sure." I tried to sound adamant rather than annoyed, which I was. "I'd tell you if she had. I want to know why she talked to my mother as much as you do."

He regarded me for several moments. "You and your mother have a lot of secrets?"

In the seconds before I responded, I imagined my mother with that stiff-jawed look she got when confronted with a question she didn't want to answer. I wondered if my jaw hardened in the same way.

I took a sip of coffee. "No more than most mothers and daughters." I hoped that sounded light enough. Because I had the feeling I was only beginning to discover the things she'd kept from me.

CHAPTER 14

After Hedges left, I had only minutes to get ready to leave for Mick's, which was good seeing as I didn't have any time to ponder whether I needed to redo my makeup. There simply wasn't time.

Still, I was fidgety the whole way over. I swear, one of the reasons I drive stick shift is so I've got something to do with my hands. I spent most of the drive examining my own ideas as to how to steal Sassy. It would have to be at a time when Blood was not in the stall, because I wasn't about to go through Blood to get to the goat, and I doubted that Mick relished the idea either. But there had to be an opportunity, and I assumed Mick would have some input there. No matter how calming an influence Sassy was, they couldn't be together constantly. Blood had to be exercised. Sassy undoubtedly needed a break from his high-maintenance companion. Maybe a time when Sassy was outside, alone. It would help if it was dark. But then the stable had to be under surveillance. Cameras. Maybe even a security guard. And what if Sassy didn't come willingly? I guessed that he weighed at least a hundred pounds, so tossing his little cloven hooves over my shoulder wasn't going to happen.

I saw nothing but problems littering my scenario. But I figured, what with Mick's reputation for skullduggery, he was bound to have a better idea.

I pulled into Mick's drive at 11:36. Those six minutes were important to me. My being on time—or early—might suggest an eagerness I didn't want to convey at this point.

Mick looked like he'd come from the gym. His hair was slicked back and damp and he smelled of sweat and soap. He stepped back as I entered and then clicked the door shut behind me, leaning against it. I could feel his gaze sweeping me, finally coming to rest on my eyes.

"You ready?" he asked.

"I'm here," I said, then realized that wasn't an answer. "And, yes. I'm ready."

After a moment, he nodded, and said, "Okay. Let's go outside."

As I followed him through the house, I was a little surprised to find myself admiring the way his pale blue T-shirt emphasized his broad shoulders and comparing him to Jack. Smaller, but still real nice. Good to know that my state of agitation hadn't affected my appreciation for a sculpted torso.

I refused Mick's offer of wine or beer but accepted a can of soda because nerves cause my saliva glands to shut down. And when he asked if I wanted to sit on the porch, I suggested we walk around his yard. There was something about plotting a crime while lounging in matching patio chairs with a ferret listening that seemed mildly absurd.

The three large maples mitigated the effects of the midday sun, and a northwesterly breeze made the day as near to perfect as you can get in August. The only other time I had seen Mick's yard it had been dark. I guess I was a little surprised to see the flower beds bordering the yard and the mass of variegated ground cover under the trees. A wooden bench painted a pale shade of green nudged up against one of the maples.

Mick walked slightly ahead of me, hands in his pockets and that hitch in his leg more pronounced on the uneven ground. He glanced over his shoulder, "You sure you're up for this? I mean—"

"Yes," I said, more forcefully than I'd intended. "I haven't changed my mind in the last minute and a half." He kept eyeing me, and I found myself adding, "But I'll admit that I'm scared."

He squinted. "Of what?" he asked, as though he really had no idea what part of this might be offputting to me.

"Getting caught."

He wagged his head. "Not gonna happen."

I touched a patch of tiny blue flowers with the toe of my sandal. "And changing. Scared of this changing me." I hadn't planned to say that, and wasn't even sure where it came from. But, once spoken, I knew that for better or worse, I'd be different.

When he didn't respond, I had to look his way. As he watched me, his greenish-brown eyes softened. "Everything changes us, Robyn. Sitting around doing nothing changes us."

"But it doesn't necessarily diminish us. Me."

"You're the only one who can do that."

"Thank you, Dr. Phil."

He shrugged and crossed his arms over his chest, tucking his fingers under his arms. "So why are you here?"

I swallowed. "I have run out of choices."

He nodded as though waiting for me to continue.

I took a sip of the citrus-flavored soda. The carbonation burned my throat. "I've run out of options for my mother. I can't move her. Not to Willoway. I'm not that bad a daughter. But I'm also not a good enough daughter to move her in with me and Bix. We tried it once and it didn't work." I took a deep breath. "And with all the checking I've done on Bull and Gwen, I can't think of a couple more worthy of … extortion." Saying the word out loud gave voice to its ugliness. But I kept going, because I also believed it was less vile than what Bull had done. "He rips off old people and she's his number-one cheerleader."

He nodded as though that motive passed muster.

"And what about you?" I asked.

I wasn't sure he was going to answer, so I prodded with, "There must be easier ways to make a couple hundred thousand than teaming up with a woman whose last act of civil disobedience involved using the handicapped stall in the women's room."

He smiled a little, then sobered as he said, "I'm in a bind. I need the money by Saturday." He paused and looked past me toward the next yard over. "And this goat thing is the only shot I've got at it. Besides, it's a damned good idea."

"What would you have done if I hadn't called?"

His mouth twisted into a wry grin. "I knew you would."

I didn't believe him—I wasn't so easy to read. Was I? But I also believed that he'd never give me a straight answer about why he needed the money.

"Have you done this … sort of thing before?"

"Extortion?"

I shrugged. "For starters."

"No."

"But you do have some criminal experience to call on."

He frowned slightly and then said, "Depends on how you define criminal."

"Illegal."

With an impatient sigh he said, "I don't get caught."

"Of course not." And I suppose that was true, seeing as he still had his CPA credentials. Then I said, "Okay, if it's so easy, then you must have a foolproof plan."

"I've got most of it worked out." He gestured toward the bench. "Mind if we sit?"

I settled in at one end, sitting so I was partially facing Mick. He sat leaning forward, elbows on his knees. Working to keep my own knees steady, I felt like I'd just downed two Lizard ventis without the milk buffer. I clamped down on my jaw to keep my teeth from chattering.

"Thursday night," Mick began, "Bull is throwing his Plymouth Million party—to which about seventy-five people are invited. He does that every time he races. Sort of a send off." He frowned a little. "On Saturday morning he'll take Blood over to Plymouth Downs."

"And he does that because Blood will have less time to stress out."

"That's right."

In a way, I empathized with Blood. It was Tuesday, so I wouldn't have much time to fret about this either.

He nodded as though agreeing with himself. "The goat's role as a steadying influence will be even more critical."

Of course.

"It'll be an indoor affair," Mick continued, "but at some point during the evening, probably around nine, Bull'll bring Blood out and parade him around so everybody can gawk at him." I didn't think I imagined the bitterness his tone had taken. "The goat will either stay behind in the stall or he'll be outside in this little fenced-off area they've got for him by the barn."

I crossed my legs and began bobbing my foot, the back of my sandal slapping gently against my heel. "And Sassy gets snatched while everyone is oohing and ahhing over Blood?"

"You got it."

I took a sip of soda into my mouth and my throat froze up. I had to make a conscious effort to calm myself in order to swallow. After an audible gulp, I took a couple of deep breaths and tried to focus. I had questions, so I decided to start there.

"I'm seeing lots of problems." I paused. "First, I take it we're both going to be at the party."

"No," he said without a trace of regret, "it'll just be me."

I stopped bobbing. "And *I'll* be taking Sassy?"

He sat back and faced me, gesturing with one hand. "Yeah. You see, it's gotta work that way. If the goat goes missing and I'm nowhere in sight, then I'm one of the suspects."

"Why would Bull suspect you? Doesn't he think you're his friend?"

"Bull would suspect his mother." He shook his head. "He doesn't believe in loyalty. Whoever's got the sharpest knife and moves the fastest gets to stay alive."

"Are you speaking metaphorically, or is Bull really capable of that?"

"He's a shark." Then he laughed a little. Probably reacting to the pearly shade of white I must have turned. "Don't worry. He doesn't do any of the enforcing himself."

"I don't care if Bull pulls the trigger or his hired thug does. I'm still just as dead."

"Don't worry about that. First, he's not going to find out—"

"That's easy for you to say. You're going to be sipping champagne and popping canapés while I'm sneaking a goat out of a secure stable."

I just looked at him for a long moment. Aside from the breeze lifting and lowering the branches of the maple, and the warble of a nearby wren, it was quiet.

"This is some plan you've got." I paused to take a steadying breath. He opened his mouth, but I kept talking. "I'd have to be an idiot to do all this myself."

"Okay," he said. "Then you tell me another way. I'm all ears." He hooked one arm over the back of the bench and shifted so he could look me straight on.

When I didn't immediately offer an alternate plan, he continued. "We haven't got a lot of time or options, Robyn. It's got to be before Saturday. We need a day to arrange for the ransom and then pick it up. Get the goat back to Blood. Bull has to believe there's enough time to get Blood settled in before the race or he's not paying. And it's got to be at a time when we know the motion detector is off and the camera's not on the goat. So the goat can't be with Blood. And, I don't know about you, but I'd rather not do it in broad daylight." Now he paused for a breath. "If you can come up with a better plan, I'll be happy to swipe the goat."

I considered this, and really did try to come up with a scenario where Mick could do the deed, and I'd just sit in the background drinking champagne and whispering, *You go, boy*, in his ear. But he was right. Bull couldn't see us together.

"Are you bringing anyone to the party?" I asked.

"No."

"Won't that be suspicious?"

"Not really."

Interesting. "Okay, how do I get in? The last time we were there, the gate magically opened."

"The security guy knows me and my car."

"Well, that's nice for you. But I won't be with you. And I'll be watched. On camera."

"Right."

"And I'll be driving a van," I said. "It'll have to be big enough for Sassy and with a ramp to get him in."

"Right. I'll get it for you—don't worry about that. You drive it in, park it, and stay in it until I call you."

"We still haven't got me in yet."

I thought about who might be attending one of Bull's parties in a van. "Who's the caterer?"

Mick smiled like he'd already arrived at where I was going. "Gwen always uses Naomi and Nathan's Catering."

"Can we match the truck and the sign on their truck?"

"Yeah," he said, drawing the word out. Then, with more certainty, "Sure. Easy enough. Get one of those magnetic signs we can write on. Stick it on the side." He nodded again. "That'll work. You just show up after the caterer is already there. Nobody'll question some-one in a catering van. Park and wait until I call you to let you know that Blood's out of the stable."

"Does the caterer have more than one truck?"

"Sure," he said. "They're big in this area. I've seen three or four at an event."

"What do they wear?"

"Whenever I've seen them, they wear something like black pants and a white shirt."

"You're sure you can match the sign?"

He nodded. "From what I remember it's nothing fancy. But I'll check it out this afternoon."

"So the guard will see a catering truck and let me in?"

"There's an intercom there, but I doubt anyone will even ask. Not once they see the van." Then he shrugged. "If the guard asks, just tell him you're bringing dessert."

"If the guard sounds at all suspicious, I'm leaving."

"Fair enough," he said, then added, "They won't. Catering trucks are always coming and going from these things. It's Gwen. She sees the caterer as her personal servants. I've seen her send one of them out for caviar because some guy Bull was trying to impress had just come back from Russia."

This didn't seem out of character for Gwen.

"Okay," I finally said. Maybe, just maybe, this could work. But I was the only one at risk, and that wasn't right.

Perhaps sensing my reluctance, Mick added, "Not only do I have to be there when the goat gets snatched, but I've gotta be with Bull when he's showing off Blood. Truth is, Bull's scared shitless of that horse." With a shrug he added, "I'll be handling him."

"I see." I wasn't sure whether Mick was referring to Bull or Blood, and I supposed it didn't matter.

I swallowed more soda, which was no longer cold and didn't burn going down. My throat wasn't closing up anymore, and I decided that was a good sign. "Okay, let's get back to that in a minute, then." I eyed him. "The barn has security cameras, right?"

"Right."

"Aimed at Blood's stall?"

He nodded.

"But when they move Blood, they'll move Sassy out of that stall. You're sure? What if Sassy wants to tag along? Or, what if Bull brings the whole crowd to the stable?"

Mick smiled and shook his head. "Won't happen. Bull hates that goat. Thinks it makes Blood look like a sissy. He won't want any of his guests seeing the two of them snuggling up together."

With that, he leaned forward and pulled a folded up paper from his back pocket. Unfolded, it was a drawing of the stable's layout and the surrounding area. I slid a little closer to him.

"Here's the stables," he began.

"I can see that. Are you sure it's accurate?"

"Of course I'm sure. I helped him design it."

All the stalls were there, all but one noted as unoccupied, and dark Xs where the surveillance cameras were mounted. Next to Blood's stall was a smaller stall. Mick tapped his thumb on it. "There's no camera aimed here. This is where the goat will be. Either that or he'll be wandering around the stables. Or outside." He dragged his finger down to a fenced-in area just east of the stable. "No camera there either. If he's not outside, you come in this way," he indicated the main entrance, "your pockets full of goat goodies you can coax him with."

"What if he won't follow me?"

"The goat likes you."

"Yeah, I know." Denying it was pointless. "But what if he doesn't remember me?"

"Goats remember."

I snorted.

"Seriously. If he liked you a couple of days ago, he's going to like you on Thursday. It's not like he'll recognize your face. He must like the way you smell or something."

I let that waft by me. "If he doesn't?" I paused. "I can't battle a goat the whole way."

Mick shrugged. "Then you walk away."

That I could do. "And the motion detector will be off."

"They'll turn it off when they take Blood out of the stable." He cocked a wry grin. "He's the only thing in the stable that Bull figures is worth stealing. Hell, he's practically the only thing in the stable."

He looked at me. "And, you know what? Like I said, if you can't do it, you can't do it." He paused. "You move your mother in with you and I … I do something else."

"You forgot the third option. One or both of us winds up in jail. And if it happens, it'll be me."

"You won't go to jail. Not if you're caught stealing a goat. That's a misdemeanor. You don't move into the capital offense bracket until we ask for money. And that's the easy part. Getting the goat is the hard part."

"What do I do with the goat? I can't smuggle it into my apartment. And your place would be too obvious."

He smiled. "Where's the best place to hide a goat?"

"With a goatherd," I ventured.

"Close," he said. "I've got a friend. Meyer. He's got a small farm. A bunch of goats. Couple of horses. In fact, it's the farm where Sassy came from. He's gonna be out of town for a long weekend at some county fair." Then he said, "While he's gone, his brother's staying at the farm." He smiled again. "His brother knows squat about animals, just tosses them some food when he figures they're hungry, and he starts drinking around five p.m. and doesn't quit until he falls asleep."

"Where does this goat man live?"

"Ten minutes from Bull's place." Then, "We only need to keep him there for a day. While we make the call and collect the money."

"What if they put Sassy's photo on TV and Meyer's brother recognizes him?"

Mick just looked at me for several moments, and I think he was trying not to laugh. "This is a goat, Robyn. There are no Amber Alerts for goats."

But it was extortion. "And who makes the phone call?"

"You need to do that."

"Why me?" As Mick pointed out, the phone call was where the crime went from something rather minor—swiping a goat—to a more criminal offense.

"Because I'll be at Bull's. With any luck, I'll be the one delivering the money."

"What if you're not? What if Bull decides to do it himself?"

Mick frowned, and I kept going. "It's got to be somewhere public enough so one of us can pick up the money without being noticed, but not so public that there could be twelve of Bull's people watching either of us do it."

He nodded, chewing on the corner of his mouth. "How about the Wired Lizard on the corner of Seventh and State. You get there—"

"Why me? If you're not dropping off the money, then surely you can pick it up."

"Maybe. But I'm guessing that Bull will be keeping me pretty close. I don't want to have to beat him to the drop."

Again, he had a point, but why were all the points on his side? "Go ahead with the plan."

He shrugged. "You get ahead of him so you can see who's coming and going. Work on your book or something."

I snorted, and Mick continued. "Tell Bull to leave it in the garbage in the men's room. After he leaves, you wait a few minutes then, when there's nobody back there, you duck into the men's room, grab the bag and beat it."

"I have a better idea."

He cocked an eyebrow at me.

"I tell him to drop it at Phinny's Tap, which is across the street from the Wired Lizard. I can sit in the coffee shop and watch him go in and leave. Then I go in there and pick up the money."

He nodded. "Yeah, that is better."

It could work. "I could do a minimal disguise. Odds are he wouldn't see me at the Wired Lizard. I know Phinny's, and the restrooms are in the back off a narrow hall to the left. Someone heading that way wouldn't be seen by the customers in the main room. The women's room is a single seater without a stall. I assume the men's room is the same."

"It is." He nodded. "I think the garbage is in one corner."

I just looked at him. "You've got amazing recall of a john."

With a shrug he said, "I notice details."

I slumped back into the bench. "Let me see if I have this straight. I sneak onto Bull's grounds in a van marked as the caterer's." Mick nodded, and at this point I began to wonder if disguising me as a caterer hadn't been part of his plan all along. He'd just let me think—

for whatever reason—that I was contributing. But it didn't make much difference in the long run, so I continued to describe the plan as I saw it. "You phone me when I'm good to go. I steal the goat while avoiding the cameras, hustle him into the van and drive to the goat place where the caretaker will be inebriated, and I can slip in an extra goat without him noticing. Then I make the ransom call, and if you're not the one to deliver the money, I'll have to pick it up as well."

He shrugged. "I'm the inside man."

"I'm the do-everything woman."

"Okay," he said with an annoyed sigh. "What's your suggestion?"

"We're asking for a half million?"

Mick nodded. "That's probably as much as he can come up with on short notice."

"I get three." I really didn't care that much about the fifty grand; two hundred and fifty thousand dollars would be enough to take care of my mother for a while. But I was taking more of a risk than Mick, and I knew what it was to be undervalued.

"What if you do get caught?"

I could see where he was going with this. "It was my own idea. I had no help."

"Fair enough," he said. "It's a three/two split."

There was that warbling wren again. As if it were warning me that we weren't finished negotiating yet.

Mick glanced at me. "One question."

I waited.

"Once you get this three hundred grand, what are you going to do with it?"

"I told you. I'm using it to keep my mother in Dryden."

He nodded. "Yeah. I know that. But where are you going to tell the IRS it came from?"

Shit, I thought, *you're the taxman, you tell me.* But I wouldn't give him the satisfaction of saying that out loud.

"I could say it's my mother's money," I told him, but I knew that would present the same problem. Besides, I'd just convinced the state of Illinois that she had no money. "Okay," I said, holding up my hands. "I guess I haven't figured that out yet."

"You know who could help you?"

Cocky bastard. "My accountant."

He grinned. "He could be a lot of help."

"So, basically, I'd be paying you fifty grand to launder the money?"

"I'm not in the business, but I know people."

For someone who hated being without options, it was happening to me a lot lately. "You got me."

He looked at me. "You mad?"

"Yes."

"Guess I'd be too."

I pressed my hand on the seat of the bench and tucked my fingers under its edge, gripping it hard. "It was my idea. I'm the one who can get caught."

"I'll do it for twenty-five," he said. "You get two-seventy-five and I get two-twenty-five."

After a few moments I leaned back and crossed my arms over my chest, feeling my sigh as I said, "Okay."

"What's wrong? That not enough?"

"No," I said. "That's fair."

"Then what's wrong?"

Where to start?

"Oh, shit, Mick. This is getting too complicated. It's too scary, and I've got to be crazy to be sitting here talking to you like we're planning a party or something."

"But it's not complicated, Robyn. This is done all the time—"

"Not in my universe."

"Welcome to Bull's world." He leaned toward me. "Hell, that's how Bull gets away with ripping off investors."

"Well, that drops me into a category I'd love to squirm out of."

"Robyn," he said and waited until I looked at him, "Blood will miss the goat for a day and then they'll be back together. He might even win that race. The only one who gets hurt is Bull. And it's his ego that'll take a bruising. And it's not like you're taking what belongs to him."

"But it doesn't belong to me either."

"Okay, if it makes you feel better maybe you can designate the money for a fund to compensate the people Bull ripped off." He waited. "How much sense does that make?"

"None," I admitted. Pulling this off might be easier than learning to live with it.

"You'll have to show me how to get to Meyer's farm," I finally said.

"I'll come by to get you tomorrow afternoon. Meyer's brother won't be there."

"Okay."

"I'll pick up a cell phone for you," he said.

"That's okay," I said. "I'll pick it up."

"Pay with cash."

"Of course."

And, because he must have known what was on my mind, I said, "You'll have to forgive me if I don't completely trust you."

"Yeah?" He didn't seem surprised. "What part of me don't you trust?"

"Most of you."

He inched a little closer, and then he moved in and kissed me. I responded. He was a good kisser, and I wasn't so staggered by the events to dismiss him. But when he drew back, his hand still touching my cheek, I rested my fingers on his wrist and said, "That's nice, Mick. Really. But that doesn't make me trust you."

"What do I have to do?"

"I don't know. And maybe that's the point. I play by the rules. You do my income taxes. You know what I'm talking about. I won't take a deduction I don't deserve."

"I know. I wouldn't be asking you to do this if I didn't trust you. So maybe that's enough?"

"I don't think it is."

"How come?" His confusion seemed genuine.

"You have a reputation. You must know that. I suspect you've cultivated it."

"I work for some unpleasant people. If I show my belly, it's all over."

"Why do you work for people like that?"

With a sigh he collapsed back against the bench. "I'm returning some favors." He turned toward me. "Believe it or not, a jockey with a bum leg isn't in big demand. It'd have been real easy to slide into a bottle or pain meds." He picked up my can of soda and took a swig. "But I'd had some good rides and—contrary to legend—had an honest reputation. I'd done some riding for a guy whose family was in the business. He paid my way through U of I. When I finished and set up my own practice, he was my first client. Started doing some investing for him and made him some money. The rest I got through references."

"You still work for that man?"

He shook his head. "He died about five years ago. But the business is still there." Then he added, "Most of my clients are legit."

"How do you know about money laundering?"

He twisted his mouth in good-natured annoyance. "Every CPA knows how to launder money. There's a big difference between knowing how to do it and doing it."

"I see." I stared off toward the house, letting the colors blur and blend. I wanted this to be over. I wanted it to be Sunday, when either I'd have a sudden influx of cash or I'd be posing for my mug shot.

Beside me, Mick said, "We're gonna make a great team."

Right.

After leaving Mick's I drove straight to the nearest box store and purchased a disposable cell phone. I felt a tad illicit paying for it in cash, as though the clerk knew I had something to hide, and he would record the purchase on some "watch list" the moment I was out of sight. Then I went to another store and bought a voice changer. The clerk assured me that it would give me "endless" voice options. I had considered disguising my voice naturally, which I can do. When I was in high school, my girlfriend and I occasionally made prank phone calls using our "Arnold" voices. It came from somewhere deep in the throat where all the phlegm lived. We sounded a bit like Gollum, hobbit gone bad. But now I figured why risk it when someone had been thoughtful enough to invent the voice changer? Several years ago, I'd read an article advising women how to protect themselves, and one of these devices was recommended so a female voice would sound like a man's when answering the phone. At the time, I thought it was a bit paranoid and never imagined myself buying one. But now I had to believe that no extortionist who knew what she was doing would leave home without it.

When I got home, I dug a wig from a box shoved into the corner of a closet shelf. It was a blond bob, which I'd purchased years ago in an attempt to find out if they did have more fun (not in my case), and then I plucked a pair of black slacks that I had worn three sizes ago from another corner of the closet. It was the only article of clothing I kept from my heavier days, and I kept it around to serve as a ghost of pounds past. If I ever fit into them again, I would have to have some serious words with myself. I'd wear a white blouse while waiting and bring a black, long-sleeved T-shirt to change into when I needed to be sneaking around in the dark.

The pants were still quite large, but if I wore panty hose with some stuffing, I could make them work. It would be warm, but I'd handle the discomfort. I also found a pair of old glasses that I could still see out of fairly well. They were no seamless bifocals, but I didn't plan to do any reading that night. My eyesight is bad, and I require rather thick lenses, so normally I don't leave the house without my contacts. Vanity was a necessary casualty of deception.

I tried on my disguise and, standing there in front of my full-length mirror, barely recognized myself. Just the look I was going for.

Wednesday had its ups and downs. But, by the end of the day, as I sat down with my scotch, I was as prepared for the Sassy caper as I possibly could be. I'd taken to referring to it as a "caper." There was something about the word that implied frivolity and good-natured hijinks. "Extortion" sounded like what it was. In the morning I had cruised past Naomi and Nathan's Catering, which was based in High Grove, a town about five miles east of Fowler. I wanted to know if Mick's makeshift sign would stand a chance of passing muster.

It occupied a large portion of a strip mall and, in addition to private catering, it also had a nice deli open to the public. I picked up a price list, coffee, and, while I was at it, a black bean and corn salad that looked pretty tasty. The lettering on the one van parked in front of the shop was, as Mick promised, an unpretentious serif style font without a logo. Black lettering on white. It shouldn't be difficult to produce a reasonable facsimile. Once again I had to wonder if Mick had the idea before it ever occurred to me. Maybe he already had the sign made and the truck hired. Seemed there'd never been much doubt in his mind that I would go along with this insanity.

Jack never called, and I wondered if he was put off by my canceling the "date" with my mother. Mostly, I hoped he hadn't shown up there alone. I'd thought about calling him, and then figured what with all that was going on, I didn't need to be pursuing romantic possibilities.

I tried to do some work on an article that was due on Monday. Strange the way I assumed my life would go on as before, with this goat thing just a bump in the road. But I found it hard to concentrate, and in the middle of a sentence, I opened a new document and typed three lines in 14-point Helvetica: five hundred thousand dollars, Phinny's Tap, 1 p.m. I inserted a note card into my printer and hit the "print" button. As the printer spit the card out, it occurred to me that I must be one sorry extortionist if I needed a cheat sheet for my ransom call. Well, I was. I hesitated, then decided I'd better print notes for each of the calls I would make. I hoped I wouldn't need any of them, but didn't want to be at a loss for words with Bull. I tucked these cards into my handbag, right between my new phone and the voice changer, and then deleted the Word documents without saving them.

Mick had come by at three o'clock to drive me out to Meyer's farm. It was a straightforward route—even if it was a bit more than ten minutes from Bull's. There were only two turns with prominent landmarks, but I paid close attention, seeing as there might be a goat bleating in my ear the next time I drove the route for real. As promised, Meyer's brother was gone, so we had time to check the place out. There must have been a dozen of the pygmies, along with a couple of nubians, two horses and a llama. Several of the goats nuzzled up to me, and the rest regarded us with benign expressions. I didn't push for interaction. I might not be a goat whisperer, but I also wasn't a goat agitator.

I'd half expected Mick to ask me out to dinner, and I would have accepted. I really didn't want to be alone with my thoughts and my nerves. Between Bix and me the edgy energy would have been unbearable. But when Mick dropped me off at my apartment, he said he'd call me in the morning and let me know where he'd drop off the panel truck. Then he hooked his forearm over the steering wheel and said, "I think that's it."

There had to be more. I shook my head. "When do I call Bull?"

He nodded. "Wait for me to call you first. I want to make sure the party has broken up and there aren't people around when he takes your call."

"Won't he be looking for Sassy?"

Mick chuckled. "I doubt he'll even know the goat is missing until he gets the call."

That made sense. To Bull, Sassy was a peripheral.

"Okay," I said. "Then I guess I'll hear from you tomorrow." This was where he was supposed to suggest dinner. But he just nodded and leaned back into his seat, watching me with an expression I couldn't read.

He'd been quiet this whole afternoon, and I just wrote it off to nerves. But, really, what did he have to be nervous about? I was the one doing most of the work. Now he studied me with that unreadable gaze of his. Almost like he was looking through me, but not at anything specific.

"You okay?" I finally asked.

After a moment he said, "Yeah, just got a lot on my mind."

"Gee," I said. "So do I."

"I know." He shifted in his seat. "You'll do fine tomorrow. Just get a good night's sleep."

"I'll try," I said, unfolding myself from the car. At that moment I had the unpleasant and vaguely familiar sensation I used to get when the guy told me he had a great time, but I knew he was never going to call me again. Mick would, of course, call me tomorrow as he promised. But our social foray had ended. That left me feeling used—at some point he'd decided that I was attractive to him only in terms of my usefulness—and also sad. I wondered at what point I had shifted from prospective lover to conspirator. It did little good to tell myself that he may just be the kind of person who didn't like to mix work and pleasure.

But as I got ready for bed—a good hour ahead of my usual time—my head was jammed with whirling thoughts and images. I knew I'd have trouble sleeping, so I combed through my "medicine drawer" and found a bottle of over-the-counter sleep medication just barely past its expiration date. It did the trick. I was out shortly after my head hit the pillow. However, Morpheus chose to visit, and I spent the night dreaming about the heist and a shadowy figure that kept flitting in and out of my dreamscape. I didn't remember much upon awakening, except that at some point Sassy began talking to me, and we had a long, interesting discussion on the afterlife.

CHAPTER 15

At ten fifteen the next morning, my mother was waiting for me in the lobby. She seldom did this, preferring to have me call upon her. But I could tell by the way she stood as I walked in and barely gave me time to sign her out that she'd been looking forward to this séance with an eagerness I didn't often see in her anymore. And sure enough, she was wearing her silk blouse.

On the way over she chatted about the dinner last night, saying that the macaroni and cheese needed salt, but that the rolls were warm. Then she said, "Oh, I forgot to tell you. We had a lovely visitor yesterday afternoon. He said he knew you."

Fortunately, we were at a stop light, so I could turn toward her. "You did?"

"Yes. Now I can't remember his name, but he knew you. He thought you were to meet him." Her accusing eyes focused on mine. "But you didn't."

"Something came up." I shifted into gear and moved ahead with the traffic. "Jack Landis."

"Yes, that was his name."

"I called him and left a message, but he must not have gotten it."

"Well, he was delightful. Played guitar and had us singing along."

I pictured him sitting in the middle of a circle of old people smiling as he strummed and sang. The residents—eighty percent of them women—singing along with the chorus of "Golden Slippers" and drinking in his looks and talent. I would have liked to have seen how he interacted with them.

"It made for a pleasant afternoon."

"I'll bet." And what was I doing at the time? Planning a goat heist.

"You say he's a friend of yours?"

"Sort of."

"He's quite handsome, don't you think?"

"Yes, I guess he is."

I could feel her watching me. "He seemed quite interested in you." And then, almost as an aside, she added, "Although I can't imagine how he felt with you standing him up."

"I'm sure he's gotten my message by now."

"Perhaps." After a moment, she added, "Have you heard from him since?"

"I haven't been home much," I said, then leaped on the first subject that came to mind. "The séance. Have you thought about what you're going to ask the, um, spirit?"

She didn't answer right away, and so I said, "I think it's got to be something he can answer with a yes or a no." Then, I added, not without sarcasm, "Unless, of course, you both know Morse code."

Glaring, she said, "Why do you take that tone with me?"

"It's not you, Mom," I said, sighing. "It's just that I'm not at all sure this woman is legitimate."

"Well, then all we'll be wasting is my money."

I thought about telling her I'd pay for it, but then decided that at this rate whatever it cost to speak to her late husband wasn't going to make any difference.

Instead, I asked, "What was his favorite food?"

"Why do you ask?"

"Well, at the last séance, they had a Whopper and fries because the guy we were trying to contact had been a fan."

"Hmm." She seemed to be giving it serious thought. "I don't recall what he had a special fondness for."

"That's okay. Probably doesn't matter."

"He did like the smell of gardenias."

"Gardenias?" This small-time thug had a sensitive side.

I considered stopping at a florist shop, but figured the chances of them having gardenias on hand were slim, and we didn't have time to waste. If Robert had been a Quarter-pounder guy, it would have been much easier.

Erika stood from her desk and came around to greet us when we arrived, smiling at my mother with a warmth I didn't think the woman capable of.

"It's so nice to meet you, Mrs. Guthrie." She took my mother's hands in hers.

This morning she wore a black, gauzy top over a pair of black slacks and a turquoise scarf wrapped around her neck.

I looked around, maybe expecting to see Jack.

"It will just be the three of us," Erika said.

"I thought we needed five," I countered.

"Five is, of course, ideal, but since this spirit broke into our session, I believe he has something he needs to communicate. I don't think the number will matter to him."

"I'm sure it won't," I said. Both Erika and my mother gave me rather sharp looks. I could see how my mother recognized the sarcasm, but I didn't think Erika knew how to read me yet.

She took us into the same small room, with the same table, only this time there were just three chairs around it. Heavy shades were drawn to keep out the light.

We settled into our chairs; Erika had my mother sit to her right. She put on some soft environmental music—birds and wind. She lit the candles and lowered the lights, but instead of holding hands, she turned to my mother and said, "Could we talk for a moment, Mrs. Guthrie?"

My mother's eyes widened in a look I'd come to know as her don't-call-on-me look and she dampened her lips with a flick of her tongue.

"Can't I just talk to Robert?" she said.

"It would help if you first told me a little about your husband. Anything you can tell me may assist me in reaching him on the other side."

When my mother didn't respond, Erika asked her, "What did he call you? Did he have a special nickname for you?"

"Elizabeth," she said, after a moment. "He called me Elizabeth."

This was news to me. I'd never heard anyone call her Elizabeth except for Wyman when he was annoyed over some minor transgression.

"That's good," Erika said, sounding encouraged. "What else can you tell me?"

My mother swallowed. "May I have some water?"

The psychic hesitated. "Of course." She left the room.

"I don't want to talk *about* him," my mother said to me. "I just want to talk *to* him."

"What do you want to ask him?"

"First I want to make sure it's him."

"Then ask him a question that proves it. But one he can answer with a yes or no."

She looked panicky for a second. "Well, I don't know."

"Did he give you something that only he would know about?"

"Well, yes, but—"

Erika returned with a round, black tray carrying three water glasses. After serving each of us, she propped the tray against the wall and sat again.

"What is his last name?" Erika asked.

My mother said, "Please. Just call him Robbie."

"I think—"

"If he's there, he will answer to Robbie."

Why "Robbie" all of a sudden? But we were holding hands now, and Erika had begun her chanting, so my question would have to wait.

My mother looked calm at first, but then she became a little agitated, and I could see her lips twitching. (I was making no pretense of closing my eyes. I wanted to see everything.)

And then, like the last time, I saw the curtain flutter. And, again, the window was not open. A few moments later I caught a whiff of something sweet. Flowery.

My mother wrinkled her nose but did not say anything. Her sense of smell has all but deserted her. She clung to my hand with her own—soft, warm and dry.

"... Please walk among us, Robbie."

The candle flames on the table wavered, and I swear the room darkened. The sarcasm began to seep from my body, making room for a mix of fear and annoyance. I knew there had to be some way she pulled it off but I had no idea how. The alternative—that this was all as real as I was—was just too hard to deal with right now. I figured as long as I kept telling myself this ritual was a fraud, I could keep my nerves in check.

"Robbie, I have someone special who wishes to speak with you." The breeze had turned cool and now there was a soft thump against the table.

"Robbie?"

Tap.

"Elizabeth is here with me. She wishes to speak with you. Will you talk to us?"

Silence.

"Robbie?" Erika asked.

My mother had opened her eyes and then, perhaps responding to the same squeeze Erika gave my hand, she snapped them shut again. Without turning my head and risking Erika's scolding, I took in as much of the room as I could. The light was dim, but I could still make things out—the little table beneath the window, the CD player in the corner. I had the strangest feeling that there was something under the table, whatever had made that sound was just inches from my knee. That thought caused an involuntary leg spasm and earned me another squeeze from Erika.

"Robbie," Erika said, sounding as though the name were awkward for her. "Elizabeth would like to speak with you. Are you here for her?"

The silence pressed into my ears and it was a full ten seconds—I was counting—before the single rap came. Apparently Robbie didn't need to be coached again on the psychic code—one rap for yes, two for no—because Erika took his response for a yes.

"We welcome you here," she said.

At that moment I wondered where Jack was, and then I imagined him behind some emerald green curtain—flipping switches that caused custom-made hammers to pound inside the walls.

"Mrs. Guthrie," Erika said, "you may ask him a question now."

"How does she know it's really him?" I asked.

Erika shot me a shivery look, and then said to my mother. "Go ahead and ask him a personal question."

The tip of my mother's tongue darted out again, and I imagined she needed some water, but she'd have to let go of Erika's hand, and I knew there was no way my mother was breaking the circle at this point. "That ring you gave me," she finally said, her voice strained and scratchy. "Was it shaped like a star?"

No.

"A bow?"

Yes.

I could practically feel the ring she'd just described gripping my finger. Why hadn't she ever mentioned that my father had given it to her?

I refocused when I saw my mother nod as though he'd answered this correctly. And then she did something very strange. She smiled. One she'd been saving for a while. There was a sigh attached to it, and her body relaxed. Like at last she'd come home. I thought for a moment that she'd died right there and then. All this time she'd just been waiting for an escort. But then she drew in a new breath and exhaled.

It was all I could do not to ask her to explain the ring. But Erika was there, squeezing my hand so hard I jumped a little.

So, instead, I said, "What did you want to ask him, Mom?"

My mother closed her eyes and said, "I didn't know you'd died. I'm so sorry."

I couldn't believe she was talking like this to the guy who'd taken her sofa money.

"What did you want to ask him?" Erika prompted.

"Nothing. Really. I just wanted to talk to him."

Erika and I exchanged looks.

"Did you miss me?" she asked.

Yes.

"Good." She nodded and then glanced at Erika. "Do they sometimes lie?"

"No," Erika told her.

I wasn't sure, but I thought I'd just witnessed a kindness. How would Erika know?

"I think I'd just like to sit here with him for a few minutes."

"I don't know how long he can stay," Erika said, and I detected some strain in her words. Then she took in a sharp breath and her eyes widened, staring at a space between my mother and me. Almost as if …

"Can you see him?" I asked.

"Yes," she said after a moment. "I can now."

My mother glanced over her shoulder, than back at Erika. "How does he look?"

"He's quite tall. Well over six feet. Distinguished. He's wearing a green sweater over a denim shirt. He has intense, alert eyes. Your daughter's eyes."

Tall? In the one photo I'd seen of my father he stood next to my mother. Saying he had three inches on her was being generous. And at her tallest, my mother was maybe five-foot-five.

I squinted. Saw nothing.

"She does have his eyes," my mother agreed. Then she said, "Is he still handsome?"

"Yes, he is."

We all sat in silence for several moments, and I imagined I could hear a fourth person breathing in the room. Of course that was silly.

"Mrs. Guthrie," Erika said, her breath catching, "he is speaking to me." We looked at her. Her sight was trained on the place beyond my mother.

"What is he saying?" Both my mother and I asked at the same time.

After a few seconds, Erika spoke again, "He said Robyn is beautiful."

"Thank you," my mother said.

"He says she looks like you."

Without glancing my way, my mother said, "I think she resembles Robbie."

Another strange statement. Robert Guthrie had reddish brown hair and there was nothing in his face that I could find in my own. Maybe the only photo I had of my late father was not an accurate one. My mother had lied about his death for so many years, I guess I wouldn't put it past her to have shown me a photo of someone else.

After a few moments of listening, Erika said, "There's something he wants to say to you, Mrs. Guthrie—he wants me to tell you that—he wants me to tell you he's sorry."

My mother's cheeks reddened and she sighed. "I know. So am I."

"He worries that you had forgotten about him."

My mother glanced at me. "How could I?" Then she said, her voice kind of dreamy. "I remember everything. The day you gave me the ring. We were on the pier ... I can still hear the gulls."

Pier? Gulls? "In Colorado?" I hadn't meant to say it out loud.

"Hush, Robyn," my mother hissed at me, all the tenderness gone.

I didn't want to start anything—not right this second—so I backed off.

"He wants to know why you never came back."

"You tell him, Mom," I said under my breath.

She darted a look my way. "You know why."

"Yes, I think you do," I added and my mother jerked my hand.

"You should have called," Erika translated. "He wanted to know where you were."

I was tempted to ask him if he was planning to steal more money from her, but I was leery about annoying a ghost. And then my mother said, "Too much … too much had happened."

What I didn't understand was why she was being so sweet to this guy who had beaten her and stolen her sofa money.

Then Erika said, "He wants to know if Robyn knows."

From the widening of my mother's eyes I knew we were heading someplace she didn't want to go.

"Knows what?" I asked.

For the second time she said, "It's none of your business, Robyn." But this time I wasn't going to let it go.

"I think it is my business."

"This is my life," my mother said, "not yours."

That just about rendered me speechless. Our lives were braided together. And for her to dismiss me like that, well, it pissed me off. I squeezed her hand. "You tell me now or so help me I'll snatch my hands away, blow out the candles and throw open the shades."

Instead of pitching an eye dart at me, Erika said to my mother, "He says that you should tell her."

My mother bowed her head, and all I could see was her pink scalp under the threads of white.

"Tell me what?" My question was met with stone silence. Even the birds in the CD had lost their voices. I commanded myself to think. All the questions tumbled together at once. Why didn't I resemble the guy in the photo, but did resemble this dead man? What was it my mother had kept from me? What was so important that she'd keep the lie for forty-five years? When I trusted my voice enough to speak, I said, "Am I allowed to ask a question?"

Apparently she had to consult with the spirit first, but finally Erika nodded.

"Did you desert my mother in Cortez and run off with the money she was saving for a sofa?"

This time it was me clamping down on my mother's hand to keep her from bolting.

"No, he did not." Erika relayed.

"Are you Robert Guthrie?"

"He says that is not his name."

Something burned in the pit of my stomach. "What is your full name?"

"Robert Alan Savage."

I had never heard this name before. Never.

My mother's eyes were squeezed shut and her mouth was pressed into a thin, bloodless line.

Still watching her, I asked the ghost, "Are you my father?"

After a moment, Erika said, "Yes. He says he is."

I clung to my mother's hand as I asked, "Were you ever married to my mother?"

Erika cast a glance at my mother, who would have gone sprinting were it not for us holding on to her.

"He says he loved your mother."

"That is not what I asked." I fought to keep my tone even.

"No," Erika finally said, "they were never married."

Oh, Jesus. I did not know this was coming. Or had I? I must have. It answered questions I hadn't even thought of yet. I had to sort out the details. Had he just said what I thought he'd said? Or had I misinterpreted something? The fine hair on my arms rose. "Are Robert and Robbie two different people?"

At the same time, my mother and Erika said, "Yes."

Double Jesus.

"Robyn." It was my mother, and her tone had that little whiney crescendo.

I couldn't stop myself from turning to my mother. "Why?"

Staring at the table's surface, she just shook her head.

Erika looked past us, and then she nodded and turned toward me. "He's afraid your mother has forgotten."

"Forgotten what? What—"

"I did not." My mother looked to be teetering between tears and anger. "Robbie, how can you say that?"

Bile was working its way up my throat. I couldn't swallow. "Sounds like a reasonable concern," I said. "You forgot to mention he was my father. For forty-five years."

"I'll not have you taking that tone with me—"

"You have no idea where me and my tone are going. Why, I—"

"This must stop." Erika abruptly released our hands. "I cannot conduct a séance under these conditions."

She gave first me and then my mother a pointed look.

"I am very good at what I do. I will not risk that by having you two conducting your personal vendettas when spirits are present. They deserve better than that." She paused. "Especially this one."

Then she looked at me and said, "One of you will have to leave the room."

"I'm not leaving," my mother said.

"Robyn," Erika's eyes were hard, black steel, "you must leave the room."

"No."

"Then this session will have to end."

"Robyn, please." It was my mother, and I could hear the tears in her words.

"Okay," I finally said, standing. Then I turned to my mother. "When you finish here we've got some talking to do."

My mother bowed her head. "I know."

"None of this 'oh, I can't remember' stuff."

She wagged her head back and forth. "Yes, dear."

"I'll wait right outside the door."

I stood and skirted the space my father occupied in his disembodied way.

I had the door halfway open when Erika said, "Robyn …"

I stopped, looked back at her as she nodded toward the floor. "You forgot your handbag."

"Oh," I said, noting the smug aura rising off of the medium. I had no choice but to scoop up my purse and take it out with me. So much for my pathetic attempt at subterfuge. I doubted she knew for sure that I'd had the recorder going during the last séance. It was probably a lucky guess, but it was a smart one, and I reminded myself that no matter how phony a medium Erika Starwise was, she wasn't stupid.

The air in the hall was cooler and all I could smell were the candles and incense for sale in her shop. At first I paced outside the door, but I couldn't hear anything. I didn't trust Erika. She'd led me into this. Why, I wasn't sure, but I knew better than to be flattered anymore. And while I knew it was easy enough to make up stuff that some spirit was saying, in order to do that she must have done her homework. And if she did do her homework on my mother, I needed to know why. After several minutes with no psychic energy seeping out from under the door, I went to the outer office to pace and fume. I had learned enough in there to make me angry, confused and curious. I wasn't sure which emotion prevailed. Who the hell was Robert Savage? Other than my real father. Or was he? My head spun. So much of my life had been spent remembering a guy who died before I was born. Now, I just learned that this man—Robert Guthrie—was some guy my mother married to make me legitimate. I kicked the doorjamb. Well, Mom, it never took. My head spun like a bad hangover.

Savage. Shit. I wasn't even Scottish.

I was dying to know what was being said. And without my recorder working for me in there, I had no way of knowing how much truth I'd get out of my mother. And I saw no reason, after all these years, for her to start telling the truth now.

After fifteen more minutes of pacing, my mother came out from the back. She was smiling, chatting with Erika like they were old friends.

"Thank you so much, Erika." My mother took Erika's hand. "This has been a most amazing experience."

"I'll make an appointment for you for Monday."

All I said to my mother was, "You've got some explaining to do."

"I know." She sighed, but she didn't slip into her cowering puppy pose.

"I'd like a drink, if I may," my mother said to me as we walked out of the Psychic Place. The way she spoke, she sounded like she was making her last request. As in: *May I have a blindfold, please.*

I relented, but only because I needed a drink at least as bad as she did. Fortunately, in Fowler you're never more than a few doors away from a drinking establishment. I directed her into the Depot and then to a corner booth. I didn't see anyone resembling a waitress, so I left my mother and went to the bar where I placed our order. The bartender said he'd bring it to me, so I was able to return to the table before my mother had a chance to escape.

I scooted into the booth across from her, my hands folded on the pitted surface of the wooden slab of a table, and watched my mother squirm. I was going to wait until we had our drinks, but wanted to see if she'd blurt something out before I brought it up. I doubted she would. My mother could hold her silence better than Marcel Marceau. She busied herself examining the contents of her purse, withdrawing an embroidered handkerchief and dabbing her mouth with it, finger combing her soft, white hair. She gave me a pleasant smile.

I kept my jaws clenched, afraid of what I might say if I were to unleash my tongue. Acid burned in the hollow pit in my stomach. It was a mixture of anger, sadness and confusion. I could not believe that my father had been alive all these years, and I didn't know about him until after he died. Did she have any idea what that meant to me?

"Are you working on a book now?" she asked.

Unfortunately, the bartender arrived with our drinks before my mother could fully appreciate the depth of my glare.

"Famous Grouse," he said, setting the amber on the rocks in front of me. And then he said, "and a Chablis." Actually, it was Chardonnay. They didn't have Chablis so I asked him to fib a little. I sighed. Now I was asking other people to lie for me.

"What's Famous Grouse?" my mother asked as if she cared.

"Scotch."

"I didn't know you drank scotch." She'd taken on that disapproving tone. "It's hardly a social drink."

"I've been drinking it for years."

"Hmph," she said, sipping her wine. "Famous Grouse. What an odd name."

"As a matter of fact," I said, getting comfortable, "it's what the crown prince of Nepal was drinking the night he murdered his family."

Her eyes widened and she swallowed.

"Let's cut the crap," I said.

"Your mouth, Robyn," she murmured.

"It's time for you to tell me everything. And I mean *everything*."

She used her handkerchief to dab at the damp spot on the table where her glass had left a wet ring. "I don't know where to start."

"The beginning is such a good place."

When she hesitated, I could see the anguish in her features—her tucked brows, the way her eyes looked like pools of blue. The lines on either side of her mouth had deepened, giving her face a grayish cast.

"Let me ask you this," I said. "Were you married to a guy named Robert Guthrie just before you had me?"

She seemed shocked that I'd ask such a thing. "Of course I was married."

"Was Robert Guthrie my father?"

She cocked her head to one side as though to bend the answer. "No, he wasn't."

"My father was also named Robert. Robert Savage."

She finally nodded. "Yes."

"Tell me about him."

She placed both hand hands on the table, palms down and leaned toward me. "You have to understand. You weren't supposed to know anything about this until ..."

"Until?"

"Well, until after I died. I was going to leave you a letter." She didn't give me a chance to comment before continuing. "You see, I had to give you a name."

As stunning as this deception was, it made perfect sense in my mother's world.

"Did you intentionally marry a guy named Robert?"

"No," she smiled. "But it was convenient, wasn't it?"

"Tell me about my father."

She smiled. "He was a wonderful man. I met him in Los Angeles in the early sixties."

"Why were you in Los Angeles?" It was one place my mother had never said she wanted to go.

"I wanted to be an actress."

I had to bite my tongue.

"Hollywood was an exciting place then. I moved out there and waited tables in a coffee shop while I auditioned for movie roles. Had a couple of bit parts. But then I took a job as a production assistant to a film director. He was demanding and a tough boss, but I learned a great deal from him. I learned I was better at that job than acting. It paid better too."

"Was that my father?"

"Oh, no, the director was, well, a homosexual." She whispered the word. "But we were working on a film that was being produced by a couple of men, and they would show up on the set every now and then. Made Larry nervous," she added. "Felt like they were looking over his shoulder. But then it became clear that it wasn't Larry's shoulder one of those men was looking over. It was mine." She nearly blushed at the memory and I got a glimpse of my mother at that age. "The one man—Robert—was very kind. Charming. I had an easy time talking to him. When he asked me out for coffee, I really believed it was just that."

I gave her a look.

"I know," she sighed. "And, you know, I think I'd still have gone even if I'd known exactly what he wanted."

I almost smiled.

She swallowed some wine. "We began seeing each other then."

"Was he married?"

"Yes. She was …" She paused. "She wasn't a nice woman."

I nodded. Sure. They never are.

"No, I know what you're thinking, but she really was a horrible person. Drank too much, was rude to people. Had a yappy little poodle she took with her everywhere."

Dear God, she sounded like me. "Why didn't he divorce her?"

Her jaw hardened as she swallowed. "Well, she was the sister of a rather powerful man. He was, um, with the mafioso."

"Oh."

"Robbie couldn't divorce her."

"But if she found out he was cheating on her that was okay?"

"I don't know if she ever did find out. I don't think so. But I also don't think she would have cared."

She swallowed again. "It was nice for a while. We went lovely places. He gave me beautiful gifts … my ring." She reached across the table for my hand, and I let her examine the ring. "It looks very nice on your hand."

"It's a beautiful ring."

"What's that style called?"

"Art deco."

"Yes, that's it. He loved old things, you know. Collected all kinds of things from the first part of the century. Wines, coins, jewelry. He thought they carried stories."

Yeah, sure, I thought, not thinking many kind thoughts about any of my fathers at this point. I pulled my hand away.

"And then I got pregnant." She shook her head. "I was so careful. We were so careful, but, well, some children just want to be born."

"Yeah, that's me."

"We talked about ... what to do. He said he'd pay ... for whatever. He'd take care of me ... us. But I knew that wouldn't work. I told him I'd go away and he'd never hear from me again."

"Did he believe you?"

"I think he did. I asked him for some money to get me started in a job and get an apartment—"

"How much?"

"Not very. I think it was ten thousand."

I waited.

"But his advisors were afraid I'd blackmail him later." She shook her head. "I'd never have done that to Robbie."

"So what happened?"

"I left town. Without the money. Without telling him where I was going." She sipped more wine. "He never found me. At least I didn't think he had. Not until that woman came."

"Mary Waltner?"

"That's right."

"She didn't come to see you about Robert Guthrie."

"No."

"Is he still alive?"

"I have no idea," she said and from her tone implied that she didn't care.

I tended to think that the hundred and fifty dollars in the canister had also been part of the myth, but I didn't want to sidetrack her. "Why did Mary Waltner come to see you?"

Her features clouded. "What was it that happened to her?"

"She died, Mother."

"Oh, my. That's right. That's what that policeman said. I don't know if I had anything to do with that."

"You didn't, Mother," I said, not certain that was the case anymore.

"He'd known my whereabouts for years, but he understood it was best keeping me a secret. At least while that horrible wife of his was alive." She smiled a little. "But then she died." She scowled. "Eighty-nine years old."

"Only the good die young," I offered.

She looked at me. "I'm going to live a very long time, aren't I?"

"You won't die of natural causes soon," I said.

She wouldn't meet my eyes. I kept going. "If he knew where you were, why didn't he come out here after his wife died?"

"She died less than a year ago. And then Robbie's health was failing." She paused. "At least that's what the letter said."

"What about me? Did he know about me? Did he know I was here—with you?"

"He did." She straightened her napkin and continued. "He wrote me this letter. Oh, Robyn, it's the most beautiful, loving letter. He mentioned you. And in it he says he had provided for me."

"Really? How?"

"I-I'm not sure." Her brows tightened. "There was something that woman said about it, and I can't remember what that was. It was just too much at once."

"Was it something he said in the letter?"

"Why, yes, I think there must have been something in there."

"A check?"

"No. Nothing like that." Her face screwed up and she pressed a fist to her forehead. "Oh, Robyn, why can't I remember these things?"

"It's okay, Mom. Maybe if you let me see the letter."

"Well, yes, I suppose I could do that."

"Do you have it?"

"It's in my room."

I pushed aside my half-finished glass. "Let's go."

My mother drained her wine and collected her purse.

She shed her sweater on a chair and hustled over to the table beside her bed. I folded her sweater and slipped it into a dresser drawer, thinking I'd ask if she had a photo of my father. Even if she didn't, if he was a wealthy Hollywood type, there would be photos. Once this craziness was over, I wanted to see where I came from.

"Well, that's strange," she was saying.

"What?" Even as I spoke the word I knew that the windfall was slipping from our reach.

"I was sure I put it in here." She looked up at me.

I walked over to the table. My mother was perched on the edge of her bed and had the contents of the drawer spread out on the duvet. I recognized her address book and a card I'd given her for Mother's Day. An extra set of my apartment keys. A deck of playing cards and a package of mints rounded out the contents. I ran my hand along the bottom of the drawer, feeling around. Jammed into a crack in the back of the drawer was a cigarette. I pocketed it without comment. Clearly, there was no letter here.

"Did you show it to that policeman who was here the other day?"

"No." She hesitated. "I . . . I should have, but it was a very personal letter. I didn't even know that man." She looked up at me. "Should I have done that?"

"That's okay." I looked around the room. "Could you have put it in your purse?"

"I-I don't think so. No." She shook her head. "I'm sure I didn't."

"Do you mind if I look?"

"Of course you can look, dear. If you don't trust my memory."

"You're always warning me about it." I unzipped the nylon purse she carried with her everywhere, and she started to reach for it. I handed it to her. "Why don't you look?"

A few moments later the contents of her purse had joined her emptied drawer on the bed. Aside from her wallet, a napkin blotted with lipstick, lipstick and a compact, her purse was empty.

"Robyn, I-I don't know what—"

"Maybe it's in your dresser."

"No."

I believed her.

"Could you have put it in the pocket of something you were wearing?"

I rifled her closet, feeling for anything other than tissue and hard candy. Then I went through her books. She sometimes used whatever was convenient for a bookmark. I found a stamped envelope with a return address in California. It was empty. I held it up. "Did the letter come in this?"

"Yes. I think it did."

"Is it okay if I take it?"

When she didn't answer right away, I added, "Just to keep it safe." I wanted to check out the return address.

"All right," she acquiesced.

When my search turned up nothing, we sat in silence for a few moments, my mother on her bed and me in the chair she usually sat in.

"Was anyone in your room?"

"Why, no. Just the nurses. They all have keys. And the young Hispanic woman who cleans. She might have come in." I could hear the rawness in her voice. "But why would they take the letter?"

It didn't make sense to me. Then it hit me. I think my mother had the same idea at the same time. "That man," she whispered.

"The one who was here playing guitar?"

"Yes. Your *friend.*"

"He was in your room?"

"Well, yes, we were talking about you, and I mentioned I had some photos of you as a little girl. He was so interested. I-I offered to show them to him." She shook her head. "The door was open all the time."

"Was he ever in the room alone?"

"No." She stopped. "Well, it was time for my medications, but I was gone only a few minutes. And the door was open."

It could have been a long few minutes. The residents lined up for their medications like they were getting … well, drugs. It was a first-come-first-served arrangement, and everyone wanted to be first. Besides, it wouldn't have taken Jack more than a minute or two to find the letter.

"Robyn, what did I do?" She was on the verge of tears.

"It's okay, Mom. I'll talk to him. Maybe he didn't take it." Right. And maybe I hadn't been hoodwinked. "Or maybe he just borrowed it."

I punched in his cell phone number. He didn't answer. No surprise. I didn't leave a message. I had to think about what I was going to say.

"Robyn, I have to have that letter. It's all that I've got. You understand, don't you?"

"I do, Mom." Then I said, "Did you and Erika talk about this at all?"

She worked her mouth a couple of times before saying, "Well, yes. I mean, Robbie brought it up."

Sure he did. "What did you tell Erika?"

"I didn't remember. I mean that's what I told her. She—I mean Robbie—got a little short with me. I—"

"It wasn't Robbie who was short with you, Mom."

"What …?"

I grabbed my purse. "You take a nap. I'll take care of things."

"Do you promise?" She seemed both relieved and unsure.

"I promise."

On my way out of Dryden, I checked the sign-in book. There he was—Jack Landis. And he was there to see Lizzie Guthrie.

Bastard.

"Is April in?" I asked the receptionist, Bobbie, a young blond woman who got a kick out of my mother.

"She's out to lunch, Robyn. Can I help?"

"You know that guy who was playing guitar here yesterday?"

She perked up. "Yes, he was wonderful. Everyone loved him."

"He took something from my mother's room."

"No—"

"His name is Jack Landis. Please make sure he doesn't get any-where near my mother. Better yet, make sure she doesn't have *any* vis-itors."

Her eyes widened. "Should I call the police?"

"No," I said, perhaps a bit too quickly. "It may be a misunder-standing."

She nodded. "I'll let April know."

"And would you tell the nurses? Especially whoever is working Mom's floor."

"Will do."

She was punching numbers on the phone when I left.

I was fuming by the time I got to my car. And part of the anger was self directed. Did I really think this guy was interested in me? God, how gullible can you get, Robyn? Charmed by a good-looking guy. I thought I'd learned.

I pulled out of the lot and ground a gear as I shifted into second. Damn. I imagined the gear shift knob was a sensitive part of Landis's anatomy and I squeezed hard. Bastard.

I thought about driving back to the Psychic Place, but I needed to collect my thoughts. And there was another thing I needed to do even before I paid Erika a visit. Although, the last thing I wanted to do on the day I would commit my first major crime was call the police. But I had to do it. Detective Hedges might not know about Jack Landis. And if he knew that Mary Waltner was bringing something to my mother—something Landis wanted enough to attempt to steal—well, I didn't need a badge to know that made Landis—if not her killer— at least a suspect. At the same time, I warned myself to be careful. If Landis was desperate, and if he'd killed once already, then nobody involved in this was safe. That included my mother and me. So I needed to call Hedges not merely as this might pertain to Mary Waltner's murder, but also for my mother's—and my own—sake.

I waited until I got home to call. As I was keying in the number, I thought of how my mother had been this morning. I'd seen the way she'd looked at that space that Robbie had occupied. Whether Erika had conjured him up or not, it was as if she'd seen him there with his tousled hair and his sweater and denim shirt, and for a few moments it was as though the years lifted off of her.

To me, it was both puzzling and sad. I had never known my mother to be head over heels in love with any man. With my mother and Wyman there was a level of partnership they developed. They worked together well, complemented each other. But I seldom saw them exchange longing glances from across the room. They probably had a pretty good sex life—there was the bank vault, after all—but I wondered how much affection was exchanged. But during the part of the séance I'd witnessed, my mother had sounded, at times, downright flirty and at other times almost tearful with longing.

That was the thing about unrequited love. It never has the chance to sour.

I put the call through to Hedges and got his voice mail. A little relieved, I left a message saying I'd learned something he might find interesting. At that point, I again debated returning to the Psychic Place and confronting Erika. I knew she had more she could tell me about Robert Savage. Did she know about Mary Waltner's death? If she didn't, that would prompt some kind of response. On the other hand, if she did know, she might be involved. I sat down. Maybe I needed to rethink this visit to Erika's. If she had something to do with Mary's death, then what was to stop her from bashing my head in?

I settled down to do some of my own digging. I started by examining the envelope my mother's letter had come in. It was addressed to my mother at her old address. The one in Westchester, where she hadn't been in almost two years. There was a return address—in

Thousand Oaks, California—but no name. And the stamps had not been cancelled, so it had never been mailed. But at one time he had intended to mail it. Maybe he had known that my mother moved. The address was printed in neat, black letters, all in caps, but the first letter in each word was larger. I believed this was my father's hand, and I tried to see some of my own writing in the blocky letters.

Deciding I'd need the contents of the envelope to get any further, I snuggled up to my laptop and started by Googling "Robert Alan Savage."

By the time Hedges called me back an hour later, I had learned some interesting things about my father—like the fact that I had a half brother and sister, and that he had been a wealthy man, but there were no clues as to what had been in that letter. And there'd been plenty of photos—a number of them taken around the time I was born. He'd been a handsome man, with wavy, dark hair; a wide, white smile and arresting eyes. I wasn't sure I saw a resemblance when I looked in the mirror, but I wouldn't have minded.

"What've you got?" Hedges asked.

"Well, I'm not sure this is anything, but Mary Waltner gave my mother a letter when she visited her. It was from a man my mother had a relationship with decades ago. And that letter is missing now. I think I know who took it." I went on to explain about Erika and Jack Landis and Erika's connection to my father. As I attempted to explain, I began to wish I had rehearsed, written it down. I was rambling and he wasn't interrupting to ask questions or give me better focus. When I finished, he didn't say anything for several moments.

Finally, I heard his intake of breath. "You say this woman is a psychic?"

"That's what she claims."

"And your mother talked to your father—your dead father—through this woman?"

"Yes."

"And you just found out he was your father?"

Sensing where this was going, I didn't prompt Hedges.

"And after all these years of lying, your mother—who is a little confused, right?"

"Right."

"—your mother tells you all this and you believe her?"

I flapped my jaw a couple of times, then realized there was no way to explain why I did believe her this time. "You'd have to know her," I said, realizing how feeble that sounded.

"You never saw the letter?"

"No. But I did see the envelope. It was from Thousand Oaks, California."

I heard him sigh and imagined him rolling his eyes at the guy sitting at the desk facing him. The other cop was trying to grin and drink weak coffee at the same time.

I pressed on. "Look, I don't know what's going on or even what's in the letter, but I do know that Mary Waltner and Erika Starwise are from the same area." I paused, realizing this tack wasn't helping any. "I just thought you might want to talk to her. Or to my mother again."

After another moment or two, he said, "Maybe I will later, Miss Guthrie. Thing is, we brought in a suspect last night who's looking pretty good for it."

"Oh."

"Yeah, he was caught using one of the victim's credit cards, and he's got a history of assaults on women."

"Oh," I said again.

"But I appreciate you calling. And depending on how this goes, maybe I'll come out and talk to your mother again. I'll give you a call."

I was about to tell him I wouldn't be home tonight, but decided the less said the better.

When I hung up, I sat there for a minute. At first I was perturbed with Hedges. Some cop he was. But then I considered all of the elements this story contained—a psychic talking to my dead father, a love letter the psychic's brother stole, and their connection to a dead woman—well, I guess I couldn't blame him for being dubious. But that didn't make me doubt my theory any less. Mary Waltner's purse had not been found at the scene. If Landis had killed her, he could have tossed it into a dumpster, figuring someone would find it and start using her credit cards. And maybe get arrested for her murder.

Bix uttered a guttural moan from his doggie bed. His eyes were closed and his jowls twitching as though an electric current were running through him. Then his feet started jerking as he pursued some dream creature.

I glanced at my watch. Almost four. I needed to get to Bull's by seven. That meant I had a couple of hours to spend in a state of anxiety. Or, I could stroll over to my neighborhood psychic's place and ask a few questions. Granted, if my theory was right and Jack Landis—and possibly Erika as well—had something to do with Mary Waltner's death, then confronting her could get me in trouble. But if this nebulous promise of my father leaving something for my mother were true, and if that something translated into money, then that meant I would not have to sneak into a party disguised as a caterer, steal a goat and then hold it for ransom. I could call Mick and tell him to find another woman to do his dirty work. I decided I'd risk confronting a killer.

CHAPTER 16

When I arrived at Erika's shop she was standing behind her desk with the phone to her ear. As I opened the door she looked up. Into the phone, she said, "I'll have to call you back," but her expression didn't change. I had to admit, this woman really had a lock on cool.

Even when I said, "We need to talk," her composure remained intact. But when I added, "Your brother took something from my mother and I want it back," I saw something flicker in her eyes. Anger? Surprise? Again, she was tough to read.

When she didn't say anything, I blundered on. "That is if he *is* your brother."

Crossing her arms over her chest, she regarded me with annoyance. "Of course he's my brother."

"You must be proud," I said, nodding as though I never doubted it. "He steals personal letters from little old ladies." After waiting a beat, I added, "I think you know what letter I'm talking about."

Her eyes widened and she drew in a deep breath. "I don't know anything about this, Robyn. I can't imagine he would do that."

"Then you won't mind telling me where he's staying so I can ask him about it myself. He's not returning his voice mail messages."

Her mouth twisted into a wry smirk. "Are you sure this isn't personal? Just because he didn't call you back doesn't mean he's out to do you or your mother any harm."

"Don't let yourself get caught up in your brother's appeal. He's a nice-looking man, but he's about as exciting as steamed polenta."

For a second there, I thought she was going to laugh. But then she thrust her chin forward. I moved a step closer. She didn't back up, but she coiled.

"Where is he?"

"I don't know where he's staying."

"Right." Then I said, "He told me he was in town for a pharmaceuticals conference. Surely you know where that's being held."

"He doesn't have to keep me informed."

"There was no conference, was there?"

Nothing.

"Gee, I thought he shared everything with you. He made it sound like you practically raised him."

"That was a long time ago."

"How did you know Robert Savage?"

Her eyes widened again and she drew herself up. "I didn't know him, and I don't know what you're talking about. Now, I have an appointment in a few minutes, so you'll have to leave."

"I will. When your appointment shows up, I'll leave."

That didn't make her happy.

I repeated my question. "How did you know my father?"

She shook her head.

"And don't tell me you met him just this morning."

Crossing her arms over her chest, she said, "It doesn't matter what you think of my abilities—I am not a charlatan."

"Just sometimes."

She didn't respond.

"You knew my father, didn't you?"

Her jaw muscles flexed.

I continued. "It's no coincidence that your shop in California was close to where he lived. He was a customer. He had a fascination with the afterlife. He saw you as a psychic, didn't he?"

Finally, she swallowed and said, "Yes, he did."

I nodded. There it was.

But then she continued. "His spirit—your father's spirit—is very powerful."

"I'll bet it is."

"Your attitude is not helpful."

"Oh, gee, I'm sorry about my attitude. Your brother finagled his way into my mother's room, stole a letter from her, and it's just breaking her heart. I'll do whatever it takes to get it back."

This time she sighed. "I wish I could help you, but I can't."

"You can't or you won't?"

Again, no response.

"When you and my mother—or rather, my parents—were talking this morning, after you got rid of me, did you talk about something he left for my mother?"

"We talked of many things."

"You know what I mean." I paused. "You talked about that letter, didn't you?"

"Robert only asked if she had received it."

"What's in the letter?"

"How would I know?"

"Your brother knows."

"I haven't seen him since last night."

"Have you talked to him?"

"No."

"If that letter were specific, you wouldn't still want something from us, then would you?"

She blinked once, slowly. "You don't know what's in the letter, do you?"

"I haven't seen it. Thanks to your brother."

"Your mother seemed ... confused by it."

"Okay, so you don't know what it is he left her, do you?"

"Not specifically." Her mouth twitched. "You don't strike me as the material sort, Robyn."

"Whatever he left her, it's not mine. And it's certainly not yours.

Or your brother's. It belongs to my mother. I don't know what my father gave her or how much it's worth, but I'll bet it doesn't come near to what child support payments would have cost him over the years."

"You sound quite certain that there is some money." She paused. "Perhaps it's just a letter."

"Then why did your brother steal it?"

"I think," she said, "if your mother's memory were clearer, she would recall that she let him take it."

"That's bullshit and you know it." I kept pushing. "My guess is that the letter doesn't spell it out. And neither you nor your brother are good at reading between the lines."

"I've never seen a letter."

"You still need something. Otherwise there'd have been a 'For Rent' sign on your shop window when my mother and I showed up this morning."

"My brother is not an unreasonable man. He would be willing to talk to you."

"If?"

"Well, if he thought you'd be reasonable."

"Why should I be reasonable?"

She breathed a couple of times, all the while staring at me.

Finally, I said, "At least tell me where he is."

"You would be foolish to cross my brother."

"Are you threatening me?"

"I'm warning you." She waited a beat. "You don't know my brother."

"You don't know me."

When she didn't respond, I said, "Did you know a Mary Waltner?"

She hesitated. "Why is that name familiar?"

"She was a lawyer. Robert Savage was a client."

I waited until she caught up with me. "You said 'was.'"

"She was found dead in the Warren Forest Preserves two days ago. Strangled." Erika's eyes widened, but she said nothing. "I believe she was here to deliver that letter to my mother. The one your brother stole from her."

She didn't respond for several moments and when she did, her words were measured. "I heard about this woman on the news. I also heard they have a suspect they're questioning."

"But they haven't charged him yet."

"Perhaps it's just a matter of time."

"You won't listen to anything you don't want to hear, will you?" I decided there was nothing more to be done here. She wasn't inclined to help me, although she also didn't sound like a big sister fighting tooth and nail for her little brother. I reached into my purse for my car keys. "If you can't see that there's something really rotten going on here, then either you're blind or you're a part of it."

As I pulled out my keys, they caught on my purse strap and I lost my grip on them. They fell to the carpet, landing at Erika's feet. She bent to pick them up, and as she held them in her hand, her eyes widened as though she'd just seen something odious.

"What?"

She held onto them as she said, "I had an image. It was of an animal. It's throat is …," she squinted, "it's either cut or torn. There's blood."

"What kind of animal?"

"It's black with … I see a moon." She looked at me. "It's some kind of animal." She nodded. "About the size of a large dog."

Then she handed my keys back to me with a stiff little smile. "But you don't believe in this sort of thing, do you? So I'm sure it won't trouble you."

She left me standing there, trying to keep my mouth from flopping open.

As she opened the door to the back of her shop, she turned to me and said, "If I talk to my brother I'll ask him about the letter."

CHAPTER 17

As I turned the panel truck into Bull Severn's long and winding driveway, I was humming the third movement of Beethoven's Seventh. Time slowed. And in the few seconds the turn required, I did a flashback to the afternoon's preparations—Mick delivering the catering truck along with a large-dog-sized crate, me getting dressed in my catering outfit. I'd saved the wig until I got out to the van, which Mick had parked on a side street near my apartment. The catering signs adhered to either side looked authentic enough. I'd peeked under one and learned that the van belonged to the Riverside Players. What Mick's connection was to an acting troupe, I didn't want to know. I had both my phones—each set to vibrate—tucked into the pockets of my pants, which helped to add another half size to my frame. The last thing I did before leaving the house was call my mother just to check in on her. She complained about dinner; I promised I would get the letter back for her and said I didn't know if I could stop by tomorrow, but would call her. The very last thing I did was pick up Bix and give him a big hug. He's not a cuddly dog—a bit too dignified for that— but he gave me a lick on the cheek as though he understood I was hugging him out of some personal need.

I pulled up to the Severn estate, stopped at the gate and turned off the CD player. I hoped I wouldn't have to talk to anyone while I was here. I waited. Finally, after what my watch measured as fifteen seconds, during which time all I had to listen to was my pounding heart, the gates swung open. They moved ever so slowly, and I had to force myself to wait until there was plenty of room for me to drive through before proceeding. Once through, I felt my shoulders sag with relief, but I warned myself that this was only the beginning. I arrived at the place where the drive splintered off in two directions and took the south route where most of the guests had parked, partially on the lawn and partially on the large, paved area. Many of the guests had arrived already, because I didn't see anyone around the cars. I wedged the van between a Hummer and a Ford Expedition, so I was practically invisible.

I turned off the van and leaned back into the seat, sighing. Now, all I had to do was hunker down and wait for Mick to call. Staying calm would be the challenge. I tried to scratch my stomach through the padding and managed to only irritate the itch. It was going to be a long hour or two. I'd have to try some breathing exercises.

Instead, my thoughts homed in on Erika and what she knew. And as the minutes ticked by, I thought about our meeting and all the questions—troubling questions—it raised. Starting with: how did she know about the goat? That black, big-dog-sized creature she'd "seen" had to be Sassy. The "moon" could have been his white crescent-shaped mark. If she wasn't truly psychic, then she knew something about the plot I was participating in at this moment. And she wanted me to know that she knew. And if she did know, she must have heard through Mick or someone he had confided in. I preferred to think she really was psychic. Because that other option was scarier.

I opened the window on the passenger side for some cross-ventilation, and tried, once again, to clear my mind. But then it settled on my mother and what would happen to her if this didn't work. What would happen to her if I got caught? Imagining those scenarios would have me careening out of here and tossing the cell phone, so I let my thoughts scurry back to where they might do some good. I traced the last few days in my mind trying to figure out how Erika could have known, but nothing made sense. It must have something to do with Jack, who was a better suspect to my mind. He might not be a murderer, but I knew he was a thief. And wasn't there something about him that made Erika uncomfortable? Sure seemed that way. But Mick and Jack?

A latecomer pulled into the parking area, and I slumped down in the van. The car parked behind me, and I was able to watch in my sideview mirror as the couple emerged from the white Mercedes. They were young, trim and attractive, and he put his arm around her as they walked toward the festivities. I envied them—not for their youth or looks—but for their unencumbered lives. Then again, who knew? I spent a few minutes concocting sordid story lines for each of them. But when I cast the man as a bully, his image morphed into that of Jack Landis. Then I put Jack together with Erika and remembered the odd way they played off each other when I'd met him at her shop. I'd assumed it was me that made her so edgy, but wasn't there also some odd undercurrent between the two siblings?

I glanced at my watch and saw that I'd spent almost an hour sorting out my thoughts. I took a sip from the water bottle I'd brought, but only a sip. I had to watch my liquid intake. The sun's last rays burst into flames against the hood of a silver Thunderbird. I leaned my head back against the seat and closed my eyes.

Did Erika have a connection to Bull? It was bad enough the woman knew more about my father than I did. How did she know about the goat? Had Jack been following me? My eyes blinked open and I sat up, the sense of being watched overwhelming. Apparently the mere thought of Jack set my pulse racing. Had he followed me here? Waiting to see what I was up to? I kept coming back to Jack and the letter he'd stolen from my mother and tried to connect it all with Erika's knowledge of the goat. And then I settled on Mick again. Did he have some connection to either of the siblings?

And then, like an annoying song, the possibility that Erika actually was psychic kept playing in my ear. I'd switch it off, but it kept coming back.

I pictured Jack with his frat boy looks and charm. Hedges told me they had someone who "looked good" for Mary Waltner's murder.

"Looking good" was a long way from "guilty." The more I thought this all through, the more I believed that Hedges had the wrong man in custody. But I was hardly in a position to point that out to him.

Maybe Jack was sitting outside Dryden right now, just waiting for an opportunity to go in so he could threaten my mother. I looked down at my faux catering outfit and wondered how closely they checked repairmen at Dryden.

These thoughts were still rioting in my head when my phone vibrated against my hip. "Showtime," I breathed. Problem was, it was the wrong phone. I thought I recognized the number as Detective Hedges. Just as I decided not to answer it, my other hip buzzed. I swapped phones. This time it was Mick.

"You ready?"

"I am."

"Severn's talking now. I'll be on my way down to the stable to get Blood in a minute or two. I'll meet the groom down there. We'll both come back with the horse. Ten minutes. Tops."

"I'll be there."

"Good luck," he said, and disconnected.

I tried to quiet my mind as I put on my black T-shirt and collected the leash and the bag of goat treats. I also opened the dog crate and pulled the plank into position, so I would just need to open the back of the truck, pull the plank down, lead Sassy into the truck and then into the cage. So simple. After stuffing my pockets with goat treats, I headed toward the stable.

I made good time, seeing as I was trying to be invisible but still moving at a fast clip. I half expected to find a few people leaving early and figured I'd have to be extra careful. But no one ever left Bull's parties while he was talking.

When I reached the stable, I stood outside the door for a moment, just listening. I heard some shuffling around in there, and assumed—hoped—it was Sassy.

I ventured in and saw that the aisle between the two rows of stalls was empty. I checked the diagram Mick had given me that indicated what areas were under surveillance. If I stayed on the side I'd entered, I figured I could go in about ten more feet before risking entering the camera's line of sight. That would put me just this side of Blood's stall, and I should be able to see if Sassy was in there.

When I'd entered just about as far as I dared, I squatted with my back against one of the stall dividers and peered through the goat door and into Blood's stall. I didn't see anything.

"Sassy?" I used a stage whisper. Nothing. "Sassy?" A little louder. Still nothing. Finally, in my normal voice, I tried one more time and was rewarded with a high-pitched bleat and then Sassy's head poked out of the stall just past Blood's.

"Sassy!"

With another bleat, he emerged from the stall, slowly at first. Once he saw me, he let out another, more upbeat bleat, and began trotting toward me, his little hooves making clicking sounds as he crossed the pavement.

I dug into my pocket and produced a couple of treats, shoved one into his mouth and ran my hand along his back.

Then I clipped the leash onto Sassy's collar and gave him another treat. "You're going on a little vacation, fella." I stood and began walking toward the door. Sassy gave me a gentle butt that I barely felt and followed along with me, sidling up to me and acting genuinely pleased to see me. When we got to the door, I stopped to listen. I could hear voices in the distance, in the direction of the exercise track, but I was pretty sure that Sassy and I had this area to ourselves.

I'd been prepared to bribe Sassy all the way to the van, but he followed me like Mary's little lamb. I probably didn't even need the leash. I took the long way to the parking area, leading him through a grove of trees to the south of the stable and then past several garages and into the parking area, threading our way through the vehicles until we came to the white van. All was quiet as we approached. I pulled open the rear door and opened the dog crate. With a layer of straw on the bottom and a bag of hay for Sassy to munch on, I figured he ought to be fairly comfortable. He climbed the ramp like a goat who is used to going places and marched right into the crate. He seemed pretty calm, but just to be safe, I took one of Bix's "doggie downers" and stuffed it into one of Sassy's treats. He gobbled it up like a good goat.

I stopped at the gates and it was only a few seconds before they swung open. I was nearly light-headed with my accomplishment. I wanted to call Mick, but he had instructed me to wait until I had Sassy settled into his new quarters before I did that.

As I pulled onto the main road I saw no headlights in either direction, and as I drove toward the farm, no headlights appeared behind me. Maybe I'd been paranoid in thinking that Jack would be lurking about.

I tried to push him to the back of my mind as I concentrated on finding my way to the farm. And, yes, there was a goat bleating in my ear.

Bouncing along on a dark road in the late evening in a vehicle as large as my bedroom and with a mouthy goat as a passenger, I reflected on the absurd turn my life had taken. But only briefly. I was too uncomfortable—my wig itched like crazy and I was sweltering in the pantyhose and stuffing. I couldn't dwell on my discomfort for long either, because in less than fifteen minutes I had arrived at Meyer's farm. I pulled off the road about twenty feet from the gravel drive leading to the house and, beyond it, the barn, and turned off the engine. Lights beamed through the small house's windows, but I'd known to expect that. Although Meyer's brother drank, I assumed he didn't do it in the dark. I didn't like the idea of having to walk Sassy by the house in order to get to the gate that opened onto a small pasture and the barn where the herd was kept. But there was no other way to go, unless I wanted to scale a fence while juggling a goat. I expected that Meyer's goats would be in the barn. I'd read that pygmies didn't like sleeping outside. Just as well. I'd also read that they could fall prey to dogs and coyotes.

When I got out of the van I could hear music—Eric Clapton if I wasn't mistaken. I pulled the catering signs off the sides of the van and stuffed them behind the driver's seat. Then I opened the back of the van and the crate, and Sassy hopped out before I could put the ramp down. He nuzzled me and I gave him another treat.

And then I stood there, watching him chew, and thought about what I was doing and why it felt so wrong. I hadn't had a living being put so much trust in me since—well, since Bix. And, of course, my mother. Now I was going to leave Sassy here with this drunken bum. Possibly at the mercy of coyotes and wild dogs. And then, I will admit, my practical side also weighed in. This little goat was all I had. If I let him loose on this farm and walked away, I relinquished my only bargaining chip. Maybe Mick would be there to convince Bull to pay the ransom, and maybe he wouldn't leave the whole pick-up-the-money part to me. And he was right—I couldn't launder money, and if this were to succeed, I needed him to do that for me. The way we'd laid everything out made sense. But what if he had something else in mind? Something that I hadn't even dreamed of yet because I was basically, prior to the last few days, an honest person. Right now I had Sassy. If I let him go, I had nothing. And really, how well did I know Mick? Fine time for this thought to hit. The thing was, I *had* thought of it. I'd thought of all of this. I had gone through with the plan because I was really that desperate. But I was still allowed to think for myself. And one thing was clear, even to a novice crook like me: I had precious little control over this situation, but without Sassy I had absolutely none. I watched the little goat nibbling the sparse grass on the side of the road.

Throughout this inner dialogue, I refused to acknowledge Erika's goat "vision," and I made a point of telling myself that my decision to keep Sassy had nothing to do with the fact that a coyote could do a lot of damage to a goat. That's what I told myself.

Of course, now I had to consider what I was going to do with Sassy. I might be able to keep him with me for now, but I couldn't let him tag along when I went to pick up the money. I glanced back at the farmhouse just as a light in one of the front rooms flicked on. Meyer's brother would not be there during the day tomorrow. Mick had been certain of that. I was convinced that the less time Sassy spent on this farm, the better off he'd be. Why couldn't I just drop Sassy off at the farm before I went to pick up the money? I looked at that idea from all directions and couldn't find anything wrong with it.

With a sigh, I yanked the wig from my head and tossed it into the back. The cool air hitting my damp scalp made me shiver.

"C'mon, Sassy." I lowered the ramp and patted the floor of the van. He trotted back up and right into the dog crate.

I climbed into the van and slowly pulled back onto the road. Now what?

I needed to think. I drove west, farther into the country. I felt safest where civilization was thin. I'd never had reason to go out this way, and I knew of only a few small towns, strung together by farmland, that existed this far west.

I'd have to call Mick eventually, but decided to wait until I'd decided what I was doing. That was when I remembered the call from Detective Hedges. I pulled over again and retrieved his message. "Yeah, this is Detective Hedges. Just wanted to let you know that we had to release our suspect. His alibi checked out. So we're going to look at Landis. I'm not convinced he's a threat, but steer clear of him. And let me know if you do see him." I wondered if he knew how much sense that made. He finished with: "Give me a call as soon as you can."

Great. After giving it some thought, I decided to pretend I hadn't gotten the message. I needed to avoid both Landis and Hedges while I had this goat in my life.

We were just entering the outskirts of a little town called Bookman and I was wondering how far west I would go. We passed a couple of motels before I got to a gas station, a bar and a pottery shop. There was also the requisite diner and a convenience store. Not much else to do in Bookman. When I'd cleared the town I thought of the sign on one of those motels. I turned around and drove back through town. On the right was a long, low motel with a string of about eight rooms. On the lower half of the Wayside Inn sign were four lines of black, battered lettering that read: "Air conditioned. HBO SHO Videos. Hrly rates." But this little place was trying to be everything to everyone because the bottom line said: "SMALL PETS WEL-COME."

Behind me, Sassy stopped chewing. A pygmy goat was probably not what the owners of the Wayside Inn had in mind as a small pet, but I knew of an animal that would surely qualify that could, in a way, act as a cover. I accelerated out of town, driving east, back toward Fowler.

CHAPTER 18

Bix did his usual happy dance when I walked into my apartment. I'd left Sassy in the van, which I'd parked on Holden, a side street one block west. It was a street of mostly businesses and a couple small factories, so I hoped any bleating he did would go unnoticed. I didn't plan to be here long. I just needed to get out of these towels and into comfortable clothing, grab a few things for a night away and leave with Bix in tow.

I changed into a pair of jeans and a sleeveless top, threw on a hooded sweatshirt, tossed a change of underwear and some essentials, Bix's travel bowls and some dog food into a tote bag, and clipped Bix's leash onto his collar. When he started to snuffle around the floor for a few crumbs beside his dish, I decided I didn't have time for his dithering and scooped him into my arms. Then I stepped out the door and pulled it shut behind me.

"When Erika said you wanted to talk, I didn't think you'd be so scarce."

I clutched Bix so tight he yelped, and I looked up to see Jack Landis standing on the top step leading to my tiny porch. I loosened my grip on Bix, and he began to squirm.

"Now's not a good time," I said, doubting he cared.

"Where you off to?" He climbed the final step so that he stood in front of me on the porch. The forty-watt bulb did a meager job of illuminating the area, and it cast shadows across Jack's face, burying his eyes so it was as if he watched me from two deep, black pits.

"I've got some errands to run," I told him.

He snorted a laugh. "At ten thirty?"

Just then the phone in my sweatshirt pocket vibrated. But it wasn't completely silent and in the stillness between us here on the porch, the faint buzz was audible. It had to be Mick.

"Why don't you get that later," Jack said as he stepped closer to me.

He wore a T-shirt and jeans and his arms were folded over his chest. I couldn't see any weapons on him, but he was a good deal larger than me and those muscles I'd admired earlier weren't nearly so appealing now.

"I want the letter back," I told him, hoping he wouldn't think I knew about anything else. "I don't know what it is to you, but I do know it means a lot more to my mother."

I saw him nod. Now he raised one hand to his mouth and began to pull at his lower lip as though giving this some thought. "Yeah, I'll bet," he said.

Gone was the affable charm he'd exhibited the other day. The icy tinge his voice had taken on was probably more natural for him. I could imagine him taking those huge hands and wrapping them around Mary Waltner's—or my—neck. And while I was scared, I was also angry. I hate bullies. I drew in a deep breath and pulled myself up. Bix stopped his squirming.

"You're some nice guy, aren't you? Finagle your way into an old lady's room and then steal something that has no monetary value, but is priceless to her. If you're looking for extortion money—" I nearly choked on that word "—you've come to the wrong person. I have no money."

"You're sure about that?" Then he chuckled and added, "Your mother's an interesting lady. A little too trusting, though, don't you think?"

"You'd better stay away from her."

But he went on as though I hadn't spoken, "Especially when there's a nice-looking man involved ..."

"There you go again. Being modest." I shifted Bix in my arms. Even a little dog can start to get heavy. "Okay, Landis, just what is it that you want?"

He took a step back and leaned his butt against the railing. "So you're prepared to make a trade?"

"For what?"

His face was no longer in shadow, but the yellow light didn't do much to soften his features. He wasn't blocking the stairs anymore, but he could still keep me from getting past him.

"You're a pretty bright woman, Robyn. But a lousy actress. You don't play stupid very well."

He seemed convinced that I knew what he was talking about, so I decided I'd let him keep thinking that. Eventually, I might be able to figure what the hell he was talking about. "Okay," I said. "Maybe we can deal."

"Now you're talking." He eyed me and the tote bag and purse that hung from one shoulder. "You got it with you?"

"Of course not," I said, and added, "you just said I wasn't stupid."

He nodded.

"I'll have to go in and get it."

"Fine. I'll go with you."

"Let's see the letter first."

He studied me for a moment and then pulled a folded piece of paper from his back pocket. After unfolding it, he held it up for me to see. I had a chance to read only the first line, which said: "My Dearest Elizabeth." Then he snatched it away and stuffed it back into his pocket. I wanted to tell him to be careful with it.

"Okay?"

I nodded once.

He jerked his head toward the door. "Let's go."

I knew once I let him into my place only one of us was coming out alive. And the smart money was on the one with the bulging biceps. So this was my only shot.

He pushed himself away from the rail and stood over me, waiting.

"Here," I said, "you hold him while I get my key." Before he could protest, I handed Bix to him. Landis raised his hands, probably as a reflex, either to take Bix or to fend him off, and once Bix saw those flailing hands his head shot out like a viper's and his jaws clamped down on the little finger of Landis's left hand.

"Shit!" Landis pulled his hand back at the same time I retracted Bix who, after giving the finger a good shake, released him. Landis fell back against the rail, grabbing at it to keep from going over.

I clutched Bix to my chest and tore down the steps. With a dog in one arm and my two bags hanging from the crook of my other, I bounced off either rail most of way down. But I made it.

As I cut through the cars in the small lot and headed toward the bank's drive-up window, I could hear Landis coming down the steps. I had maybe twenty feet on him. Then I heard a crunch and a loud thud and Landis swore. I allowed myself a glance over one shoulder and saw him sprawled at the bottom of the steps. But he was still moving.

I cut through the drive-up window lane. Once I got to the sidewalk, I considered running the opposite direction, to throw Landis off, but knew I didn't have the time to lose him or the energy to outrun him. As I rounded the corner onto the street where I'd parked the van, I saw Landis coming out of the bank lot and heading my way. I had a half block to run and a key to dig out of my handbag before he caught up with me. If there'd been houses in the area, I might have run up to one and pounded on the door. But I'd carefully chosen a place without residences to park the van.

Sassy had been silent as I'd approached the van, but now he took up his bleating again. One doggie downer hadn't done much for this goat. I set—dropped—Bix to the ground and began dredging my handbag. Why do our mothers always chime in at a time like this? I could hear her: "Robyn, a place for everything and everything in it's place." And her new adage: "Robyn, if you had a compartment for your car keys you wouldn't have been bludgeoned to death."

Landis was closing in on me—slowed by a slight limp—as my hand found the smooth, plastic key holder. I jammed my thumb on the lock button, threw open the door, hoisted my bags and Bix onto the passenger seat and had the key in the ignition as I was slamming the door. Jack Landis filled my side-view mirror as I pulled away. He ran after me for about fifty feet, but didn't follow me around a corner. I'd turned west even though I planned to head directly over to Dryden, hoping that would throw him off. Maybe he'd look for me in that direction. He might have gotten my license plate, but he wouldn't be looking for me out in Bookman.

I drove around several blocks before heading back toward Main Street. During that time Sassy was hollering his little horned head off, and Bix had joined in the chorus with incessant yapping while he tried to climb into the back. I didn't want to open the windows, so I cranked up the air conditioning. As I neared the intersection, a car pulled off a side street and headed in my direction. I wished I knew what kind of car Landis drove. But I knew he wasn't the kind of guy who gave up easily, and so I had to believe he was driving around looking for me.

Once I got to Main Street I turned right. Although I needed to head the other direction, there was just enough traffic to keep me from making a left. In my rearview mirror I saw the other car make a right. Could be coincidence, but I had to assume it wasn't. At the next opportunity I made a sharp left, earning myself an unfriendly gesture from the guy I'd cut in front of, and then I headed back west at the next block. No one seemed to be following me as I made for Dryden. I considered calling Dryden, but there would be no one at the desk now and the place would be all locked down. By the time I got one of the nurses on the phone, I'd be there already. Besides, my cell phone was in my purse, and I'd have to pull over to find it. I can't multitask in a car.

I kept off the major streets and drove a mile or two under the speed limit. This went against my inclination, seeing as I figured I might be in a race with Landis to get to Dryden. But I couldn't risk being pulled over. I didn't know how I'd explain Sassy to a cop. I could try telling him that the goat was being used for a production of an Albee play, but even if he bought it, he wasn't going to forget a black goat with a crescent moon around its belly. Mick had insisted that Bull would not go to the police with this, but I wasn't so sure.

Dryden's parking lot was quiet when I pulled in and took a place in the residents' area. The trip had taken less than fifteen minutes and during that time, the boys had quieted down, Bix taking refuge on the floor in the front. I cracked the windows. "I'll be back in ten minutes and I don't want you two annoying each other."

Before I went in there, I needed to take the time to call Mick. First I checked the message he'd left me.

"It's me. Where are you? Call me." He sounded more concerned than annoyed, and I hoped once we finished our conversation, he would continue to think kindly toward me.

I hadn't rehearsed what I was going to say to Mick, and there was no time to write a script. So I just hit the speed dial number.

"Yeah," he answered.

"It's me. Are you alone?"

"I'll call you right back." He disconnected.

I waited almost a minute, and had just about decided that "right back" could mean anywhere from one to fifteen minutes, which I didn't have, when the phone jiggled in my hand.

"Where are you?" he asked.

"I'm with my mom," I said.

"Everything go okay at Meyer's?"

I didn't want to lie, and it took me a second or two to figure out that I could answer this without lying and without telling him the truth. "Yes," I said.

He sighed his relief, and I felt a stab of guilt.

I hurried on before he could question me further. "Is it time for me to call Bull?"

"Yeah. He doesn't know the goat's gone yet. Let him know. Then tell him you'll call him back. Remember how we rehearsed it?"

"Of course I do." I wasn't driving around in a third-rate acting company's van for no good reason.

"Call me."

"I will."

I disconnected the call, plugged in my voice changer, pulled in a deep breath and hit speed dial #2. Although I'd committed Bull's number to memory, I didn't trust myself to dial it. I mean, what if I were to misdial and wound up telling some insurance salesman in Topeka that I'd stolen his goat?

As I listened to it ring, I had another one of my absurd moments. Here I was, sitting in the parking lot outside of Dryden Manor making my very first extortion call.

Bull answered on the third ring, barking a "yeah" into the phone.

"Mr. Severn?" I read from my cheat sheet.

"Yeah?"

"I have your goat." I wondered what I sounded like to him. Mean, I hoped.

A pause. "What're you talking about?"

"I have Blood's goat."

"The hell you do."

"Then where is he?"

"I don't know." Another pause. "He's around somewhere."

"Why don't you check on that, Mr. Severn? I'll call you back in fifteen minutes." I disconnected, knowing it would be longer. But Mick had said it wouldn't hurt to make Bull wait.

I had just about enough time to collect my mother.

It was after hours at Dryden, so I had to be buzzed in. While there was no reason I couldn't take my mother off the premises at any time, it was not something I'd ever done at eleven p.m., and I knew I'd need a good excuse—or at least a reasonable one.

Why I thought my mother would be safer with me and the boys, I wasn't sure. But Landis had gotten into her room once before. He might have a tough time gaining access at night, when the place was locked down, but there was always tomorrow. And tomorrow I couldn't be around. I had to have her with me. Even as I was running afoul of the law.

I was buzzed in by a nurse I knew only by sight. She wasn't the one who usually called me when my mother was having a bad night. For this I was relieved. I'd come to learn that the better I knew someone, the harder it was for me to lie to her.

The nurse was a short, thick woman with harsh red hair and severe bangs. Her black and white badge read Meg Savoy.

"I'm Robyn Guthrie," I told her. "I'm here to take my mother out for the evening."

She looked as though she hadn't heard me correctly.

"I'll need to sign her out," I prompted.

"Is there something wrong?"

"No." *Wrong? How could anything be wrong?* "I want to take her to see an old friend in Ohio tomorrow. We're getting an early start." I shrugged. "I meant to get over here sooner, but it's been kind of a crazy night."

She regarded me for a moment, her hands clasped in front of her. "Did you tell anyone about this?"

"I didn't think I had to." I held her gaze. "I *am* her daughter."

"Of course," she said, sounding none too convinced. "I'll have to get her meds together."

"Thank you."

We traveled up the elevator together in silence, but I could feel her eyes on me. When the doors opened, she said, "I'm sorry, Miss Guthrie, but I'm going to have to ask to see an ID."

"Sure," I said. If an ID check was all it took to keep her from giving me the hairy eyeball, then I welcomed it. I dug my wallet from my purse and showed her my driver's license.

After giving it a thorough scanning, I could see some of the tension leave her shoulders. "Thank you. You do understand, I—"

"It's okay. Really. I'm glad you do check."

"I'll bring the meds down to her room."

I thanked her and hurried down the hall.

My mother was up watching television. When she saw me at the door she looked stunned and then alarmed. "What's wrong? What's happened?"

"Nothing, Mom." I walked past her into the room and dug an overnight bag out of her closet. "We're going for a little trip."

She sat there in the pink flannel nightgown I'd given her, her feet encased in blue fuzzy slippers. She didn't respond, nor did her expression change.

"It'll be fun." I packed her toothbrush, cold cream and hairbrush. I figured if I kept moving, acting like I knew what I was doing, she wouldn't start with the questions.

"Robyn?"

It was as though she wasn't sure who I was. I stopped packing and walked over to her. "It's me, Mom. Robyn. You always say you'd like to get away from here for a while. Well, that's what we're going to do."

"I'm not sure," she said, starting to whimper a little. "Did you tell them?"

"Of course I did. I'll have to sign you out."

"My room. Will they give my room away?"

"No, they won't." I have her hand a squeeze. "I'll bring you back tomorrow."

As I tossed her underwear into the bag, I realized it was past time to buy her some new ones. Why didn't I ever think to go shopping with her? I folded up a navy blue sweat suit and a yellow knit shirt I didn't recognize.

"Do I have to put that on?"

"No, no. You keep your nightie on," I said as I helped her into her flannel robe. "We'll just go to bed when we get … there. You'll be that much ahead of me."

"Robyn," she began, bending to accept the sleeve. "I don't know about this."

"Sure you do, Mom. You like adventures. Remember?"

There was a soft rapping at the door and Savoy stuck her head in.

"Lizzie," she said, coming into the room. "I hear you're going to visit an old friend in Ohio. Who would that be?"

My mother looked at her as if she had begun speaking in tongues.

"Are you feeling up to a long ride?"

Again, that look of complete disconnect. I patted her shoulder. "It's okay, Mom." To the nurse I said, "She sometimes gets confused in the evening."

"We know," she said, sounding rather sharp. "That's why I'm a little concerned with you taking her out tonight. Why don't you wait until morning?"

"Like I said, we have to leave very early."

"What time? I'll have someone get her up and ready by then."

"Oh, no, thanks but that's okay. I've been promising her a night at my place."

My mother grabbed my wrist. "Robyn—"

"That's okay, Mom."

"Robbie?" Her whole face lit up. "Are you taking me to see Robbie?"

"Not exactly." Although that would have been the easy way out, I couldn't lie to her about Robbie. Not after seeing her face at the séance. "But it's someone you've been looking forward to seeing."

I got her cane and handed it to her. "It's going to be an adventure, Mom."

"An adventure?" I sensed a little excitement in her tone.

Nurse Savoy was giving both of us a dubious look.

"I need to sign her out now," I said.

I felt as though Savoy's odd little eyes were on me the whole way to the residents' lot.

"It's a lovely night, isn't it?" my mother said.

"It is. It really is pretty."

Still hunched over her cane, she looked up at me. "Robyn, you need to take more time with your hair. It looks a fright."

"I know, Mom."

Much to Bix's dismay, I moved him to the back of the van. There was plenty of room around Sassy's crate, but he ensconced himself in the corner farthest from it. Sassy was curled up in his hay, content for the time being.

"Where did you get this vehicle?" My mother asked as I helped her up into it. She wasn't used to that large a step, and I practically had to lift her onto the seat.

"A friend loaned it to me. My car's in the shop." The little lies had become so easy.

"You wait here for a minute, Mom. I need to make a quick phone call."

As I walked away I heard her mutter, "What is that smell, Robyn?"

I put about fifteen feet between the van and me, positioning myself under a maple tree so I wouldn't be standing out in the open, and punched in #2 again.

Bull answered on the first ring, unleashing some colorful language. I imagined his face turning red and bits of spittle hitting the phone. What he said in effect was that I'd better bring his goat back or I would be very, very sorry.

I let him finish and then, keeping my voice as calm and as even as my racing heart would allow, I read off my notes again. "If you want the goat back, it's going to cost you five hundred thousand dollars."

There was a silence I can only describe as stunned. "A half mil? Are you out of your mind? It's a fucking goat."

"It's *Blood's* 'fucking goat,'" I ad libbed. "And it's going to cost you five hundred grand to get him back." I waited for more cursing and when it didn't come, I said, "I'll call you at ten a.m. tomorrow to tell you where to bring the money." Now I could hear him sputtering. "If you follow instructions, you'll have him back by three." This was getting easier. Maybe I was feeding off his anger.

Then he stopped sputtering. "I don't know who you are, but you are not getting away with this. Nobody messes with me, and—"

"We'll see," I said, and disconnected, hoping I had sounded bolder than I felt. Now it was up to Mick to convince him it was worth the trade. I had to concede that, at this point, Mick had the tougher job. He'd have to deal with the raging Bull and work him at the same time.

Before I returned to the van, I switched phones and punched in Detective Hedges' number. As I'd hoped, I got his voice mail. "It's Robyn Guthrie. Jack Landis was at my apartment this evening. He wanted something he thinks I've got. I don't know what it is, but he's got me scared. That was about ten thirty. I'm taking my mother and staying out of town for the night. Talk to you later." I supposed he would call me.

When I got in the car, my mother said, "Robyn? Is that a goat in the back?"

"Yes. Yes it is. A pygmy goat." I turned to her. "But I could get in a lot of trouble for having this goat, so you've got to remember not to tell anyone about him. I hate to ask you to lie, but can you do this for me just once?"

"Are you in trouble, Robyn?" I could hear dry tears in her words.

"Not really. No. It's just something I need to do …" I trailed off.

"It's not for a cult or anything like that?"

I had to laugh. "No."

She sniffed. "Oh, well that's good."

Then she said, "Are we going to your place?"

"No. This is a little farther. Why don't you try to get some sleep?"

"All right." Then she said, "Did you bring my cigarettes?"

"I'll stop for some."

"See that you do."

CHAPTER 19

When we arrived at Wayside Inn, it was almost midnight. I figured I'd be waking up the proprietor, but that couldn't be helped. The light was still on and the "no" in "no vacancies" hadn't been lit. We were in luck.

I pulled up to the office door and turned off the van. My mother roused from her sleep long enough to tell me she was hungry, then tilted her head back and dropped off again. For that I was grateful. I went around to the back of the van and opened the door. Bix had fallen asleep, as had Sassy, and my dog didn't protest as I lifted him out of the van and tucked him under my arm.

The office door was open and the blinds clanked against the glass as I closed it behind me. The office consisted of a short counter with a closed door behind it and an area with two green frayed chairs with a small table between them. Against the wall was a Coke machine. At first all I could hear was its humming, but then I noticed the faint sounds of a TV show emanating from behind the door. I looked around for a bell to ring and, finding none, went around behind the counter and knocked on the door. I had to knock another time before I heard the TV being muted. Then, a moment later, the door opened and a tall, thin kid with dark eyes and hair poked his head out the door. Great, I thought. Of all the motels in all the world I get the one where Norman Bates works.

I pasted on a smile. "Hi, I need a room for the night."

He looked at me and then at Bix, then back at me. He couldn't have been much more than sixteen or seventeen. I wondered if his parents owned the place.

"You and your dog?"

"And my mother." I looked down at Bix. "The sign says you take small pets." I lifted him up. "I think he qualifies."

"Yeah," he said, then ran his hand through his hair and shut the door behind him. It occurred to me that he must have been asleep.

He eyed me again as he opened the registration book. "Sign in here." Bracing his hands against the counter, he said, "You from around here?"

"No. Wisconsin." I signed the book with an alias.

He turned the book around so he could read it. "Cindy Hutton." Then he looked up and smiled at me. "I'm Matt Cirico."

"Nice to meet you." I was about to ask how much, when he cocked his chin and studied me as though he'd seen me somewhere.

"Anybody ever tell you you look like that actress …" He stared down at the counter as though her name might be carved there. "… can't remember her name." He looked up again. "The one in the Star Wars movies."

"Carrie Fisher?" Who I look nothing like.

"No," he shook his head as though I had guessed badly. "The new ones."

"Oh." Of course. Not *my* generation's *Star Wars*, which I had seen countless times. I had perfected the art of sexual fantasy with Han Solo in the cockpit of the *Millennium Falcon*.

Matt persisted. "You know. She played Queen Amidala."

"Natalie Portman?"

"Yeah. Her."

Okay, I didn't look like her either. And I wanted to tell him to never assume a woman liked to hear that she resembled a woman fifteen years her junior. If anything, Natalie Portman resembled me.

He must have sensed my mood, because he quickly added, "In a way." He kept going. "The first movies were better."

"They were," I agreed, then nodded at the register. "How much?"

He told me, and I paid in cash.

"Is there any place around here that delivers pizza at this hour?"

"Uh," he furrowed his thick brows. "Yeah. Not sure how much longer. I can give them a call if you like."

"No, that's okay. Just tell me who I can call."

"It's no trouble."

It had taken me all this time to realize this kid liked older women. Whether they looked like Natalie Portman or not. I decided not to argue further. "Okay. Make it a medium thin crust half pepperoni and half mushroom and onion. Thank you."

I glanced behind him at the string of room keys.

"Can you put us in a room a ways from the office? My mother is quite elderly and she's a light sleeper."

He handed me the key to room eight, which he told me was the end unit.

As I left I asked him how long he thought it'd be on the pizza.

"Half hour."

"They'll deliver it to my room?"

"Sure."

"Thanks again."

My mother was still sleeping. I hoped she would continue to do so once I got her in the room. I'd wake her long enough for some pizza and then tuck her in for the night. But I knew she wasn't much for sleeping at night, so I was prepared for a long one.

I drove the van down to the room and parked it in a space on the side of the building, less obvious from the road. I decided to leave Sassy in the truck until after the pizza arrived. He was snoozing now. I hoped he didn't mind waking up and finding himself alone. If he did put up a fuss, being in the end unit, we'd be the first to hear.

I gave Bix the chance for a pit stop before taking him into the room. He was nearly too agitated to pee. He doesn't deal with change well.

The room had two twin beds, stained carpeting and smelled of cigarettes. It made me wonder if it had been cleaned since the ban took effect, but then I decided I didn't care. I'd stopped at an all-night grocery store for cigarettes and a lighter. I think my mother slept through that pause in our journey, but I was willing to bet that she would ask about them. Well, when she did, her smoking wouldn't change the room's ambiance. A Danish modern desk held a lamp with a permanently crooked shade, and a chair that resembled the two in the office, along with a small table wedged between the two beds, rounded out the furniture. But it was only for one night, and we would prevail.

I left Bix snuffling about and went to get my mother. She woke a little dazed, but when I told her pizza was on its way, she rallied. I deposited her on one of the beds, found a blanket in the closet and covered her with it. In a motel that rented by the hour, there was no way any of us—including Sassy—were letting our bodies touch these sheets.

"Where's the ash tray?"

I felt a stab of guilt sharp enough to make me gasp. Here I was, telling myself I was doing my best for my mother—keeping her in Dryden—and I was bribing her with cigarettes, the thing most responsible for her being there. My palette was running out of gray.

"You awake enough?"

"Of course I am."

I hunted for an ash tray and wasn't surprised to find one stashed under the bathroom sink. It was blue plastic and looked like a warped UFO. I gave it to her, along with the pack and some matches.

When I cracked open the window, she said, not without some sarcasm, "I'll blow the smoke in that direction."

In truth, I'd opened it because I wanted to hear if Sassy started to put up a fuss. But I said, "I'd appreciate that."

We were in for a long night. I sat on the bed nearest the door and after a moment, put my feet up on it. The headboard felt hard against my back, but I didn't move. It was good to just sit and breathe. I closed my eyes.

"Robyn?"

"Hmm?"

She didn't respond, so after a few moments I opened my eyes and looked at her. Twin streams of smoke exited her nostrils.

"Why am I here?" she asked. "Why do you have that goat?"

Bix, who had been traversing the room, nose to the ground, stopped and looked at me, almost as though he, too, wanted some answers.

I thought if I explained the situation with Jack Landis first, maybe I'd distract her from the goat, which was much, much more difficult to explain.

"Okay," I said. "You remember that letter that Robbie sent you?"

Her eyes widened. "Did you get it back?"

I shook my head. "Not yet." I swallowed. "That man who played guitar at Dryden—Jack Landis?"

She nodded.

Bix had gone back to his frenetic room inspection.

"He took the letter when he was in your room."

"I should have known."

"We both should have."

"But why?"

"I don't know. He's looking for something." I shook my head. "But whatever he was looking for wasn't in the letter, and he came back for it."

"To my place?"

"No. To my apartment."

"Did he do anything to you?"

"No, Mom. Nothing. But he thinks I know what that something is. And I don't. I was afraid he'd come and bother you again and, well, I'm convinced he can be a pretty nasty guy when he wants to be."

"I don't understand."

"What else did Mary Waltner give you?"

She shook her head. "I—I can't remember. Other than the letter." Her eyes softened at the mention of it, but then she focused again. "That's all I remember, Robyn. Just the letter. It was so—so much to take in."

I nodded. "Do you think there was some kind of code in the letter? Some message that only you would understand?"

"Well, I don't think so. It was a long time ago, Robyn. Unless it was something I was supposed to remember. Something that was special to the two of us. Oh, my. How could I forget such a thing?"

"Maybe that wasn't it," I said, sorry that I'd brought it up. "It's got to be something else."

I grabbed my handbag and dug out the envelope. I read the address to her. "Does that mean anything?"

"Of course not."

I nodded. Then I ran my thumb over the stamps. There were four of them: two two-cent stamps with red-headed woodpeckers on them, a ten-cent stamp with an eagle standing on a clock, and a twenty-four-cent stamp with an old-fashioned stunt plane. At least, I assumed it was a stunt plane, seeing as it was upside down.

"Did Robbie collect stamps?"

"Well, I don't remember. He did love old things. Maybe old stamps." Then she added, "But it's been a long time."

I needed a few minutes on the internet. I didn't have my computer with me, but I wondered if Matt down in the office might have one I could use. Maybe if I batted my Natalie Portman eyes at him he'd show me his laptop.

When I left our room, I stepped right into the start of a drunken argument between the man and woman staggering toward room number three. Something about his scuzzy friends. He had so much trouble getting the key in the lock that I didn't hold out much hope for their evening.

Matt was slumped over the counter drinking a soda when I walked in. He perked up when he saw me. "Hey," he said. "The room okay?"

"It's fine," I assured him. "Would you happen to have an internet connection I could access? Just for a few minutes." Then I added, "It's really important."

He shrugged and gave me a little smile. "Yeah, sure." He ducked into the dark room behind the counter and returned a moment later with a notebook computer, screen facing me. "It's wireless. Want me to sign you on to my account?"

"I'd really appreciate it."

He grinned as he logged onto the computer.

I pictured the stamp, which was in my back pocket along with the envelope it was adhered to, and typed in "stunt airplane postage stamp" and hit the return.

I scrolled down the page, looking for something about an upside down plane and a postage stamp. I tried Googling "upside down airplane postage stamp."

A few seconds later the page filled with sites. Bingo. I clicked on a promising hit and when the page assembled, there was the stamp. As I read the news story, my breathing slowed, and then the universe slowed, too. Even the chill that gripped my shoulders took its time creeping down my spine.

Matt said something, but I couldn't make it out.

Was it too late to take back the last four hours?

"You okay?"

I heard Matt that time.

With a nod, I severed the connection and closed the computer. "Thanks, a lot. Just something I needed to check out." I glanced at my watch. "Pizza ought to be here soon?"

"Sure. I told them to put a rush on it."

"Thanks." I managed a smile. "My mother isn't patient when it comes to pepperoni."

I walked back to our room, almost oblivious to the sounds coming from unit number three. I had my key in number eight's lock, when a firm hand on my shoulder nearly made my knees give way. I sensed it wasn't the pizza delivery guy.

"We weren't done yet, Robyn."

I looked over my shoulder and up at Jack Landis. Something hard dug into my spine. "Open the door."

I didn't see that I had a choice.

When we walked in, my mother looked up from the television. "Where's the pizza?"

Jack pushed me toward the bed and my mother scrunched out her cigarette. "What's going on?"

Bix had started barking, but was keeping his distance from Landis.

"Don't worry, Mom."

She drew the blanket up over her chest and ran flighty fingers through her hair.

"I've seen you before," she said to Jack, but Jack was watching me and, it seemed, Bix, who still wouldn't come within five feet of him.

"Shut that mutt up," he said.

I scooped up Bix and held him to my chest. Probably the only reason Landis hadn't killed my dog was because he didn't want to fire his gun. Bix started squirming, but I pulled him tighter.

Focusing on me, he said, "You know what I want." He paused. "Now, hand it over."

Actually, I did know what he wanted. Now I did. But I figured Jack was as clueless as I'd been up until a few minutes ago.

I decided to play with this and see where it went. "I want the letter," I said.

"You give me what I need, and you'll get the letter."

"Let's see it."

He pulled it from his pocket. It was a little rumpled, but my mother must have recognized it because I heard her breath catch. "Your turn," he said.

"It's in my handbag."

"Get it."

I set Bix on the bed. He jumped to the floor and scooted under it. I dug into my bag and pulled out my key ring. From this, I removed the key to my locker at the gym, slid it off the ring, handed it to Jack, and stuffed the keys into my pocket. He looked at it, turned it over a couple of times, then focused on me.

"It opens a storage unit on the east side of Fowler."

"What's in it?"

"Bearer bonds. Worth at least a half million."

"Really?" It was my mother. I pretended I hadn't heard her.

"Okay," he said, turning toward my mother. "Get up, Grandma."

My mother looked from me to Jack and back again, her mouth opening and closing a couple of times.

"You know what's going to happen to your mother if I don't find what I'm looking for."

Then he added, "And don't get any bright ideas about calling the police. If I get nervous, she's dead."

"Robyn?"

How could I have thought my mother would be safer with me than at Dryden?

I pulled the envelope from my pocket and dropped it on the bed. Without taking his eyes—or his gun—from me, Jack bent down to pick it up.

As he examined the front of the envelope, I said, "That stamp is from 1918. That upside down airplane is called an inverted Jenny. It's a mistake. One recently sold for more than a half million. I don't know what the other stamps are worth."

The smile came to him slowly, and when he started to nod, I knew he believed me. "That's more like it." He tucked it into his rear pocket.

I didn't have time to mourn the loss, because I was too busy wondering how he was going to kill us.

Jack cocked his chin. "What the hell's that?"

Sassy was awake. Faint bleats wafted in through the window.

I was thinking of how I could use that bleat to my benefit when a sharp rap on the door turned us into a tableau.

"Pizza."

"Just a sec," I said before Jack could silence me.

"Tell him to leave it by the door," Jack whispered.

"He's going to want money," I whispered back.

"Cindy?" That was when I realized Matt had brought the pizza.

"Just a sec," I said again and started to dig through my purse. I couldn't try anything and risk Jack firing that gun. Too many targets in this room were precious to me.

"Ask him how much," Jack said.

"How much?" I called.

"Seventeen thirty." Then he added, "I gave the guy a twenty."

Jack took a position behind the door, so that I could open it and hand Matt the money in exchange for the pizza. Matt would never know that a former date of mine was holding a gun on my mother.

I folded the bill into my palm, desperately trying to think of some way to tip off Matt. Finding none, I opened the door about a foot.

At that moment, Bix darted out from under the bed and bolted out the door. Sheer reflex drove me out after him. I didn't want him running out on the road or getting lost. Of course, I didn't want to leave my mother alone with a murderer, but that didn't come to me until I heard the door slam shut behind me. What had I done?

I grabbed Bix before he got past the parking lot. When I turned, I saw that Matt had followed me with the pizza. He was laughing a little, perhaps at the sight of Bix under my arm. The door was now locked, of course. So I knocked.

"Mom? Open the door please."

Nothing.

"Mom?"

Still nothing.

"Mother?"

Just as Matt asked if he should get the key, I heard a click and the knob turned. The door opened about three inches and I saw a narrow portion of my mother's face.

"Come out here, Mom."

She didn't move.

"Is that man with you?"

I reached in and gently drew my mother out onto the concrete slab, then stepped into an empty motel room. When I turned to my mother, she said, "He went to the bathroom."

"What's going on?" Matt said, attempting to take control. "I thought you said it was just your mom and the dog."

"We had an uninvited visitor." I walked into the room, past the twin beds and opened the bathroom door. Empty. And a window over the tub was wide open. Just then I heard a car ignition and tires spinning on gravel as they sought traction.

"Want me to call the cops?" Matt was saying.

"No. He's gone." Along with the stamp.

My mother came back in and lowered herself onto her bed, almost in slow motion, as though fighting off exhaustion.

I gave Matt the twenty. I wanted to give him a much larger tip, but my cash supply was running low. "Thanks for showing up when you did."

Stuffing the bill into his pocket, he looked around the room. Then he said, "Did you hear a sheep a minute ago? Could of sworn I heard a sheep."

I nodded toward Bix. "That's Bix. He's a herding dog."

Matt gave me an uncertain nod, then said, "Give me a call if you need anything, I'll be in the office."

"I will. Thanks again."

After Matt left, my mother leaned her head back against the pillow. I slumped onto the other bed.

"He never gave it to me," she said. "I think he was … distracted."

"We'll get it back." I didn't believe this any more than I believed we'd see the stamp again. But it was the only thing to say.

"Was that true what you said about the stamp?" she asked.

I didn't trust myself to speak, so I just nodded.

"Robbie left that to me."

She was looking down at her laced fingers.

"I guess he did."

"He loved me."

"He must have."

She sighed. "Thank goodness we don't need the money."

I just looked at her.

"Do we?"

"No, Mom. Not yet."

I opened the carton of pizza, peeled off a slice from the pepperoni side and gave it to my mother.

"I need to get Sassy now. I may be gone for a few minutes, Mom, but don't worry."

Fortunately, she was too taken with the pizza to complain about sharing a room with a goat. I watched her picking a slice of pepperoni off the cheese and popping it into her mouth. I had to get that letter back for her. At the same time, I wondered if it had ever occurred to her that I needed a letter too. One I'd never get. Knowing that my father, my real father, loved my mother enough to send her a valuable stamp after forty-five years felt good. I was glad to know that my mother had that kind of love in her life. But what did he think about me? *Did* he think about me? I guess I spent my life missing the wrong father, though truth be told I didn't miss him much. How could I? I never knew what it was like to have a father—Wyman wasn't much in that department—and even if my mother hadn't lied about him, I doubt I ever could have known Robbie Savage.

I pulled the door shut behind me and locked it. When I returned to the van, Sassy was awake and bleating. He must have gotten scared when he woke to find himself alone because when he saw me, he quieted down. I wasn't sure how I was going to do this. Finally, I decided to bring him into the room and come back for the crate where I hoped he'd spend the night. I wasn't sure how smelly goats were, and

I figured I'd blame any odd odors on Bix. He was small, but he could be potent.

I led Sassy out behind the motel, which edged up to a wooded area. I knew he wasn't housebroken, but I hoped maybe if we hung around long enough, he'd get the urge to relieve himself. I waited. Time really flies while waiting for a goat to pee, but I settled on the ground, and as I watched him nibble at the grass, I thought about where we would all be in twenty-four hours. And, although I tried to ignore it, this obnoxious voice in the back of my head kept reminding me that if I'd noticed the odd stamp sooner, none of this would be necessary. Sassy came over to me, looked at me with his disconcerting eyes and uttered a protracted "Whaaaaa." And again. "Whaaaaa." I had some pellets in my pocket, so I dug a few out and held them out to him. With the mouthy request, I expected him to gulp them down and then start yammering for more, but he ate what I offered him with dignified enthusiasm. I stroked his back and rubbed behind his ears. He lowered his eyelids and sighed. We were lucky that Sassy was an easy-going creature; I guess that was one reason he and Blood got along. He went back to grazing, jerking tufts of grass from the ground. And then finally, my patience—or lack thereof—was rewarded. Never thought I'd be so happy to watch a goat relieve itself.

When I led Sassy through the door, Bix started barking. Helluva time to get territorial.

My mother set her slice of pizza on the open carton. "That animal is not spending the night here."

"I'm afraid he has to, Mom." I patted his back. "He's clean. He's empty. He'll be in the crate." I sat next to her on the bed. "No one can know I've got him."

"You need to tell me what's going on, Robyn. I don't like this one bit. And why am I here?"

"I will, Mom." I would tell her something.

When I returned with the crate, Sassy was munching a slice of pizza and my mother was trying to shoo him away from the carton.

"Get away, you filthy thing."

Sassy jerked his head back, taking the slice with him. Bix, siding with my mother for the first time in his five years, stood on the bed next to her and barked at Sassy.

"Everybody, be quiet."

My mother's eyes widened, and Bix sat down and shut up.

"We need to get through this night. All of us. Together." My mother opened her mouth, no doubt to protest, but I cut her off. "There will be no discussion. We are here." I glanced at my watch. "It is almost one a.m. The night's almost over." I wished. "We need to do this. Please don't ask me any questions."

Neither my mother nor Bix interrupted as I set up the crate. Once I tossed a slice of pizza in, Sassy followed. I'd also brought some straw in for him. And now I filled the ice bucket with water and placed it in the crate.

"Robyn—"

"Please try to go to sleep." I wished I'd thought to bring some Grouse.

My mother sighed, and then she said, as though addressing no one in particular. "I just wanted a glass of wine."

"Yeah, that'd be nice."

"You don't have any?"

"No."

"Could we watch television?"

"Sure." I turned on the set and was lucky to find a John Wayne movie. *Sands of Iwo Jima.* He died in the end, but I hoped my mother would be asleep before then.

I looked over at her and the question just came out: "How long were you and my father together?"

"A year," she answered without taking her eyes off the TV.

"I must have been an unpleasant surprise."

She continued to stare at the TV, and I thought she'd chosen not to respond. But then she said, "You weren't a mistake," and added, "I thought if I were to become pregnant, he'd leave her."

I watched some actor in a commercial cheerfully gargle, then dip below the camera to spit. I guess I could see how after a year she might think that extreme measures were necessary. How different would our lives have been if he had left his wife? In a way, I was surprised she'd kept me. My mother has no pro-life leanings whatsoever.

"It wasn't your fault," she said, and I thought I understood then. If I'd been an accident, I might not be sitting here. But I wasn't—a bad move, perhaps, but not an accident. And so she had to deal with me. And, maybe she held out the hope that Robbie would come after her. When he finally did, it was too late.

I was mulling this over when, out of the blue, my mother said, "Why don't you think we ever got along?"

"I don't know." Maybe because you resented my intruding on your life. Even though I'd been invited.

"I think we may be too much alike."

I looked over at her and saw that she was serious. "How do you figure that?" I asked.

"Well, we're both rather self-centered."

Here I was sitting in a motel with my mother, my dog and a goat, biding my time until I could collect the ransom money, all so she wouldn't have to move out of Dryden. Words failed me.

She continued, "That must be why you won't let anyone into your life. Other that that dog." Who happened to be curled up at the foot of her bed. "You can't even make room for your mother."

"We tried it, Mom. It didn't work."

"We did?"

I nodded. It was possible that she remembered the time after her stint in the nursing home as a dream. A bad one. "You stayed with me for a few months. Remember?"

The haze of confusion lifted slightly and she nodded. "It might have been better if you'd had a larger place."

"It's what I had." The two-bedroom had been small. Even for one person.

"Well, once I get the money from that stamp, maybe I could buy a larger place for you."

A glance in her direction revealed that the suggestion had not been made to provoke me. She lay on her back, hands folded at her chest with her head propped up against the flimsy veneer headboard.

The room went silent then, and after a few minutes I realized she'd fallen asleep. Bix was scrunched up next to her leg and Sassy lay in his crate, watching me with his strange, amber eyes.

I stretched out on the other bed thinking I should have been relieved that my mother had decided to explore our personal relationship rather than interrogate me about our present situation. I looked over at her, taking a moment to marvel at the fact that she was asleep. I knew she often spent much of the night wandering the floor, chatting with the nurses or dozing off in a chair. But tonight, with a goat in her room and a dog at the end of her bed, she slept. Strange where you found comfort.

It was after one. I needed my strength for what was to come. I had to call Bull, but I would also place a call to Erika. I doubted I'd get hold of her. She and her brother were probably on a flight out of the country by now, with my mother's stamp and her letter in a carry-on bag. But I would call her. If only to hear the no-longer-in-use message.

I thought of the letter, saddened by its loss. I wanted to read it, to hear the voice of my father. Now I wouldn't get that chance.

I tried to decide if I did fit into my mother's "self-centered" frame, but I couldn't hold on to a thought anymore and was starting to doze off when my phone vibrated against my hip. This time it was Hedges. What could I tell him? I almost didn't answer, but then thought better of it. Didn't want him thinking I'd come to harm and have the Fowler PD looking for me.

"You okay?" was the first thing he said.

"Yeah, but I had another run-in with him."

"What happened?"

"I was worried about my mother and I took her to a motel. West of town. I guess he managed to follow us. As it turned out it wasn't the letter he wanted. It was the envelope. There's a stamp on it worth a lot of money. It's called an Inverted Jenny."

"And he's got it now?"

"Yeah," I sighed, then proceeded to explain what had happened, omitting any references to a goat.

"Where are you? I'll send someone out there."

"No, that's okay. My mother's sleeping now. I'm half asleep. He's gone. He's got what he wants. He won't be back. Maybe his sister knows where he is."

"We thought to question her," he said, sounding a little sarcastic. But when he added that I should call him in the morning, he sounded concerned again.

I promised him I would, wondering to myself if that would be before or after I called Bull with the drop-off instructions.

I closed my eyes hoping that even the wicked deserved what was left of a good night's sleep. But all I could think of was how Erika had known about the goat. Every path my mind took led me to the same conclusion: the woman really was psychic.

CHAPTER 20

It was true. The wicked really couldn't count on rest. I woke to a darkened, unfamiliar room, and it took until I dug my phone from my pocket for me to remember where I was. It took another moment to focus and when I did I saw Mick's home number glaring at me from the phone's display. Just above it, the time digits read 3:18.

"What's wrong?" I answered.

"Tell me you've got the goat," Mick said.

"Hold on." I didn't want to conduct this conversation with my mother in the room. My eyes had adjusted to the dim light and the shapes of her and Bix on the other bed. Sassy shifted in his cage, but didn't make a fuss. I shut myself in the small, yellow bathroom, lowered the toilet lid and took a seat. Then I pulled in a deep breath and said into the phone, "Okay, Mick. I can talk now. What were you saying?"

"Tell me you've got the goat," he repeated, sounding rather ominous.

I swallowed. "I have the goat."

"You do?"

"Yes, I do."

I heard him sigh—definitely a sigh of relief—and at first I felt my own tiny burst of relief. But then he said, "What the hell, Robyn? Why didn't you tell me?"

"What happened?"

"Right after I talked to you, Bull decided he's going to find another goat for Blood."

"That was really late."

"No shit. Dexter, Blood's trainer, remembered where we got Sassy, so he calls Meyer's place, talks to his brother, who says for us to come on out."

"In the middle of the night? With the drunken brother there?"

"You got that right. Imagine my surprise when we're looking over a barn full of goats and not one of them is Blood's goat."

I knew I would have to explain, but my next question was more urgent. "Did Bull find another goat?"

"He brought three back, but Blood'd have nothing to do with any of them."

"So we're still on. Right?"

I heard his intake of breath, and then all he said was, "Yeah."

I tried to spin it to my advantage. "It's a good thing Sassy wasn't there. I mean, weren't you relieved?"

"At first. Then I was worried. And then I got pissed." He breathed into the phone a couple of times. "You'd better start talking, Robyn. For starters, where are you?"

"I'm in a motel."

"Where's the goat?"

No use lying. "He's here with me."

"In a motel room?"

He didn't know half of it. "Yes."

"What the hell were you thinking?"

"Well, I couldn't take him to my apartment, so—"

"No. I mean what the hell were you thinking when you didn't take him to Meyer's?"

"Well, I wonder if it doesn't matter so much what the hell I was thinking, only that I was thinking. That I kept Sassy and—"

"Why? Why'd you keep the goat?"

He wasn't letting go of this. "Leaving him. It just didn't feel right."

"*It* didn't feel right or *I* didn't feel right?"

"It wasn't you. Not really. But the place was dark, you said Meyer's brother was a drunk. I didn't want to leave him with a drunk."

"It's a goat, Robyn. Not a two-year-old."

"And the coyotes. They target goats."

Nothing.

I blundered on. "And, you know, that's another thing. You never call the goat by its name. It's always 'the goat this, the goat that,' you never use Sassy's name. It's almost like you don't want to get real attached to him."

"Jesus, Robyn—"

"It's all those things combined."

All he said was, "What the hell?"

"Well, I'm under a little pressure here, Mick. I've never done anything illegal in my life." I was speaking in a harsh whisper, for fear that my mother might be awake, ear pressed to the door. "And ..." I considered telling him where I was and why but knew it would only add credence to Mick's diminishing opinion of me. So I cut to the finish: "And I am just about certain that there is no possible way I'm going to get through tomorrow without winding up dead or in jail. Something's going to go wrong." My eyes burned with tears, and I fought to keep them out of my voice. "I've got no control. And, to be honest, I guess I've wanted a little control."

"Well, congratulations. You got it now. And if that's the way you want to play it, then that's the way we'll play it." Then he said, "You figure out what you're going to do with the goat when you're supposed to be picking up the money."

"I thought I'd take him to Meyer's right before then."

"Yeah, well, that's not going to work now."

"Why not?"

"Think about it. I've just been there with Bull and Dexter. We all know that Blood's goat isn't there. If he shows up there tomorrow afternoon, it'll be a coincidence too hard to explain."

He was right. I sighed. "Can't you be just a little relieved that I did keep Sassy?"

"Not as relieved as I am pissed off."

I couldn't even imagine what he'd think if he knew I was sitting here, in a motel room, with my mother, the goat and my dog in the middle of a murder investigation. "I'm sorry, Mick."

"Yeah, sure," he said. "You made this mess, you fix it."

And then he was gone.

I sat there, on the chipped white toilet lid, pressing the phone to my cheek, and thinking how many ways I had screwed this up. If I wound up in jail or dead, it was my own fault.

I turned off the bathroom light and returned to the other room where I sat on the edge of my bed and let the whole mess wash over me. I could hear my mother breathing in the next bed. If we'd had the kind of relationship where we shared our problems, I might have woken her. I shook my head. No. This one had gone way past dire, and there was no explaining it. It had taken on a life of its own, and like some wild creature I thought I had under control, it had turned on me, and I could feel the heat of its breath on my neck.

Goats wake early. I was roused from a muddy sleep to a steady, clanging sound followed shortly by bleating. And then there was the smell. Apparently Sassy didn't mind soiling his own bed. Or, maybe that's why he was putting up a fuss now.

I'd slept in my clothes and felt rumpled and grubby as I lowered my feet to the floor. My back screamed from a short night spent in a lumpy bed, but that would pass. It was time to tend to the livestock.

The clanging sound had been Sassy's horns banging up against the side of his crate.

"You'd like to go out, wouldn't you?" I kept my voice down. Bix raised a sleepy head, and then lowered it again. His little body was thrust up against my mother's back, and she was snoring.

I didn't know what to expect in terms of goat dung, and was relieved to find small, dark pellets that I was able to clean up with toilet paper and flush. I wished I'd thought to bring air freshener.

My watch said it was going on six. If Sassy needed some outdoor time, this was our opportunity. I decided to let my mother sleep, hoping she wouldn't wake to find me gone and panic.

I took Sassy out behind the motel again. The morning was cool, but the air heavy, as though the clouds were storing up the rain for some major downfall. While Sassy munched, I thought about what I'd do with him now. I didn't want to sneak him out of the motel in broad daylight, which was when I'd have to move him. I could take my mother back to Dryden—clearly she was no worse off there than with me—and Bix could go home. So it'd just be Sassy and me driving around in a white van, waiting. And then I still had to pick up the money. I'd have to leave him at the motel, because Mick was right about moving Sassy back to the farm. Too big a coincidence. I'd give him a double dose of Bix's downers, since the one I'd given him yesterday had little effect. I hoped that Mick, having some time to cool off, would not leave me hanging. However, as I replayed our conversation in my head, nothing that he said made me think that a change of heart was coming any time soon.

When we returned to the room, my mother was awake and eating a slice of leftover pizza. It had spent the night on top of the air conditioner, so I hoped it wouldn't hurt her.

"Robyn, when are you going to tell me why that goat is here?"

"It's a really long story, Mother." I sat on the edge of the bed I'd slept in.

"Well, we would appear to have some time." She gave me a look. "Unless, of course, you want to leave early so I can see that long-lost relative of mine."

"Mom, the less you know, the better off you'll be. But I'm doing this for us. I'm just asking you to trust me."

"Well, then why can't I ask you to trust me?"

I sighed. "When this is over, I'll explain." Maybe by then I'd have time to think of something that didn't involve kidnapping and extortion.

Her expression didn't soften, and so I said, "How about I get us some coffee?"

She gave me a look that implied she knew what I was doing, but then she said, "Coffee would be nice. Perhaps a donut."

"Good idea."

But then when I looked for my handbag, it wasn't on top of the dresser. Had I moved it? I stood in the middle of the room and did a three-sixty, scanning the furniture, the floor. I checked in the bathroom.

"Did you see my purse, Mom?"

"Why, no," she said, tucking her brow. "Was it on that dresser?"

"Yes." I didn't know where this was going yet, but already I didn't care for the direction.

"Well, that man last night—what was his name?"

"Jack."

"Yes, him. He took something off the dresser."

My purse.

"Oh, shit," I said, crumpling to the floor.

"Oh, Robyn, I'm sorry. I didn't realize. Until just now." Her voice tightened.

"It's not your fault, Mom."

"What was in it?"

"Everything," I managed. "Everything."

"Oh, I'm so sorry. Why do I foul everything up?"

"It's not your fault," I said, straining to keep my voice even.

I pushed myself up from the floor and took stock. My keys weren't in my purse, so I had them. I had my own cell phone. But the "extortion phone" and the voice changer were in my purse. Along with my money and credit cards. Perfect.

"Do you have any money, Mom?" I knew the "sofa money" was a myth, but figured she probably did have a stash.

"Well," she said, drawing it out. "I do have a few dollars."

It turned out to be almost fifty dollars. I had no idea how she'd gotten it, and I didn't want to know.

As I thrust it into my pocket, she was giving me her look.

"Mom, I have no money. No credit cards." But it wasn't until I said, "I promise I'll pay you back," that she relented.

I took the van and found a convenience store where I bought some yoghurt and donuts and a bag of chips. I also bought three large cups of coffee. As luck would have it, there was a public phone at the gas station next door. It wasn't my extortion phone, but it wasn't my personal phone either.

Before I drove back to the motel, I tried calling Mick from my cell phone. His answering machine kicked in on the fourth ring. "Mick, it's Robyn. Call me. Please."

While my mother was munching on a donut, I went to the office where I found Matt stretched out in one of the chairs with his notebook computer on his lap.

He sat up when I walked in. "Hey, Cindy. How's it going?"

"Good." I handed him one of the coffees I'd bought. "Sorry for the commotion. Thought you might need this."

"Thanks." He set his computer on a low table. "Sleep okay? I mean after that guy left."

"Yeah." I gave a half shrug. "An old boyfriend."

Matt nodded. "That's what I figured." He removed the coffee's lid and blew the steam off the top before taking a sip.

I sat in the other chair, holding my cup between by hands. With a yawn, I said, "My mom is a little tired from the commotion. I think we're going to stay another night."

"Sure," he said, "not like we're booked."

"I'll need to run out in a little while for a couple of hours. But my mom really needs her rest. If I put up the 'Do Not Disturb' sign, can I count on the cleaning people not bothering her?"

"No problem," he said. "I'll talk to Anita."

"If you need to get in touch with me, here's my cell number." I scribbled it on a slip of paper. "I'm sure you won't need it, but just in case."

"Sure," he said, taking the paper.

"I appreciate it." I gave him a smile I hoped would remind him of Queen What's-Her-Name and make him feel inclined toward chivalry.

Before I returned to our room, I called my home voicemail and found a couple of messages. One was from Detective Hedges, before he tried my cell phone. The other was from Erika asking me to call her. It was important. I had planned to talk to her, but that wouldn't be possible this morning. Not that it mattered. I'd given up on the stamp. If it was going to be recovered, Hedges would have to do it. Erika could wait.

When I got back to the room I turned on the TV and my mother watched the *Today Show* and smoked while I fed Bix and changed the straw in the bottom of Sassy's cage. He nuzzled my ear as I bent to the task. I gave him a hug. Were all goats this sweet?

As I stuffed the soiled straw in the plastic bag I'd brought, I thought about calling Mick again. As much as he'd like to leave me hanging out to dry, he wouldn't. Or, rather, he couldn't. I was the one picking up the money, but he'd have to let me know who was delivering it. I wished I'd thought to ask him about that last night.

I left for the convenience store just before ten and placed the call at about five after. Without my magical voice changer, I would have to invoke my "Arnold" voice. I punched in Bull's phone number and settled back into my throat. As the phone rang, I went over the instructions in my head. Bull picked up on the third ring, and I said, "Have you got the money?"

"Not yet. I—I've made arrangements."

"One o'clock this afternoon."

"Listen—"

I had to wing it without my note cards. "No, you listen. At one p.m. bring the money to Phinny's Tap in Fowler at Seventh and Main. Put it in the wastebasket in the men's room and then leave. If all the money is there, I will call you within the hour to tell you where you'll find your goat."

"How do I know it's alive?"

"It is."

"Look, whoever you—"

"One p.m. Phinny's Tap. Don't be late."

I disconnected and let my throat relax. Less said the better. I didn't blame him for wanting to know if Sassy was okay, but there was literally no way to do that short of posing the goat with this morning's *Tribune*.

When I returned to the room, my mother hit the remote button that turned off the television. "I'd like some answers, Robyn."

I shook my head. "I told you I'd explain this all later."

"You're not supposed to have that creature, are you?"

I didn't respond.

"Did you steal it?"

"Steal a goat?" I tried to convey a mix of disbelief and amusement.

"You don't keep a goat in a bedroom if you're not trying to hide it. I may be somewhat senile, but I'm not stupid."

I just looked at her.

"Don't treat me like I am."

I nodded. "It's really complicated. And I think the less you know, the better."

Now she looked hurt. "You're afraid I'll run off at the mouth."

I shrugged. "You wouldn't do it on purpose."

She sighed deeply and took another cigarette out of the pack. "I hate this." It was as though she were speaking to herself. Then she said to me, "How long do we have to stay here?"

"We'll be gone before the end of the day," I said, grateful to have something I could tell her. "I'm going to have to leave you here with Bix and Sassy for a while. But when I get back, we'll leave."

She put the cigarette between her lips and pressed her thumb against the lighter's wheel. As she exhaled a stream of smoke, she said to me, "Are you going to leave my cigarettes here?"

"I can't."

She nodded. "Then I won't stay here." Now she looked at me. "Take me with you."

"I can't. It's—" I almost said "dangerous" then caught myself.

"Why not? Are you ashamed of me?"

"Of course not."

"Robyn, I don't know how I'll manage with these animals. And I don't know what you're doing, but I want to help." Then she added, as I knew she would, "You are using my money, aren't you?"

I wanted to tell her she could help by staying right here. A second option would be to take her back to Dryden before I went to the Wired Lizard, but I was running out of time. I still had to stop at my place to switch cars. And then, to my shame, I thought of how, should Bull happen to look inside the Lizard, we'd look like a mother and daughter sharing coffee and scones and not like the pathetic mastermind behind an extortion plot and her somewhat addled mother.

"Okay, Mom." I moved over to the bed to sit next to her. "But you've got to do what I tell you to do. We'll just be going out for coffee, but I really can't have you talking with people. I've got to be low-key about this."

"Coffee?"

I nodded. "And a pastry."

"All right."

"And I'll have to leave you alone for a few minutes. Just a few. Promise me you'll be okay?"

"Yes, dear."

This time I gave Sassy two of Bix's pills stuffed into a glazed donut. He weighed three times Bix. Why was this goat so—well—Sassy? Then I poured a little more food into Bix's dish, hung the "Do Not Disturb" sign on the outside of the door and walked my mother to the van.

CHAPTER 21

My disguise was subtle this time. I wore my hair pulled up and tucked under a Cubs cap, and an oversized T-shirt with jeans. Typical coffee shop wear.

I stopped at my apartment, swapping the van for my Honda. The white van was way too obvious a vehicle. I also grabbed a tote bag and threw a few items into it so it wouldn't look empty. Then I drove my mother over to the coffee shop. It was just before twelve when I pulled up in front. There were no parking spaces nearby, but I noticed one across the street a couple doors down from Phinny's. If I was lucky it would still be there when I drove around the block. But it would be bit of a walk for my mom, so I dropped her and her cane off in front of the shop and told her to wait while I parked the car.

"Just what is it we're doing here?" she asked for the umpteenth time.

"I have to meet someone. And, remember, if you're going to sit here with me, you've got to be patient. We may be here a while." And then I added before she could ask again, "And there's no smoking here."

She looked at me with her mouth pinched. "Of course, dear." She unzipped her purse and felt around in it, then assumed a panicky look before saying, "My money! What happened to my money?"

I leveled a cool look at her and said, "You loaned it to me. Remember?"

"Oh, yes," she said, zipping her purse, then looked at me and said, "Lucky for us I didn't get my purse stolen."

I could have reminded her that Jack would not have entered our lives had it not been for her past dalliances. But then, had it not been for those dalliances, I wouldn't be here.

The spot was still there when I circled the block, but after I pulled in and got out, I saw that my mother wasn't standing by the Lizard's entrance. My gut clutched with panic, and I ran across the middle of the street, dodging traffic and praying that in a fit of either obstinacy or impatience, she had gone in without me. When I yanked open the door I felt a rush of relief when I saw her tousled white hair and the navy sweatsuit. But it was short lived when I realized she was sitting at a table with Erika Starwise.

Shit.

I glanced at my watch. Twelve twenty-eight. Surely she'd be gone in thirty minutes. Whatever she had to say to me and my mother couldn't take that long. But when I approached the table and saw her chatting amiably with my recalcitrant mother, I had a bad feeling about the way the next hour would play out. I hadn't told my mother that Jack was Erika's brother, thinking she was already on information overload. But now I wished I had because she'd clearly taken to the woman. The fact that Erika Starwise was able to connect my mother with the love of her life no doubt had a lot to do with it.

When Erika saw me approaching the table, she rose and claimed an empty chair from another table, which she tucked under ours. Then she gestured for me to sit with them. As if I were the one intruding. I saw that both Erika and my mother had a cup of coffee and a scone, so I secured my usual—a large regular with no cream, steamed milk, sugar—no nothing.

As I waited for the barista to fill the cup, I glanced around. It was crowded, as I figured it would be, with only one other table empty. I didn't see anyone I knew—fortunately—and as I scanned the faces I had to admit to myself that if Bull had someone in here, I had no way of knowing which one of these coffee drinkers that might be. As I took the ceramic mug in my hand, I conceded that there was nothing to do but sit down with my mother and her psychic.

"Erika has something to tell us," my mother said as I scooted up to the table and tucked my tote bag underneath it.

Erika looked up from her mocha coffee and into my eyes. "That detective came to see me this morning."

Just then my cell phone thrummed against my hip. It was Mick.

"Just a second," I said to him. Then to Erika, "It's noisy in here. I'll be right back."

Fortunately, the women's room was open. Once I'd locked myself in there, I realized I had worked up a bit of anger toward Mick. If he wanted to get pissy regarding my goat judgment, then I'd give him some back.

"Bull's bringing the money," Mick told me.

"Will he be alone?" I leaned against the wall, feeling the cold metal of the toilet paper dispenser against the side of my right knee.

"Far as I know."

I wanted guarantees this was going to go smoothly. But I knew I wouldn't get them. "You're sure there won't be someone else there?"

"I don't think so. Unless he's doing it behind my back."

That was no comfort at all. Was this what it felt like when things started to spin out of control? Or had the spinning started last night and I was just catching up with it? I rested my head against the wall, fighting a sense of displacement.

"I think we should forget this, Mick."

Someone knocked on the restroom door. I ignored her.

"What're you talking about?"

"I don't think I can go through with this."

"Robyn, you have to."

"Actually, I don't." It wasn't too late to back out. Was it?

"Robyn," he said, lowering his voice, "we are an hour away from pulling this off. If you fuck this up, I'm ..." He trailed off.

The knock came again.

"Just a minute!" I said, raising my voice.

"What—" he started.

"I'm in the john and someone has to go."

"Pull it together, Robyn. You can do this."

I sank to the floor, my legs crossed beneath me. The tile felt damp and disgusting.

"All you have to do is wait for Bull to leave, go into the bar and collect the money. Don't—"

"Oh, no," I said. "Oh, shit."

"What?"

I put my hand to my forehead, which felt cool and damp. "I left the duffel in the car."

"Where's the car?"

"Just down from Phinny's."

"Then it's not a problem."

"I don't know, Mick."

"Robyn, you have to—" he began. His delivery was calm and quiet, but I thought I heard an implied threat.

Just then the woman knocked again. "Could you hurry?"

"Would you wait just a goddamned minute!" I screamed through the door.

Then I jumped up and started pacing the short length of the room. When I stopped in front of the sink I didn't recognize the wild, terrified eyes looking back at me. She scared me. I turned water on full blast and let loose: "And if I don't? What're you going to do, Mick? Kill me? Shoot my kneecaps out? Kidnap my mother? I am doing my best under really difficult circumstances. I have just—and I mean just—learned that I am the product of an affair my mother had with a married Hollywood producer who died and left her a stamp worth hundreds of thousands of dollars only neither of us realized that until it was too late." I splashed my face with cold water. "The guy who stole my purse also stole the stamp. I think he also killed someone. And now I'm sitting in this coffee shop with my mother and the killer's psychic sister, and I'm ready to shoot out my own kneecaps." I stopped there. Fat tears rolled down my cheeks, cutting through the dripping water, and I did not want him to hear them in my voice.

For a few moments I suffered through complete silence, pulling in deep breaths. I began to wonder if I'd been dropped. "Mick?" I said. "Are you there?"

"Shit, Robyn." Then, "Shit." And, finally, "Shit."

I waited.

"What the … psychics? Stamps? Hollywood producers? You got a UFO or some little green men to throw in the mix?"

"No." I swallowed, sensing I'd best let him work through this on his own.

After several long seconds, I heard his sigh. "Why didn't you tell me this, Robyn?" The anger was gone.

"I didn't think it was all going to come toppling down on me at the same moment." Then I said, "Maybe we should just forget this. I'll leave Sassy somewhere and call Bull."

"Robyn, he's about to drop a half million dollars in the men's room across the street from you. If you don't pick up the money, the guy who empties the trash will."

When I didn't respond, he kept going, "We're almost there."

She knocked again. "Please."

"I've gotta go," I said.

"Okay, Robyn, listen to me. The rest is easy." Then he said, "Can you do this without your mother and her psychic knowing what's going on?"

I pictured the two of them chatting over their lattes and scones. They didn't need me to stoke the conversation. Maybe this would work. No, I had to do better than that. I needed to get back to the place where I believed I might be able to do this. I set the phone on the sink and splashed more water on my face, stared back at the frightened woman and told her to grow a pair. Then I picked up the phone and said to Mick, "No problem."

I heard him sigh. "Okay, Bull's gonna be at Phinny's any minute now, so I gotta go. After you get the money, what're you going to do?"

He was testing me to make sure I hadn't completely melted down.

"I'm taking Sassy to the farm on the northwest corner of Route 75 and Hammond."

"And then what?"

"I'll call Bull and tell him."

"Right." Then, "Good luck."

Easy for him to say.

I wiped my face with a paper towel, then opened the door to a short, plump woman with spiky, red hair. She was glaring at me. I apologized. When she saw the look on my face and the phone in my hand, I said, "Bad breakup."

"No problem," she said after a few seconds.

When I returned to the table, my mother said, "Is everything all right, dear?"

"Fine, Mom." I took a sip of coffee, grateful I could keep the mug steady. The way my insides were jumping I wished the Lizard had a liquor license.

Fortunately, Erika had chosen a table near the window and my seat faced the street so I had a clear view of Phinny's.

In a matter of minutes I was going to have to leave my mother, probably in the care of Erika. I needed to know whether I could trust her.

I turned to her and said, "What did Detective Hedges want?"

"He came about Jack." She shook her head. "I did not know what he had planned, and I most certainly did not know that he might have killed that woman."

"Why were you helping him?"

She took her time answering, setting her mug down. "Jack is not my brother." Looking up at me, she said, "He is my ex-husband. We were married for less than a year."

Another member of the wow-was-this-a-bad-idea club. "I have an ex too, and if he tried to use me in a con I'd tell him to pound sand."

"Robyn," my mother scolded, "this isn't easy for her."

Without acknowledging my mother's defense, Erika said, "The rest is not important. Not right now. You need to listen to me."

My mother, divine judge of human character, touched my wrist. "Listen to her."

I chomped down on my tongue and waited.

"I did set up the séance so that you could be …" She seemed to be searching for the appropriate word.

"Manipulated?" I suggested.

"Yes. That is true." But then her tone softened as she continued. "But I did see your father." She looked at my mother and said, "Robbie." My mother gave her a fond smile.

"Right," I said.

"When your mother was with you that time, he was as clear and as real to me as your mother and you were."

Even as I said, "Sure, Erika," that crawly feeling slid down my back.

"I have a gift—if that's what you want to call it. You may choose to believe me or not."

I didn't know yet. "What's your point?"

Her gaze locked onto mine and held me there for a few seconds before releasing me. Then she said, "I see that you are in trouble right now."

My mother looked from me to Erika and back again. "What's this about, Robyn?"

"Nothing, Mother."

"Don't tell me—"

"I'd like to try to help you."

I sighed. I wanted to believe she was telling the truth. But even if she was, what the hell could she do for me except tell me I was driving off a cliff? And I knew that already.

Then she said, "I saw something again." She sipped from her coffee, and when she set the mug down she continued to stare into it.

"What?"

"Water. I saw water."

She looked up and her throat constricted, and I remembered how she had told me that her first image ever was of her sister drowning.

"Was someone in the water?" I asked.

"You were." Then she shook her head, as though confused. "But you were breathing."

"Underwater?"

"You were alive."

"What else?"

"Nothing." But she added, "These visions that I have, they're not always literal, you know. And they aren't always inevitable. It may be a warning."

I hoped she was right because I didn't plan to be anywhere near water today.

My phone buzzed again. This time I didn't recognize the number.

"Ms. Hutton?" The voice was young and sounded panicky.

I almost told him he had the wrong number, but then I remembered who Miss Hutton was—me—and knew that Matt Cirico was calling me, which could only mean trouble.

"Matt?"

"Yeah, I'm really sorry, Cindy. There wasn't anything I could do."

"What happened?'"

"That guy came back."

Oh, shit.

"Your old boyfriend."

"What happened? Are you okay?"

"Yeah. But he had a gun. I had to give him the key to your room."

"That's okay, Matt." But it really, really wasn't. "Did he—"

"He didn't take anything," he said before I could finish.

"You went in?"

"No. But I saw him leave." Then, "But maybe I should go in to see if your mom is okay."

"She's with me, Matt. She's fine. You don't need to go in. Really. He didn't find what he was looking for."

I heard him sigh. "You sure? I can check?"

"No. It's okay. Really. You've done enough. When did this happen?"

"Um," he paused. "It was a little while ago. I'm sorry." And he really sounded it. "I couldn't find the number you gave me. I—"

"It's okay, Matt. Really."

"You sure?"

"Absolutely," I said. "And thank you ... really, thank you for calling."

"Should I call the cops?"

"No. He won't be back. I promise." Then I said, "I'll be back in an hour or so. You've been great, Matt."

After disconnecting, I just sat there for a second, letting it all sink in. Thinking maybe I should call him back and tell him to check to see if there was still a goat and a dog in the room. Both alive and well. But once he saw Sassy—first in the room and then later featured on the news—I was sunk. What did Jack still want? He had the stamp. He had the letter. And for whatever it was worth, he had my handbag ... and its contents ...

... Oh, *shit*. My notes! If he'd looked through the purse he'd have found my extortion script. And it was obviously about extortion. Focus. I couldn't do anything about that right now, so—

Someone touched my arm. "Is the goat all right?" It was my mother.

I felt Erika watching me as I tried to silence my mother, too late, with a narrow-eyed look.

"The goat?" Erika said, leaning toward me, with a touch of smugness.

All I said was, "Erika, if you forget about the goat, I will forget that you helped set us up."

"Did the goat have a crescent moon across its belly?"

I didn't back away from her gaze. "Yes. It did."

"Then do you believe that I am who I say I am?"

I did. And it wasn't the psychic thing. Yes, I believed that. But, mainly, she was asking me, as a woman who had also suffered the consequences of a very, very, bad choice, to trust her. And I did.

I was about to say something—I'm not sure what—when I saw a Mercedes pull into a parking space in front of Phinny's Tap. I set my mug down. Bull Severn climbed out, looked around, his gaze skimming the Wired Lizard, and I knew exactly how a sparrow felt trying to blend into a bush as the hawk flies overhead. But he didn't hesitate. Once he looked around, he turned and walked into Phinny's. He carried a sports bag, which kind of fit with the shorts and T-shirt he wore.

"Robyn? Are you all right?" It was my mother.

"Yes. Yes, I'm fine."

I had to wait this out. I looked at Erika, who had followed my gaze out the window and across the street, and I nodded, then turned to my mother. "How's your scone?"

"It's got currants in it." She continued on about the pastry, almost as though she felt she was the one who had to keep the conversation going. Erika and I contributed, but mostly it was my mother, virtually tap dancing. She must have sensed the tension, and I have to admit I was surprised that she knew me that well.

Several minutes passed before Bull left Phinny's. I watched him get into his Mercedes and pull away, then I rose from my chair, gave my mother's hand a squeeze, and said, "I forgot something. I need to go to my car. Stay here." When she didn't respond, I repeated myself. "Promise to stay here."

Erika was looking out the window, trying to figure what I was up to, but she didn't question me.

"Of course. Where would I go?"

Then I said to Erika. "Would you stay here and watch my mother? I'll just be a minute."

"I can watch myself," my mother said, sitting up straight and doing a little shoulder toss.

"You know what a worrier I am, Mom."

"I will watch her," Erika said to me.

I left the Lizard and walked to the corner and across the street with the light. I thought about the call from Matt, trying to work through it. Jack had seen the goat, but he'd left it there. For whatever reason. Maybe he just didn't have the means to move it. And he knew it needed to be alive. I tried to reassure myself with this theory, but I wasn't easy to reassure.

I got into my Civic on the driver's side and reached into the backseat for my duffel. Feeling the stiff nylon straps in my grip gave me a little courage. I yanked it into the front seat and clutched it to my chest. Just as I swung my legs out of the car, the door to Phinny's flew open, and Jack Landis came running out with a backpack flung over his shoulder. I froze. Moments later another man came barreling out the door in pursuit. This guy was big and bald with a full beard. My brain told me to duck, but before it conveyed that message to the muscles required to do it, Jack saw me. And before I could react, he had the door on the passenger side open and a gun pointed at my head.

"Drive."

Prior to last night, I had never had a gun pointed at me before and, judging my response, I wasn't getting any more used to it. My voluntary actions shut down. I still breathed, my heart pounded like a jackhammer, and somewhere the blood must have been churning through my veins, but I could not move. Not until Jack pressed the gun to my temple and I felt the sting of the steel.

"Drive," he said again.

Outside the car, the bald guy was yanking at the door, which Jack had locked. Then he backed up a step and reached beneath his jacket. Just as I saw the glint of silver, Jack took the gun off of me long enough to fire it through the window. Glass exploded and someone grunted. Then the gun was back on me again. Its acrid smell filled my nostrils. I jammed the key into the ignition and found the gear.

"That's right," he said, "let's get out of town."

Without checking behind to see if I was backing into anyone, I jumped the car out of the space, jammed it into drive and floored it. Traffic had stopped—cars and pedestrians—and a small crowd had gathered outside of the Wired Lizard, but this all came to me in slow motion as we sped west out of Fowler.

I assumed someone was calling the police. Shots fired and a car speeding through red lights didn't happen every day in Fowler. And then there was my mother, alone in a coffee shop with a psychic and no money.

Jack directed me, telling me to drive down one street and up another. We had turned around completely and were taking side streets east. I tried to spot places I recognized—a Burger King, a Methodist church and Forster's Veterinary Clinic. Jack kept glancing behind us and shouting directions, holding the gun on me the whole time.

I prayed the police would intercept. Earlier, I'd seen the day ending with me either wealthy, dead or in jail, with heavy odds on the latter two. Right now, jail was starting to look better and better.

He had me turn left on Route 73 so we were heading north. It was a less traveled road and the next town was almost ten miles away. But then we jogged east and then north again and were on a two-lane highway that wound its way past farms and small areas of business. I recognized the road because sometimes I'd take my mother this way for a drive, and there was a bakery in a little strip of stores that made astonishing shortbread. I thought of my mother again and hoped that Erika was taking care of her. Had to believe it. They must have seen some of what went down, and my mother was probably a handful by now.

I guessed we'd keep going north while angling west, toward the less populated areas.

"You were there for the same reason I was," Jack said, shoving the backpack under the dashboard.

No point in arguing.

"How many people write a script for extortion?" He didn't wait for an answer. "You think I didn't know what those notes were about." He snorted. "Haven't had much practice at this, have you?"

I glanced at Jack and his gun.

"A half mil." He nudged the backpack with his foot, smiling and nodding like he'd actually earned the money.

We were about a mile from the strip mall with the bakery when Jack told me to turn left at the next light. Here I was unfamiliar with the territory, but I assumed the road would take us across the Crystal River so we'd have our choice of roads heading north.

"Are you planning to escape to Canada?" Which would be absurd, what with border security.

"Not until we stop at my motel room. Got a few things to pick up."

Not to mention a few things to get rid of—starting with me. "You don't honestly think you're going to get away with this, do you?"

"You'd better hope I do." And then he patted me on the shoulder. I wanted to smack him, but it wasn't smart to hit a guy with a gun.

We turned, and he looked back over his shoulder as I came to the Crystal. I flirted with the idea of taking the car off the bridge. The rail didn't look too sturdy, and I'd done an article on escaping from unpleasant situations such as dog attacks, avalanches and submerged cars. But the bridge was about fifteen feet above the river, and it wouldn't do me much good to know how to extricate myself from my Civic if the crash killed me.

Once over the bridge, he told me to turn right, which I did, and we were heading north again, this time on the west side of the Crystal.

Still intent on something behind us, Jack said, "You know anybody who owns a red Porsche?"

"I wish." It could be Mick, but I didn't dare hope.

"Speed up," he said.

"I'm already going ten over."

"You heard me."

I nudged it up another five miles and after a minute, Jack seemed to relax. He couldn't expect me to outrun a Porsche. I love my car, but its four cylinders didn't stand a chance.

For several miles we passed open fields and patchy wooded areas. Then a green and white sign told us we'd entered Eden and the population was 1539. Eden had some businesses lining the street, and I wondered what would happen if I were to crash into a parked car. But then I glanced at Jack and he wasn't getting careless with the gun. At one point he saw me looking, nodded and said, "That's right. I'm taking you with me." Then he added, "Watch your speed limit." I swallowed and slowed as we drove through town. We left the commercial area behind and passed a group of small homes with clever mailboxes at the end of each long drive. It all looked so cozy I nearly choked up. How stupid had I been to bet it all on this? Just past the homes we came upon a wooded area where the road followed the river as it bent west. As we came around the turn, I saw lights ahead of us and began to slow. About thirty feet down the road, two squad cars formed a blockade. In the distance, more flashing lights were headed this way. On the right was the river. I saw a bridge farther down and, beneath it, someone fishing from a small green boat. On the left the woods stood like a palisade with maybe six feet separating the trees from one of the squads. I tapped the brakes.

Jack swore. "Go for the patch by the woods," he said.

Police stood around the blockade with rifles pointed our way. Maybe I could steer through that patch and maybe I couldn't.

"Are you nuts?" I asked.

"Floor it!"

"No!"

He leaned over and hoisted his left leg over the console, stomping his foot on the accelerator. The car lunged forward. My surroundings blurred. I saw myself underwater and remembered Erika telling me I was breathing. I jerked the wheel to the right. The Civic bounced over a short stretch of grassy bank and then plunged into the river.

At first we floated. I heard muffled yells and what sounded like a small airplane.

"You stupid bitch." Jack swung at me. I didn't see the gun, but did see the bloody gash on his forehead.

I ducked and lunged at him as far as my seatbelt would allow, trying to avoid his flailing arms and a blow to the head. The stick shift jammed into my ribs as I tried to pin him against the door. My Civic wobbled, then tipped. Water gushed into the compartment through the broken window and we began to sink. I gulped, filling my lungs with air. I felt for the door, found it, but the power of the surge tore my grip from the handle. I grabbed for the steering wheel, trying to keep my sense of up and down. Jack kicked at me, and the car pitched to the right. Moments later, fully submerged, we hit bottom. The impact jerked me hard against my seatbelt. I could barely see, but we weren't far down. God, it was cold. I groped for the door handle again, found it, but it wouldn't budge. It was supposed to open. I fought the urge to open my mouth and scream. Think. Okay, the car was running, so the locks must still be engaged. Shit. I fumbled for the lock, but felt the window buttons first. I pushed down on the top two and reached for my window. It was moving. Slowly. My lungs burned. I kept one hand on the window button and with my other hand I fumbled with the safety belt release, cursing as it refused to disengage. No panicking. I gritted my teeth, tried again and it gave. As I propelled myself out of the seat and through the window, I looked back at the passenger side, but all I could make out in the murky dark was what looked like Jack's left foot jerking slowly in the water just above the gear shift.

Once out the window I was afraid to let go of the car; that article I wrote didn't include a strategy for getting out of the water. But I couldn't breathe, so I didn't have a choice. I released my grip, the world brightened as I rose, and I burst above the surface with a ragged gulp. I bobbed underwater again as the current tugged at me. But then someone had my arm and was pulling me out of the current. I kicked, trying to work with my rescuer, and then I felt something solid against my shoulder. I blinked my eyes open and saw a wall of green and then a voice commanding me to "Hold on to the side," and a pair of hands pulled me out of the water enough so I was able to grasp a hard edge. A moment later, I cleared my eyes and my head enough to realize I clung to a small boat and someone was helping me maintain my grip atop the bow.

But the current was powerful, and the lower half of me wanted to travel downstream. I tried to get my other hand up on the boat, but couldn't find the strength. Just as my secure arm started to give out, someone grabbed me around the waist. I almost fought it, thinking the current had grabbed me. But then a voice behind me said, "Let go. I've got you."

My mind still fought it. After all, I was holding on to a solid object, but the force behind me persisted. "Let go!" he repeated.

His urgency convinced me, and so I did. Then there were more arms wrapped around me, and when I felt for the rocky bottom, it was there. I stumbled, but whoever had hold of me lifted me out of the water and carried me several feet, setting me down on the grass. But he still held on.

I kept pulling in deep breaths, which turned to sobs, and then I let myself lean against whoever held me as someone else threw a blanket over my shoulders. And all I could think was, this never would have happened if I hadn't thought about stealing that goat. All this was my fault, and I deserved to be at the bottom of the river right now.

But I wasn't. And I could still be grateful.

I let myself be held, drawing strength from another body. And when I finally looked up, there was Mick. "That was you behind us," I said, still gasping for breath.

He pulled me closer.

"You okay?" I looked up and saw Hedges crouched in front of me. Did he always wear a sports jacket?

"Yeah." I nodded, then glanced back at the river. "What about him?"

With a wag of his chin in the direction of my sunken Civic, he said, "Somebody's going down there. Wouldn't hold out much hope. Or whatever you want to call it." He patted my shoulder. "You rest for a minute. Get some strength back. We'll need to ask you some questions." Then he stood and headed toward the cars still blocking the street.

I looked up at Mick.

He kissed my forehead but didn't say anything. That was okay. I had a few items we needed to cover.

"We need to talk," I said.

"I know."

"My mother. She's …" Despite the blanket, I was shaking and my breath was still coming in gasps.

"Is she at the coffee shop?" Mick prompted.

I nodded. God, I hoped she was. "She was with Erika."

"Sure. Who's Erika?"

"Our psychic," I said.

To my relief, he didn't pursue that. "How about I ask her to take your mom back to Dryden?"

I nodded again. She had seen me underwater. Surviving.

I felt his warm breath on my ear as he said, "Where's Sassy?"

"Wayside Inn in Bookman. Room eight. With Bix. "

"I got it."

There was more to tell him, but my thoughts were scrambled.

"The van?" he asked.

"Side street one block west of my place. Keys are under the seat."

"I got it covered. Anything else?"

I forced myself to focus and took a couple of slow, deep breaths. This part was important. "If Matt— the guy at the Inn—gives you any trouble, tell him Queen Amidala says it's okay."

"Am I supposed to know what that means?"

"Doesn't matter."

I rested my head against his shoulder. "Damn, I really needed that money."

"Don't worry about it." He kissed my forehead again. "It doesn't matter."

I didn't get to Dryden Manor until after seven when Detective Hedges dropped me off.

It had been a long afternoon. He'd offered to take me by my apartment so I could change into some dry clothes, but my key was with all my others in the ignition of the Civic and my extra set at my mom's. So we went straight to the Fowler Police Station where they found some sweats for me to change into. Then came the questions. And a few answers.

They treated me well, offering me food, soda, coffee, and I felt a little guilty. But my guilt couldn't even begin to compare to my relief when I learned that the guy Jack shot outside of the bar in Fowler was going to be okay, and that Jack Landis was not. When the car tipped toward the passenger side and sank, he'd been partway out the window and wound up pinned beneath the car. They'd brought Landis's body up but my Civic was still down there. No hurry.

Most of Hedges's questions involved Jack and what I knew about him. I did my best to cover for Erika but figured they'd have plenty of questions for her. When asked why I was parked near Phinny's Tap, I told them the truth. Sort of. Said I was having coffee with my mother and had gone to my car for her blood pressure medication, which was in her overnight bag, now at the bottom of the Crystal River.

Hedges seemed satisfied that they'd found Mary Waltner's killer. Not only did Mary and Jack have a history together in California, but a receptionist at the hotel where Mary had stayed identified a photo of Jack. He'd been seen with her in the lobby on the day she was killed.

When I asked how they'd found Jack and me, Hedges told me that Mick had seen it go down and had followed us out of town, contacted the police and kept them informed as to our route. "Mainly," Hedges said, "it was a matter of waiting until you stayed on one road long enough to set up a blockade."

I was surprised to learn that Mick worked with the cops so well.

At one point Hedges asked me if Jack had mentioned another person who might have been in on the goat heist with him. I could truthfully say "no."

Mainly, I hoped that after today the lies were over.

When I arrived at Dryden, Hedges pulled up in front of the building and said, "You'll be able to get home from here?"

"Sure. If not, I can always stay with my mom." I considered that for a few moments. "No, I'll find a way home."

"You got an extra set of keys?"

"In my mom's room."

He nodded his approval.

Then I asked, "Do you know if the goat was returned to Bull Severn?"

"Yeah. We got a call around four thirty. Found the goat in a pasture with a bunch of cows."

"Do you know who called?" I sure hoped he didn't.

"No. Could've been an accomplice. But the goat's photo had been on the news, so it also might have been someone who saw it there and didn't feel like leaving his name."

"That's good. That he's back where he belongs," I said, so relieved my fingers tingled. Then, "Severn never did call the police about the goat, did he?"

"Nope." He practically spat the word out. "First inkling we had was when shots were fired on Main Street."

"If he had, what would you have done?" I paused, searching for the words. "I mean, it was a goat."

"Yeah." He chuckled a little. "But there was a half million attached to it." He paused, tapping a finger against the steering wheel. "Hard to believe someone would come up with that kind of money for a goat."

"Must've been special," I said.

Before I got out of the car, he reached into his jacket pocket and pulled out a folded sheet of paper—the letter—and the envelope with the inverted Jenny stamp. "We checked out Landis's motel room.

These were there. The envelope was addressed to your mother. Clearly, Robert Savage wanted her to have them."

I took them and looked at the odd little stamp.

"What're you going to do with it?" Hedges asked.

"Sell it," I said, then glanced up at the door to Dryden. "This is an expensive place."

He nodded his understanding, but there was something else there, like maybe a question unasked. Fortunately, he left it that way.

I thanked him and got out of the car. On my way up in the elevator, I read my father's words; I saw his handwriting. The letter was sweet, sad and peppered with the guilt he must have carried with him for years. *If only I'd believed in our love the way I believed in the power of money.* It had the dying person's determination to atone for his perceived wrongs. *I can't get back those years, I can't ever set things right. But this letter is sealed with a kiss that I hope will bring you some comfort.* His love for my mother was in his words. And his sadness over never meeting me, well, that was there too. *I imagine she's like you, Lizzie, a beautiful, clever and tenacious woman.*

If he only knew.

I knocked on my mother's door, waited a brief moment, then opened it.

"Oh, Robyn." My mother pushed herself up from her recliner and did a fast shuffle toward me, her hands clasped at her chest.

As I wrapped my arms around her bony shoulders, she shook with dry sobs. I patted her back and rocked her slightly where I stood. That was when I saw Erika Starwise. She'd been sitting in the chair I usually occupy, and now she stood, reached for the television remote and lowered the volume on the TV. All I saw were blurs of color on the screen.

"Don't you ever do something foolish like that again," my mother said into my shoulder. "You could've been killed."

"I won't, Mom."

"Then what would have happened to me?"

Erika and I exchanged a smile.

"You're a survivor, Mom."

Erika picked up her purse. "I'm going to leave now, Lizzie."

My mother detached herself from me and took Erika's hand. "You're a dear, Erika. I don't know what I'd have done. What with Robyn leaving so suddenly."

I gazed heavenward.

"I was glad to be here," Erika said, giving my mother's hand a squeeze, then began moving toward the door, stopped, and said to me, "Do you need a ride home, Robyn?"

"Um, yes, I do. Yes. I'd appreciate that."

She gestured toward the door. "I'll wait outside."

Once she was gone, my mother said, "That woman is an angel. She sat with me this whole time. I didn't know what had become of you." I could hear the tears in her voice again.

"I know, Mom." I led her to her chair and helped lower her into it.

"The nurse offered me a pill to relax, but I didn't want to sleep. I needed to know that you were all right." She'd removed a tissue from her pocket and was kneading it in her hand.

"I am. I'm fine." I patted her knee. "Are you okay now?" I took a couple of steps back and sat on the edge of the rocker.

"Well, I'm somewhat better." She sort of trailed off with a sigh.

"We're going to be okay," I said.

She blinked once. "Well, of course we are."

I nodded. "Maybe you'd like that pill now?"

"Why, yes." She looked up at me. "Perhaps I would."

I got up. "I'll talk to the nurse when I leave."

"Thank you." Then, "Robyn, do you have my money?"

At first I thought she was talking about the stamp, and was about to tell her that I'd have to find a stamp dealer, but then I realized that, of course, she was talking about the fifty dollars—the "sofa money."

"I'll get it to you tomorrow. Okay?"

"Thank you," she said again. "I just don't like not having any cash."

"I understand."

She leaned back in her chair, sighing, and closed her eyes. After a moment she opened them again and said, "Are you leaving?"

"I'd better," I said, prepared to present my reasons, but that turned out to be unnecessary.

"Be sure to tell the nurse. About my pill."

"Yes, Mom. I will."

"Will I see you tomorrow?"

"You bet." I reached into my bag and pulled out the letter. "I've got something for you."

She took it, her slender hand shaking slightly. As her eyes rose to meet mine, I nodded. "It's Robbie's letter."

She tilted her head and blinked her eyes as she ran the pad of her thumb over the ink. "Thank you," she whispered.

"He really loved you."

"Yes. Yes, I think he did."

A moment later she asked, "Did you read the letter?"

"I did." And then I said, "That's how I know."

She looked up at me. "We—you and I—are alike, aren't we?"

I nodded with a sigh. "I'm afraid so."

She leaned back into the chair, still smiling.

I got up and gave her a kiss. And then as I turned to leave, she said, "Robyn," I looked back at her, "remember my pill."

"I will."

"She was very worried about you," Erika said as I closed the door behind me.

"I know. And thank you for taking her home and staying with her."

"It was no trouble."

After I alerted the nurse to my mother's needs, Erika and I walked out to the parking lot and got into her car. I told her where I lived and along the way I filled her in on what had happened, although she'd seen and heard most of it on television.

"Once your mother learned you were all right, she couldn't watch enough of it."

"I'll bet."

We rode in silence for several moments. Erika's demeanor was calm, but her insides must have been churning.

"What will you tell the police?" I asked.

After a moment she said, "I'll tell them the truth."

"What is the truth?"

As she turned onto Main Street, she held herself erect, with both hands on the wheel, at the ten and two positions, her knuckles sharp points of white. Now she flexed the fingers of her right hand, then tucked them around the wheel again.

She wet her lips and said, "Your father was one of my clients. Had been for many years. He wasn't a religious man, but he did believe in the afterlife. More so after he learned of his illness." She glanced at me. In his letter he had said he was dying, but wasn't specific. "He had colon cancer, and he knew he didn't have very much time. He wanted to meet you and to see your mother again before he died. I was helping him to determine a time to go. A time when the stars were right. He was very nervous about it, and he insisted the planets and stars be aligned just so."

"That's too bad." I felt her look at me. "If he hadn't insisted that he got the universal thumbs-up sign, I might have gotten to meet him." That made me angry.

"Perhaps," she said, then added, "I also think he was hoping he'd outlive his wife. He did, but not by much."

"So what was the plan?" I asked, then added, "And I still can't figure why you went along with it. What did Jack have on you?"

I heard her sigh. "Our daughter. He had our daughter. She was the *only* good thing to come of the marriage. At first Jack wanted nothing to do with her, and for that I was grateful. But Jack Landis doesn't leave until he's ready. Over the years he would appear now and then. I believe he did it just to prove he could and to remind me that I should never forget about him. As if I could. He'd threaten to go to court for partial custody of Holly. I would do anything to keep that from happening."

I recalled the photograph in Erika's office, and for a moment I envied the strength of that mother-to-daughter bond. I'd only experienced the daughter-to-mother end, and I supposed I'd never completely understand what drove my mother to carve out a fake history in order to protect me. And herself.

"Where is your daughter?" I asked.

"She's at school. In the east." Apparently Erika didn't want to elaborate, because the next thing I knew she was telling me what Jack did after learning that my father was one of her clients. "Jack couldn't see a wealthy man without finding a way to steal money from him. He found out who Robbie's lawyer was, and he started a relationship with her." She glanced at me. "He was good at that. After Robbie died, Mary told Jack she had to go to Illinois to finish his bequests. Although she wouldn't tell him what that was, I knew she was going to see your mother. Jack promised me if I were to help him with this one, final ... deception ... he would be out of my life forever."

"And you believed him?"

She glanced at me, then back at the road. "I wanted to. Badly."

That I could understand.

"You came to Fowler to see if you could find out what Mary was bringing to my mother."

"Yes." She shook her head. "I never dreamed Jack would kill over this. Never."

But once he crossed that line, he never looked back. "And since you didn't know what Mary was bringing to my mother, you needed to concoct that séance and your 'seeing' my father."

She didn't answer for several moments, as though testing her words. "The first séance was staged—although the women there thought it was real—but the second, with you and your mother, that was not. I did see Robbie."

I looked at her profile as she drove and considered whether I would choose to believe her. My father had. I still felt some anger. At her—if she'd told him to quit waiting for Venus to align with Mars and get his ass to Illinois, I'd have had the chance to meet him. On the other hand, he could have done that himself, and maybe as much as he thought he wanted to see us, it was easier to wait until it was too late. I sighed. "I wish I could have seen him."

"I'm sorry," she murmured. But then she added, "It was not meant to be."

I snorted in response, and she said, "You don't have to believe in my abilities, Robyn, but I'm surprised to find your mind so closed."

While I was mulling that over, she said, "Tell me. Why did you choose the river?"

"Water is softer than wood."

She glanced at me and nodded. "Of course."

And then I added, "Besides, you told me I'd grow gills."

I thought I saw a trace of smile, but it was almost dark so I couldn't be sure.

She pulled into the parking lot behind my building. The purple of dusk cast the cars in an eerie light.

"Are you going back to California?" I asked.

Turning toward me, she said, "Why do you care?"

"My mother will ask."

With a sigh, she leaned back in the seat and tilted her head up toward the sky. "I don't know. I may not have a choice. The authorities may want someone to answer for this mess, and even though Jack died, they may find me worth pursuing."

Feeling guilty and a bit chastened, I said, "Let me know if I can help."

She looked at me again, maybe a little surprised. "I'll be fine."

"Probably."

As I climbed out of the car, I said, "Thanks again for looking out for my mother."

"Your mother is a delightful woman."

"You know, some people tell me that."

As I began walking toward the steps leading to my apartment, it occurred to me that Mick had probably taken Bix home with him. I'd miss the critter's presence. But I told myself I should quit wishing for what wasn't and count my blessings—I was alive, I wasn't in jail, and the stamp would go a long way in taking care of my mother's needs.

I'd climbed two steps when I heard the sound of little claws clicking their way down the stairs. I looked up and saw a small shape wiggling its way toward me. "Hey, Bix!" I scooped him up and began climbing again as he slobbered kisses on my chin. And when I got to the top, there was Mick Hughes sitting in one of my lawn chairs, feet propped on the railing. He just smiled and said, "Welcome home."

As good as it was having Mick help pull me from the river, I wasn't sure how I felt about finding him on my porch. For now, a little distance might be good. When I looked at him, all I could think of was these last few days. It was a little like waking up after a night on the town. The light of day and the hangover combine, and the desire to erase the whole evening rolls over you like a tank. But first you've got to do something about that guy in bed next to you.

"How long have you been here?" I asked.

He lowered his feet to the porch and pushed himself up from the chair. "Let's see." He locked his fingers behind his neck and, took a good stretch and said, "Once I dropped Sassy off and got rid of the van, Bix and I stopped for a burger, then we came here." He shrugged. "Maybe an hour."

"Thanks for bringing him home."

I couldn't tell him to leave. Not now. So I let him follow me into my apartment. As I walked into the kitchen of my little home above the framing store, I realized that when I'd left it yesterday, I didn't think I'd be seeing it again for a long time. Maybe never. But now I just stood for a moment and enjoyed the assault on my senses: the faint smell of garlic, the hum of the refrigerator and the watercolor of Edinburgh's skyline above my café table.

And then Mick had me in his arms and was kissing me. The part of me that wanted to respond with gusto fought with my ambivalence. I didn't push him away, but neither did I give him much back.

"God, you had me scared," he said when he'd finished.

"I had me scared too."

"If you had …" he broke off.

Feeling the closeness in the room, I pushed up the arms of my sweatshirt. I didn't want to help him out.

"I think you oughta give up crime," he said. "Makes me too nervous."

I hesitated, but then said, "You should've thought of that before you decided I had to be the one to pick up the money."

He looked like I'd struck him.

"I need to change." I looked down at the my police-issue gray garb. "Will you make us a couple of drinks?"

He nodded. Bix followed me into my bedroom and jumped up on the bed while I took a quick shower and found some clean, comfortable clothing. He watched me as I pulled on some sweats and a T-shirt, as though afraid if he looked away he'd find I'd been replaced by a goat.

Mick had poured a nice, dark Grouse for me and helped himself to a Sam Adams. I sat on the couch with him, but not right next to him. With my feet propped on the coffee table, only inches from the singing bowl, I thought about all that had happened in just a few days. One week to a whole new you. The scotch was wonderful, and I took a couple of sips, concentrating on its peaty taste, the smooth glass, the click of the cubes against it.

"You okay?" Mick asked.

I glanced his way and saw he'd shifted so he faced me, with his back to the arm of the couch and his ankle propped on his knee.

"I will be," I said.

After another sip, I rested the glass on my thigh. "Earlier," I began, "you said it was okay about the money."

"I did."

"Did you mean it?"

He nodded and lowered his foot to the floor, then leaned toward me.

But before he could say anything, I continued, "If it wasn't about the money, what was it about? And why did you pretend it was the money?"

He sighed, looking up at the ceiling. Then, as though finding some answer there, he nodded once, turned to me and said, "Blood wasn't Bull's first horse. About two-and-a-half years ago he bought a two-year-old named Pay Dirt. Terrific animal. Bull raced him every chance he got. Raced him too much. Thoroughbreds, for all their size and heart, are fragile. Those skinny legs of theirs take a pounding. Bull didn't care what his trainer said. Didn't care what I said." He paused, and I saw some pain in his eyes. "And when Pay Dirt blew a bone in his leg and had to be destroyed, Bull blamed everyone but himself. The trainer quit. I should've." He took a drink from the bottle and leaned back again.

"Why didn't you tell me this before?"

He snorted. "Like you'd have believed I was doing it in memory of a horse."

He was right. Still, I had to work this through.

"What?" he said as though he knew where my thoughts were headed.

"I'm just trying to decide if I feel better about all this now." I turned toward him. "I mean, there were so many ways this could have gone wrong. What would've happened if I had gone into that bar to get the money? What if Jack had been in there? What if he hadn't, and

I had to face that big guy Bull had in there? What if he had died? What if I'd walked out of the men's room and found a dozen of Fowler's finest pointing guns at me?" I felt my eyes brimming, so I had to look away. "I don't do stuff like that." Mick opened his mouth as if to speak, but I wouldn't let him. "And I'm asking myself if I feel better knowing you weren't doing it for the money. You were striking a blow for equine …" I struggled for the right word and came up with "… justice."

I kept going. "But no matter how noble our motives—you with the horse and me with my mother—we still committed a crime. And that means we're no better—or not much better—than Bull." I pulled in a deep breath. "And I don't know why none of this occurred to me earlier. Or why it didn't matter earlier."

"Maybe because it was a little exciting."

I snorted and took another drink. "And to top it off, Bull lost nothing." Bix was curled up next to me, warm against my thigh. "I'm tired, Mick."

I felt him watching me, but I wouldn't look at him. Finally, he said, "You're going to the race with me tomorrow, aren't you?"

"Are you kidding?" Now I looked to see if he was serious. He was. Entirely. "How can I be in the same room with Bull after what happened?"

"Because you are not going to want to miss tomorrow."

He wasn't just talking about the race. "Why not?"

He shook his head. "Can't say. Trust me. One more time."

CHAPTER 22

The Plymouth Million was Illinois' version of the Kentucky Derby and the attendees dressed accordingly. Bull had reserved a suite at Plymouth for a few "close" friends. We'd be viewing the race two floors above the grandstand at the clubhouse turn. There would be food, drink and, depending on the race's outcome, potential revelry.

In my usual quandary as to what to wear, I eventually opted for the black and white halter dress I'd chickened out of the night I went to dinner with Mick, and I splashed it up a bit with a red shawl and black sandals with a small heel. Maybe I wasn't all that ambivalent about my relationship with Mick after all.

When Mick came to pick me up, I could tell from his raised eyebrows, not to mention the low whistle, that he approved. He'd cleaned up well too, wearing a pale, tweedy, silk sports jacket with threads of oak and mulberry running through it.

August had continued to sully its reputation as the beastly month by producing another incredible day—sunny, high seventies with a scattering of puffy white clouds, just to give the sky some depth. Weather reports had the temperature increasing daily until we hit ninety by the end of the next week. But, for now, the humidity was low and my hair was behaving.

We didn't talk much on the ride to the track. I was still bouncing all over the emotional scale, and Mick seemed to be focused on some thoughts I wasn't privy to yet.

When we arrived at the track, we went directly to the barn. Mick wanted to see how Blood was holding up, and I wanted to see for myself that Blood and Sassy had been reunited.

The track provided security for all the racehorses, but Sassy had received some protection of his own. Racehorses came and went, but a half-million-dollar companion goat was a novelty.

I was glad everyone was focused on Blood so they didn't notice how Sassy trotted over to me, nudging my hand for some treats. I slipped a few out of my purse and fed them to him.

Mick was conferring with Blood's trainer, and they both agreed that the horse was up to the race. To my untrained eye, Blood appeared a bit hopped up, like any athlete would before a big event, but also somehow focused.

I watched Blood resting his forehead against Mick's chest as Mick rubbed the animal's cheek. Blood closed his eyes and blew air out his nostrils.

From the barn, we went up to the suite Bull had rented where forty or fifty people navigated among the hors d'oeuvres table, the bar and our very own betting window. When we arrived, last bets were being called for the first race.

Watching the races from an air-conditioned suite seemed a little artificial, but we did have a great view, and it was probably the closest I'd come to feeling like royalty.

Bull and Gwen arrived just after the fourth race. He wore the suit of a man who expected to make an appearance in the winner's circle, and Gwen had on a snug little number that matched her husband's pale blue shirt and she wore a drop necklace consisting of a mix of diamonds and some pale blue gems. I didn't notice anyone mentioning the goat to Bull. Apparently having his money returned intact had done little to repair his pride. Bull Severn's horse needed a goat nanny, and that fact did nothing for Bull's image.

On the news last night I'd enjoyed watching Bull being led through a phalanx of reporters asking him about his goat that was held for ransom. Questions like: "Mr. Severn, did you really pay a half million for the goat's release?" and "What kind of relationship have the horse and goat got?" Bull had surged through the crowd, shoulders first and didn't respond to any of these questions. But his face, red and tight, had said it all.

Now, being in the same room with the man I'd been extorting on the phone yesterday made me nervous. Suddenly the voice changer was a flimsy mask. But I detected nothing in his dark, rather harsh eyes that made me think he was onto me.

Mick said to Bull, "How're you holding up?"

Bull glanced around before answering, his voice low. "I've got the cops working 24/7. The dead guy wasn't in on this alone. The fucker who did this is going to pay. I'm going to personally disembowel him."

Mick nodded, and I tried to imagine Hedges telling his men that their careers depended on apprehending the dreaded goatnapper. It would have been funny, except that Bull was so deadly earnest. I took a sip of beer and then looked up to find Bull giving me an intense stare.

"How're you doing?" he finally asked.

I forced myself to swallow. "Okay." Then I asked about the man who'd been shot.

"He'll be home in a few days."

"That's good to hear." Another thing I'd never considered—collateral damage.

"How's that book coming?" he asked.

I forced myself to maintain eye contact. "Still doing some research. Should be starting it soon."

He nodded his approval. "Like to read it when you're done."

Mick was giving me an amused look.

"I'll be sure to send you a copy," I said, hoping this didn't mean I'd have to write the damned thing.

Gwen came up to us then, threading her arm through her husband's. "Mick, I'm glad you could come." Then she turned to me, hesitated, assumed a painfully awkward expression and said, "I'm sorry, what was your name?"

Mick answered. "It's Robyn."

"Of course." She looked me up and down. "Cute dress, Robyn."

I looked her up and down, smiled, and said, "Thank you." Then I turned to Mick, touched his arm and said, "Come help me pick a horse for the fifth race."

As we walked to the betting window, I pulled a five dollar bill out of my purse. "I'm feeling lucky today."

As I placed a bet, I glanced over my shoulder and saw Gwen still watching us. I tucked my hand around Mick's arm and gave Gwen a bright smile, which she didn't return.

Moving on, I tried to figure out what was about to happen. Mick wasn't giving me any clues, although he was being attentive, and when the bet I'd placed, based on his suggestion, paid off nicely, I decided that, no matter what happened, I was glad I'd come out.

While waiting for the fifth race to start, I noticed my old friend Rudy, drink in hand, standing at one of the windows looking out toward the track. He certainly got around.

After I collected my winnings, Mick asked me if I'd thought about a buyer for the stamp.

"Not yet. Haven't had the time to do much thinking." I bit the corner off a wedge of cheddar. "Why? Are you interested?"

"No. But I know a guy who is."

"You do know people, don't you?"

He just smiled.

The Million was the tenth race, and by the time it came around, you could feel the tension thrumming in the room.

Horse races don't last long, but the festivities preceding the Million were about as lavish and lengthy as Super Bowl half time. The Plymouth queen was introduced, a tenor sang the Illinois state song,

"Illinois," and a local woman belted the race's theme song, which was, for some reason, "Wind Beneath My Wings."

While introducing each horse during the post parade, the announcer dwelt on Bull's Blood a bit longer than the others, mentioning Sassy and the commotion surrounding the horse during the past forty-eight hours. Blood was tied for favorite. He and Merle's Magic would be going off at five to one, which was better than Mick had guessed, given Blood's recent history.

As they were loading the horses into the starting gate, I said to Mick, keeping my voice low, "Do you want him to win or not?"

"What do you think?" he said with a smile.

I honestly didn't know.

Blood broke fifth from the gate and by the first turn his jockey had gotten him out of a small knot of horses and running clear on the rail. I glanced over at Bull and Gwen. Bull's face showed no emotion, just hard concentration, while Gwen was jumping up and down on her little spiked heels. Bull held a drink glass between his hands in a throttle-grip.

Blood edged into the lead along the backstretch, and my fist kept time with the hoofbeats I was hearing in my head.

But then a horse named Sight Unseen edged in front of him, and it was clearly a battle between the two horses. Almost everyone in the suite was crying, "Blood!"

In the end, it was a matter of a nose. Not even three inches. Amazing how such a small measure would plummet a room into silence. I could feel the energy drain.

When I finally looked over at Bull, he was sitting, barely holding on to his glass by the rim. Next to him, Gwen sat with her legs crossed, and a truly pissed off expression added a few years to her features.

Someone said something about "a good race" and was silenced by the look Bull shot at him. It *had* been a good race. The kind a crowd loves. Close, with the headliner nearly winning and a come-from-nowhere horse stealing the race. I couldn't help but wonder if Blood might have had just a little more—that was all he'd have needed—if he hadn't been without Sassy for a day.

Finally, Bull stood and walked over to the bar and set his drink on the counter. "The same," he said, pushing it toward the bartender. The party would go on. And what a happy time we'd all have.

As people began to talk and move about again, I sort of slumped against Mick. "This sucks," I said, truly bummed.

"Not really."

"Oh, yeah?" I turned to him and saw that smile again.

"Bull dumps his losers. People, property, horses. It's all the same to him."

"And you're thinking ..."

He shrugged. "Wouldn't be the first time I bought one of his discards."

"Goat too?"

He winked. "Goat too."

I was about to pursue that when I noticed three men entering the suite. They stood out from the crowd because of their dress. They wore suits, but not the race-day casual kind. These were dark suits with white shirts. One of them approached Bull at the bar while the other two stood by the door, hands folded.

"William Severn?"

Bull looked at him, his eyes at a creepy half mast. "Who's asking?"

The man, a good four inches shorter than Bull with receding red hair and freckles, pulled an ID from his pocket and proceeded to introduce himself as an officer with the Fowler police department, finishing the sentence with, "I have a warrant for your arrest."

Bull seared him with a look and said, "For what?"

"Insurance fraud, for starters," the officer said, and began to read him his rights as he produced a pair of handcuffs.

Something flashed across Bull's face—alarm—but then his expression turned dark like a storm about explode. But, before he could unleash himself, a heavy-set man with thin blond hair had cut his way through the crowd. This man said to the cop, "I'm Richard Blackstone, Mr. Severn's attorney."

The cop just nodded.

"Let me see that warrant."

The cop produced it from his pocket and handed it to Blackstone.

Bull had apparently recovered his sense of humor, because he was almost smiling down on his arresting officer as he said to his attorney, "Make sure you get this guy's name, Rich. I don't—"

Blackstone silenced Bull with a look and handed the warrant back to the officer. "I'm going to advise you not to say anything right now, Bull."

Bull's anger and indignation deserted him, and I could almost see him sag under the loss. As the cuffs were clicking shut on him, he started looking around the room. For a moment I thought he was looking for me. Guilt fades slowly. But then his gaze landed on Gwen, who was still sitting on a settee with the look of one recovering from a gut punch. "Are you coming?"

Before she could answer or change her expression, the two men standing at the door led him out of the room and the arresting officer followed. Bull's ravings faded, then stopped as the elevator door closed.

Mick and I exchanged a look, but his expression remained neutral as, I hoped, mine did.

No one spoke for several moments, and then a man came up to Gwen and whispered something to her. She started, as though just awakened, then stood and let him lead her from the suite. She stumbled once, and I almost felt sorry for her. Almost.

After she left, there was a bit more silence and then a guy who'd been leaning against the bar said to the bartender, "You still open?"

"Sure," came the answer with a shrug.

It was like someone flicked a switch. People started talking, laughing, filling their drinks and looking for more shrimp at the appetizer table.

Mick and I left, neither of us speaking as we stood waiting for the elevator.

Then the doors opened, and I stepped in. Mick had started to follow me when he stopped and held the door.

Rudy stepped into the lift, and they were both grinning. The door shut and I said, "Okay, guys, what just happened?"

Mick nodded toward Rudy. "Rudy's an insurance investigator. Specializes in gems and jewelry."

Something clicked, but I didn't have enough yet. "And?"

Rudy turned to me. "A year ago, Bull's home was robbed and his safe broken into. Some valuable jewelry was stolen. He filed a claim and his insurance company settled."

The elevator bumped to a stop and the three of us got out and began moving through the crowds. Rudy looked at me with his pale eyes and said, "I never believed him."

"This still isn't coming together for me." I turned to Mick. "I don't have all the pieces."

Mick conceded that with a nod. "I'm Bull's accountant. I know how much money—how much cash—he's got. And I knew if he had to come up with a half million on short notice, he'd never be able to do it. He'd have to sell one of those 'stolen' pieces."

I stopped. Mick and Rudy waited as it sank in and washed over me. "And how did you know he sold it?"

Rudy smiled again, "I know a few people in the gem acquisition business."

I looked at Mick. "He was set up."

When he nodded, I said, "But how did you know for certain that he'd do this?"

"We really didn't. But it was a good bet. And then, even if it didn't pan out, we'd still have the money."

"Good thing it panned out, huh?"

"Indeed," Rudy said.

He folded the racing form and slipped it into his jacket pocket. "Well, I'd best be going. There are one or two parties I'll need to attend." He gave me a nod and slight bow. "It's been a pleasure, Robyn."

After Rudy left, Mick circled my waist with his arm and we kept walking.

"So this wasn't about that horse that had to be put down," I said, thinking it through.

"Yeah, it was. I just needed a way to take Bull down." Then he shrugged. "Look at it this way, Robyn. Maybe he's not going away for what he did to that horse or to your mother, but he's going away. Doesn't that feel good?"

"Yes," I said after a moment. "It really does."

We walked a little farther, and then I looked down at him and said, "Why didn't you tell me any of this?"

"Need to know."

"Yeah, well, here's something you need to know." I tucked my arm through his. "You don't know anything about secrets."

"Oh, yeah?"

"You don't know my mother."

THE
END

D.C. (Deb) Brod has written fiction most of her life, but didn't think she had a novel in her until after she graduated from Northern Illinois University with an M.A. in journalism. It was then that she decided if she could spend 120 pages discussing postal oppression of the radical press, she could write a novel. She was right. Her first novel, *Murder In Store,* featuring private detective Quint McCauley, appeared two years later in 1989. Four more novels in that series were followed by a contemporary Arthurian thriller, *Heartstone.* Her short stories have appeared in *Alfred Hitchcock Mystery Magazine* and several anthologies; two of these stories received Reader's Choice Awards.

She lives in St. Charles, Illinois with her husband, Donald, and their two cats, Skye and Jura, who are possibly the world's most aww-inducing felines. (If you don't believe that, check out her website: www.dcbrod.com.) When she's not writing, reading, or finding excuses not to clean the house, she enjoys watercolor painting, traveling, and watching crows. And, sadly, the Cubs.